AGAINST THE GRAIN

BOOKS BY PETER LOVESEY

SERGEANT CRIBB SERIES

Wobble to Death

The Detective Wore Silk Drawers

Abracadaver

Mad Hatter's Holiday

The Tick of Death

A Case of Spirits

Swing, Swing Together

Waxwork

THE PETER DIAMOND SERIES

The Last Detective

Diamond Solitaire

The Summons

Bloodhounds

Upon a Dark Night

The Vault

Diamond Dust

The House Sitter

The Secret Hangman

Skeleton Hill

Stagestruck

Cop to Corpse

The Tooth Tattoo

The Stone Wife

Down Among the Dead Men

Another One Goes Tonight

Beau Death

Killing with Confetti

The Finisher

Diamond and the Eye

Showstopper

Against the Grain

HEN MALLIN SERIES

The Circle

The Headhunters

THE PRINCE OF WALES MYSTERIES

Bertie and the Tinman

Bertie and the Seven Bodies

Bertie and the Crime of Passion

OTHER FICTION

The False Inspector Dew

Keystone

Rough Cider

On the Edge

The Reaper

Reader, I Buried Them &

Other Stories

AGAINST
THE GRAIN

A PETER DIAMOND INVESTIGATION

Peter Lovesey

Published by
Soho Press, Inc.
227 W 17th Street
New York, NY 10011

Library of Congress Cataloging-in-Publication Data

Names: Lovesey, Peter, author.
Title: Against the grain / Peter Lovesey.
Description: New York, NY : Soho Crime, 2024.
Series: The Peter Diamond Mysteries ; 22
Identifiers: LCCN 2024007642

ISBN 978-1-64129-615-1
eISBN 978-1-64129-616-8

Subjects: LCGFT: Detective and mystery fiction. | Novels.
Classification: LCC PR6062.O86 A73 2024
DDC 823/.914—dc23/eng/20240223
LC record available at https://lccn.loc.gov/2024007642

Printed in the United States of America

10 9 8 7 6 5 4 3 2 1

This book is with love and gratitude
to my family, Jax, Kathy and Phil.
Living with a full-time writer is not always a joyride.

AGAINST THE GRAIN

1

THIS IS A death trap, his brain told him. You have a few seconds left. Maybe a minute.

A minute to curse his stupidity for being conned. Like an idiot he'd taken up the challenge with no thought about the danger. A couple of drinks had made him bolder, but he certainly wasn't drunk, not even in party mood. He had been focused. This was a game he'd needed to win.

In the moonlight, he'd climbed the twenty-metre ladder and lifted the inspection hatch in the conical roof. It had been left unbolted. A promising sign, he had decided. He'd looked in and at once spotted what he had come for. The pink prize was lying in the centre only a short way off. He felt a rush of excitement.

He should have sussed he had been set up. Should have worn a safety line. And shouldn't have gone in alone, after dark. But he didn't hesitate. Gripping the hatch door and the side for support, he lowered himself inside. The silo was filled almost to the top with wheat grain, so he didn't need to jump. His feet met the surface before it needed to take his weight. A crust had formed on top and felt reasonably firm.

He wasn't troubled that the hatch didn't stay open. It was

within reach so he could easily push the door up to get out again. And he had his phone to see with. He switched on the flashlight for a better view of the smooth-sided galvanised steel cylinder. Ten metres across. He would only need five.

His shoes broke the crust and sank in a short way. That didn't register as a warning. He could still get to the centre. The effort of freeing his foot gave extra force to his next step and caused him to sink in some more. The crust was thinner out here, away from the wall. Stored grain is unstable, he told himself. What else do you expect?

Almost at once he was knee deep. Movement was like wading through a swamp. Still the lure of the reward drew him on. I won't be beaten, he told himself. I've gone to too much trouble already. Pushing on, thighs straining, upper body twisting, elbows at shoulder level working like machinery, he inched towards the target. He leaned in, stretched and felt his fingertips touch the lace trim. At a second try he grabbed it.

Success.

And so simple.

He drew the garter on to his arm to leave both hands free.

Now he needed to get back to the hatch and climb out. He made the effort to turn and felt a troubling loss of control. All this disturbance had produced a shallow crater in the surface that was clearly getting deeper. He was at the lowest point with the grain streaming down. It was taking a huge effort to move his legs. Already he was up to his thighs and sinking. For the first time in this misadventure, he knew he was in danger of being buried alive.

In alarm, if not panic, he shouted for help. His voice echoed off the steel sides and roof, only confirming that he was in an enclosed space where nobody would hear.

Seed was bouncing down the slope, stinging his face.

Some of it got in his mouth. Shouting will only make this worse, he thought. I must keep my airways clear.

His legs and feet were being crushed. His descent might have slowed, but it hadn't stopped. He was held fast, up to his armpits. With each movement of his shoulders a million suffocating seeds ran down the sides of the crater.

Idiot. You have a phone in your right hand. Use it.

No service came up on the status bar.

He was in a dead zone.

2

PETER DIAMOND STARED at the email on his home computer screen. "Smelly lanes and horse flies. I'm not cut out for country life."

"I never said you were," his partner, Paloma Kean, said over his shoulder. "Doesn't mean you can't go out of town. You've been before."

"Only on police duty. This is something else. She's asking us to stay."

"Not forever. It's a visit."

"A whole damn week out of my annual leave."

"She was your deputy. You're always telling me what a gem Julie was. Aren't you interested to see her again after all this time?"

He hesitated. He'd never told Paloma why the staunchly loyal Julie Hargreaves had quit and applied for a transfer. The harsh truth of the matter was that the day came when even Julie had wearied of his overbearing conduct. She'd smoothed the way for him through case after case until she'd finally buckled under the strain. Her announcement that she was leaving Bath CID had been one of the great shocks of his life. He couldn't blame her any more than he could change his own personality. For

Julie it had been a gut-wrenching decision, unknown to him until later. She had discussed it all with Stephanie, his late wife, and Steph had supported her. "Let her go, Pete," she had told him after Julie had dropped her bombshell. "A trouble-free life isn't necessarily what you want or need." Another way of saying she's too good for you. Anything Steph had said was gospel. He bore no resentment towards Julie.

"But a day visit will be more than enough," he told Paloma. "I don't do overnight. It's only Somerset, for pity's sake. We can be there and back in a couple of hours."

"Maybe she has a reason for wanting you to stay."

"Like what? Putting up shelves? She'd regret that."

"Something professional."

"Julie is retired now. She had the sense to put it all behind her."

Paloma vibrated her lips. "Says you."

He managed a self-conscious grin.

Retirement beckoned for him, too, but he wasn't looking forward to it. His job defined him. Without it, he would lose self-respect and, more importantly, the satisfaction of seeking and discovering nuggets of truth in a chaotic world. "I had a run-in with Georgina yesterday."

His boss, Assistant Chief Constable Georgina Dallymore, had endured his prickly personality for almost twenty years and thought it should have earned her the King's Police Medal for service of conspicuous merit.

"She asked me my age."

"Doesn't she know it already?"

"You bet she does. Years, months and days. She started talking about the NPA as if I should know about it. She knows my blind spot for abbreviations."

"NPA?"

"Normal Pension Age."

"Ouch."

"My reaction exactly. I was forced to remind her about the RPO."

"What's that, the Royal Philharmonic?"

"The Retention of Police Officers scheme. For those of us—I quote—'due to retire, who wish to continue to supply their valuable skills and experience.' Bit of a shock for her. She almost burst her tunic buttons."

Paloma smiled. "But I don't think you should stay in the job just to spite Georgina."

"I do it for myself. You know that."

The truth was that he and Georgina had worked on their mutual dislike over the years and attained a level of understanding, if not tolerance. The fighting never stopped, but the chance of a knockout had long since gone by. They knew too much about each other. She had his misdemeanours on file going right back to violence episodes when he had been in the Met. But the only time she had tried to get him sacked at a disciplinary hearing at headquarters, it had been cancelled at the last minute because he had broken his leg performing an act of heroism in the line of duty.

Diamond didn't have a dossier on Georgina but he knew her weak points. She had once been desperate to find a house-sitter, mainly to cosset her pampered Persian cat, Sultan, when she went abroad. Through no fault of his own, he'd ended up doing the job himself, whisking Sultan away from Georgina's luxurious house in Bennett Street to the more humble Diamond homestead in Weston to share with his own tough tabby called Raffles. Georgina never knew Diamond could have had the run of her house, everything from her Mills & Boon collection to her underwear drawer. And he was privy to more of her innermost secrets, the afternoons out for golf, hair appointments and choir practice.

"We've never experienced village life," Paloma said as if the thought had just occurred to her. "Julie's invitation could be an opportunity."

Danger signals sounded for Diamond. "Opportunity for what?"

"Finding out if the country suits us."

He didn't like that at all. "It wouldn't. We're townies, through and through. Nothing ever happens there. You can soon get tired of frolicking lambs and helping the farmer pick his apples."

"What's that Sherlock Holmes quote about the smiling and beautiful countryside having a more dreadful record of sin than the vilest alleys in London?"

"Detective fiction," he said with a curl of the lip. "I deal in true crime."

"You may have to go looking for true crime if you want to exercise your brain after, em . . ."

"Retirement?"

Paloma hadn't wanted to use the *R* word again. She knew how it troubled him. "But you'd help Julie if she had a problem. It's not in your nature to spurn a cry for help from an old colleague."

He checked the screen again. "Cry for help? I don't see one here."

"Did you notice the name of the village?"

Baskerville. "Is that real?"

"Doesn't it have some appeal to you, of all people?" Paloma said.

"Is that why you just quoted Sherlock Holmes?"

"It may have popped into my head."

"It's only a name," he said. "The countryside is dotted with stupid names. One more reason for avoiding it."

"That's rich for a man who lives in a town called Bath."

She knew better than to press old Grumbleguts when he was in this mood. She would let him brood on the matter. A few hours might make a difference.

As for Diamond, he had a more urgent matter to deal with, a visit to the vet with Raffles, his elderly cat, for the annual booster injection. The needle never seemed to bother Raffles. What troubled him was the waiting room and the smells and sounds of other people's pets, especially dogs. He would be safe in his carrier but that didn't stop him from mewing loudly enough for Diamond to get looks from all the other owners.

Mercifully, when they got there, the waiting room was empty except for a man with a large bird cage under a black polyester cover. Whatever was inside was silent.

Diamond didn't have to ask.

"He's a beautiful cockatoo," the man said. "He's been off colour for a week and I want the vet to take a look. I'd show him to you, but it could be psittacosis. Heard of that?"

"The parrot disease," Diamond said in a tone meant to shut the man up. He didn't want conversation right now. But he made the mistake of softening his response by adding, "Let's hope it's not that."

"It can easily be transferred to humans," the man said as blithely as if he were doing a TV commercial. "Little airborne particles. Breathe any of those in and you could go down with pneumonia."

"Nasty," Diamond said, thankful that the cockatoo and its owner were on the other side of the room.

The man was nervous and needed to fill the silence. "The symptoms are like Covid. Bit of a cough, temperature, headache. You could take one of those lateral flow tests and come up negative and think you're safe, but you aren't. If you're taken seriously ill and don't tell them you've been near a parrot, they won't know how to treat you. It could be curtains. I'm doing the right thing, bringing him here."

"No question," Diamond said without meaning it at all. "You can't be too careful."

"I'm going to warn the vet to wear a protective mask."

"Excellent idea," Diamond said, thinking he, too, should be wearing protection.

"Not just a face covering, a proper surgical mask that filters out those particles."

A young woman in a green uniform appeared at the door of the inner sanctum. "Mr. Screech?"

The man twitched. "That's my cockatoo, not me."

"The vet will see you now, both of you."

After they'd gone in, Diamond picked up a magazine. Not to read, but to flap the air and disperse any particles that had come his way.

Raffles treated him to one of those disdainful looks cats give their owners.

"How old is he now?" the vet asked Diamond when their turn came.

"I wouldn't like to answer that in his presence. Last time we were here I told you he likes to check on the birds from the windowsill but can't jump up anymore, and you suggested a chair would help. Now he needs a footstool to get on the chair."

"Good thinking," she said. "And how is his appetite?"

"Smaller, for sure."

She put Raffles on the scales. "You may need to raise his feeding dish to shoulder level."

"His shoulders or mine?"

She smiled. "An upturned shoebox would be about right."

"Good idea. I'll find one." A shoebox wasn't going to cost anything. Elderly pets can get expensive.

"We are recommending new medication for the arthritis that will help him," the vet added as she lifted Raffles on to her table. "Let's look at his teeth."

Some dental work under anaesthetic was going to be necessary. They'd need another appointment for that. The bill was mounting. The new medication for the arthritis wouldn't come cheap. And the annual jab wasn't free.

On the drive home, Diamond had a rather good idea. He would use Raffles as the excuse to get him out of that week in the country. A phone call to Julie to explain that the cat needed special care now and couldn't be boarded anywhere.

"GUV, ARE YOU talking about Raffles?" Julie said when he called her the same evening. "I remember Raffles. He must be a good age now."

"That's the problem. Arthritis mainly. He needs surgical aids." A shoebox was a surgical aid if the vet recommended it.

"Like his own mobility scooter?"

"Haha. Other stuff, too much to bring. He's of an age when he's better off in the place he knows."

Julie didn't seem to have heard. "Bring him with you, poor old thing. Bring his equipment, everything. I'd love to see him again. That's not to say I wouldn't like to see you and Paloma too."

And that was how a week later he and Paloma came to be driving south under the clear blue sky of Somerset with Raffles in the pet carrier on the back seat, as well as a New Balance sneakers shoebox filled with tins of gourmet cat food.

"Was Julie on your team from the beginning?" Paloma asked.

"You want to know more about her?" he said unnecessarily, and answered his own question. "Of course you do. She's our hostess for a week." In his head, he was deciding how much to tell. None of it reflected well on him personally but he hadn't deliberately hidden the story from her.

They were using the old route south of Bath. The dull city suburbs gave way to eye-pleasing fields edged with poppies and elderflower.

This would be uncomfortable to relate. "She was in CID when I rejoined the police," he said, recalling the bizarre episode of his blow-up with Mr. Tott, the Assistant Chief Constable, triggering his resignation and the year scratching a living in London, until Bath had begged him to come back because of an emergency only he could deal with. "Detective Inspector Julie Hargreaves. Good rank for a woman in that male-chauvinist era. Difficult at first. We circled each other like cats."

"Because you were prejudiced?"

He sniffed. "Smells like Somerset to me." They had the windows open. Overnight it had rained heavily and the air was rich in earthy scents, tolerable on the breeze although not at closer range. "Prejudiced, did you say? Possibly. There was a phrase around at the time for blokes who were politically correct: the new man. Remember? Well, I wasn't one of them."

Paloma laughed. "Who would have thought it?"

"Actually, most of the tension with Julie was because I was parachuted in and I came with baggage, a dodgy reputation with the Met before I even started here. It was made worse in Bath through a troublesome brat I put in hospital. By accident," he added. "So Julie had every right to treat me with caution. But I soon appreciated how bright she was. Loyal, too. Watched my back and kept me out of trouble."

"You've always needed a minder," Paloma said.

"She was my deputy," he said in a tone of injured virtue. "Two, in fact. One at home and one at work."

"Have it your way. She was marvellous. Solved a locked-room murder for me when I was floundering about. But on the next case, I made a huge mistake. I assigned a murder investigation to DCI John Wigfull, mainly to get him out of my hair. He's another cop you never met, a right pain in the you-know-what. Then Julie told me she would have jumped at the chance of taking it on. From then on, nothing went right."

He had to suspend the story. They were on the A361, and the great mound of Glastonbury Tor was ahead. He needed to concentrate on his driving through the town, the centre of the New Age universe. It was always full of hairy tourists crossing the street as if traffic didn't exist.

"Back to Julie and me," he resumed when they were out the other side without running over a single hippie. "We started sniping at each other. At one stage, she made a sympathetic remark about the murder victim, a foreign woman who had been working the social care system to her advantage, and I said she was being too sisterly for my taste." His slightly more enlightened modern self winced at the memory. "That really got to Julie, but it was just the latest in a series of sexist things I said to her and came to regret. She decided the chemistry was wrong. She couldn't work with me any longer. She put in for a transfer."

"And still wants to see us?"

"She's a good person. Phoned me after Steph was murdered and saw me through the worst time of my life. She really helped me deal with it. And it was a tip from Julie that put me on to the killer. She found something in one of those Scotland Yard bulletins I never bother to look at. Yes, I'm eternally grateful. Those old skirmishes are long gone."

They drove through Taunton, the county town, more staid and less folksy than Glastonbury. Soon after, Baskerville started to appear on the signboards. The village was well off the main road, accessible only along narrow twisty lanes with not many passing places. The atmosphere changed. A huge black cloud had materialised out of nothing in that blue sky. Their sunglasses had to come off. Driving here was an act of folly, Diamond thought to himself. It never entered his mind that he was about to be treated to the one thing missing from his long career—a village murder.

"If we meet something, they'll have to do the reversing. My days of driving backwards are well in the past."

"If it's a farm vehicle, they won't back down," Paloma said.

"They've got a reverse gear, same as I have."

It wasn't a tractor that came round the next turn. It was a herd of Friesian cows advancing at a steady rate. Cows don't reverse. They don't even brake well. You don't argue with big beasts.

"That's all I need." Forced to eat his words, he braked, turned in his seat and started the move back.

Raffles saw his face and mewed.

"Belt up, you."

"You're talking to the cat, I hope," Paloma said.

"I'm looking for a passing point."

"There was an open gate some way back. That could be where they're heading."

"How far is some way? I don't see it."

"I'll tell you."

"Leave the driving to me and watch the cows."

"Can you go a little faster?"

"That will just encourage them." His control of the wheel wasn't confident. He was intent on avoiding contact with a drystone wall. "Isn't anybody with them?"

"I can't see."

Neither of them cared to entertain the thought that these could be runaway cows making a bid for freedom.

He'd reversed for almost a minute when he reached the opening. First, he spotted a patch of road gleaming with mud and cowpats. He knew what would happen. Even if he judged the turn successfully and steered off the hard surface, his wheels would sink in and spin and he'd be stuck.

How right he was. Just as he'd turned the wheel and Paloma was saying, "Well done," he felt the sickening lack of response from the tyres. His instinct was to put his foot down harder. They sank deeper into the mud. He switched off.

The cows hadn't stopped. The leaders headed past the car's nearside and into the field. There was space if all of them were sensible, but that was too much to expect of cattle on the move. The side of the car took several bumps.

"That's my no-claims bonus up the spout."

A cow with an eye for adventure moved around the front and continued along the lane. Others followed.

"This can't be right," Paloma said.

"You're telling me."

"I mean the ones going on up the lane. I think they're meant to go in the field."

"What am I supposed to do—get out and do traffic duty?"

"I don't advise it. You'll get trampled. Hold on, someone is coming."

The last of the cows were followed by a youth on a quad bike. He couldn't have been much over fifteen. He had two sheepdogs with him. He shouted like someone twice his age, "What the bloody hell?"

Diamond put down the window and shouted back, "Are you supposed to be in charge?"

The kid didn't even stop. He yelled, "Close the fucking gate," and drove straight into the field with the dogs following. The quad bike made light work of the mud and hummocks and was soon lost to view.

"What was that about?" Diamond said.

"I expect he knows a way to head off the strays. Better do as he says."

He didn't enjoy taking orders from a foul-mouthed teenager but he saw the sense in it, emerged from the car, trudged through thick mud and shut the gate before the cows in the field took it into their heads to go after the escapees.

"Do I smell?" Diamond asked when he was back in the car.

"It's to be expected," Paloma said.

"The car's going to need a good cleaning, inside and out, and that's if we ever get it moving again."

Paloma took out her phone. "Want me to call Julie?"

"And tell her we're up to our hubs in cow shit? I'd rather not. We must think of something."

"Like a tow truck?"

"Something we can do for ourselves."

"Like me getting out and giving it a push?"

"I'd need about six of you." He felt helpless and annoyed with himself. He was supposed to be resourceful. His reputation was summed up in this standstill. He was the ultimate stick-in-the-mud.

Paloma looked at her phone. "It says here you should lighten the car's load by asking passengers to get out and stand at a safe distance."

"You'll ruin your shoes, same as me."

"And I suppose we should unload the cases as well. They're heavy."

"Makes sense, but I'm not optimistic."

"You never are, Pete."

"It's starting to rain. That's going to make it worse."

As soon as he got out, a huge drop hit his head and splattered. He felt the water run down his neck. He heaved out the suitcases and set them down at the side of the road. Paloma got out and stood nearby under an umbrella reading instructions from her phone.

"You can also try deflating the tyres a bit."

Crouching beside the muddy tyres trying to find the valves was a messy business. The rain was stinging him. The tow truck became more appealing by the second.

He got back in the car to try again. Lowered the window. "When I'm sitting here, I can't see the damn wheels."

Paloma moved closer to the car. "I'll tell you." She was doing her best to sound calm as she read from her phone. "Move the steering wheel back and forth to give the front tyres room to manoeuvre. Use second gear to get the best possible traction. Push slowly on the accelerator. Slowly!"

She got a faceful of mud. "Do you mind?"

He apologised. He could see her in the wing mirror. "We're running out of options."

"They suggest wedging pieces of cardboard in front of the tyres. This is starting to sound like desperation."

Muttering, he listened to the rain rattling on the roof. He needed a few seconds to compose himself. "Where am I supposed to find cardboard?"

"Raffles's shoebox."

"Are you serious?"

"We can get him another one. Julie probably has some."

He left the engine running, got out, opened the rear door, emptied the shoebox of tins and released some of his tension ripping it into two flat pieces of cardboard that he then forced under the rear tyres.

Raffles protested loudly, adding to the misery.

Diamond got in and tried again.

The wheels spun and didn't engage with the cardboard.

Paloma closed the umbrella, pocketed her phone and knelt beside the nearest wheel. "Try again, I'll see if I can get it under the moving tyre."

"You'll get covered in filth."

"We're in a filthy hole and we've got to get out of it somehow."

He didn't argue.

Magic. The extra pressure from Paloma did the trick. The tyre treads found some purchase on the cardboard and the car eased out of the ruts and down the slope to the hard surface of the road. Paloma climbed in.

She looked like a coal miner at the end of a shift.

"If this is country life," she said, "I'm starting to come round to your way of thinking."

3

JULIE LIVED AT the heart of the village on the edge of the green in a thatched black-and-white cottage with a front garden stocked with shrub roses and a patch of lawn that hadn't been mowed all summer.

"The long grass surprises me," Diamond said. "She kept her desk really tidy."

"It's wild," Paloma said.

"I can see that. It's a riot."

"Wild by choice," Paloma said. "Helps the bees and the butterflies. It's rather lovely. Harebells, red campion, meadowsweet, lady's bedstraw."

"The only ones I can name are dandelions."

He knocked and they both heard the bark of a dog inside.

He prickled. "Why didn't she tell us she has a dog? Raffles won't like that."

Paloma made light of the matter. "It would have given you another reason not to come."

"But she knows we have a cat. We'll have to keep him in the car. A dog guards its territory."

"From all I've heard about Julie, she will have thought it through."

Footsteps sounded from inside and Julie opened the door. She was slimmer than he remembered, or was it time that had taken away the softness of her flesh?

She said, "This is such a treat. I'm so pleased I was firm with you and insisted you came. But don't stand there. Come in."

"We'll take these shoes off first," Paloma said.

Julie laughed. "No need, my dears. It's no palace, as you'll soon find out."

"Even so." Paloma lifted her heel and removed a muddy shoe.

"Oh, come on, you only just stepped out of the car." Julie's head was angled upwards as if to check the state of the cloud cover. "It stopped raining ten minutes ago."

"That's not the whole story," Diamond said with a sidewards glance at his bedraggled partner. "Haven't you noticed the state of us?" But before the words were out, everything came together in his brain: the barking dog, the overgrown garden and the strange tilt of the head.

Julie had gone blind.

"We're covered in mud and god only knows what else," he managed to say while his thoughts raced. Julie, whose observational skills were a legend, had been dealt a life-changing blow. "We had a close encounter with a herd of cows and the car got stuck."

Julie laughed again. "You need a shower and a complete change of clothes by the sound of it."

"You have a shower here?" he said in surprise.

"What were you expecting—a tin bath? This may be deepest Somerset but we do have modern plumbing. Come on in and I'll take Paloma upstairs first and find towels and a shower cap."

They left their shoes on the doormat.

LATER THAT EVENING, cleansed and wrapped in bathrobes Julie had found for them, they ate warm quiche and salad while seated on an L-shaped sofa in the largest room in the cottage. "Before you ask," Julie said, "it happened unexpectedly three years ago. Macular degeneration. In most cases it's slow to take effect, but mine was the wet form that can take your sight in a matter of days. It's a good thing I was already well established here. People are very helpful. I have a marvellous guide dog called Bella who you'll meet in a minute. Where's Raffles?"

"Still in the car."

"Poor mite. Fetch him in, guv, and all his equipment. Bella won't trouble him. She's too well-mannered for that."

Shamed by her openness, Diamond cleared his throat. "When we spoke on the phone, I laid it on a bit thick. His equipment amounts to a shoebox we rest his dish on."

Paloma added, "And it had to be sacrificed to help get the car out of the mud."

"You need another shoebox? No problem," Julie said and put her tray to one side.

Diamond was already on his feet. "Tell me where and I'll fetch it."

Julie said in a firm tone, "You won't. My legs are capable of going upstairs." And she crossed the room at speed.

"Don't patronise her, Pete," Paloma said when they were alone. "She'll know every inch of this cottage."

"I'm shocked," he said. "She didn't mention this on the phone."

"She wouldn't. She's refusing to let it dominate her life. Better bring Raffles in, like she said."

He also brought in the tins of cat food. His elderly pet didn't hesitate when a dish of tuna was placed on the shoebox Julie provided.

"Sounds like he's taking it," Julie said.

"You bet. He's still got a good appetite."

"After he's settled in, we'll introduce him to Bella. Once they've met, I don't expect any trouble. Before that you must tell me about your adventure with the cows. I think I know who they belong to."

Paloma told the story. It was easy to laugh now.

"The boy on the quad bike will have been Hamish from the farm," Julie said. "He's a good lad, growing up fast. And I'm guessing he gave you a mouthful of grown-up language."

"It wasn't the time for polite conversation," Paloma said.

"Kids on farms learn to make themselves useful from an early age. It's no bad thing. He'll have crossed the field and met the stray cows in the lane as they reached another gate. His parents run the farm as tenants. The owner is serving a prison sentence."

"Whatever for?"

"Gross negligence manslaughter. She got three years. There isn't much sympathy for her in the village."

Diamond had been starting to doze off. Raffles was a warm bundle on his lap. The mention of manslaughter acted like adrenalin. "What?"

"You may know all about this. Claudia Priest."

"It rings a bell faintly. Someone else must have dealt with the case. Tell me more, Julie."

Like old times, she got straight to the salient facts, turning to face him. The muscles of her grey-blue eyes functioned as if she could see, steady as any sighted person. He had to watch closely for a sign that she couldn't. The giveaway was the absence of focus, as if she were gazing through him. "She's in her forties now and lived here as a child. Her father Mervyn was well liked and respected. He went out of his way to welcome me when I first arrived.

They're one of the few village families left. Been here for generations. The name Priest is all over the church on tablets and brasses."

"Quite something to live up to."

"Mervyn did. He built up the farm, modernised it and made a huge success of it. He kept most of the village employed one way and another. He lived in the farmhouse, which is huge and much restored. He was tower leader for the bell-ringers and supplied the village shop with half its produce."

"What about his wife?" Paloma asked.

"I don't know much about her. She died years before I got here. A freak accident, struck by lightning in one of the fields on the farm."

"Dreadful."

"They're a tragic family. Mervyn was left to bring up Claudia. Many of the locals believe he overcompensated and spoiled her. I was told she was quite a tearaway in her teens, really naughty, got in bad company, was caught passing drugs to her school friends more than once and cautioned by the police. She only escaped detention because Mervyn's lawyers were the best."

"All this was when she was underage?"

"Still at school."

"A fee-paying school, no doubt."

"A series of them. She was expelled from several. In the end the drug-dealing was too much for the magistrates and she was given a year in a secure institution. By the time she was released she was sixteen and free in more senses than one."

"Left home?"

"Wasn't seen in the village again until after Mervyn's death."

"What did he die of?"

"That's another tragedy. He never really got over his wife's death. He took an overdose. A few close friends and people he worked with knew about his depression. He hid it well. He was found dead in bed. He'd drunk half a bottle of whisky and taken a lot of sleeping tablets."

"Then Claudia inherited the farm?" Paloma said, eager to hear more. She wasn't just making polite conversation. She was leaning forward, hands smoothing the robe against her legs.

"Yes, more than twenty years after she left home, when most of the locals had forgotten about her. At that time she was living in Bath on a generous allowance from Mervyn. He'd continued to support her financially through the years even though she'd had little to do with him. To everyone's surprise she came to live here."

"To farm?"

"That's what we supposed. Of course, it wasn't hands-on. She asked the family who'd been running it for Mervyn in his last years to stay on and they're still here."

"Still being paid?"

"On the same terms."

"These are Hamish's people?" Paloma was asking all the questions while checking regularly to make sure Diamond was paying attention. There was a possibility he wasn't. He had spread himself inelegantly across most of the sofa like Madame Récamier on a night off, the stresses of the journey having taken their toll.

"His parents, Jim and Agnes Douglas. They're lovely. I'm hoping you get a chance to meet them."

"The three of them do the real work?"

"Plus a team of farm workers. It's a big undertaking."

"Wise decision, then, wouldn't you say, Pete?"

"Hm?" He gave a start. His eyes were open, but he hadn't been listening as closely as Paloma. "Oh, yes. No argument."

Julie didn't show she'd noticed. She was addressing him as much as Paloma. "None of us could think what was in Claudia's mind, moving out of Bath to a backwater like this, but we were given a clue when the parties started."

"Parties as in raves?" Paloma said.

"Not exactly. These weren't kids. They were yuppies. The yard filled with expensive cars. Music blared from the farmhouse windows until three and four in the morning. On summer nights the guests spilled out into the lanes, drunk or high on drugs. You can imagine the reaction in a hardworking community where everyone is in bed and asleep by ten."

"How often was this?"

"Once a month, starting Friday night and often running over until Monday morning."

"The guests slept over?"

"I didn't enquire into the sleeping arrangements."

Diamond smiled and proved he hadn't drifted off. "You were always discreet."

"I imagine they crashed out wherever they happened to be and slept well into the next day. One of the sheepdogs had a nose for cannabis and kept finding used joints in very odd places like the church porch, the lambing shed and the bus stop. A packet of condoms turned up in the kids' playground. And a haystack went up in flames one Sunday morning, definitely caused by a cigarette."

"How does the manslaughter fit in?" Diamond asked, more engaged now that they'd reached the juicy part of the story. "I'm thinking Claudia will have made herself so unpopular locally she was more likely to be the victim than the killer."

"A decomposing body was found in a grain silo."

Paloma screwed up her face and said, "Ugh!"

"Sorry. I needn't have said that so bluntly."

Diamond said, "Carry on, Julie. She's heard worse from me. In a silo, you say?"

"You know what I'm talking about? Large round towers for storage. The farm has two. Something was stopping the grain from running freely out of the bottom. When they investigated, they found the, em, corpse."

"One of the party crowd?"

Julie nodded. "Roger Miller. An art dealer, lived in a nice house up near the Circus, in Bennett Street."

Diamond flattened his palm against his brow. It wasn't easy switching his tired thoughts from rural Somerset to Georgian Bath. He was trying to recall an art connection from the not-too-distant past. He squeezed his eyes as if that would make a difference and it did. A priceless memory from three years ago of his solemn colleague DI John Leaman, who never got out much, standing on a wall at the back of the Circus trying to work out where the painter Gainsborough's studio had been and getting spotted by a passing police patrol. "You wouldn't find a better address, Bennett Street." He paused for someone to ask why.

"Cheek by jowl with Gainsborough?" Julie said, taking the wind out of his sails. "You're right, guv."

Paloma said, "Roger Miller. I remember the name from way back. Can't place him, but he must have been around some while."

"Paloma's business is all about art and illustration," Diamond said as if confirming a melancholy truth. "Tell us more about this bloke."

"He had a bit of a fling with Claudia that fizzled out, but he was still in her group of friends until he disappeared from the scene four months before the body was found. He was in party gear, Hawaiian shirt, flared jeans and smart buckled shoes and—this was the clincher—on his right forearm was a frilly pink garter."

"A woman's garter?"

"I don't think men wear them much."

Paloma smiled and added, "Certainly not on their arms."

The garter brought a lighter touch to a gruesome topic. Diamond saw an opportunity to keep it going. "Does anyone wear garters these days?"

Paloma said, "In some situations, yes."

"Like brides wearing something blue on their wedding day? But you said this was pink."

Now both women were smiling. Paloma said, "Come on, Pete, you're not that much of a puritan."

"Sex? Is that what this was about?"

Julie explained. "It emerged during the trial that some sort of game was played. Claudia had hidden the garter somewhere around the farm and it was up to the men to find it."

"Hunt the garter?"

"Sort of."

"She admitted this? And what was the prize?"

Paloma was ahead of him. "If you have to ask that, Pete, you really are tired."

"I like the rules spelled out, as you know."

"This was a drunken, drug-fuelled party, my love, not a cricket match."

Julie said, "Prosecuting counsel at the trial thought along the same lines as you, guv. He put the question to Claudia about what was on offer to the winner."

"Sex—like I said?"

"Not necessarily. Claudia's answer in court was that garters come in pairs."

"And?"

"One of the ladies would be wearing the one that matched it and identifying her would be the next challenge."

Paloma laughed. "Saucy. I like it." The image of the rotting body was erased from her thoughts.

Diamond doggedly picked his way through the practicalities. "Getting back to what we know for sure, the garter must have been put in the silo before the game got under way."

"And the silo was a death trap," Paloma said.

He was trying to picture this. "How do you get into those things—through the top?"

"There's a ladder up the side and a hatch in the roof."

"The game was thought up by Claudia, so she will already have climbed up and put the garter inside?"

"At some risk to herself," Paloma said.

"That's the assumption," Julie said.

"Didn't she say?"

"She said she had no memory of going up there."

"This is fascinating."

"She wasn't believed, especially when it emerged in court that she'd taken drugs and drink. They all had. If she was on a high, she might well have done something as reckless as climbing the silo."

"That I can believe."

"The silo was full to the top with stored grain." Julie was back on a wavelength with her old boss. "All she needed to do was throw the garter where it could be seen. Anyone retrieving it would need to wade through the grain."

"With a high chance of being sucked in? Horrible way to die. Sorry, Paloma. Think of this as more shop talk."

Julie said, "There's a term for it: grain entrapment. At the trial, an expert witness said up to thirty deaths a year occur that way in the United States alone, where silo storage is most used. A crust forms on the surface after some months and it can give the impression it's safe to walk on. It isn't. It's treacherous. The victims are mostly farm workers. They start sinking in and soon lose control. Struggling makes it worse. In a very short time they're up to their necks in grain and they suffocate."

"Did Claudia understand the risk?" Diamond said. "If she did, you could argue there was premeditation and that could be murder."

There was an awkward silence. Julie was frowning. "That was never seriously suggested in court, guv."

"Outside, perhaps?" he said, hearing the tension in her words. Another hesitation before she said, "Some tongues wagged in the village."

"There's always some mean bastard."

"I overheard it myself from some women whose voices I didn't know. She's been treated horribly."

"Is that why you're telling us this?"

Julie didn't answer at all, so he added, "I'm glad you did. It's an intriguing case. In her defence she wasn't a farmer and she probably didn't know enough about the danger of sending someone into a silo."

"She was raised by a farmer," Julie said. "She spent the first fifteen years of her life on the farm where it happened. She must have been warned that you don't go inside a silo."

"Then why would she endanger the people she invited to her party? You said there was some kind of affair in years past with the victim? Tell me his name again."

"Roger Miller."

He sat forward and brought out his phone. "You'll be proud of me, Julie. These days I can do a background check on the PNC." He tapped in his security number to access the police computer. While painstakingly entering the letters, he said out loud, "Full name: Roger Miller. Bennett Street, BA1." He stared at the screen, waited and got only a "not known," a humbling anticlimax. "Unfortunately, he doesn't feature. Sorry, I interrupted the story. You were telling us about Claudia. She'll be on the database for sure."

"What do you want to hear?" Julie sounded uncomfortable with the way the conversation was heading.

"How she's supposed to have done this." Diamond pressed on regardless. "Let's say it *was* premeditated and Miller was making a nuisance of himself, wanting to rekindle the flame when Claudia didn't. An unwanted lover can be a real pain. But then if she meant to get rid of him she'd have to make sure Roger and not one of the other men climbed into the silo. How many played this game?"

"Not many, I heard. Some of the guests were too spaced out to join in."

"Did they all start the search at once? You don't know?"

"I don't think anyone asked at the trial."

"If she's really evil she may have tipped Miller off."

"What do you mean?" Julie said.

It was distracting that the sightless eyes could still look disapproving. Her tone of voice reinforced the reaction.

The word "evil" had been a bad choice. He tried to explain more mildly. "Had a quiet word with him and told him to look in the silo. You don't care for that? You think she's innocent?"

Paloma could see he was in deep water. "Get Pete started and he's sure to think the worst."

Julie nodded and tried to smile. "I should have remembered."

"Do you think Claudia is innocent?" he pressed her. "Innocent of anything at all?"

"I can't say that for sure, guv. I just feel she didn't get a fair hearing. No one was willing to speak up for her character, not one of her so-called friends from Bath and certainly nobody in the village. The judge will have known about her record, the troubles in her early years." She felt for the arms of her chair and started to get up. "But that's enough about Claudia. I think it's time Raffles met Bella."

IN THEIR ROOM while getting ready for bed, Diamond said, "That Bella is remarkably well trained. She drew back in the nick of time."

"It was only a gesture. Raff didn't want her too close."

"I'm not so sure."

Paloma rose to Raffles's defence. "If he'd really meant to scratch her nose, it would have happened."

"I'm not so sure. His tail was swishing. That's never a good sign."

"He was out of his comfort zone. You can't blame him."

"I don't. He was acting on instinct. No use telling him we're visitors and you don't behave like that towards the resident dog, least of all a guide dog."

"Don't fret. They'll work it out between them. In a few days they'll curl up together on the sofa."

"One with a scratched nose."

IN BED AFTER they'd turned out the light, Paloma said, "It's a huge effort for her, inviting us to stay."

He was yawning. He didn't want a discussion now. "Yes, she'll sleep well and so will I."

"Have you worked out why we're here?"

"Mainly because you insisted."

"I thought it would do you good, getting a break from work."

"Sampling country life? I've had enough already, thanks."

"Aren't you interested in what's on Julie's mind?"

"Do we have to go into that?" he said. "It's late."

"It's only just gone ten."

"After the day we've had, it feels like midnight."

"I told you there must be a reason why she wants us to stay for a week and now we know what it is. Could be quite a challenge, Pete. It's not like you have your team with you."

He didn't answer. He was asleep already.

4

JULIE'S BREAKFAST WAS a revelation. She moved around her kitchen as if she was fully sighted. She judged the cooking to perfection.

"I don't know how you can tell when the eggs are ready," Diamond said.

"You get an ear for it. You put a lid over the pan and listen for the sizzling sound and if you judge it right they get cooked without being overdone. I like eggs and bacon myself, so I get plenty of practice."

"And you scoop them out of the pan without breaking them."

"Accidents are not unknown," she said. "It's a learning process. When I drop things, Bella is only too happy to clean up."

"Mind if I ask another dumb question? How did you manage to write that email inviting us here?"

"On my laptop."

"Yes, but . . ."

"I could always touch-type. And I have a software programme called a screen reader that sounds as friendly as a police radio, but tells me what's on the screen."

She suggested a stroll through the village later. The

overnight rain had given way to bright sunshine. "We're small, but we still have a shop and a pub, which is more than many others can claim."

"What's special about Baskerville that it keeps going?" Paloma asked.

"Careful how you pronounce it," Julie said. "We're nothing to do with the famous hound. Round here, it's Bask, as in basket."

"Baaarskeville, m'darlings," Diamond said in a dreadful faux-Somerset accent. "I like it."

Julie answered Paloma's query. "We're isolated, as you will have seen when you drove here, but there are people living across a wide area and most of them shop in the village rather than the supermarkets in town. It's out of loyalty, I'm sure, and the shop is community owned and well stocked with farm produce, so we are well known. Customers drive out here from Bridgwater and Taunton, where they have shops of their own."

"You depend a lot on the farm?"

"Without it, we'd really be in trouble, which is why there was such a crisis when Mervyn died. We didn't know Claudia would take over. Fortunately, Jim and Agnes—Hamish's parents—had been running it for some years and they were happy to continue. Their terms of employment didn't suffer. I'm told they are well paid, as they should be."

"Claudia didn't plunder the profits, then?" Diamond said while doing some plundering of his own, a rasher of bacon Paloma had pushed to the edge of her plate.

"As far as I know, the financing of the farm was never under threat. She splashed out on a few luxuries like a new car and a foreign holiday. You'd have to be a saint not to have a bit of a spree when you first inherited over a million."

"She can't do much where she is now."

"Poor soul, yes." Julie pushed back her chair. "Did you leave any scraps for Bella?"

Diamond glanced down at his empty plate.

Paloma was quick to say, "It was so delicious there isn't much. I'll scoop ours into her dish." She had some scraps left.

"And I'll wash up," Diamond offered—for which he got a surprised look from Paloma. He wasn't known for being domesticated. "What time is it? Generally I've driven to work by now." Being a houseguest would take some adjustment.

"It's only a matter of loading the dishwasher," Julie said. "We'll give it a whirl later in the day."

WITH BELLA HARNESSED and leading, they stepped out for the tour of the village.

"The first thing of note is my filthy car," Diamond said in a tour-guide voice before they came out of the front gate. "Your neighbours will already be asking what sort of scumbags are staying here."

"I don't think so," Julie said. "This isn't the Royal Crescent. The folk here are used to mud. If it worries you, I'll find you a bucket and sponge when we get back."

"It doesn't worry him enough for that," Paloma said.

"Give me a break," he said. "I cleaned your shoes and mine before you were up and about this morning."

They started along the path skirting the village green. Bella steered them around a puddle. "Good girl," Julie said. "She'll stop altogether if we come to a large one. All I have to say is 'Find the way' and she does."

"Where are we heading?"

"She knows. When I'm out in the morning the shop is where we make for."

They passed a terrace of stone cottages. The top of the church tower was visible above the roofs, greyer in colour than the creamy limestone buildings closer to Bath.

"By the way, Julie, you can drop the 'guv,'" Diamond said. "We've all moved on since the Manvers Street days."

"Unless you really mind, I'll stick with it. I'll always think of you as my guv'nor. I wouldn't be comfortable using your first name."

Paloma said, "If you're introducing us to other people, you'll need to call him something."

"Preferably something polite," Diamond chipped in.

"You're Peter, my ex-boss. But I won't say you're a senior detective. I've never told the locals I was in the police. They think I was a social worker of some sort, which is basically true."

"Why the secrecy? You should be proud of your old job. You were damned good at it."

She reddened. "It takes a while to get accepted here. I don't want them all on their best behaviour each time I walk into the pub."

"You want me to keep quiet about the day job?" he said. "I get it, Julie, but there's more to this than your wish for privacy, isn't there?"

She smiled. "You don't miss a thing."

"Feelings are still sore in the village?"

"After the body was found, we had officers here for days questioning everyone. People got upset at being treated as suspects when it was obvious Claudia and her Bath friends were responsible."

"And you don't want anyone to get the idea that the case is being opened up again? I understand. Why don't you call me Peter Dee, just in case anyone has heard of me? It's easy to remember."

Julie seemed to like that.

For a short time, no more was said except the odd word of encouragement to Bella for changing course at puddles. Then Diamond started up again. "You don't really believe it was wrong to question the residents? Someone from here could have decided a fatal accident would put a stop to the partying."

"It crossed my mind, but I can't think how they'd manage it."

"Neither can I right now, but if I were on the case I wouldn't rule anyone out. Whoever was in charge must have felt the same way. I wonder who the SIO was."

"Jack Crandley, from Taunton CID."

"You were here, of course. I'm forgetting. DI Crandley. I've never heard anything to say he isn't a good detective. Did he question you?"

"One of his sergeants did."

"Anyone you knew?"

She shook her head. "Personnel have changed since I was on the payroll."

"But you didn't tell this sergeant you were a retired DCI?"

"He didn't ask so I didn't volunteer it. That's a side benefit of being blind. People assume it was forever."

They were moving round two sides of the green, which wasn't the sort where village cricket is played. A large pond was in the centre and a children's play area on the far side.

As well as taking in the features of the place, Diamond was thinking about the drift of Julie's remarks. The body in the silo was much on her mind. She was the one who had brought it into the conversation this morning. Paloma was right. They had been invited for a reason. Julie wanted his opinion on the case.

He didn't mind particularly if it didn't amount to more

than that. The mystery fascinated him but he had no authority to reopen the inquiry. He could get into real trouble if he did.

"The shop used to be our post office and when that part of it closed, we were in danger of losing it altogether," Julie said when they got near.

"When was this?"

"Soon after I moved here. People were so alarmed that Mervyn suggested taking over the shop as a community venture and that's what we did. I'm a shareholder like most of my neighbours. The bulk of the money was put up by Mervyn. We run it as volunteers. Well, I can't do much now, but I took my turn behind the counter while I still had my sight. We have a vested interest in supporting it."

"This is happening in villages all over the country," Paloma said.

"Yes, and it's good in all sorts of ways. We know each other better than we ever did before."

Which can also have its downside, Diamond was tempted to say, but didn't. "Mervyn seems to have been a twenty-first-century lord of the manor."

"That's pretty much how we thought of him, except there was no lording it. He mucked in and got things done. I liked him a lot."

"Is that why you have some sympathy with his delinquent daughter?"

"I wouldn't call it sympathy. She was a pain."

"Empathy, then."

"That's more like it. I sometimes think of her in her cell brooding over what went wrong. The manslaughter sentence was too heavy for what happened. I'm sure they were all acting stupidly. She was the one who carried the can."

"Her house, her party, her game," Diamond said. "It was

about responsibility and she made bad decisions. The story of her life, from all you've told us." He had a high respect for Julie's deductive skills, but he could only give an opinion on the facts as he'd heard them and he couldn't find the sympathy Julie clearly felt. The image of the prisoner in the cell lamenting her situation didn't sway him. Every prisoner felt like that.

Julie didn't comment. Her silence was eloquent.

Paloma felt the tension and tried to deflate it. "I can understand a young girl brought up on a farm looking for a more glamorous life outside."

"That was when she was a kid," Diamond said. "We all rebel as teenagers, or most of us do. Claudia doesn't seem to have grown out of it. She's in her forties now, Julie told us."

"I did," Julie said. "I can't defend her behaviour. And yet I hear my friends and neighbours discuss her as if she's evil and I can't accept that she is. She admitted thinking up the game but she denied ever placing the garter in the silo."

"Where did she claim to have hidden it, then?"

"In the bull pen, but she wasn't believed. She didn't say it with any conviction. The prosecution picked up on it straight away and turned it to their advantage, asking if she was bent on putting her friends in harm's way. They asked a series of questions about the layout of the yard. She got flustered, contradicted herself several times. The thing is, her brain was fogged by all the rubbish she'd taken."

"Drugs?"

"And alcohol. She wasn't a good witness. She remembered the main events of that night but when it came to detail, she was hopelessly confused. The prosecution tore her to shreds."

"Was her state of mind queried in court?"

"Oh, yes. Under questioning she admitted she was on medication. Sedatives. I suppose she thought she would get a sympathetic reaction, but of course she didn't. It undermined her evidence."

"I'm not surprised the judge took a hard line." He was being honest even though Julie believed Claudia had been hard done by.

They had reached the shop, double-fronted and with a *Somerset Gazette* board outside announcing COAL ORCHARD TO CLOSE.

"What the heck is that about?" Diamond asked. He sensed the need to lighten the mood but he had forgotten Julie's blindness.

Paloma read the words aloud and Julie smiled and explained that the Coal Orchard was a pub in a part of Taunton being developed as a riverside attraction with restaurants, a large arts centre and theatre, but the project had run into difficulties during the Covid lockdown. "You'd better buy the paper if you really want to know."

"I don't suppose it will tell me what a coal orchard is."

Julie did. "Way back in the past it was an apple orchard beside the River Tone where Welsh coal was unloaded."

"So it doesn't grow on trees. What a disappointment. Do you ever get into Taunton?"

"Quite often, on the bus."

"Really?"

"I'm not helpless, guv."

Some things haven't changed, he thought. She was always able to cut me down to size when I said something thoughtless.

In the shop, a tall, silver-haired woman behind the till greeted Julie by name, looked over her rimless glasses at Paloma and said, "I don't think we've met."

Julie was quick to say, "These are friends of mine from Bath, Peter and Paloma, spending a few days here."

"From Bath? What do you do in Bath?" the woman said, putting them on the defensive sooner than they'd expected. She was probably in her fifties, but she dressed like someone of seventy, in a long-sleeved white lace blouse with a stand collar and pearls worn over it. Hair combed back, pinned and gathered into a Queen Victoria bun.

"What do we do?" Diamond said, on his best behaviour for Julie's sake. "At this time of year we try not to get trampled by tourists. I was about to ask where you keep the newspapers."

"Behind you." She wasn't sidetracked. Her penetrating brown eyes almost pinned him to the magazine rack. "Do you actually work in Bath, Peter?"

"I don't think of it as work," he said, stonewalling. "It's a privilege to be in a city as handsome as it is. But you have the advantage of us, ma'am."

"In what way?"

"What's your name?"

"Miss Harrap." As formal as her get-up. "I take my turn as shop manager."

"Well, Miss Harrap, I'll let you get on." He turned to the newspapers.

She wasn't done. "Is that your car standing outside Julie's cottage?"

"I hope so. It was when we started out," he said over his shoulder. He was becoming irritated.

"When I came by this morning, I happened to notice a pet-carrier on the back seat. If you want to stock up on tins, the pet food is in the centre aisle. A cat or a dog?"

"We brought all the tins we need, thanks."

"Which paper are you looking for? We have them all."

"I just like to check the headlines." He muttered to Julie, "Get your shopping before I blow my top."

After they got outside, Paloma said, "She was only doing her job, Pete, welcoming us to the shop."

"Felt more like a workover than a welcome."

Julie said, "It always is with Maggie. As soon as I heard her voice, my heart sank. We call her our Miss Marple. She's not a gossip, but she likes to know everything."

"Village life, Pete. Get used to it," Paloma said. "People take an interest in each other."

"Fair enough. Miss Marple, eh? People like that can be useful."

Paloma eyed him with amusement. "You're starting to get your teeth into this."

Without comment, he turned to Julie. "It must be a challenge not being able to recognise people until they speak."

"I'm used to it now. And living in a small community helps. What really throws me when I'm out is someone touching my arm when I don't expect it. They mean to be helpful but it comes as a shock. I wish they'd say something first."

He was learning things about sightlessness that hadn't crossed his mind before now.

"Where next?" Julie asked. "The church or the pub?"

"Do you really need to ask?" Paloma said.

He surprised them both. "The farm gets my vote."

For that, he got a look from his partner as sharp as anything he'd got from Maggie Harrap.

5

WHEN THEY RETURNED to the cottage to drop off the shopping, Raffles wasn't where they'd left him, in his cat bed near the radiator. He was in a prime position on the sofa, asleep, or pretending to be. He may have registered that they were back, but didn't stir.

"How the heck did he get up there?" Diamond said. "He can't jump. He can't climb."

"That's his secret," Paloma said, "and he has no intention of telling us."

"I hope he hasn't been conning me about the arthritis."

"I expect the new tablets have something to do with it."

"He can't stay there."

"Where is he?" Julie asked. "On the sofa? Leave him. He's doing no harm." She had brought in two pairs of wellies. "These will do for Paloma and me. Sorry, guv, I don't have any you'll get your feet into."

"I'll just watch my footing."

"On a dairy farm that may not be enough. I hope you're not wearing your best shoes."

He looked down as if by some miracle he was not. He had long ago decided it was in the stars that he would never be wearing appropriate dress for anything. He was in the dark suit he habitually wore for work, the trousers still marked from last night's misadventure, for all the efforts he had made to scrape off the dry mud. "I'll follow Bella."

"Even Bella is going to need a bath when we get back."

The first part of the walk had a few hazards they avoided.

"Let's hope we don't meet the cows again," Paloma said. "We could get unpopular with young Hamish."

"They won't be on the move yet," Julie said. "I can hear the milking machine."

"Your hearing's sharper than mine."

"I know what to listen for."

"Do we need the owner's permission?"

"To visit the farm? She's in no position to give it. Anyhow, there's supposed to be a right of way."

Sure enough, a footpath sign was opposite the entrance. A large triple-gabled farmhouse with an oak front door stood to their right. Two-storied, with leaded windows tall enough for a manor house, it had numerous architectural features in the stonework that delighted the eye.

"Fine old building," Diamond said.

Difficult to estimate how many bedrooms it contained. Certainly enough to have housed numerous generations of the family it had been built for. Or, more recently, numerous partygoers.

"How old is it?"

"Getting on for five hundred years, I'm told," Julie said. "They knew how to build an attractive house. Most of that time it was tenanted, so there weren't the alterations you often get when the owner lives in."

"There must have been money in farming in those days."

"It's much restored in recent years," Julie said. "And I do mean restored, not altered. Before Mervyn inherited, it was rather run-down."

The yard beyond the house was a minefield of cowpats. Diamond soon gave up trying to avoid them.

"I know where we are by the pong, some of it fresh this morning," Julie said.

"Better than traffic fumes," he said. "Bath is officially a clean air zone, but you wouldn't know it."

Paloma flapped a hand in front of her nose. "This is rather overpowering. I was brought up to believe farming is all about fresh air and honest toil."

"Not much fresh air round here," Diamond said. "There might be some further on. I'd like a closer look at the two silos. Anyone mind if we head that way?"

"What a good idea." Julie couldn't conceal her satisfaction at Diamond's interest in the case.

"The cows do well here," she went on. "There's plenty of good pasture land and Mervyn believed in letting his ladies, as he called them, into the fields to enjoy it as much as our climate allows. When I still had my sight, I saw them being turned out after their winter stay indoors and they were like kids at playtime, gambolling about. You could feel their joy. Half the village turned out to watch. I treasure that memory."

"Sweet," Paloma said. "I like the idea of traditional farming, cows in fields."

"You didn't mention that when we met the stampede last night," Diamond said.

"You know what I'm talking about. They don't want to spend their entire lives in a shed putting their heads through iron bars to feed. And before you say it, no, I've never asked them."

"That's the way it has to be in the winter months," Julie said. "They're looked after here, as you say." She giggled. "There's even a bull called Chummy."

"And is he?" Diamond asked.

"That's a question for the cows. Not to visitors, particularly. I wouldn't stand in his way if I were you."

"Now you tell us." He took a nervous look around. "Where is he kept?"

"He has his own pen somewhere here. Unless he gives a bellow, I can't tell you where."

"I can see a big thatched building."

"He won't be in there. That will be the tithe barn, used now as a games room and for village events. Mervyn said it was right to give it to the people after their ancestors worked for centuries to fill it with their produce. He had it modernised inside and made safe."

Mervyn sounded like a true altruist.

They were close to a tall open shed with a concrete floor that housed up to twenty tractors, harvesters and other vehicles. "I can't get over the scale of all this," Diamond said. "It's a big investment."

"Are you talking about the tractor shed?" Julie said. "They need a range of machines for all the different jobs."

The milking parlour was ahead. Some distance farther on and across a field, gleaming in the morning sun, were the twin silos Diamond wanted to see close up. Functional and stark, no one could say they added anything to the view.

A voice behind them called out, "Oh, it's you, Julie. For a moment I panicked, thinking you were a DEFRA inspection, and then I spotted Bella."

Julie turned and waved. "This will be Agnes, the farm manager." She waited for Agnes—a short, smiling woman splashing across the yard in her boots and blue overalls. "Meet my friends, Paloma and Peter, here for a few days. I thought I'd show them round."

"Sorry if we alarmed you," Diamond said. "I'm told suits are not worn hereabouts."

"Or anywhere much," Paloma said, "except funerals."

"I'd offer you all a coffee," Agnes said, "but Jim and I bring our own flasks. We don't live on the farm, you see. Our cottage is the other side of the village."

"So that lovely farmhouse isn't lived in?"

"Not right now. Julie will tell you the situation."

"I already did," Julie said. "They know about Claudia."

This was as good a cue as Diamond could have wished for. "She still owns the farm, I understand."

"It's the family business. Jim and I were recruited by her father, Mervyn, when he got too old to cope with the work. He was a lovely man. We don't know Claudia so well but she's content for us to manage the same way we did with her dad."

"She's in no position to run the farm herself."

Agnes smiled. "She's not really into farming. If you met her, you'd understand."

"More of a party girl?"

"Yes, and she doesn't mind anyone knowing. She's open about everything. Or was. Prison may have changed that. I hope not." The note of concern was interesting. Agnes hadn't written Claudia off.

"But she isn't so popular in the village, Julie tells us."

"Fair comment. They didn't like the company she kept. The noise at night and the cars everywhere. It stopped after the dead man was found."

"And how did that happen?"

"We couldn't empty one of the silos. The grain should fall through the hole in the base but it was blocked. It's a common problem. The best way to deal with it is to lower an auger inside, specialised equipment we don't keep here."

"What's an auger—like a drill?"

"A kind of giant corkscrew."

"You had to hire one?"

"And it still didn't do the job. In the end, Jim had to go inside from the top—which can be dangerous, so he was wearing a harness and a safety line. You can imagine the shock when he found what was in there. We were inundated with policemen and people in protective overalls. I forget what you call them."

"Forensics, usually. Did they tell you much?"

"The body had been in there for about four months. He was dressed in party clothes, poor guy, and he had a pink garter round his arm that was apparently used in a game."

"Was Claudia informed?"

"Right away. She called the police at once and told them everything she knew. She identified the body and told them about him being one of her friends who came to the parties. She couldn't have been more helpful and a fat lot of good it did her."

"It had been there four months, you say. Hadn't anyone reported him missing?"

"Apparently not. Claudia assumed he'd left the party early. Not everyone stayed overnight although plenty did."

"Wasn't his car found the next day?"

"No. Some of them always came and left by taxi, so that they were free to drink as much as they wanted." Agnes turned to look at him. "You're getting interested in this gruesome story."

Sounding awfully like a policeman, she might have added. Before Diamond could answer, Julie said, "Typical Peter. He always wants to know every detail. We mustn't hold you up."

She was doing her job, just like old times, stopping him from getting too heavy with the questioning.

"Come and see the milking, then," Agnes said. "Jim is in there with our boy, Hamish. They won't have time to talk but you're welcome to watch them at work."

Diamond was about to say they'd met Hamish yesterday but Agnes was already on the move, heading past the vacant byre where the herd wintered. Julie said she would walk around the outside of the milking parlour and meet them at the other end in case her dog unsettled the cows, so Diamond and Paloma were left alone.

"This was Mervyn's pride and joy," Agnes told them inside the main shed.

"What a spectacle," Paloma said. "A cow carousel."

Thirty stalls were in use on a rotary platform, the soiled rear ends of the herd facing outwards defiantly in what was clearly a highly controlled operation. The cows had entered the slowly turning booths five at a time from a walkway on the opposite side, lured in by cattle-cake pellets in the filled feeding troughs. Barrier frames descended and clanged shut behind them, keeping them from backing out. Sprays washed the udders before the teat-cups were attached manually.

The not unpleasant smell of cow shit left no doubt where they were. The heat from the big animals was immediately apparent. Wetness, warmth and the whiff of dung prevailed here: steaming pools of urine, fresh cowpats, gallons of milk filling the glass collectors.

Jim Douglas, wearing waterproof overalls, was at ground level working alone, a powerfully built man whose hands in rubber gloves performed the routine with delicacy that the cows accepted without flinching. He didn't once look up from his work. There was no sign of Hamish.

"They don't know how lucky they are," Paloma said.

"They must be content because we get higher yields," Agnes said. "We used to work with the herringbone layout most dairy farmers still use but there was a certain amount of jostling you don't get in these stalls. Kicking is a thing of the past, too. They feed on concentrates while they wait. What is more, the time we spend milking is halved. One of us can manage the entire process in just over an hour."

"And I suppose it gets sprayed clean after they leave?"

"All automatic."

"The outlay must have been heavy," Diamond said.

Agnes gave a shrug. "Mervyn knew it wouldn't be cost-effective for the small herd we have, but he wasn't short of money so he could indulge in something that pleased him. We had an entire refit as soon as the rotaries came into production. The doors at the far end lead to the tank room and the mechanism. All new and up to the same standard."

Paloma asked, "How was all this funded, then? A government grant of some kind?"

Agnes shook her head. "Nothing like that."

"Mervyn paid? He must have been super-rich to afford facilities like this. Is the rest of the farm so well equipped?"

"We aren't short of anything."

"Old money? Or another source of income?"

She looked away.

It was a good thing Diamond wasn't still doing the probing or he'd soon be outed as a professional policeman. Agnes was clearly uncomfortable with the questioning, which only prompted Paloma to press harder. "Julie was telling us Mervyn committed suicide. Was he in some sort of trouble?"

"Yes and no." She clasped her arms across her chest as if she was in a sudden draught. It was touch and go whether she would say any more, but Paloma's sympathetic, enquiring face was difficult to ignore. "He suffered from depression and hid it from almost everybody. He was all right when he was busy at the heart of village life, making a difference to all our lives, but when he got too old for work and retired, the demons closed in. Towards the end, he was drinking heavily at home. His family life was non-existent."

"I can understand," Diamond said. Only too well, he thought. Retirement is the waiting room for death. Some people decide the waiting is too much.

"His wife died young, Julie told us," Paloma said.

"You heard about the lightning strike? Dreadful. He wouldn't share his grief. And later he felt he'd failed Claudia as a parent. There was never a reconciliation. Isn't that awful, when a father and his daughter can't find a way to bridge the past?"

"Did everything pass to Claudia after he died?"

"Every penny as far as I know."

"No other family?"

"His brother Howard died some years before him."

"Was he a farmer like Mervyn?"

Agnes smiled faintly. She was more relaxed speaking about this remote family member. "Howard? He wasn't the sort to farm. We hardly ever saw him. He had a white beard, I remember. I was just a kid then. He was a bit eccentric. Some kind of artist, but I've heard since that he never sold anything or put it in exhibitions. Lived alone in a rented house in Bathampton. After he died, Mervyn had a terrible job sorting out all the clutter. Anything worth keeping—and there wasn't much—he stored here, in the farmhouse. There was some furniture that had once belonged to their parents but it was riddled with woodworm so he had some huge bonfires." Without pause, she changed the topic. "I'm sorry

Hamish isn't here. He's probably outside with his quad bike ready to move the ladies back to their field."

Diamond had to think about that for a couple of seconds. "We met the ladies briefly in the lane last night." No point in denying it. The story of their arrival would be public knowledge by now.

Agnes knew all about it. "He can seem surly. It's his age. He's a good lad underneath it all. Why don't you make your way out now and link up again with Julie? You may see Hamish there." The tour was at an end.

As soon as they were out of earshot, Diamond asked Paloma, "What did you think of that?"

"Agnes or the milking parlour?"

"The way she spoke about Mervyn."

"There was sympathy, I thought. Sad story."

"She was happier talking about the brother rather than where the money came from. She must have some idea how all this was paid for but she wasn't keen to share it with us."

"She thought I was being nosy and I was," Paloma said. "Can't blame her for giving us our marching orders."

"I needed fresh air anyway," Diamond said. "What happens to all the dung?"

"It gets hosed away, I expect. They call it slurry, don't they?"

"And then?"

"Doesn't it get spread over the fields as fertiliser?" She was frowning. "Why are you so interested?"

"I may be an ignorant townie, but I know a slurry pit can be lethal. Farms are dangerous places—and that's regardless of any bad people who work there."

"There's nothing bad about Agnes, is there?"

"Who knows? There are things she doesn't want to share with the likes of you and me. You said yourself she couldn't get shot of us quickly enough."

"Can't blame her," Paloma said. "Her livelihood and Jim's depends on the money Mervyn had in the bank. If there's anything dodgy about it, she's not going to tell us. I wonder whether the brother left him money. Some people who live as recluses turn out to be millionaires."

"I got the impression he was a struggling artist."

"We can find out from the probate records," Paloma said. "Want me to check?"

"Right now?"

She took out her phone. "Anyone can sign up for the free trial on a family history app and access the records."

Diamond wished he'd thought of it, but he was proud of her.

Paloma's thumb worked the keypad at high speed. "His unusual name and place of birth should get us his other data. The family had lived in Baskerville for generations."

It turned out that Howard Priest had been born in 1925 and died in Bathampton in 1993. His estate was registered in Bath and had amounted to £1351.

"That wouldn't have made anyone rich," Paloma said.

"There goes another promising theory. Can we find out how much Mervyn left?"

"These records only go up to 1995, but you can apply to the probate registry."

"That would take a lot of time."

Outside in the morning sunshine, Julie's relief at hearing them approach was obvious. She had been trying to hold a conversation with Hamish, who was seated on his quad bike ignoring her, staring into the distance, the embodiment of adolescent angst. "Impressed by what you saw?" she said to her two guests.

"Super impressed," Diamond said. "I almost envied those cows. Morning, Hamish."

A scowl was all Hamish was willing to supply, but Julie made a valiant effort to involve him. She was being infinitely patient. "You guys met already, right?"

Diamond chipped in. "Helped him get some of them back into their field, didn't we, Hamish?"

For that he was treated to more lower lip than he cared to see.

"All except the ones who wanted to take the scenic route," Diamond breezed on, speaking to Julie with words intended more for Hamish, "and they would have been in Taunton by now if a certain young man hadn't headed them off on his quad bike. The way he handled that thing across a bumpy field was something to see."

The flattery caught the certain young man off guard. He actually turned to look at Diamond.

"He handles that bike as if it's an extension of himself. He's a natural, a complete natural."

Hamish couldn't keep down a flush of pride.

"Are you on the payroll? You should be," Diamond said directly to him.

Hamish spoke. "Wassat mean?"

"Do you get a regular wage, or is it treated as pocket money?"

"Not old enough."

"That surprises me. I just hope your parents fork out for all the excellent work you do. You're a key man. Are you responsible for seeing all those cows back to their field?"

A nod was all the answer he got but plenty was going on behind those pale blue eyes.

"We'd better move on as fast as possible, then," Diamond said. "It looked to me as if the milking was coming to an end and unlike you we don't have quad bikes."

They let themselves out through a gate, leaving the boy to reflect on his terms of employment.

"What mischief were you up to there?" Paloma said. "You have no idea if he deserves more pay."

"Getting on his good side. A bit more schmoozing and he could be a useful ally. Are we heading for the silos now?"

"By all means," Julie said. "Let's go."

"The quick way is across the field. Can you cope with that? It's not ploughed or anything."

"Of course. Lead the way and Bella will take her cue from you."

Once it was clear that Julie was walking freely, he took the opportunity to ask about the source of Mervyn's wealth. "We raised it with Agnes. She wasn't keen to discuss it. Made me wonder whether there's any local gossip about him."

"If there was, I never heard it. But you need to have lived here longer than me to move in those circles."

"Like Miss Harrap?"

She smiled. "You *have* got us summed up. She might know something I don't. But Maggie doesn't often volunteer things. You need to trade some titbit she's keen to know about." A few steps further on she asked, "How does Mervyn come into the equation, guv? He'd been dead for some time when the body was found."

"You know me, Julie. If something doesn't add up, I want to know why. He had buckets of money to splash out on that milking parlour that Agnes herself said was an indulgence. Where there's easy money, there's often lawbreaking somewhere up the line. Claudia may have inherited more than just the farm and whatever was in the bank."

"Like what?"

"Like a link to organised crime. Was her father into something dodgy and did she know about it?"

"I knew you'd think of angles I hadn't," she said with an anxious sigh. "If this turns out to be true, I'll be shocked to the core. Mervyn was quite the hero in these parts."

Diamond looked behind him, making a visual check. "How far is this from the farmhouse where the parties were held? What do you reckon? Three hundred metres?"

"More like five," Paloma said.

Julie's mood had changed. She was laughing.

"What's funny about that?" Diamond asked.

"I'm sorry, guv. You finally embrace the metric system after how many years?"

He chose to ignore the comment. "If he took the quickest way, across the field, it's a tricky walk in the dark. And if he followed the track the vehicles use, it's closer to six hundred metres. He'd have to be keen to try it. Or well tanked. Or high on drugs, but we can do it because we're clean-living, healthy types who exercise daily and drink nothing stronger than water."

"Oh, yes?" Paloma said.

They were breathing hard when they finished the cross-country part and approached the nearest silo, cone-shaped at top and bottom and mounted on a sturdy metal frame, looking to Diamond's fanciful eye like a missile waiting to be fired. The height alone was daunting and the ladder fixed to the side looked a stiff climb. "Two people must have gone up: the victim and whoever planted the garter in there in the first place."

"Claudia, if the prosecution had it right," Paloma said.

"She denies it," Julie said.

Diamond couldn't picture any woman wanting to tackle the climb just to gee up a party game but he didn't want to be called sexist so he kept the thought to himself. "I wonder if the jury were brought here to see the silo for themselves. They were probably shown photos, but that isn't the same as seeing it close up like this."

"Which one had the body inside?" Paloma asked.

"I can't tell you," Julie said.

"Presumably it's empty now."

"They both are. The second one as well, in case there was another body. I was told the seeds were spread over a big area to be searched."

"So two loads of grain had to be destroyed? That must have been a hefty loss to the farm."

"That was the least of Claudia's worries."

Diamond looked at the cone-shaped base of the huge steel cylinder. The grain had been emptied through the outlet at the bottom. Normally it would have been collected mechanically.

"Was anything else found?"

"The dead man's phone, I believe."

"Would he have got a signal inside the silo?"

"Probably not. They thought he must have been using it as a torch."

He could picture it. "Poor beggar."

Paloma was becoming restless. "Have you seen enough? This place is giving me the creeps."

He understood. "Why don't you two go on? I'll check a couple of things and see you presently."

"In the pub would be a good idea," Paloma said. "Enjoy your fresh air. We're thirsty."

Left to himself, he felt like a kid out of school. Each of his companions had played a major part in his life, partnering him in quite different ways, steering him through the challenges thrown at him. Both understood him and tolerated his faults. He'd been uncertain how they would get on with each other. In reality they had bonded so well he felt slightly ganged up on. He enjoyed female company but right now he needed a break. He circled the silos slowly, looking to see how far away the two women had gone. Far enough. He stopped at one of the ladders, put a foot on the first rung and started climbing.

6

IT DAWNED ON him halfway up that investigating Roger Miller's death could easily cost him his job.

This wasn't playing games to spice up a boring week in the country. An injustice might have been done and if that was what Julie suspected there was a probability she was right. The case was crying out for the full treatment, a reinvestigation, questioning witnesses and examining statements. No use kidding himself he could do it on the quiet. People at every level would want to know what right he had to question them. When word got back to headquarters, as it would, all hell would break loose. He was already well known as a loose cannon. The high-ups who remembered him from previous episodes would be queuing up to boot him out. The fast track to retirement.

Stuff them. Not one of them had ever walked the mean streets and tracked down a killer.

He'd do what he'd done before: crack the case, prove himself right and give them no option but to keep him on.

He was gathering knowledge as he climbed, getting a sense of the effort needed to put the garter in place, out of reach on the fragile surface of the stored grain, then come down again. If Claudia hadn't put it there, as she claimed, someone else had.

Already he was panting, but so what? Overweight and out of condition, he knew he couldn't compare with a fit young woman. Still, he made it to the top without stopping, gripped the sides of the ladder and took a moment to draw breath and look behind him.

The view was exhilarating. He didn't have any problem with heights. Paloma, Julie and Bella the guide dog were already out of sight, obscured by farm buildings not much bigger than Lego models. He could see as far as the farmhouse itself and beyond. He was getting a sense of the size of the village, the old part and a less appealing new estate to the north. Not much more than two hundred dwellings, he reckoned. A small community had been impacted heavily by the scandal and disruption Claudia and her friends from Bath had inflicted. Everyone would have an opinion about it. You never want to be a target of gossip.

He recovered his breath enough to lift the hatch and look inside. He managed it with one hand.

Too dark to see much. He could just make out the faint gleam of steel on the other side. The space below was a black void, as sobering an image of death as he could imagine. A morbid thought. Snap out of it, he told himself. On an impulse, he shouted, "Anyone at home?"

"Home . . . home," the echo called back to him.

The terror the victim had suffered was all too easy to imagine. He yelled, "Help!"

The voice was his own but it still made an eerie sound.

"Help . . . help . . . help." The last of them touchingly faint.

He drew back and closed the hatch.

The descent was less work for his legs but more testing because he couldn't see the rungs. He hadn't gone far when he missed his footing and slipped. For a moment he hung from his hands. Just as quickly, his foot found one of the rungs and supported him again.

Close call.

He was reminded of the twin ladders sculpted on the west front of Bath Abbey and the twelve stone angels apparently trying to climb up to heaven, some so weathered and worn that their heads and wings had gone. Most were heading resolutely upwards, although two had turned to look down, two unfortunates plunging headfirst towards hell.

At key stages in his career he had stood in Abbey Churchyard staring up at those figures, identifying with them, thinking deeply about his own life and which way he was heading. He wouldn't care to explain the logic to anyone else, how the angels served as a kind of oracle for him. He looked to them for guidance. Call it superstition, but over the years he had found answers there in times of stress.

Today, just thinking about them was enough.

This was another ladder and another defining moment. His mind was made up. Better cling on. Avoid the long dive. Make enquiries about the dead man in the silo, but with caution.

At ground level, he rubbed his hands clean, stepped back and went rigid when a voice spoke close behind him.

"Had a good look, mate?"

He swung round and was face to face with the farm manager, Jim Douglas, in his blue overalls, arms folded, legs slightly apart, a combative stance.

No use denying what he'd been doing. His only option was to play the ignorant townie. "You don't mind, I hope? These are the highest buildings around here. Fantastic view from the top."

"Don't give me that. I saw you arse upwards with the hatch open."

"Ah." He must have been watching for some time. "Curiosity, I suppose."

"What the fuck were you doing?"

"I was told it's a right of way."

"The footpath is. You've no right climbing the silo. That's trespass."

"Awfully sorry. Couldn't resist. Are you the farmer?"

"Farm manager."

"You must be Jim." Diamond thrust his hand forward. "Peter's the name, here for a few days visiting Julie Hargreaves, the blind woman. She's an old friend."

The hand was ignored. "Julie sent you to nose around?"

"Not at all. That's down to me entirely. Bloody cheek, I admit." He was wittering on to cover his embarrassment. "You're wondering what the hell I was up to and I don't blame you. Three of us were looking around the farm, my partner Paloma, Julie and me, and we met the lady who must be your wife. She very kindly showed us inside the milking shed. Amazing. I think we caught sight of you in there. You were too busy to notice."

"Agnes showed you round?" Jim Douglas said with astonishment.

"Charming lady. You and I seem to have got off on the wrong foot." All of this grovelling was becoming a strain. It didn't come naturally. He took a step away. "Forgive me. Must fly. I'd better catch up with the ladies now—the human ones. They'll be wondering where I am."

PALOMA AND JULIE were in the Feathers drinking coffee. The village pub is the dimly lit, cheaply furnished, stale-smelling staple of English country life that the patrons know is a disgrace but would die in a ditch to save. Diamond hadn't come there to drink coffee. "Parched. What's the local brew?"

"The Exmoor is popular," Julie said.

"That's for me, then. Where's Bella?"

"Under the table sleeping," Julie said. "She's had a busy morning already."

"Doesn't she get a drink?"

"She's fine."

The young woman behind the bar had overheard him and was poised with her hand on the Exmoor Ale pump. Nothing went unnoticed in this place. He handed her a five-pound note and told her to keep the change. She opened a jar and told him to hold out his hand.

"What's this?"

"Treats."

"Not hungry, thanks."

She stared at him as if he was unreal.

"Ah." He tumbled to what was happening. "Treats for Bella. Obviously one of your regulars."

"Best behaved of the lot."

The only other people in there were two old men in cloth caps playing cribbage. They didn't look badly behaved. "Seems quiet this morning. You have some wild nights here, I daresay."

"We have our moments," she said, and looked him up and down as if he might be one of those moments himself.

He carried his drink to the table and asked Julie to hold out her hand. Bella was quicker to those treats than a greyhound out of the trap.

"I thought she was asleep."

"She smelt them. Did you find anything of interest?"

"Nothing special," he said, not yet ready to share the story of his meeting with Jim Douglas, "but I've done some think-ing." He lowered his voice to a level the barmaid wouldn't overhear. "I need to spend some time in Bath tomorrow."

Paloma gave him a sharp look. "Doing what?"

"Getting some background on Claudia Priest and her friends. I'll return before dark."

"Can't it wait until we get home?"

"The whole point is that everyone thinks I'm away all week. I can make a few enquiries unofficially without my team knowing. And in case you're wondering, Julie, it's nothing to do with your cooking."

She gave a slight smile, but she, too, had doubts. "Are you sure you want to do this? I only told you about Clau-dia to get your ideas on the case. I wasn't expecting you to get involved."

"Really?"

"Well . . ." She coloured slightly. "Not in a professional way."

"That's not the plan."

"You know how the grapevine works, guv. If Taunton CID get to hear, you're sunk."

"Which is why I'm doing it on the q.t. Give me some credit, ladies." He didn't like sounding huffy, but he was too late to stop himself. "And if I need to share any of this with a couple of work colleagues, I know the ones I can trust to keep their mouths shut."

Paloma didn't let that pass. "Hold on. A moment ago you said no one from the team would know."

"Julie mentioned the grapevine, that's why. It's all hypo-thetical."

"Driving back to Bath isn't hypothetical. We're supposed to be enjoying a week in the country."

He didn't persist. However hard he tried to justify his

plan, he'd fail. No use saying the stone angels had spoken. "Who wants another coffee?"

They shook their heads.

"I'll take the tray back and have another chat with the barmaid."

Paloma sighed. She knew what he was up to. Julie must have heard the sigh. She smiled.

It emerged that Dolores had run the pub for nine years, right through the time of Claudia's parties and the incident that finished them. She didn't mind talking about it.

"That was a fun time. Some of them used to come in here for liveners before moving on to the farm. They didn't mix much with the locals."

"I'm sure they chatted to you," he prompted her. "Can I buy you a drink while it's so quiet?"

She fluttered her eyelashes. They were big enough for a drag queen. "You're a sport. I'll pour myself a G&T and put it on your tab."

"Did I start one? I usually pay as I go."

"Your lady friends did, before you got here."

"That'll teach me to turn up on time." He waited while she fixed the drink. "Those partygoers. I guess they were Bath people, like Claudia."

"She was from here originally. Spread her wings and flew the coop as soon as she was old enough. Can't blame her. Some folk here have never been further than Taunton."

"Funny she should have ended up in Bath, where I live."

"Small world. Do you know her?"

He shook his head. "I might know some of her friends, although I'm not a party animal."

She eyed his suit and tie. "Who would have guessed?"

"Do you remember any of them?"

"Her playboy friends? The one who stood out was

the shortest and the funniest. Fab could easily have done stand-up."

"Fab as in Fabio?"

"You got it. Cheeky fella with a buzz cut, moustache, wandering eyes, a Porsche and a million stories. Know the type? Done a bit of everything, travelled the world, had the wheels, the charm and a quip for any occasion."

"Did he have a job?"

"Not what I call a job."

"Go on."

"Wealth management, whatever that means."

"Nice if you can get it."

"It worked for Fab. He flaunted it, too. Made sure you saw his Rolex when he paid with his Platinum card. All the chat, and no problem finding clients. He had a story—how true I couldn't tell you—about a bus driver who won the jackpot on EuroMillions, more than twenty million, and the only thing this bloke wanted to spend his money on was train rides, the treat of being driven by someone else, you see. The Orient Express, the Trans-Siberian, you name it."

"The ultimate busman's holiday."

She wasn't amused at having her story interrupted. "More of a retirement plan. All Fab had to do for this guy was order the right currency for each country. Is that what wealth management is?"

"There's more to it than that. I can't speak from experience. I think they invest your money for you if you save any up."

"Me?" she said. "You're joking. Anyhow, the point of the story was that Fab said something to the bus driver about his portfolio and the guy thought he was talking about another place to visit. Port Folio, geddit?"

"Haha."

"It was funny the way he told it."

It wasn't funny the way Dolores had told it but Diamond had raised a smile. She was already a helpful contact. "I can't place Fab among the people I know but then I don't have any wealth for him to manage. Do you remember his surname?"

She shrugged. "He was only ever Fab to me. Or Fabio when he got saucy."

"How about Claudia? Did she come in here much?"

"After she first moved in, she did. She met the regulars and bought rounds for anyone who was in, but things changed fast when the parties started. She wasn't popular after that. She was snubbed a few times and got the message she wasn't welcome."

"She stayed away?"

"Except at quiet times like now. We supplied her with booze for the parties, you see, so she'd come in and order stuff and I'd drive up to the farmhouse and deliver it. Business is business. I took some flak from the locals for supping with the devil but I give back as good as I get."

"Did she ever share anything about the poor fellow they found inside the silo?"

Dolores eyed him as if he was something she'd trodden in. "You a reporter?"

He'd been expecting this. "I wish! I don't get out much. Like a few million others, I spend most of my working hours at my desk staring at a computer screen."

"Why all the questions, then? No offence, ducky, but you're a bit old to be chatting me up."

"I'm curious, that's all. Julie told us about all the aggro the parties created and my ears pricked up when she mentioned

Claudia's friends were from Bath. She couldn't describe them, being blind, so I hope you can fill me in. How about another drink?"

"Not while I'm working." She grinned. The only work she'd done in the last five minutes was lifting her glass. But she seemed to decide he was harmless and the information flowed again. "The guy they found in the silo was Roger Miller, one of Claudia's exes. She had the job of identifying him." She pulled a face. "Imagine that, after four months in there. At least he was in the same clothes he'd worn at the party, which made it easier."

"When you say he was an ex, had they split up before he died?"

She nodded. "A few months. That was the pattern with Claudia. Roger was one of many. The thing is, while most of the others got the message and moved on, he stuck around hoping she'd change her mind."

"Was he a pest?"

"Not the way you mean. He tried to make himself loved, poor sap. The standard moves, sent her flowers and stuff, still in hope, which is hard to handle if you're a woman and the spark has gone."

"Was she seeing someone else by then?"

Dolores pulled an ironic smile. "Only on the days with an *a* in them."

"Who did she take up with after she dumped Roger?"

"While he was still alive? Now you're asking. I can picture the bloke. He was in here a few times. Thin as a toothpick, blond ponytail, public-school posh with a deep, deep voice, which was probably what appealed to her. Didn't have a proper job, of course."

"Do you remember his name?"

Dolores shook with laughter. "This was the weird bit. I

was expecting Rupert, Tristram or some such. She called him Bert."

"*Bert?*"

"Working behind a bar gives you a pretty good bead on names, but that creased me up."

"It must be short for something grander. Bertrand, Egbert—who knows? Have you seen him lately?"

"Not since Claudia was taken away by the police. The parties stopped and her noisy friends disappeared like rats down a hole. I expect they started up somewhere else."

He wanted more about the toff with the deep voice. "To be clear about this, Bert was the boyfriend who replaced Roger, right?"

She gave him a penetrating stare. "Are you sure you're not press?"

"I'm sure, but I don't think you are. I like a good story, that's all. If I were a reporter, I wouldn't have a couple of ladies in tow, would I? You were telling me about Bert. Did he keep coming here until Claudia was arrested?"

"They all did. I'm not sure anyone realised Roger was missing. Nobody asked where he was."

"Are you sure about Bert?"

"Sure in what way?"

"He didn't stop coming the same night Roger went missing?"

She shook her head. "Don't get carried away, sunshine. There was only one body found in the silo."

"I'm talking about the night they played the garter game."

"Did Julie tell you about that? She doesn't miss much considering . . ." She didn't complete the sentence. "I've talked to more reporters about those stupid garters than I can remember. That sort of stuff sells papers, doesn't it?"

She still hadn't made up her mind about him.

"You tell me."

"Well," she went on, "it hasn't made me any richer. Gets boring when you've told it ten times over. Claudia and her pals were always playing games like that. Room keys, calling cards, garters. The object was the same each time, pairing people off for sex. They were all so far gone they didn't care who they ended up with."

"Did you hear this firsthand?"

She reddened. "To be honest, no, but it all came out in court and got in the papers."

He let that pass without comment. Helpful as Dolores was, he needed to remind himself that her salacious take on events was mostly second hand, a patchwork of pub talk and news stories.

She continued: "Claudia opened up about it. She admitted everything except hiding the garter in the silo. She categorically denied that. She wasn't believed by the judge and jury and that's what did for her."

"What's your opinion? Do you think she was lying?"

"I honestly wouldn't know. I wasn't at the trial so I didn't hear her giving evidence. I can usually tell if someone is telling porkies."

"Did anyone from here go?"

"A couple of them did. One was Maggie Harrap."

"From the community shop? We were in there a short time ago."

"She'll have got your number, then. Anything you want to know about this village, ask Maggie."

Which was what he'd heard already from Julie. "Does she come in here?"

"Often. It's the best place to hear things. Sits alone on a barstool and makes one lemonade last an hour. We'll never get rich from Maggie's bar bills."

"And does she talk about the trial?"

"Not unless she's asked. She's more of a listener than a talker. Most of it washes over me but our Maggie misses nothing."

"Doesn't anyone object?"

"They scarcely notice her and they're not bothered anyway. Ninety-nine per cent of what gets said in here is public knowledge already, so why would they care? She's harmless. And she does more than her share of managing the shop." Dolores looked up at the clock. "Nice chatting but I've got to get food ready for the lunch bookings. Enjoy your visit and don't misquote me when you go to print."

Better to be taken for a reporter than a cop. He reckoned a competent newsman would have extracted the facts in half the time—which reminded him of a reporter called Ingeborg Smith who had appeared at a press conference and practically hung him out to dry. It was the year he had investigated the Bloodhounds of Bath, the group of mystery-lovers who met in the crypt of St. Michael's Church to talk about books they were reading. Over the next two years, Inge was a thorn in his side through case after case until he had the smart idea of suggesting she join the police on a fast-track scheme. A learning process had followed. The learner was Diamond. He soon discovered that being over-protective towards her was a big mistake. She was as tough as any of the team, intelligent and well able to cope. Fast track was an understatement. She had rocketed from detective constable to sergeant to inspector at a rate no one expected nor begrudged. It wouldn't surprise him if she ended up as head of the murder squad.

"Not yet," he told himself. Then: "Why am I thinking about my team when I'm trying to cut it as a solo sleuth?"

He returned to Julie and Paloma. Bella emerged from under the table and padded towards him.

"Someone forgot to bring more treats," Paloma said.

"She's had enough already," Julie said. "Shall we move? There's more of the village I want to show you."

Diamond had got more than he'd expected: a contact with someone who had bridged the gap between the locals and the visitors, an insight into how the village telegraph worked and two new names to investigate in Bath.

What could possibly go wrong?

7

DIAMOND TOLD PALOMA he would leave for Bath early in the morning. Raffles would get his arthritis tablet and his breakfast and, "You ladies can sleep on as long as you like."

"Do you really think this is worth doing?" Paloma asked him in the privacy of their room. "I don't know what Julie makes of you disappearing all day."

"She'll be okay with it. She asked for my help."

"That isn't quite right, is it? She hasn't asked for anything. When we got talking about Claudia last night it was only a bit of gossip, but you wanted every detail and now you've turned it into an investigation."

"It's a long way short of that, love. I'm not acting professionally."

"Hmm," she said, implying that a whole lot more lay behind his interest in the case.

"Well, then."

"Be honest, Pete, this is a dream come true for you, the chance to test your skills on a village mystery. The beauty of it is that the cause of the man's death is officially settled. It's not like a killing that just happened and needs the full police treatment. Julie has given you what every private detective needs: a licence to roam. You can nose around like one of those amateur sleuths in an Agatha Christie and amaze us all by discovering what really happened."

He hadn't seen it that way but she was spot on. As so often, Paloma's thinking was ahead of his. If there was anything wrong about the manslaughter verdict, he was uniquely placed to find it. Nobody needed to know he was head of the murder squad. Julie had given nothing away to the locals about her police career or his. He could play this game for the rest of the week if necessary.

A village mystery. It had some appeal.

HE GOT UP early, saw to Raffles's needs and was on the road by 7:30. The traffic was light. People living out here in the sticks didn't know how lucky they were. The roads would get busier when he was closer to Bristol and Bath, but by then he'd be on the motorway, chugging along at a civilised speed with the usual trail of frustrated speed-hogs behind. He'd pull in for a leisurely breakfast at Gordano services on the M5 until the congestion eased. He planned to do some googling. Although he hadn't yet found the joy most people seemed to experience using a mobile phone, the thing had its uses when you were travelling.

For once, everything went to schedule. The Gordano breakfast couldn't match Julie's but by then he would have eaten old boots if they were put in front of him.

Finding Fab, the wealth manager, shouldn't be too much of a problem, he told himself when he got his phone out. That was before all the little red icons sprouted across the map of central Bath. Thirty? Forty? Bath was awash with wealth managers. He'd walked the streets for almost thirty years without knowing this was going on. There were more of these hotshots with alluring company names like Profits

Galore than coffee shops. Usefully for him, most of the sites had a Meet the Team page with photos of young men and women trying to look trustworthy and not succeeding any better than the ones in the rogues' gallery on the police computer.

It didn't take long to find Fabio online. The buzz cut and big moustache clinched it. Fabio Fortunato was the chief of a firm called MYA (Maximise Your Assets) in Prospect Place, BA1. A perfect address for a wealth manager. The postcode suggested central Bath, but BA1 extends further than you would expect and a check showed the location was three miles from the centre, in Bathford. He would visit there first.

Fabio Fortunato. Could that be real? About as real as Mr. Seawright, the optometrist, he thought. Mr. Fortunato the wealth manager. For the present, that was how the guy was known and it would do.

The other partygoer Dolores had named was Bert. Simply Bert. Dolores didn't do surnames. Bert had been Claudia's lover at the time the silo man Roger Miller came to his unfortunate end. The only other clue was that he was a public-school type without a proper job.

Bert could be a key witness. As Claudia's current man he would have attended the party. He would have to be found. An internet search would be no use without more information. This was where Diamond would normally have asked the well-named Jean Sharp to ferret out an address. The newest member of the team, she had quickly proved herself a brilliant researcher, better even than the obsessive-compulsive John Leaman, whose nose had been put out of joint, one of many issues requiring Diamond's attention. But his immediate need was to find Bert. A voice in his head (not Jean's) said, "Tough. You're on your own, mate."

His best hope was to get a steer from Fabio Fortunato, the life and soul of the Bath crowd, the source of all the stories and Dolores's favourite. It could be as simple as that. He was in an optimistic mood today.

He headed north of Bath on the M4 and took the turn that makes the long descent from the Cotswold ridge, past Dyrham Park to the city. At the intersection at the bottom he diverted east along the Avon valley through Bathampton to the Georgian suburb of Bathford.

Already he was having second thoughts about becoming an Agatha Christie detective. How do the likes of Poirot have any credibility? he mused. No one challenges their right to be at the scene of the crime and interview every witness. It's about reputation. They are tolerated because of all the cases they've solved. Anyone who complains goes to the top of the suspect list.

His own debut as an amateur sleuth couldn't be more different. His hard-earned status in the police had to be concealed. Working undercover wouldn't come naturally. Without authority he would need to justify himself each time he questioned anyone.

He had no patience with TV detectives like Jessica Fletcher, Miss Marple, and Hercule Poirot. The characters might be entertaining, but so is a fairy story. Real murders get investigated by professionals. If the sheriff or the inspector appears in a television drama, he is hopeless at the job, needing the brilliant unpaid celebrity sleuth to reveal the truth.

Laughable.

Prospect Place was a turn-off from the High Street, a turn-off in more senses than one. The only "prospect" was the leafy view along the Box valley, rather than the promise of abundant wealth, for this was a humble terrace built in the 1800s on a steep section of hill to house workers in the local paper mill. The sides of the houses met but the roofs didn't. They were stepped. They could have functioned as a staircase for the Somerset giants of legend, Goram and Ghyston, who were said to have competed to drain a huge lake that extended the length of the Avon valley from Bristol to Bradford on Avon.

Strangely, the headquarters of Maximise Your Assets turned out to be a two-up, two-down cottage with paint flaking from the door and sash windows. The patch in front couldn't be called a garden. And the large, middle-aged man who came to the door didn't look anything like Fabio Fortunato or any of the others on the MYA website. He was in a grubby string vest and ill-fitting trousers held up with braces. Body hair covered his shoulders and thick, muscled arms. The smell of cooking wafted from the house and didn't appeal. Tripe and onions, at a guess.

"Yeah?"

Diamond asked after Fab.

"Not here. Who told you he was here?"

"I must have got the wrong address. This is Prospect Place, is it?"

A nod.

"Maximise Your Assets?" Diamond said, feeling stupid as he spoke the words.

"What about it?"

"You know what I'm talking about." He'd seen a glimmer of understanding.

"He doesn't live here. It's only junk mail that comes. I've got a heap of it in here."

"Got you," Diamond said. "He puts Prospect Place on his letterhead because it sounds like a nice address for an investment manager. But most people use email or the phone nowadays. Is that how it works? He calls here once a week, picks up his mail and gives you a few quid for the service?"

"Once a year, more like," the man said.

"So where does he live in reality?"

"He never told me."

"Come on, you must have some way of contacting him. I'm here to do business with the guy."

There was no answer. But the door remained open. The tenant of Prospect Place had seen the prospect of a handout.

Diamond felt for his wallet and fingered the few banknotes inside.

The man took the fiver he offered with one hairy hand and gestured with the other for Diamond to step inside the flagstoned room.

Wary of being mugged, he stuffed the wallet in a back pocket and buttoned it.

A phone number was written on the wall above the light switch. He memorised it, backed out and returned to the car, where he wrote it on the palm of his hand. He drove further up the hill along a narrow lane that brought him to Browne's Folly nature reserve, where he was able to park. It was good to breathe fresh air and get the cooking smell out of his lungs. And it had a commanding view of Bath, deep in the Avon valley, deceptively pale blue from four miles away, fringed by the tree-covered hills. Today the atmosphere was hazy, yet he could make out the pinnacled Abbey tower at the centre and the spire of St. Michael's. The terraces and crescents rising on all sides had to be imagined. He knew them all.

His heart felt the pull of the city. He'd never want to leave. Talk of seeing out his days in some village out in the sticks was outrageous. For all its drawbacks—the politics, the cost of living, the tourists, the oppressive heat of high summer—this was home. He even had an affection for dull old Manvers Street and the nick where he'd worked so many years.

Bollocks to retirement.

He took out his phone.

"May I speak to Mr. Fortunato?"

A female voice asked, "Who is it please?"

He'd already decided how to answer this awkward question. "Peter Dee. He won't know me. It's just an enquiry. I drove to Bath hoping to meet him and ended up here in Bathford, which I've now discovered is a mistake."

"One moment, Mr. Dee."

He heard voices pitched low, too low to make out what was being said.

She came on the phone again. "Is this about a business matter?"

"Definitely."

"Mr. Fortunato is at a meeting right now, but if you wouldn't mind coming here he will be happy to speak to you in person."

"Excellent. Where exactly is 'here'?"

"Do you know Bath, Mr. Dee?"

Did he know Bath? Better than you or Mr. Fortunato do, he felt like saying. "A bit."

"One moment."

He was tempted to say that her "one moment" was already two. Wisely, he didn't. He waited again.

"Do you know a restaurant near the Abbey in Cheap Street called Bill's?"

"I do."

"Mr. Fortunato wishes to treat you to a coffee after the trouble you've had finding us. He can meet you there at eleven."

"That sounds agreeable."

THE LITTLE MAN with the buzz cut and the walrus moustache was at a table outside with a glossy brochure in front of him. Diamond went straight over and shook hands. "Recognised you from the website."

"You must be Mr. Dee, then. You prefer a table inside? More of an al fresco chap myself."

"Actually, I would." Diamond knew too many people in Bath to feel comfortable seated in public view. It would be just his luck if one of his own team came by and greeted him by name.

After they were settled and had placed the order, Fortunato said, "You must have met the ape-man."

Diamond had to think about that. "Ah. I know who you mean."

"What I can't understand is why you went all the way out to Bathford without phoning first. Our number's on the website."

"Didn't think to look for it," he answered truthfully. "Obviously I need the help of someone like you to smarten up my act."

"Excellent. We pride ourselves on looking after our clients. May I ask what attracted you to MYA?"

Caution was needed here. This was going to be a tricky interview and Diamond didn't want to show his hand yet. "Isn't that obvious? You stand out from the rest."

Fortunato almost purred. "Me, or the company?"

"Both."

"Good call. Branding is vital in my profession. Personal image, corporate identity. We have a million blue-sky phrases for something that's as old as the steam baths in this very city. Do you know what I'm talking about?"

"Actually no, but I'm sure you'll help me out."

"Trust, Mr. Dee. Trust that no one will stick a knife in

your back when you're slipping out of your toga, to stretch the analogy."

Diamond was lost for words.

"Let me spin this another way." To reinforce his words, Fortunato made a winding motion with his hand. "You wouldn't believe how many wealth managers there are in Bath."

But he did. He'd seen all the red markers on his phone.

"There's no shortage of wealth."

"Well said, sir. We have to be competitive or we wouldn't stay in business. To put it bluntly, wealth attracts sharks. So how does an executive such as yourself navigate the treacherous waters? Who do you choose to handle your investment opportunities?" Fab leaned forward, elbows on the table, smiled broadly and steepled his stubby fingers. "One you trust." The words were spaced for maximum effect.

He moved on smoothly from the sharks. "It's about cementing our relationship. Right now you and I are in a wet trench. We both wish to turn it into the concrete foundation for a great temple of trust. Am I right?"

Diamond shrugged. In the last five minutes, he'd heard more bullshit than he'd found at the farm. He'd almost given up trying to filter some of the facts he needed. "Can we cut to the chase?"

Fortunato looked hurt. "Chase? There's no chasing going on, Mr. Dee."

"It's a figure of speech," Diamond said, and added unwisely, "like the temple of trust."

"Trust, yes." The little man with big visions was off again. "Before I set up here, I used to lie awake at night deciding what we'd call ourselves—investment advisors, profit generators, financial planners, fulfilment providers—and the name we ended up with sums it up pretty well. We have a rather special client list."

Diamond did his best to look like the next rather special client.

"We set up office in the centre of town, which you need to do. The rent is absurdly high, but location is everything. Almost everything." He laughed. "There's always a snag. Top line: Maximise Your Assets. Second line: Cheap Street. What a comedown."

"Hadn't thought of it like that."

"You've seen Cheap Street. It's no slum, but a stranger to Bath wouldn't know that. Prospect Place sounds so much better."

"Unless you go there," Diamond couldn't resist saying.

"You're the first for some time."

"There's always one."

"I wasn't going to say that. How can I help you, Mr. Dee?"

"Peter."

"I'm Fab—my name, not a boast."

Diamond needed to be smart. He wanted the inside story of the garter game at Baskerville Farm. If he asked straight out, it would be obvious he wasn't interested in having his wealth managed. His cover would be blown and so would his chance of learning anything useful. Right now, he had a small advantage. Fortunato was trying to cultivate him as an investor. Best let him do his selling job. An opportunity would come.

"You'll have to bear with me. The financial world is an alien place to a peasant like me."

"Let me give you a marketing tip, Peter. Don't downplay yourself. If I were representing you, I'd never use a word like that."

"Out-of-towner, then."

"Better," Fab said. "Do you own a farm? I've looked after farmers before."

"No, I gave you the wrong idea. I don't know one end of a cow from the other but I've lived in Somerset most of my life."

"Doing what?"

"Sitting in front of a computer. Doesn't sound countrified, does it?"

"I earn my crust the same way," Fab said, "but I'm doing it in Bath. Where are you based?"

"A small village west of Taunton. You wouldn't know it."

"I might." For a moment, Diamond thought he'd clicked straight away, but Fab didn't follow through. "What exactly is your business?"

He'd known this was sure to come up. Telling lies was dangerous, so he gave an opaque answer. "I'm a problem-solver. I'd rather not go into it too closely, but it has a payday from time to time, which is why I'm here."

"Understood." Fab didn't understand at all. He couldn't. The word "payday" must have been music to his ears but he wasn't so crass as to ask if the job involved dirty money. "Listen, I'm not the type to get sniffy. Our clients come from a wide spectrum. Sometimes they come into money unexpectedly, like a legacy from a long-lost uncle. Some have earned it by hard graft and a few lucky beggars have a cash cow they'd rather not tell me about. Frankly, it doesn't bother me whether you've backed every winner at Cheltenham for a week or rifled the church collection box. All cash is capital and I can make your capital grow"—he cleared his throat—"regardless of its back story."

"At no risk to the client?" Diamond said.

"Peter, my friend, I'm going to level with you. All investment has an element of risk in uncertain times like the present, but the range of holdings we pick for you—your gold parachute, as I like to think of it—will allow for that. You say you're a problem-solver. We make sure problems don't arise." He was already fingering the brochure.

Not wishing to be given yet more of the hard sell, Diamond tried another approach. "I expect you're wondering how I heard about MYA."

"Slightly intrigued, I won't deny."

"I got chatting to the pub landlady."

"Here we go," Fab said after a pause for thought. "Is this my reputation catching up with me?"

"She spoke warmly about you, said you made her laugh."

"Which pub was this?"

"The Feathers in Baskerville."

"I know it," Fab said without any sign of defensiveness. "I've had a few bevvies there. What were you doing in Baskerville?"

"Visiting someone I used to work with. She moved there after retiring."

"Small world. I had a friend who moved there from Bath. Some of us used to meet up socially at her place and whenever I got there early, as I usually do, I'd pop into the pub and irrigate the tonsils. Can't remember the landlady's name."

"Dolores."

Fab gave a lecherous grin. "I do now."

"She told me a funny story she'd heard from you. The one about a bus driver who won a large amount of money and wanted it invested."

"The Port Folio joke? Not one of my best."

"Made me laugh. Anyhow, she happened to mention that you worked in wealth management, which is something I'd never thought much about until now. So I decided I'd look you up and here I am." He was forcing the issue here and it showed.

Fab had a more guarded look. "How come you talked to Dolores about me?"

"It wasn't just about you. And she was doing most of the talking."

A frown. "She'll have told you about the parties, I expect?"

Diamond couldn't have asked for a better opening than this. He plunged in. "At the farmhouse, yes. And the tragedy that brought them to an end, the man found dead in the silo. How did he get in there?"

With the focus shifting to events rather than himself, Fab seemed willing to open up. "I don't think anyone knows for sure. The body wasn't discovered until some months after, you see. None of us were there when it was found except Claudia, the woman I mentioned who was living in the farmhouse. Her farm manager made the discovery. The victim turned out to be one of our crowd from Bath, a chap called Roger Miller."

"What a shock."

"Seismic." But he spoke of it as casually as if it were last night's football game. "The police were called and all of us were questioned. You see, they pinned down the tragedy to a night when Claudia organised a game with a pink garter we were supposed to hunt for. It could be anywhere around the farm buildings. Poor old Roger had it with him when he was found. The theory is that it was hidden in the silo and became a death trap."

"On purpose?"

He smiled a superior smile. "That's the killer question—literally. There was an inquest and a court case. Claudia said in evidence that she'd hidden the garter beforehand but insisted it was in the bull pen, definitely not the silo.

The judge didn't believe her and neither did the jury and she was sent down for manslaughter."

"Harsh."

"We thought so."

Almost all of this was familiar. Diamond wanted the inside story. "You were there for the garter game, then? Did you join in?"

Fab shook his head. "Too energetic for me. I stayed with the serious drinkers. Only three went on the garter hunt. The idea was that once the game was under way, Claudia produced a box with more garters. Then any of the women who were up for some fun would slip one on her leg."

"I can see where this is going."

"Right. So when the lucky winner returned with the trophy he'd get an extra reward. If he made the right guess, he'd be treated to a flash of thigh."

"Was that all?"

Fab gave another broad wink. "Anything else was decree nisi, if you know what I mean."

"Not really."

"Up for negotiation. It sounds silly and it was, but silly things get done at parties."

"Can you remember the three who took part?"

Diamond had tried too hard. Fab backed off—literally. He pressed his hands so hard against the table that his chair moved. "The names wouldn't mean anything to you."

"You told me one already—the unfortunate Roger Miller. Let me guess the others. Was one called Bert?"

Fab's eyeballs almost popped out. "Bert Dombey. How the heck do you know?"

"Dolores is a mine of information." And so are you, chum, he might have added. The surname was gold dust. "After that, I'm stumped. I've no idea who the other guy was."

"The third man."

"Ha." Be cryptic if you must, you smug little man, Diamond thought. I'll worm it out of you.

Fab grinned and pointed his finger. "Go on. You know it already, you crafty blighter. Ha who?"

"You'll have to help me."

"I thought you were about to say it. Haaaar . . . ?" He was like a father urging his child to utter its first word.

Diamond didn't actually suck his thumb but he didn't show any intelligence.

"Harvey Hertzog," Fab said, eyebrows raised.

"Ah."

"A randy ex-rugby player who'd volunteer for anything?"

"Never heard of him. Is he still about?"

"I see him sometimes for a drink. He owns the Holloway Hotel."

"Here in Bath?"

"It's a glorified bed-and-breakfast place south of the river. We used to party there, but it was a bit cramped."

Diamond made another mental note. "Getting back to the garter game, was Claudia wearing one?"

"You bet she was. She had to set an example, didn't she? I can vouch for it. I didn't join in the game, so I was there when she hitched up her skirt to show the other wenches what to do. There weren't many volunteers."

"Why?"

"When the girls knew who the players were they didn't think much of the choice. We all assumed Bert would be the winner and he thought so, too. He was Claudia's latest catch, you see, but after a search that went on so long we all lost interest. He came back empty-handed and so did Harvey. It was getting late by then and everyone assumed Roger had given up as well and got in his car and beetled off back to Bath."

"Did Claudia say where she'd hidden the garter?"

"No. And Bert and Harvey were too proud to ask."

"Maybe they thought they'd been suckered and there was never a garter to find."

"Possibly." Fab looked at his watch. "Look, I don't have much time and we seem to have gone on some wild garter chase. We've barely discussed your situation. Are we talking about a lump sum or regular investments?"

Diamond had almost forgotten his cover story. "It's not that urgent. The money isn't in the bank yet. The main thing is that we've met and I must say how impressed I am by everything you told me about your business." He needed a get-out now. "I see you brought a brochure with you. Is that for me to take away?"

8

HE TOSSED THE brochure into a rubbish bin at the end of Cheap Street. All the information he needed was safe in his head. Three keenos had joined in the garter game and he had their names: Roger Miller, Bert Dombey and Harvey Hertzog. The two left alive shouldn't be difficult to find. That injection of optimism was still working.

After googling Bert Dombey and getting nothing except Charles Dickens, he tried putting Bertram in front of the surname and then Bertrand, with the same result. Albert, Egbert, Hubert, even Engelbert. The last name started a false trail of German musicians, so he put Dombey in again with a question mark and got Barnaby Rudge and Martin Chuzzlewit. Stuff this, he told himself, I can do without it. There's another party boy to see and I know his name and where he lives.

Harvey Hertzog.

The Holloway Hotel was south of the river, not far from Paloma's house on Lyncombe Hill where Diamond now lived. He'd seen the place for himself, at least from the outside, on the rare occasions Paloma had persuaded him to join her for an evening walk through the woods below Beechen Cliff.

First, he took the opportunity to drive home and freshen up. His suit had collected enough Somerset mud and animal hairs to keep a forensic scientist busy for a month. A shower and a change of clothes energised him for the next challenge. He was almost tempted to do the walk. Better sense prevailed and he drove to a spot where he knew he could park.

Holloway was both an area and a road, quite a historic one. Until the 1770s it had been the main route to Wells, a testing climb to the turnpike at Bear Flat. Halfway down, where Diamond joined it, was the old priory church of St. Mary Magdalene, once associated with a leper hospital, a facility on the outskirts of many towns in medieval times. One thing he never failed to notice was the Judas tree in front of the south wall of the church. Tradition had it that Christ's betrayer hanged himself from such a tree. Cloaked in green heart-shaped leaves at this end of the summer, it produced blood-red buds each spring that blossomed into a spectacular display more purple than pink.

Harvey Hertzog's hotel was a remnant of Georgian elegance a short way down the hill, a converted villa not far from the cheap end of Holloway, which was a stretch of unsightly post-war housing mercifully screened from the hotel by trees.

He stepped up to the pedimented doorway, went in and asked if Mr. Hertzog was available. The receptionist was a woman in her thirties, smartly dressed in a white jacket, and well in control. Her response was guarded, as he expected, so he introduced himself as Peter Dee and explained that he wasn't there to make a reservation but had come on the recommendation of one of Harvey's friends, Mr. Fortunato. Fabio's name worked a treat. She picked up a phone and made an internal call. After some earnest conversation

Diamond couldn't hear, she came from behind the desk, said, "He won't be long," and showed him into a smallish room with armchairs, a period fireplace and a silk flower arrangement on a table in the bay.

He asked whether Harvey lived in the hotel. He did, she said, on the top floor, but when visitors called, he preferred to see them downstairs.

"Does he live alone?"

Immediately he asked, the answer was obvious. She turned as red as the silk geraniums. Bashfulness in a woman her age was rare and rather sweet.

He saved her having to explain. "I should have guessed. You and he manage the hotel between you."

She nodded and hauled up a worn-out question from her well of embarrassment. "Have you come far?"

"I was already in Bath. You must know Fab, the guy who sent me here."

"I do, but he didn't tell us to expect you." If any doubt remained, the "us" confirmed she was more than just Hertzog's doorkeeper.

"Do you mind telling me your name? Fab may have mentioned you."

"I'm Elaine."

"Elaine, of course," he said as if he'd been looking all his life for her. "Were you by any chance at any of the parties at Baskerville?"

She flushed red again.

"I can see you know the place I'm talking about, the other side of Taunton," he went on, trying his damnedest to put her more at ease. "Charming little village. I expect it added to the fun, meeting up in the country with a bunch of people you knew."

She gave a shrug, unwilling to speak.

"I was told you partied here in the hotel before that."

A nod. She was even more reticent now.

He looked around him, scratching his chin. "There must be a bigger room in the hotel than this."

She was reluctant to say, but it was a straightforward question. He waited and finally got a response. "The flat upstairs."

"Where you and Mr. Hertzog live? Got it."

She took a step back, wanting to end this. "I must get back to the desk."

"Difficult holding parties upstairs when you had hotel guests staying. You can't turn up the music."

"Harvey is on his way down."

"You know what I'm saying?"

"Of course."

"I expect you had more room in the farmhouse. You had it all to yourselves." Gave it full blast in Baskerville and annoyed the hell out of the villagers instead, he could have added. "But that came to an end, unfortunately. Are the parties a thing of the past?"

"They stopped." She was quick to draw a line under the conversation. Light, rapid footsteps had sounded on the stairs.

Harvey Hertzog appeared, a head taller than Diamond, a head that testified to serious rugby: scar tissue, ears like gristle the dog had chewed and given up on, and a nose without bone structure. He may have been good-looking before he took up the game. He was a potato-head now. He was barefoot and wearing the Bath club shirt and black jeans.

"I'll leave you, then," Elaine said.

Hertzog said, "Stay," as if speaking to a dog.

She stayed.

Questioning the man wouldn't be easy with almost no prior information. Their shared interest in sport should have helped. Diamond had played rugby union himself and was a staunch supporter of the Bath team. But he'd racked his brain without success for a memory of watching anyone called Hertzog at the Rec.

"So," Hertzog set the ball rolling, "we have a mutual friend in Fortunato."

As soon as the words came out, particularly the "have" sounding like "hev" and the rolled *r* in "friend," the accent marked him as South African and cleared up the mystery about his playing career.

"I can't honestly call Fab my friend," Diamond said. "We only met a couple of hours ago, but he's a good guy, no question, and keen to help. That's how I heard about your hotel. I'm here on behalf of someone in the village where you and your friends had your parties for a time."

"Okay," Hertzog said, steady-eyed, uninterested in picking up on the prompt about parties.

Diamond was forced to put out more. "This lady is having sleepless nights about Claudia Priest, the woman who was sent to prison, do you remember?"

"Are you a lawyer?" The pale eyes in that car crash of a face had a gleam of ice. You wouldn't want to cross him.

"Far from it," Diamond said. "Just a well-wisher hoping to set a lady's mind at rest. I'm visiting Bath so it's a chance to speak to some of the people who might know what happened."

"You came all the way up from Taunton for that?"

"Along with a few other things I need to do."

"And you found Fab and he sent you here?"

"To be fair, he didn't, but your name came up." The phrase sounded more intrusive than he intended, so he softened it by adding, "I was interested to meet you anyway. I played club rugby myself at one time."

"Who for?"

The questions were coming from Hertzog, which wasn't what Diamond had planned, but at least he was on safe ground talking about the oval-ball game, or so he thought. The words "The Met" were on the tip of his tongue. He bit them back in the nick of time and named the first team that came into his head. "London Welsh."

"Old Deer Park?"

"Er, yes. And you?"

"Pretoria."

"Still playing?"

"At my age—are you joking? What do you want from me?" End of chummy chat about rugby.

"Fab told me you joined in Claudia's hunt-the-garter game."

"Did he now?" There was ice in his voice, a vast sheet of ice, as if he were speaking from the opposite bank of a frozen river.

"I'm hoping you can tell me the inside story."

Hertzog gave Elaine a hostile glance, perhaps to check how much she had revealed already. She made a tiny movement of her head in denial.

He said to Diamond, "Inside? Inside what? There's nothing to tell."

"No?"

"This so-called game was a damp squib. Only three of us joined in. Two of us found shit all."

"When you say 'two of us' . . . ?"

"Me and Bert Dombey. I can't speak for Roger Miller, the guy who was later found dead. He shot straight off when the game started, like a dog from the traps, like he already knew where the damn thing was."

"Did you see which way he went?"

"You ever tried chasing a dog in the dark?"

Diamond had heard enough imagery in one morning to last him a week. He stayed where he wanted to be, asking the questions. "Did you think of looking in the silo yourself?"

"What for?"

"The garter."

"No." Each time the garter was mentioned, a muscle twitched in Hertzog's left cheek.

"Where did you search?"

"The farm buildings, barns, milking parlour, cowsheds."

"All in the dark?"

"They have security lights. When you get near, the floods come on."

"Did you look in the bull pen?"

Hertzog hesitated, eyebrows raised, giving Diamond credit for thinking of this. "First place I tried."

"Why was that?"

He shrugged. "If I was running the jol, hiding something, that's where I'd put it. Test the players. See if they fancy a head-to-head with Mr. Bull."

"So you opened the gate and went in?"

"Climbed over." A note of self-congratulation had crept into the responses. Something to work on.

"You're brave. Did he have horns?"

"They dehorn them when they're calves, but you have to respect them. Big fellow like that could knock me over and trample me, no problem."

"He's called Chummy, I understand."

"There's a tiger called Kitty-Kitty at Jo'burg zoo. Cute, but I wouldn't get in the cage with it."

"Claudia claimed she hid the garter in there."

"She said so in court."

"Were you at the trial, then?"

"She couldn't remember shit. Didn't answer the questions she was asked. She got flustered."

"Wasn't she telling the truth?"

"All I know is the damned thing wasn't there when I checked. I had to shift a thousand kilos of beef to find out for sure. The bull was sitting down. It could have been underneath him."

"How did you manage that?"

"With a few hundred volts from a cattle prod."

"More than I would do."

"I worked on a farm in South Africa, man. He shifted his arse pretty damn quick and kept his distance while I raked the hay and looked in his feed. I looked everywhere. Take it from me, I don't do things by half. I would have found anything if it was there." His ego had made him more talkative, probably more than he intended at the outset.

"I'm in awe," Diamond said, feeding the vanity. "So you went on to search the other farm buildings. Did you see anyone else as you went round?"

"Bert crossed the yard one time. That farm is bigger than you think. I hollered across to see if he'd got lucky but he said he'd got fuck all. I caught up with him later where they park the tractors. That was when we agreed to call off the hunt and go back to the jol. We decided Roger must be back in the farmhouse with the prize, but he wasn't."

"You didn't see him at all?"

"Nah. Shitshow all round. We thought he was the winner and the poor sod was already up to his ears in grain."

"While you were playing the game, did you look in either of the silos?"

"Have you seen the height of those fuckers?"

Diamond chose not to say he'd recently climbed one.

"They're in a field on their own, aren't they? I'm asking if you searched that area at all?"

"I checked the ground. Nix."

"But you didn't climb either of the silos?"

"I ruled them out, man. I figured Claudia wouldn't put her friends at risk for some crap party game."

"So you think she's innocent?"

"I didn't say that."

Diamond could have pursued this but with Hertzog talking freely it was better probing the night of the party.

"What happened next, after you and Bert returned to the farmhouse and admitted you were beaten? Did Claudia reveal the hiding place?"

"Did she heck! She said the game was still on. Me and Bert told her we weren't playing anymore. We both needed cleaning up. We went for a shower. Roger never showed and we decided he'd given up and driven back to Bath."

"That was it? No one went to look for him?"

"Get real, man. People were having fun. They weren't going to stop because that idiot hadn't been seen for a while."

"Didn't Claudia show concern?"

"I couldn't tell you. I was more interested in another little lady." His eyes switched to Elaine, who reddened again and looked down. But there wasn't much affection in the look he'd given her.

"And how long passed before the body was found? Four months, wasn't it? Didn't any of you notice Roger was missing?"

Hertzog opened his palms. "Why should we?"

"He was one of your mates."

"Wrong, bro. As Claudia's ex, he was out on the fringe, just a drag, hanging about hoping she'd change her mind and want to start over. Nobody liked him much."

"Not even Claudia?"

"She wanted to be shot of him."

"Enough to want him dead?"

Hertzog screwed his scars into an angry glare. "Don't twist my words. What are you saying—that it was murder? No chance." He paused for thought, still frowning. "You won't give comfort to your lady friend talking like that."

Caught out. Thinking like a cop when he was supposed to be playing the good neighbour. "Do you know anything about Roger's job? I heard he was an art dealer. Did he have a shop?"

"A shop? Too much like hard work, man. He ran the business from his home in Bennett Street. He knew his clients and what interested them—pictures of Bath, street scenes and landscapes. There's a market in that kind of crap and he tapped into it. Tarted them up in nice frames and made enough to keep the wolf from the door. A lot of it was done through online auctions, and he also drove around Somerset and Wilts picking up items from antiques outlets. No one would have thought anything was wrong when he didn't answer calls."

A business trading in local landscapes wouldn't trigger a murder, Diamond decided. He needed something meatier than that.

"You said you were called as a witness at Claudia's trial."

Hertzog sighed as if a new line of questioning was over-kill. "Bert and me both. But don't ask me what went on. They kept me in a room until it was my turn in the box."

"Just now you mentioned something Claudia said in court as if you heard it."

"That was in the paper. Public knowledge." He frowned again. "You trying to catch me out?"

"Not at all. I was hoping to hear from someone who was at the trial, that's all."

"Better ask Elaine, hadn't you?"

"She was in court?"

They both turned to look at the coy receptionist, who duly coloured up again.

"Is that right, Elaine?" Diamond said.

She said something inaudible and Hertzog, back in master-and-dog mode, told her to speak up. "She was in the public gallery with one of the other women," he said. "She told me the judge gave Claudia a hard time."

"I need to hear about this," Diamond said.

Elaine found her voice. "I wasn't there every day."

Hertzog said, "But you heard the summing-up and told me it was fucking unfair."

The memory of injustice burnt through her shyness. She became emotional, ready to open up. "I felt sorry for her, the way he laid it on. He seemed to ignore everything the defence had come up with."

"Keep going," Hertzog said. "Tell the man all about it."

She gave him a withering glance and turned her eyes on Diamond, excluding her partner. "Claudia was too honest for her own good. She came out with stuff she needn't have told the court."

Diamond was all ears. "Like what?"

"Like Roger was her ex and wouldn't accept that she'd finished with him. Basically she said she got pissed off with his pestering because she was in a new relationship."

"With Bert Dombey?"

"Yes, but Roger wouldn't give up. He picked up a bunch of red roses for her from the shop each time he came. She didn't have to say all this in court but she did. And when she was asked about the garter game, she said it was completely her own idea, how she ordered the garters from some shop that sold fancy underwear online, and on the day of the party before everyone arrived she put one of them in the hiding place."

"Where? This is important."

"The bull pen. That's what she said. The prosecutor confused her a bit with his questions about how it was done."

"Did she go in with the bull?"

"No, she used a window pole. She hung the garter on a spiked railing behind the bull where anyone playing the game would see it." She gave a forceful, angry sigh. "I believed her and I think any fair-minded person would have agreed, except for that judge."

"Is that what he said?"

"He made a show of sounding impartial. He told the jury not to come to any conclusion until they'd heard all the evidence. But the very next day they were taken by bus to the farm to see the silos for themselves and one of the court ushers, a woman, was asked by the judge to climb the ladder to show what was supposed to have happened."

"He picked a woman? That was enough to put the idea in the jury's minds." He always tried to stay neutral for as long as possible about the personalities in any investigation. In Claudia's case it ought to have been simple because he hadn't even met the woman, but hearing this from the unassertive Elaine made him think Julie could be right about the miscarriage of justice. "Were the jury shown the bull pen as well?"

"Yes, they started there, but one of them had a hay fever attack, so they didn't spend long."

"Were you there?"

Elaine turned pink again and shook her head. "I read it online. The *Gazette* had a reporter there. But I was in court next day when both sides gave their final arguments and the judge summed up. It came so soon after the farm visit that I'm sure the usher climbing up the silo was fresh in their minds."

"Do you remember what the judge said?"

"He was clever, making it seem like he was favouring Claudia when he wasn't. He started off by saying they might think they had to decide whether there was intent to kill, but that wasn't their job. Claudia wasn't charged with murder. They should set aside the statements she'd made about Roger—he called him the deceased—being a former lover who was pestering her and wouldn't accept that the relationship was over."

"I see what you mean," Diamond said, "telling them to ignore it but reminding them of it."

"Yes, he said the charge was manslaughter, gross negligence manslaughter, and they needed to decide whether she had committed a grossly negligent action through the game that led to Roger's death. First they had to be sure whether she devised and prepared the game herself."

"No argument. She'd already admitted it," Hertzog said.

"Do you mind?" Elaine said with unexpected force. "This is tricky enough to explain without you butting in." A side of her character that hadn't emerged until now. She was no lightweight.

"Sorry, sunshine." Her big partner looked genuinely penitent.

"If you want to hear it," she said, "the judge said the next thing to decide was whether she hid the garter in such a dangerous place that it was likely to cause the death of whoever tried to reach it."

"Meaning the silo, which she denied?" Diamond said.

"To be fair, he dealt with her evidence. He said they might think hanging it in the bull pen was dangerous if that was what she did, but there were ways of getting it out of there without being attacked by the bull. Someone could hook it out with a window pole the same way she claimed it was put in. If they believed her version of what happened, they'd have to acquit her."

"Reasonable."

"But he went on to say that hiding it in the silo would amount to manslaughter. Whoever got there first would need to wade through grain to reach it and would be sucked in."

"Couldn't they use something to hook it out without going in there?"

"Like the window pole? They'd have needed to take it with them."

"And carry it up the ladder," he said, remembering how he had needed both hands. "Or go all the way down again to fetch it." He knew how unlikely that was. "Were the jury told about the danger of going into a loaded silo?"

"Oh, yes, they heard from an expert witness who brought in diagrams and explained about grain entrapment and how farm workers are killed each year going into silos without a safety line. Not so many here as in America, but it happens."

"That would have impressed the jury."

"I'm sure it did, but Claudia insisted she didn't go anywhere near the silo."

"That's how the man died," Hertzog said. "She couldn't deny that."

"You're talking like the judge, Harvey," Elaine said. "She was our friend for years and you're willing to believe she deserves to be in prison."

"Ferchrissakes, it's not about friendship. It's fact. The poor cuss had a horrible death and someone is responsible. It was the judge's job to point that out."

"He did. He said her defence team hadn't explained how it happened."

"Wasn't their job," Diamond commented.

Hertzog said, "If they had a theory, they would have mentioned it, for sure."

Diamond already had one: What if one of the others, Dombey or Hertzog himself, had found the garter in the bull pen and moved it to the silo and lured Roger to his death? This was not the best time to air the theory. "What else did the judge say? Was there any more bias in his summing-up?"

"I thought so," Elaine said. "He talked about the other garters Claudia ordered and how she handed them out to some of us girls to wear when the guys came back."

Hertzog said with some pride, "Elaine was wearing one for me."

"Only in case you were the winner," she said and deflated him more by adding, "I wasn't giving you an excuse to get off with one of the others."

"What exactly did the judge say?" Diamond pressed her.

"It was more of his double-speak, telling the jury to disregard stuff when really he was bringing it to their attention."

"Can you be more precise? I'm not trying to embarrass you but I'd dearly like to know what he said. For my blind friend in Baskerville."

"It will only depress her more. He said the fact that Claudia ordered the garters showed how far her planning went. He said judges are sometimes accused of being out of touch, but he was under no illusion that the men joined in the game with the promise of sex for the winner."

"Is that true?"

She tilted her head towards Hertzog. "Better ask him."

A shrug was all the answer they got from the big man.

Elaine said, "The garters were put in the hallway and any of us girls could take one. Claudia pulled up her skirt and showed us hers when she told us about the game."

"Claudia wanted Bert to win?"

"Obviously."

"But what if Roger came back with the garter thinking it was his big chance of a reconciliation? Do you think that crossed her mind?"

"If it did, she didn't say anything."

"Surely she'd be appalled. Was this possibility mentioned by the judge?"

Her mouth tightened. "You're joking, of course."

Hertzog said, "Maybe she knew all along that Roger couldn't win."

"How do you mean?" Elaine said, then turned on him in fury. "Prick! You've never believed she's innocent."

"Whoa, easy, tiger. I keep an open mind, is all. She'll be out soon, anyway. They send them out on licence after half the sentence is served."

Elaine swung round to Diamond. "How about you? You've heard how she was treated in court. What's your opinion?"

Put on the spot, he said, "From everything you say, she didn't get a fair trial. Isn't there something in the law about being innocent until proved guilty?"

"You're not man enough to speak up for her either. Wimps!" She stormed out of the room.

For a short interval the only sound was the ticking of a grandfather clock. Then Hertzog said, "She can charm the birds off the trees when she wants to. You heard all you came for, right?"

"Just about," Diamond said—which wasn't quite true.

There was another main witness he hadn't met. He needed Bert's address.

Hertzog seemed more approachable. They had something in common now, the blasting from his girlfriend. "You can tell the blind woman she isn't alone, feeling sorry for Claudia. Not much chance anyone can overturn the verdict."

"If she's innocent, as Elaine seems to think, she doesn't deserve to have a prison record. A pardon isn't impossible. There's such a thing as the royal prerogative."

"In the process you'd have the whole establishment down on you like a ton of bricks. Me, I refuse to lose any sleep over it."

Catching the casual tone, Diamond asked, "Have you spoken to Bert since it happened?"

"We met for a beer a couple of times."

"He's still around, then?"

"He was."

Diamond waited, but Hertzog didn't add anymore. "Because I'd like to meet the guy."

"You'll get nothing we haven't told you."

"His address would be helpful."

"He moved to Bristol. He didn't say where."

"Pity. I thought I might catch him at home before I leave Bath. I'd like to hear his take on the trial. He'll still have his phone."

"Izzit?"

An annoying piece of South African speak that effectively stopped the dialogue. Hertzog grinned like a baboon that has picked a louse from its fur, squashed it and swallowed it.

9

HERTZOG DIDN'T GET the last laugh. Elaine was behind the reception desk again when Diamond came by and looking as composed as a mother superior, so he asked her straight out for Bert Dombey's phone number, saying Harvey seemed reluctant to pass it on. She wrote it on a compliment slip and handed it across, an act of defiance that clearly pleased her.

He gave her his number in return. "In case you think of anything else."

Immediately he got in the car, he called the number and got through. The yarn about the troubled lady in Baskerville was still the best he could think of and it worked for the second time in one afternoon. Dombey's interest was caught. A meeting was arranged for 4 P.M. in Starbucks at Gordano services. "I'm the burly, bald bloke in the black pinstripe suit," Diamond said.

"I'm the tall, thin one in the SLEEP ALL DAY, PARTY ALL NIGHT T-shirt," Dombey said.

DRIVING OVER LANSDOWN gave Diamond a chance to catch up. This undercover sleuthing was every bit as difficult as he feared. He was supposed to be acting as a friend of Julie's, and in a sense he was, but he'd seen how Fortunato and Hertzog had each got suspicious several times over that the questioning was excessive. Reasonably enough, people wondered why he was banging away at something that was done and dusted.

And there was another difficulty. When he'd first heard about Claudia Priest, he'd believed she was the only person who could be blamed for Miller's death. Manslaughter may have been too strong a charge, as Julie believed, but some responsibility was undeniable. She seemed to have been unfairly treated in court, but what could he do about it? He couldn't have any influence while pretending to be a nobody. He'd have to break cover at some stage and then what? Overturning the verdict would mean taking on the legal establishment. Her defence team hadn't found a way to prove her innocence, so how could he?

He wasn't even sure how much he cared about this woman serving time in prison. It was Julie he cared about.

Claudia had few sympathisers in Baskerville. She'd been a troublesome teenager and she was a troublesome adult. After inheriting the farm, she'd done herself no favours by throwing it open for the parties. Her rich friends from Bath had shown no respect for the hardworking village people. It was a situation sure to erupt at some stage and it had.

Even so . . .

The prison sentence seemed vindictive. He had a shrewd idea how it had come about. He suspected that the detective on the case, Jack Crandley, had thought he had a murder to deal with when the body was found. Faced with a shortage of evidence, he would have set out the facts for the Crown Prosecution Service, which had decided on the lesser charge of manslaughter. The heavy machinery of British justice had started its remorseless grind. Claudia was already in the system as a former young offender. As the organiser of the parties, she had a duty of care she had blithely ignored when she dreamed up the garter game. The main element of gross negligence manslaughter, the act that caused the death, had been the placing of the garter inside the silo. Claudia's tiresome former lover had won the game and lost his life. The court had decided who was responsible.

But there remained the darker interpretation: that Crandley's first suspicion was correct and Claudia had committed murder. By all accounts, Roger Miller had become a nuisance. No one could say with certainty how troubling his pestering was. In Claudia's mind, it might have been insufferable. Driven to desperation, she could have thought up the garter game as an escape. A trap to catch a rat.

She could argue to herself that she wasn't completely responsible. For the trap to work, Miller had to take the bait. She had told him she no longer wished to sleep with him. He had ignored her. To win the game, he had to go to excessive lengths, getting ahead of the others and climbing the silo. His decision, not hers. She was culpable in the eyes of the law, but he would not have died if he had listened to her pleas to leave her alone.

This could explain why she had made no appeal against the manslaughter verdict. Three years was better than a life sentence.

Diamond could think of only one other person with a credible motive for wanting Roger dead and that was the lover who had replaced him. Bert Dombey had been better placed than Claudia to bait the trap. He might have done it at her suggestion, or independently, out to impress her by removing the waste of space who was such a nuisance to her. All it required was to place a garter in the silo and then tip off Miller that it was there. Was he that kind of man, devoid of morality? Shortly, Diamond would find out.

STARBUCKS AT GORDANO is not unlike Starbucks anywhere else, in softly lit earthen tones of green, white and brown. Dombey, sporting the T-shirt, was already there in one of the padded seats near the entrance with a bottle of water in front of him. His hair wasn't worn in a ponytail, as Dolores had recalled. It was braided and sticking out like a sweep's brush. If you've got it, flaunt it, Diamond generously thought (his own hair formed ski trails over his skull), but he was intrigued that a man on his own should be gazing into space grinning at nobody in particular, not even using his phone.

Diamond went over, made himself known, but as Mr. Dee and offered coffees. A friendly approach was required, whatever he thought privately.

"Never touch the stuff, my friend. I'll stay with this. Don't let me stop you. Far be it from me to keep a fellow from his favourite poison." The plummy accent would have got Dombey into Buckingham Palace dressed as he was. The grin was built into his face, dolphin-fashion, but it didn't make him lovable. It was faintly sinister. Yet the words were friendly enough.

"I can't survive without my fix of caffeine," Diamond said. Admitting to frailty is a good icebreaker.

"The daily espresso?"

"Cappuccino actually."

He was back shortly after, cup in hand. "I appreciate this. Have you driven out specially from Bristol?"

Dombey shook his head. "I was leaving the prison when I got your call."

What do you say to that?

Diamond's face must have shown his surprise because Dombey went on to explain, "Claudia's doing her time at Eastwood Park, just up the road from here. I visit her at least once a week."

A closed category place off the M5 near Thornbury. The meeting at Gordano services now made sense.

Looking at the SLEEP ALL DAY, PARTY ALL NIGHT slogan, Diamond asked himself about the character of a man who enters a women's prison wearing a shirt like that. Lacking in empathy, to say the least. Inability to recognise the emotions of other people was one of the defining character traits of a psychopath. Yet Dombey was decent enough to visit Claudia regularly, a duty that couldn't be easy. You can't say someone has a personality disorder on the evidence of the clothes they wear.

"So, you saw her this afternoon. How is she holding up?"

"D'you know her?" Dombey asked.

"Not personally. As I said on the phone, I promised my friend in the village I would make enquiries."

"A friend going by the name of who, may I ask?"

"Julie." No harm in naming her. Not to have done so would have created suspicion.

"But you don't know Claudia yourself?"

"Never had reason to speak," Diamond said and struggled to think of a reason why. "Out in the backwoods, we still hold the gentry in awe."

"Really?" Dombey said. "Life's moved on since *Tess of the d'Urbervilles*. Actually, you don't sound like one of the peasantry."

"You're right. Village life has changed a lot. There are plenty of people like me who weren't born there. I wasn't expecting to feel concerned about Claudia, yet I do." This didn't sound as sincere as he intended, so he created a small distraction, busying himself emptying packets of raw sugar into his coffee. "I gather you feel the same way."

"We were in a relationship. Still are, platonically. To answer your question, she's finding it tough and so am I."

"Your visits must be a great support," Diamond said. "Particularly if she feels she shouldn't be there." He was stirring now and not only with the spoon.

"Maybe. She's coping well. Mentally strong." Spoken dispassionately, without a hint of emotion.

"Doesn't anyone else visit her?"

"She hasn't said so. She has no family left."

"How does she feel about the case?"

"We don't discuss it. She's trying to forget."

"Weren't there grounds for an appeal?"

"I thought so, but she fell out with her lawyers and gave them the old heave-ho and no wonder."

"She could hire someone else."

"Too late. You have to apply within twenty-eight days and that's just for permission to appeal. She was informed about that, but she'd had enough."

"What does she talk about, then?"

"What you'd expect. All the rubbish that happens inside. And her plans for when she gets out."

"Let me guess: travel."

The grin widened to the point where it might have been trying to become sociable. "How right you are. A long shopping trip through Europe, taking in all the capitals. I supply her with brochures to keep her spirits up."

"Will you go with her?"

"If I can spare the time."

"Do you have a job?"

"This and that." All the answers up to now had been short and to the point. This one was short and evasive, followed up with a blatant attempt to shift the focus. "How about you?"

"More this than that," Diamond countered, quick as the blink of an eye. No need to say any more. "Do you believe she was wrongly convicted?"

"I wouldn't drive out to Eastwood Park every week if I didn't."

"What do you think happened to Roger Miller?"

"There's nothing mysterious about it. Chap climbed into the silo and got sucked in. Could have happened to me or Harvey."

It hadn't escaped Diamond that there was little sympathy wasted. The cool way Dombey seemed to regard both Claudia and Miller suggested inability to recognise other people's distress. The possibility of a warped personality was gaining currency.

"What isn't clear is who put the garter there."

"Do you have a theory?"

"Everyone has a theory." Another short response, but Dombey seemed to be growing in confidence and revealed more. "Some people think it was me, wanting to teach the blighter a lesson for pursuing Claudia after she ditched him. I'm supposed to have collected the garter from the bull pen, climbed up the silo, slung it in there and then told Miller where to find it. Makes no sense but that's the gossip. I mean, the fellow wouldn't have taken advice from me. We were in competition, for Christ's sake."

"And why would he have believed you?" Diamond said, appearing to side with him.

"Precisely. It's tripe." Dombey took a phone from his pocket and checked the time. Surprisingly it looked at least as old as the one in Diamond's pocket. "Listen, I must be candid. I only offered to meet you because I thought you might have something to tell me."

You and me both, Diamond thought. He needed more bait on the hook. He wouldn't allow this man to leave yet. "Let's look at why Roger died. You and your friends are all city dwellers, right? You all live in Bath or Bristol."

"True."

"None of you knows much about farming."

"Sweet Fanny Adams, in my case."

"Townies wouldn't realise going into a silo without safety equipment is bloody dangerous, if not suicidal. Roger clearly didn't know."

"I can't see where you're going with this." But Dombey was sitting forward, definitely hooked.

"Claudia is the exception. She was brought up on the farm. I bet her father warned her when she was a child never to climb the silos."

"Claudia wasn't playing the game, my friend. She was running it."

Diamond didn't comment.

Dombey thought in the silence and turned pink and petulant. "What are you saying—that she planned it all? That would make her a murderer. That's bunk. All that cappuccino must have scrambled your brain. I don't have to listen to this. It's bad enough that she's banged up at all."

"Hold on, Bert. Aren't you listening? I'm saying the opposite. Claudia understood the danger better than any of you, so she wouldn't have sent any of her friends up there."

After a moment to take this in, he said, "Got you." He needed a sip of water to calm down. "Maybe you have something there."

Diamond added, "But plenty of other people in Baskerville know a silo can be a death trap."

"Can you name them?"

"Far too many for that. Farming is the backdrop to their lives."

"The peasants?"

"I wouldn't call them that if I were you. You might end up in the village pond."

But the suggestion that people other than his yuppie friends might be implicated seemed to surprise, impress and please Dombey. "By heck, you may have a point. But why would they wish to harm any of us?" Like Fortunato and Hertzog, the man was armour-plated about the nuisance the parties had created.

"Apart from calling them peasants? You weren't exactly popular in the village with your noise and your cars at weekends. An accident would put a stop to all that—and it did."

"It put a permanent stop to Roger Miller." He sat back, fingering a braid of hair. "D'you know, I never thought of the great unwashed playing any part in this until now. We didn't mix with the locals. Even in the pub they shunned us, except for the barmaid—and she had a duty to serve us. Can't recall her name."

"Dolores."

"Right, so you know her." Diamond's scant local knowledge of the village paid off, rewarded with a new tone of respect. Dombey loosened up a little. "Nice lass. I wouldn't point the finger at her. But some of the others. Hm." He scratched his chin. "How would they have got involved?"

"They may be in the background but they know what's going on. Village life is like that."

"The bush telegraph?"

"Exactly. They make a point of checking what their neighbours get up to." Diamond sketched out a scenario.

"Before anyone arrives for the party, Claudia takes delivery of the box of garters, right? The postman knocks on the farmhouse door and says, 'Parcel for you.' He expects a response. She says, 'That'll be the garters I ordered.' Or if that doesn't happen, she has someone who cleans the house and notices them. Or she is spotted hanging one of them in the bull pen before any of you lot arrive. It was in place there for several hours. Somebody will have noticed and spread the word. Things may work differently in Bath, but a small community doesn't miss a thing."

Dombey sounded unconvinced. "That may be so, but not one of her neighbours spoke up for her at the trial. If some kind soul had said they saw the garter in the bull pen before the partygoers arrived, she'd be walking free."

"There isn't much sympathy in the village for Claudia. Julie is the exception. They may not say it to your face, but the feeling is she got what she deserved."

"Because of us?"

"You were part of it, certainly."

"And . . . ?"

"People couldn't believe how different she was from her late father, who really involved himself in the life of the village."

"They can't blame her for wanting a life of her own. It's not as if she put the farm up for sale."

This was developing into a fruitful session. The cautious beginning had been understandable. "You won't have known Mervyn, her father," Diamond said before adding, "Neither did I, come to that. He spent a fortune modernising the farm. It's been owned by the family for generations. Everyone benefited. The pub, the shop, the school, the church, the value of their houses. That farm is the beating heart of the community."

"Big shoes to fill?"

"Muddy boots. If Claudia had tried them on and got her hands dirty, the people would have understood more."

"What's happening now she's in prison?"

"The farm is still functioning. The couple who managed it for Mervyn when he was too old and frail keep it going. They have the help of their son and all the farmhands still doing their jobs. As far as I know, there's money in the bank to pay everyone. Mervyn wasn't short of a few bob, as I'm sure you realised."

Dombey didn't rise to the comment, so Diamond tried another approach. He had an increasing suspicion that the family's wealth was the motivation here. "What's the inside of the farmhouse like?"

"What do you mean?"

"You have the advantage of me. You've been inside for the parties. Is it in a good state? Nicely furnished?"

"It's okay." Dombey was unwilling to say more.

"In traditional style? Inglenook, log fires and seats around the hearth, plates hanging on the wall and a big square table in the kitchen?"

"Nothing so corny as that."

"Claudia prefers a more modern look, then?"

A nod from Dombey. "She hired an interior designer."

"That will have cost her." Diamond grinned. "I keep forgetting. She has money to burn thanks to Daddy, so why not? It's an investment. We're always being told farmers have been through a hard time, but her old man did rather nicely, like I said. Did he have another source of income?"

"She never said."

"That amazing milking parlour alone must have set him back a million."

"The point being?"

"I wonder whether Daddy was into something illegal."

"Out on a farm in deepest Somerset? I find that hard to believe." Spoken without much conviction.

The hollow-sounding reaction didn't escape Diamond, but now he'd started dishing the dirt on Mervyn he wasn't going to stop. "A farm in deepest Somerset may have been the ideal place for secret goings-on."

"Such as?"

"Your guess is as good as mine, Bert. Stolen goods, drugs, forged banknotes, trafficking."

"Oh, my hat!" Even more insincere. This man knew things he wasn't willing to share.

"This may be why Claudia chose to see out her term in prison rather than fight the case all over again."

"To protect her father's name?"

"No, no, no," Diamond said. "This was self-interest. She couldn't risk losing her wealth if it was found to have been the proceeds of crime."

"Ah." Dombey let a couple of seconds pass before saying any more. He was on edge but unsurprised by Diamond's mud-slinging at the Priest family, and it showed. "You may have hit the nail on the head. But I wouldn't dare ask her."

"No one could blame her personally," Diamond said. "She wasn't living with her father. But if I'm right about any of this she could have found out the truth about him after his death when she came to live in the village." He gave a matey smile. "You and I are both on her side. We're not going to share these thoughts with anyone else, are we?"

Dombey shook his head. "You know my feelings about her."

Diamond wasn't sure he did. Everything up to now suggested a shallow emotional involvement at best. At worst, the man was faking. "And none of it explains how Roger was tricked into climbing the silo. I've heard from Fab, Harvey and now you and I'm firmly of the opinion Claudia told the truth in court. She put the garter in the bull pen. Some bloody-minded person moved it." He wasn't firmly of that opinion at all, but he needed Dombey to think so.

"It's taken a while," Dombey said, "but finally something we can agree on."

In this mood of bonhomie, Diamond felt ready to plunge into even murkier waters. "We're men of the world, Bert. Do you mind if I ask you something slightly off limits? Was there any drug-taking at the parties?"

A difficult silence. The conflict was written large on Dombey's face. When he finally reacted, he found a way to distance himself from any wrongdoing. "What exactly are you getting at here?"

"It wouldn't be too remarkable. Well-heeled young professionals out to enjoy themselves. The locals are sure it went on."

"The locals? What would they know about anything?" Dombey said, and the fragile mateyness snapped again. "Generations of inbreeding doesn't raise the intelligence. They weren't invited."

"That's why you're best placed to tell me the truth."

"Some hash was smoked, if that's what you mean. Not much and not me."

"I meant hard drugs."

"What the fuck has this got to do with it?" Coming from that silver tongue, the expletive had a strong impact.

"I was told some of you were in a bad state some nights. It didn't sound to me like too much booze."

"'I was told' is often the next thing to a lie and a lie

can get halfway round the world before the truth has its trousers on."

Diamond was reading the grinning face as if it held a message he'd been told to remember on pain of death. "Bert, can you truly deny it ever took place?"

Dombey seemed to decide he could open up. "Have you heard of Zees?"

"The so-called Z-drugs?"

"Sleepers. People take them socially with drink to get a high, and it isn't illegal."

Diamond pretended not to know about this craze among the glitterati for mixing powerful sedatives and alcohol to produce short bursts of euphoria. "They do this on purpose?"

"Some of us in high-pressure jobs need a little help with our sleeping."

"I can understand that."

"And if you also drink to relax, you find the combination of sleepers and spirits can give you a buzz. Nothing more. That's all it amounts to and, like I say, it's all within the law. Hardly crystal meth in some godawful back street, is it?"

"Right," Diamond said, as if he was learning something new. "Was this a feature of the parties?"

"I wouldn't put it as strongly as that."

"Claudia took sedatives. Did she hand them out?"

"Not to my knowledge. We brought our own—if we were inclined."

"Are any of you pharmacists?"

Dombey chuckled. "No need. Zees are sold online. Using them this way is okay if you're sensible. They've got popular the last five years or so. Before that, the trick was to fill a balloon with nitrous oxide."

"Laughing gas?"

"Correct, but there wasn't much to laugh about. If you

were lucky you had a temporary turn-on when you inhaled, but some got headaches and vomiting or felt so dizzy that they fell over. Joke was on them, I guess."

"The Z-drugs are safer?"

"Nothing is safe if you overdose. Water will kill you if you drink enough of it. Why are we talking about this?"

"Had Roger taken stuff that night?"

"Him?" The contempt in that one word spoke volumes. "Miller never messed with his head. He wasn't even a drinker. He was only there in the vain hope Claudia would change her mind and start up with him again. That's why he joined in the game."

"Hoping to win, obviously."

"Yes, if someone really set out to kill him, he was a ready-made victim. He'd have gone looking in any place he was told."

"That's worth knowing," Diamond said. It was also useful to know how much Dombey despised the man. "Harvey Hertzog told me that when the game started, Roger shot off as if he knew where he was going to look."

"It was more than just a game to him."

"Did he have enemies in your group?"

"Put it this way: he'd lost any friends he may have had. We all agreed he was a drag."

"The party pooper?"

"Fair summary. And if you think I had reason to rub him out, I can't deny it, except I'd be a fool to try, considering I'd be the obvious suspect. He just wasn't worth it."

Throughout these exchanges, Dombey had put up a good front and this was his best try yet. Diamond was unpersuaded. It hadn't escaped him that there was a subtext to all this. Dombey could have walked away at several difficult moments in their discussion but he hadn't. He needed it to continue, but why? Time to call his bluff, Diamond decided. "This has been helpful. I must get back to Baskerville now." He spoke the village name the local way.

"You're leaving?" Dombey said with a twitch that made his braids dance.

"We covered everything, didn't we?"

"There's more I'd like to find out, but I can't expect you to know the answers and Claudia clams up if I ask her. You make me think I should visit the village."

Diamond caught his breath. He'd been passing himself off to Dombey as one of the locals. He could see his cover being blown away. "How would that help?"

"When Claudia comes out, she'll have a prison record and you and your neighbours are going to take some convincing that she's innocent. If I find what was really behind Miller's death, I can clear the air for her."

"You'll have a job clearing the air in a farming village."

He was slow to get the joke. Eventually he smiled.

Diamond smiled back and said, "I mean it." But he didn't expect the swift, serious response that followed.

"I can be there tomorrow. Shall we meet? Then you can show me around, introduce me to people."

Put on the spot, Diamond made a rapid calculation. There was not much chance he could bluff his way through as a local guide, but did it really matter if he was forced to admit that he, too, was just a visitor to the village? There were definite advantages in getting to know Dombey better. The man had information to trade and was still the only serious suspect apart from Claudia. "All right. Let's meet in the pub."

10

IT HAD BEEN a demanding day but Diamond was energised. His new role as private detective freed him from bureaucracy, headquarters, the inspectorate, Georgina and, shame to say, the quirks and hang-ups of his own team. This way he controlled his own destiny. He stood or fell by his wits and no one else's.

That was what he told himself.

In reality he missed the support of his team. If Ingeborg Smith, the ex-journo DI, had got to work on Dombey, she would have charmed the truth from him in seconds. Even young Paul Gilbert would have got the inside track on the parties. As it was, some input would be needed from Paloma and Julie. Over a pizza supper, he gave them a rousing account of his day, culminating in the session with Bert Dombey. "The upshot is that I'm meeting him in the Feathers at midday tomorrow."

"As soon as that? He's keen," Paloma said. "What does he expect to find out?"

"He wants to meet some of the locals."

"But you don't know any."

"I've met a few," he said, still fired up. "Dolores the landlady, for one."

"Dombey already knows her. You told us that." Paloma wasn't being obstructive. A dose of reality was wanted here.

"Agnes and Jim Douglas, then."

"Busy people. They won't be in the pub."

"And their son Hamish." Julie came to his aid.

Paloma wasn't persuaded. "Hamish won't be there on his own. He's underage."

"Maggie Harrap," he said.

"She won't have much to say."

Julie said, "She's a good listener. She won't mind meeting him."

"And, of course, you, Julie."

There was a pause for thought.

"I can see where this is going," Paloma said. "You want Julie to join you in the pub."

"Not only Julie. Both of you could be there in a quiet corner having a drink. It's better if you're already in place. You can observe him, watch his body language, see how he performs."

"Julie can't."

"That's why you must be there as well—if you agree. Then at some point I'll pretend to spot you both and bring him over."

"Who are we supposed to be, apart from barflies?"

"Yourselves. Be yourselves. It's easier being truthful than telling white lies. I'll say Julie is the lady who got me started on this mission, which is true. He knows that much, Julie, but I didn't mention your loss of sight. That will add another layer to my cover story."

Paloma was smiling. "Peter, if I knew you were as devious as this, I would never have got entangled with you in the first place."

Julie said, "It goes with the job. You learn to be two-faced, I'm afraid." And she seemed to welcome the chance of showing her own second face. "After you come to our table, guv, how do you want to play it?"

"No set plan. We take it as it comes. Just remember he knows me as Mr. Dee."

"That's worse than a white lie," Paloma said.

"A half-truth."

"And who am I supposed to be?"

"Exactly who you are: Julie's friend, just visiting. But say the minimum."

"He sounds like a strong personality."

"He may want to lay on the charm, but there's a dark side. He knows more than he's saying. He may even be a psychopath."

"Gulp," Paloma said. "You'd blithely expose us to the wiles of a twisted mind?"

"I back you and Julie to handle him, no problem."

"We're not shrinks."

"Neither am I." He shifted in his chair. Paloma had put him on the spot again. "Shouldn't have used the word. Big assumption. A lot of things were running through my mind while he was talking to me. I'd call him cold-hearted, shallow and evasive."

"And that's okay, is it? We can cope with that? What makes you think he could be a psycho?"

"He made out he visited the prison because he was in a relationship with Claudia, but he spoke about her as if she wasn't much better than a laboratory rat. I asked him several times what he does for a living and got no answer. He wanted to give the impression he's rolling in money when all the signs are that he isn't."

"What signs?"

"His phone, for one thing. It looks older than mine, more of an iPod than a smartphone. And his car."

"What about his car?"

"He didn't want me to see it. When we were leaving Gordano, I walked out with him and asked him where his was parked and he said it was a long way off, so we shook hands when we got to mine and he marched off as if he had a mile to go. Out of interest I moved to another space where I could watch him in my mirror. He doubled back and got into an old white van just a couple of rows from where I was."

"Strange. Had he overstretched himself, trying to keep up with the Bath crowd?"

"That was my reading of it."

"Doesn't make him a psychopath, though."

"Not on its own, but they are expert liars."

"They also lack empathy," Julie said. "What you said about his attitude to Claudia and Roger Miller fits the pattern."

"He visits the prison regularly, so he must have some affection for Claudia," Paloma said.

"I'm not sure. I came away with the feeling he does it for a selfish reason. They can be very manipulative."

"He's a gold-digger. Is that what you mean? He's skint and she's got money in the bank."

"No, it's not so straightforward."

"The prospect of marrying a millionairess would be a motive for killing off a rival."

"Roger Miller didn't need to be killed. Claudia had dumped him."

"But he hadn't gone away, had he?"

He nodded, appreciative of the input he was getting.

"Miller's state of mind may be as crucial to this as Bert's. Everyone agrees he was desperate to get her back. I wonder if he dug up something dodgy about Bert."

"The dirt on Bert?"

"Boom-boom! I can work on that. He won't want to share it."

"You don't like the man, but you're willing to play along with him to find out his secrets."

"It's a legitimate method." He smiled as an idea took root. "Remember Lieutenant Columbo on television?"

"Who doesn't? The reruns go on forever."

"The plots worked to a formula. A smart, self-confident crook commits a near-perfect crime. The audience are shown the villain from the beginning. All the interest is in Columbo's interaction with this character, playing mind games, doggedly teasing out the truth."

Paloma was laughing. "Give me strength. Yesterday you were turning into Monsieur Poirot. Now it's Columbo. Where can we find you a shabby old raincoat?"

"And cigar," Julie said.

He said solemnly, "I can manage without the props. What do you think, Julie?"

"About Columbo?"

"About Bert Dombey, our potential psychopath."

She had been largely silent up to now. She had been in CID long enough to know the basics about criminal psychology. He could remember her attending more than one course. At the time, he'd suspected she needed well-earned breaks from the demands of Bath CID. Later he'd learned that his domineering management style was the problem. What she had needed was respite. Finally she had asked for a transfer.

Old sores he hoped were healed now, else why would she have invited him to stay?

Julie moved the uneaten remains of her pizza to the side of her plate and set her knife and fork together at the centre. "From all you've told us, Dombey does exhibit some of the core characteristics: emotional detachment, coolness under pressure and exceptional self-confidence easy to confuse with charm. He sounds intelligent, too. It will be interesting to meet him and find out what he really wants. I don't think we should kid ourselves that he's coming here for Claudia's sake."

"Would you call him a psycho?"

"I'll tell you after I've met him. And it's worth saying that the science has moved on. Not all psychopaths are killers. Their personalities can operate in a positive way."

"This is new to me."

"Some of the qualities I just listed are needed to function in the twenty-first century. Self-confidence, fearlessness, even lack of empathy. There are times when it's better for us to be detached. We're no good to anyone if we over-identify with people's problems. You know that from your own experience at work."

"Does that make me a psychopath?"

"You're somewhere on the spectrum."

His jaw dropped.

Julie said, "We all are. Cops are closer to serial killers than we'd like to admit."

Paloma's eyes crinkled in amusement.

"I like to think I'm rational," Diamond said.

"But you are, guv. There's logic in your decision-making just as there's logic in the actions of these people who over-step the boundaries of normal behaviour. They're rational to the point of obsession. They can shut out genuine emotions while pretending to care. What I'm saying is that Bert may display some of the classic symptoms without being a killer."

"That's not where I start from. We have a suspicious death and if Claudia is telling the truth, someone other than her is responsible. Is there anyone else in the mix? Not to my knowledge."

Julie said quietly, "Or mine."

Diamond had a sense he and Julie were back on good terms after his mouthing off about Claudia the evening they arrived. "Bert is firmly in the frame. Like Columbo, I'll treat him as the main suspect, and handle him politely and patiently. At some point he'll give himself away."

Paloma said, "This Columbo act will be fascinating to watch. I wouldn't miss it for anything."

"THE DRINKS ARE on me," Dombey said when Diamond met him the next day in the Feathers. "My chance to remind Dolores who I am."

Diamond wasn't having that. "That isn't the way it's done, Bert. This is my home and you're my guest."

"Wrong on both counts, chum. It's a public house, right? And I invited myself, so it's my shout. What's yours, then? A real ale, I expect. I'm being careful. Alcohol-free lager. I can't risk some bloody-minded cop springing out from nowhere and pointing a gun at me."

The hairs bristled on the back of Diamond's neck. Was this a coded way of telling him his cover was already blown?

"A speed gun."

Dombey was already on his way to the bar.

Today's T-shirt read: COUNTRY LORE: FRESH AIR STINKS. One thing was certain: he wasn't toadying to the locals. Lack of empathy? Diamond decided it must be more than that. A calculated wish to provoke. He watched Dombey try his charm on Dolores.

Across the room, Julie and Paloma were already drinking

tea. Bella was asleep with her back against Julie's leg. Every-one down to the dog was more laidback than Diamond was—and he was supposed to be playing the ultra-cool Columbo.

Dombey spent more than ten minutes chatting to Dolo-res, which didn't ease the blood pressure, with no way of telling what was being said. Worse, Maggie Harrap was perched on a stool at the bar close enough to take in every word. Julie had called her the village Miss Marple and it seemed a fair judgement. She was some years younger than the sleuth of St. Mary Mead, but it was easy to picture her with a brown suede bucket hat and some knitting.

"Peter, my friend, I'm sorry you had to wait," Dombey said when he finally returned with the drinks, a basket of chips and a plate of chicken wings. "There was a head on the ale when it was served, I promise you. The well-informed Dolores told me the Exmoor is your tipple. I hope she's right."

"It'll do nicely, kind sir." He launched into the bum-bling detective routine. Disarm them first by appearing to be harmless, even slightly stupid. Plenty of deferential smiles. "Between ourselves, I can't tell one beer from another. No sense in pretending I'm an expert when I'm not. I'm not even sure I could tell alcohol-free from the real thing."

"Get away."

"Yours looks the same as mine. I suppose a regular drinker can tell by the flavour, but I'm told the quality is improving all the time."

"You don't want to believe everything you hear," Dombey said.

"Right. I heard someone say a non-alcoholic drink is like sex in a canoe—too close to water."

The dolphin grin didn't change but a sound deep in Dombey's throat could have been a faint chuckle.

Diamond was encouraged enough to try for some information. "But you're right to stay sober. I expect you need a clean licence for your job."

Dombey's eyes narrowed. "Who mentioned a job?"

Caught at the start. He'd come to the point too damn soon and too obviously. More subtlety was needed to get results the Columbo way. "Excuse me, I may be daydreaming, but I thought last time we met you said something about people in high-pressure jobs needing help with their sleep."

"I wasn't speaking about myself."

Was snobbery at the root of this? "No offence, Bert. Maybe I should have used the word profession."

"It's not paid employment. Nine-to-five wouldn't suit me at all. What's the sudden interest in my occupation?"

"No particular reason," Diamond said, struggling to back out of this hole. A police officer was expected to ask direct questions. Joe Public wasn't. "I was being sociable."

"Fair game," Dombey said and turned the tables, "I can be sociable, too. What's your line of work?"

Difficult. He dug deep. "Have you ever asked yourself what the word 'logistics' means?"

"I can't say it keeps me awake at night."

"When you're on the motorway overtaking lorries, big ones, small ones, smart new ones and dirty old trucks, a fair number of them have one thing in common—the word 'logistics' as part of their business name. 'Advanced Logistics,' 'Northern Logistics,' 'Logistic Solutions,' 'Little Miss Muffet Logistics.' Do you know what I'm on about?"

"There's some sort of point to this, is there?"

"But you've seen the word on the back of a lorry?"

"Of course—many times."

"And you thought this is some tinpot delivery company trying to pass itself off as high-tech, right?"

Dombey shrugged. "So what?"

"Look up 'logistics' in the dictionary and you'll find it has two meanings. The original one is about coordinating complex projects. And the modern one is more simple. Some genius thought of it thirty years ago and turned it into a buzzword for haulage firms. It's transport. The business people liked the sound of it and made it their own."

"That's your job, is it, lorry driver?"

"No. I may have misled you. My job is the other sort of logistics."

"Civil servant?"

Diamond shook his head.

"What then?"

"I'm not at liberty to say."

"Well, thanks for leading me up that blind alley. You're a bit of a tosspot, aren't you? All mouth and no trousers."

Far from disarming the man, as he intended, Diamond had turned him nasty.

And then the bigger reason for Dombey's hostility was laid bare. "Here's another thing. Dolores just told me you're not a local at all. West Country people have a word for your sort. You're a grockle. A bloody visitor. You brought me here under false pretences."

Diamond bought time with a long swig of ale. His try at the Columbo method was getting him nowhere. Columbo would have choked on his cigar. He rescued himself with a bit of sharp thinking all his own. "That isn't quite right, is it, bringing you here under false pretences? A moment ago you were saying you invited yourself."

"Ha, maybe I did, then." Dombey raised a limp hand in

apology. "I'm disappointed. I came here to network and I was banking on you to show me around."

"That can still be arranged. I'm not a total stranger to the village. What do you hope to find out?"

"I told you already. The truth of what really happened on the night of the party. I'm rooting for Claudia."

"Is that what Claudia wants?" Diamond started to ingratiate himself again, Columbo style, even scratching his head. "Forgive me for saying this. You have the advantage of me. I haven't spoken to her myself and I probably got this all wrong. The message I picked up is that she wants to put the past behind her, serve her sentence and move on."

"Fair comment," Dombey said. "But I need more than that. I had a relationship with her and I'm trying my damnedest to keep it alive. She and I have to be honest with each other or it's doomed to fail. The party is a big black hole in her life and mine unless I do something about it."

Stirring words that Diamond didn't believe for a moment.

"And what's driving you in all this?" Dombey swung the spotlight back on Diamond. "I just poured out my heart to you. Let's have some straight talking from you."

"My position hasn't changed since you asked me on the phone," Diamond said, conscious how feeble this sounded each time he spoke the words. "I'm acting for a friend who is sympathetic to Claudia."

"You gave me a name."

"Julie."

"I'll be straight with you, Peter. I'm starting to wonder if this Julie exists."

Diamond turned a mental cartwheel of triumph. He had a chance to redeem himself. "Really? I promise you she does."

"That isn't enough. You strung me along about being a resident here."

"You want to meet her? She's the woman across the room. The one with the guide dog."

Dombey raked his fingers across his head and hung on to one of the dreadlocks as if he needed support. "That's her?"

"It's why I'm acting for her. She's with a friend, or I would have introduced you straight away. I don't suppose they'll mind. Bring your drink and—please—try not to startle the dog." Diamond got up and headed for the table where Julie and Paloma were waiting. It was the best moment yet in his fledgling career as an amateur sleuth.

11

BELLA MUST HAVE heard their approach because she opened her eyes, raised herself fully, took a couple of steps towards Diamond and licked the back of his hand, an endorsement he couldn't possibly have staged.

"Apologies, Julie, I know you don't like being ambushed like this," he said, speaking more for Dombey's ears than hers, yet trying to sound as natural as anyone unexpectedly meeting friends in the pub. "I spotted you here with Paloma just when I happened to mention your name."

"Peter, how nice," she said. "And who is that with you?"

"A man with doubts about the things I say."

Dombey had no difficulty dealing with the taunt. "There he goes again, making judgements. I'm Bert Dombey, one of Claudia's gang of troublemakers, and the plain truth is that this old scoundrel and I get on like toast and marmalade." Spoken in a rich, deep tone he probably saved for women he wanted to impress. "May we join you, ladies?"

The heat of the charm didn't melt either Julie or Paloma, primed to meet a psychopath.

"By all means," Julie said. "Do we have enough chairs?"

"You do."

"And may we offer you a drink?"

"You took the words out of my mouth, ma'am." Weirdly, Dombey was using his voice like a cellist, switching from a deep register to still deeper. Presumably it appealed to some women. "Peter and I are on the beer, but it looks to me as if you are ready for more tea. Let me order a fresh pot."

"Good idea," Diamond said in the deadpan tone he always used. "And the treats for Bella are in the jar at the end of the bar." As soon as Dombey was out of earshot, he said, "It's an act. He claims he's still in love with Claudia and wants to clear her name, but he has another agenda for sure."

"And he thinks we can be useful to him?" Julie said.

"It won't last. He's already spoken to Dolores and found out I'm just a visitor myself. He talks about wanting to network."

"What's behind it?" Paloma asked.

"I can't be sure yet. I'll be fascinated to see how he gets to work on you to get the information he wants."

"I don't know anything he'll want to know."

"I meant Julie."

"Julie knows something he's after?"

"He may believe she does."

Julie said, "I can't think what. How do you want me to deal with him?"

"Like we said. Be natural. Answer him honestly." He glanced towards the bar. "He's on his way back with a full tray."

He had brought more beer, a large pot of tea and cupcakes and muffins. "What shall I do with the doggie food?"

"One at a time," Paloma said. "She'll be your friend for life."

"I wish it worked like this with people," he said as Bella crunched the first treat and then fixed her eyes on him as if he was the patron saint of Labradors. "Don't know if Peter's mentioned this. I'm trying to discover what really happened here the night Roger Miller died."

"Me, too," Julie said. "It's been on my mind a lot."

"Tell me more. You're talking to the right person." He seated himself in the chair next to her and pulled it so close that Bella had to find a new position.

"There isn't much to tell," Julie answered. "I keep thinking about Claudia in prison. I wasn't a witness to anything but I know what was said in court and I don't believe all the truth came out."

"What do you think happened?" Dombey reached for the teapot. "I'll top up the cups while you answer that."

Julie wasn't fazed by his pushy manner. "Three of you played hunt the garter, am I right? Out of mischief or malice, somebody moved it from its hiding place and put it in the silo and that raises certain questions."

"Such as, who was it?"

"We may need to answer some other questions first. Why did they do it? What did they expect to happen? And what prompted Mr. Miller to search the silo?"

"Have a cupcake. I'm impressed," Dombey said and added in the same patronising tone, "You should be in the police."

By luck or judgement he'd come disturbingly close to the truth, so Diamond took over. "But you have the advantage over Julie because you were there."

He shook his head. "I was too close to the action. Julie has it nailed."

"Better find the answers to her questions, then. Why did this unknown person move the garter to the silo?"

"Mischief or malice, like she said. I'm hoping it was mischief. If it was malice, we're dealing with murder, god forbid."

"Which brings us to question two. What did they expect to happen?"

"If they knew anything about silos—which I don't—they expected him to sink in and suffocate. Grim. Makes one shudder to think of it." Dombey looked no more agitated than a lizard basking in the midday sun.

"Finally, why did Roger search the silo?"

"Obviously someone told him to."

"Tipped him off?"

"He wouldn't have gone straight there otherwise. I didn't and neither did Harvey."

"Why not?"

"For one thing, there were plenty of places to search in the main farmyard. The silos are out in a field some way off. And for another I couldn't imagine Claudia climbing up the side to hide the garter there."

"Not in her party clothes," Paloma said.

"She would have done it before the party started," Diamond pointed out. "Before she got changed."

"Claudia wouldn't do a thing like that," Dombey said, holding up his hands in a show of outrage. "She knew a silo can be a death trap. We were her friends, for god's sake."

"Roger Miller wasn't. Not anymore. He'd become a nuisance."

"I want to hear from Julie, if you don't mind." Theatrically he turned his back on Diamond. "Tell me about Claudia's life in the village, my dear. She was brought up here, wasn't she?"

Julie must have cringed inwardly at being treated like a child, but she gave a straight answer. "I can't speak from personal knowledge. I wasn't living here then."

"But you will have heard things."

"Only bits and pieces. Her mother died when she was young, so her father Mervyn brought her up."

"An only child?"

"Yes, and spoilt, I was told. By the time of her teens she'd become quite the tearaway. Mervyn was a lovely man who kept our village going, but he was too busy managing the farm to cope with the parenting as well." She gave Dombey a puzzled look. "Hasn't she told you any of this?"

"Why would she? I'm her lover, not her shrink."

Unseen by Dombey, Paloma raised an eyebrow.

"I thought you might have shared some personal stuff like that," Julie said.

"If I buy a used car, I check the condition. I don't bother with the service history."

The analogy straight out of the psychopath's phrasebook jarred with Diamond and he saw the impact it had on both his companions. They made no comment.

"She ended up living in luxury in Bath, I know that much," Dombey chuntered on, oblivious. "She wasn't in a job when we met. I don't know how she supported herself. She dressed in the latest fashions."

"Thanks to a generous allowance from her father," Diamond mentioned, to give Julie a chance to collect her thoughts.

Dombey responded over his shoulder, "Stop butting in, old man. I want to hear from Julie." His focus fixed on her again. "Peter has an outrageous theory that Claudia's much-admired old man was into some kind of money-making scam. What do you make of that?"

"Illegal, do you mean?"

"We're not talking bingo, darling."

"I wouldn't know anything about that," Julie said.

"It's worth exploring. Now I'm back in the village, I mean

to find out all I can and Peter is with me every step of the way. He's my Dr. Watson. What a fine team we make."

Diamond didn't object to that, except he didn't like the Watson reference. He was far more effective in his Columbo role. "So who would you like to meet next? I think Julie has told you all she can."

Abruptly, Dombey turned in his chair to face the others. "One of the great unwashed." Seeing the puzzled faces, he said, "The carrot crunchers. Anyone on the payroll will do."

"The farmhands, if that's who you mean, will all be outside working."

"Let's go, then. The game is afoot!" Dombey was off, quitting the ladies without a trace of courtesy. Julie had served her purpose and he'd save the charm for whoever he met next. He functioned on his own level, as self-centred as a small child. But his real objective had yet to be revealed.

Behind the bar, Dolores had spotted them leaving. "Just one more thing, gents."

Columbo's catchphrase. They'd already reached the door. They both turned. Diamond exchanged a puzzled look with Paloma, but she shrugged and shook her head. It must have been pure chance that Dolores had used the words.

Dolores said, "How about settling up before you go?"

"Was there something we didn't pay for?" Diamond asked.

"Two pints of real ale, two of alcohol-free, the chips, the chicken wings, the cupcakes, the muffins and the pot of tea. I don't charge for the dog's treats."

At a loss as to what was going on, Diamond turned to face Dombey and got the explanation.

"You did say I was your guest, old man, so I started a tab."

You don't argue with a psychopath.

Outside, the lush grass had a velvet look in the late

September sun. A tractor and trailer were heading towards them along the lane that skirted the village green. Immediately Diamond spotted who was at the wheel, he put up his hand. The tractor came to a halt with the engine still running, so he had to shout at the sour-faced youth.

"Got a moment to spare, Hamish?"

"No."

"What?"

"I'm working."

"Don't you ever stop?"

"Can't hear you."

Diamond cupped his hands and yelled through them, "Can you switch off?"

Hamish mouthed an obscenity before silencing the tractor.

"That's better. On your way to the milking, are you?"

If Diamond thought a break in the noise would encourage conversation, he was mistaken. Hamish kept his mouth shut and sneered at the stupidity of a townie who didn't know the first thing about milking times.

Flattery had worked once before. "I was telling Mr. Dombey here, you're a hero. The farm can't function without you. Where are you making for?"

"Church."

He might as well have said outer space.

Some seconds passed before Diamond rearranged his thoughts enough to say to Dombey, "He's also a barrel of laughs." Turning back, he said, "What's in the trailer, then—hymn books?"

Hamish didn't enjoy being on the receiving end. A quip from Diamond was never going to remove his scowl.

Diamond was forced to reset. "Let's be serious. Mr. Dombey wants to speak to you."

"What for?"

"He'll tell you presently." In a short aside, he brought Dombey up to speed on Hamish's family, the fact that his parents were the farm managers, in the job ever since Mervyn had got too old to work.

For Dombey, this was networking gold dust. He took a step closer to the tractor. "Did you mean that, young man, about going to church?"

Not the question Diamond would have asked. Was Dombey so devoid of humour that he'd taken Hamish's bit of sarcasm literally?

Equally oddly, Hamish answered, "Sure." He gave a solemn nod as well.

This was becoming surreal. The screwball making landfall with the teenage grouch.

"Do you want to confess to something?" Dombey probed further, sounding ridiculously like a priest.

"Nah."

"Say your prayers, then?"

"Piss off."

Normal service was restored, but Dombey doggedly pursued the point. "I don't understand. Why did you mention the church?"

Hamish gave an answer that made no sense except perhaps on some spiritual plane. "My mum's waiting."

Dombey blinked. "Have I missed something? Mr. Dee seems to think your mother is alive and well and manages the farm."

"She is."

"So . . . ?"

"She'll give me hell if I'm late with this lot."

"Your load, you mean? What's really in there?"

"Straw."

"For the church?"

"Harvest festival, innit?"

"Got you. This Sunday?"

Hamish decided he'd said more than enough already. He started the engine and the dialogue ended. The tractor powered forward. Flecks of straw from the trailer peppered Diamond and Dombey and stung their faces.

"What a lout," Dombey said.

"It's his age, as they say. I couldn't warn you in front of him," Diamond said, past the stage of disapproval and already thinking ahead. "This is an opportunity, Bert. If some of the locals are getting the church ready for the harvest festival, we can offer to help. It's only a matter of sticking marrows and carrots on the choir stalls and we get to chat to people. So much easier than knocking on doors. What do you think?"

"I'm not dressed for it."

He had a point. The FRESH AIR STINKS slogan on his T-shirt might get some shocked looks.

"It's all right for you in your posh suit," Dombey added.

"We're not going in to say our prayers. We're a working party. I'll take off my jacket and roll up my shirtsleeves."

"You think so? All right, I'm up for it."

With a trail of straw all the way along the lane, there was no difficulty finding their way. The short walk was another opportunity to probe Dombey's mindset.

"Were you thinking you were on to something?"

"What?"

"When he spoke about church? The kid with a guilty conscience?"

"He's got no conscience," Dombey said. "I'm looking at him as the cause of all the trouble. He could shin up that silo like a monkey after coconuts."

"I'm sure of that. You've got me interested. It's the kind of prank boys of his age get up to."

"That was no prank."

"He may have thought so."

Without warning, Dombey turned his fire on Diamond. "Whose fucking side are you on? Roger Miller was buried alive and Claudia is doing time for it. You call him a boy as if he's a five-year-old. He's a teenage yob as capable of murder as you or me."

The sudden mood swing was a red light. There was obvious danger here in arguing. In Columbo mode, Diamond took some of the heat out of the situation. "Now you put it like that, Bert, I see it clearly. He'd have needed to be somewhere near when Claudia hid the garter in the bull pen. That's possible, well possible."

"Possible, my arse. It's odds-on likely." Dombey was still pink-faced.

Diamond nodded. "He's got to be a suspect."

"He's capable of anything. Did you see the muscles on him? Boys on farms get used to blood and killing. Parents make them neck a chicken before they're out of short trousers. They see killing on a daily basis. Pigs, injured sheep. It messes with their minds."

Diamond cleared his throat. "Possibly, but we don't want to let it get to us, do we? Especially when we meet the mother. Agnes Douglas is a useful contact and she doesn't need telling how dangerous her son is."

"You don't have to say the bleeding obvious. I won't let my feelings show." Hard to believe when he was practically foaming at the mouth.

The bleeding obvious couldn't be left to chance. "Hamish will be there as well. My approach is to butter him up even if it pains me to do it. Shall we agree to treat him like that?"

There was no answer. Dombey observed a sullen silence until the church tower came into view. "Is there a vicar?"

"There must be. I haven't met him—or her. Is that a problem?"

"I'm thinking ahead, wondering who we might meet."

"Apart from Hamish and his mum, there's no knowing. You like to be prepared, do you?"

"When possible. We'd better be ready." He seemed to regard vicars as bogeymen.

"Forewarned is forearmed, eh?"

"I didn't say that."

"Just me, wittering on. Unfortunate choice of words. The vicar won't be armed, I hope." Diamond grinned.

Dombey didn't.

The boxes were being ticked. Plainly he was uncomfortable with the clergy and their spirituality. He dealt exclusively in material things. The absence of humour and emotional response, the need for certainty, the superficial charm that could turn in a flash to aggression, all contained in a personality that passed for normal ninety-nine per cent of the time. That's what makes psychopaths so dangerous—the façade that can mask extreme violence.

All this speculation needed to be justified with evidence, the hidden clues Lieutenant Columbo was so brilliant at winkling out. The real detective work lay ahead.

Having parked the tractor in front of the church, Hamish was standing in the trailer tossing out bales of straw that thumped on the patch of grass by the lychgate. Dombey had been right about the muscle power.

"Want some help?" Diamond called out. A hand trolley was standing ready.

"Get lost."

"We could shift some of these into the church for you."

The response to the offer was a dollop of spit a couple of inches from Diamond's shoe.

They moved on. Outside the west door was a collection of crates, baskets and shopping bags containing contributions from the parishioners: fruit, flowers, vegetables and loaves. Agnes Douglas and another woman seemed to be debating where items should go.

This time Diamond's offer was better received. "How kind. We could certainly use some help, couldn't we, Sally?"

Dombey's T-shirt didn't seem to be a problem.

Names were exchanged. Sally Brooks was introduced as the church organist, a large lady with a bright red apron over her jumper and skirt. "She's really here to make sure we don't stack so much fruit on the organ that she's buried in an avalanche when she starts playing and everything vibrates. It's not unknown."

"We won't go anywhere near the organ," Diamond said. "Find us a simple task and we'll do it."

"The windowsills, then. A marrow on each and peppers for colour. Heap them up with anything you like. People have been very generous and they do like to see their produce on view. This is so good of you, considering you don't live here."

Dombey took that as a cue to turn on the baritone charm. "It's a privilege to join in the show, ma'am. Scouts' honour, we won't eat any of the fruit, appetising as it looks."

"The care that goes into this is amazing," she said. "Each tomato is washed and polished for display. By the time you've done the sills, Hamish will have brought in the straw and we can arrange things on top of the bales."

With armfuls of marrows, the new volunteers went

inside. The church was Norman, like so many across the west of England, too large for a small village in the present century, when attendance was down nationally. The whitewashed walls and columns testified to the care still lavished on it by the faithful.

Dombey was into his networking immediately. Leaving Diamond behind, he marched up the aisle, dumped the marrows on the chancel floor and started chatting to the women at work on the choir stalls. Peals of laughter testified to his social skills.

Diamond made a start on the real task at the windowsills. At one stage Dombey came over and said confidentially, "Hot news. I don't think we'll see the vicar. He has three parishes to manage and there's a funeral this afternoon in the next village."

"We can relax, then," Diamond said.

Dombey missed the irony.

Several middle-aged women were at work decorating the pulpit. Dombey climbed the steps as if about to deliver a sermon and then picked up some tomatoes and juggled with them. Some of the women applauded.

Bloody show-off, Diamond thought. Next thing, he'll balance a cucumber on his nose.

Agnes Douglas approached soon after and praised the arrangement Diamond had just put in place. In respect for the surroundings, she was dressed more formally, in a beige dress with a cameo brooch at the neck. "You're good at this. And your friend is a hit with the ladies."

"I wouldn't call him a friend. We don't have much in common. He latched himself on to me, thinking I live here."

"What does he want?"

"He's Claudia Priest's boyfriend."

She rolled her eyes. "One of that lot. I thought I'd seen

him before. They all vanished like breath off a mirror when she was arrested. What's he doing here?"

"Trying to clear Claudia's name, he says. Mending fences, basically."

"It's a bit late for that, isn't it? She's served half her sentence. She'll be back in the farmhouse any day now. They send them out on licence."

He knew how the parole system worked and she was right, but with everything else going on, an imminent release hadn't occurred to him. He was surprised Agnes was so well informed.

"Mending fences, you say?" She was amused at the prospect. She smiled, more relaxed with him than the last time they'd spoken. His efforts on the windowsills must have done the trick. "If that's really what this is about, he's got his work cut out. Here in Baskerville, most of them think she got what she deserved."

"Do you?"

She was back in her shell, caught off guard. "She's my employer. I'm not going to knock her."

"Do you think she'll keep the farm when she's released?"

"I've got no worries about that. She told us our jobs are secure for as long as we want. She phones me from the prison sometimes. I can't find the time to visit her. There's always work to be done here."

Now he knew how she got her information. There was more to Agnes than he'd first thought. "What does she talk about?"

"Oh, farm stuff mainly. I keep her up to date on what we're doing."

"Has she mentioned Bert Dombey?"

"Your friend? I wouldn't expect her to. Her private life is her own and we're just employees."

"Not my friend," Diamond made clear for the second time, not wanting to be lumped in with Dombey. "I thought his name might have come up. She sees him regularly."

"At the prison?" Agnes blinked. It seemed he knew something she didn't.

"He's still the boyfriend. I think he hopes to pick up where he left off when she is released."

She sighed. "We were hoping the parties were a thing of the past."

"I feel sure they are. This is more about their personal relationship." He felt a tweak of insincerity as he spoke. In truth, he couldn't imagine Dombey getting emotionally involved with anyone, whatever he claimed. The man was a predator. "I'd better get back to work. I haven't started the sills along the far side."

"We're grateful," Agnes said. "I hope Julie is bringing you and Paloma to the harvest supper."

The first he'd heard of a supper.

"When's that?"

"Tomorrow. It's a lovely event, a real village occasion with a band and dancing as well as home-cooked food. What with Covid and the lockdowns, we haven't done it for three years."

He had a rapid rethink. "Where does this happen?"

"The old tithe barn behind the farmhouse. It's always held there. We're already preparing. Claudia arranged for me to collect the set of keys held by her solicitors so we can get in and use the kitchen as a base. There's heaps of food to warm up. Quiches, lasagne, sausage rolls."

"Will you be cooking as well?"

She shook her head. "I'm needed for other duties. I'll be on the road early, driving to Bath."

"For the keys?"

"To open up the house for everyone else."

A chance to see inside the farmhouse. He couldn't pass up that opportunity.

"We'll be there. It sounds irresistible."

12

H E DIDN'T MENTION the harvest supper to Dombey. The man would go through fire and water to be invited and foul up the whole event with his manic behaviour when he got there. There was a chance he'd heard about it from the women he'd been chatting to, but nothing was said when he linked up with Diamond again by the chancel rail. "Stout work on the windowsills, Peter. Sorry to leave you to it. I got a bit distracted. They could talk the proverbial hind leg off a donkey, some of those old ducks."

"Keep your voice down. Everything carries between these stone walls."

"They won't mind," he said. "Each of them thinks she's Jennifer Lopez and the rest are only extras. How can I be useful?"

Diamond extended a hand to the ten bales of straw lining the chancel in front of the choir stalls. Without toppings of harvest products, they looked sacrilegious. "I noticed a wheelbarrow outside. You could use it to bring in some of the big stuff, the pumpkins, cabbages and cauliflowers."

"A wheelbarrow in church?"

"Saves on the journeys."

Soon enough, Dombey was trundling barrowloads of fruit and veg up the aisle.

Together, they decorated two of the bales passably enough to draw coos of approval from the ladies arranging flowers around the pulpit. One of them took a picture with her phone.

They moved to the next bale and yet another monster pumpkin, somebody's prize specimen, a white one. "Some sticks of celery would be good along the front," Diamond said. "And a cabbage either side."

"Are you enjoying this?" Dombey asked.

"There are worse ways to spend an afternoon." Like paperwork for the Avon & Somerset Police, he thought to himself.

"You were humming something just now."

"*We plough the fields and scatter.*"

"Is that Lady Gaga?"

Diamond gave him a disbelieving look. The man wasn't capable of irony. "It's a hymn."

"Stormzy?"

"Hymn with a *y*. Didn't you sing it at school?"

"I didn't go to school. My parents decided I'd get on better with private tutors."

That fitted the profile, Diamond decided. He could imagine the disruptive pest Dombey must have been. "I expect you read school stories when you were growing up. Did you feel you missed out?"

"I don't read fiction. Never did." His head shook and the dreadlocks rearranged themselves. "Waste of time. I like to know facts, not the nonsense some author makes up. I'm good at speed-reading. I can get through several long books in a day, non-fiction, every time."

"Was it difficult relating to people when you got older?"

"I don't need to. They relate to me."

All part of the pattern. Confident, boastful and self-centred.

"So I noticed. You seemed to be joking with the ladies a short while back. There was a lot of giggling."

"I was fooling around with a butternut squash. Don't ask."

"I won't. Did they tell you anything I ought to know about?"

"The vicar not coming? I told you."

"About how Mervyn got rich."

Dombey slapped a hand to his forehead. "Forgot to ask. That could be the key to Claudia's troubles, bless her heart." He sighed heavily. A psychopath can lie with total conviction.

Diamond was losing patience. "It's why we're here, I thought."

"True. I really do need to get the inside track on the saintly Mervyn."

"Meaning what?"

"Something dodgy. You brought it up yourself when we first met at Gordano. Where did the extra funds come from?"

"A wild idea. I was half joking."

"Made a lot of sense to me. Booty of some sort, I reckon."

"Stolen goods?" Diamond shook his head. "I don't think he doubled up as a burglar."

"Some scam he was working. I haven't fathomed it yet but there was obviously dirty work going on."

"He's been dead six years. You're not going to find out now."

"I'm going to try. The money hasn't dried up. How do you think the farm has kept going with Claudia locked up in prison?"

"Are you saying Claudia is involved?"

"What the fuck is this?" In a blatant move to distract, Dombey lifted a huge loaf from the latest barrowload. It was in the shape of a sheaf of corn tied in the old style before combine harvesters were invented. "Some keeno must have baked it specially."

The Columbo method of detection committed Diamond to go on sweet-talking this pillock. "What a whopper. Pride of place in front of the altar, I reckon."

"I baked it." A voice had cut through the chatter of the helpers. It was a good thing he hadn't said anything uncomplimentary. They turned to see a tall, slim woman who had materialised like an alien visitor in a multicoloured shaft of sunlight from one of the high south windows, her glasses flashing. It was Maggie Harrap, who had appeared in the aisle unnoticed by either man. They'd last seen her in the Feathers looking as if she would prop up the bar for the rest of the day.

"Did you make this today?" Diamond asked her, truly impressed. "I can smell how fresh it is."

"First thing this morning. I let it rise overnight and I was up before dawn to punch it down, reshape it and let it rise again."

"You need some muscle for that."

"Just to lift it," Dombey chimed in. "It's a good weight, believe me."

"It's the harvest loaf for our parish. It has to be larger than any other."

"Look at that golden crust," he said, oozing his brand of charm. "The form of it, the stalks, the ears of corn. Such detail. If I'm not mistaken, that's a harvest mouse attached to it."

A small round form, baked brown, with a pointed nose and ears, had been built into the design.

She looked pleased. "Well spotted."

"It's a thing of beauty, ma'am."

Dombey's flattery was working. "Maggie. Feel free to call me Maggie. The loaf is an older tradition than harvest festivals, centuries older."

"Tell us more," Diamond said, not needing more, but pleased to be on better terms with the local know-it-all.

Sounding like the voiceover in a TV documentary she said, "The origin goes back through time immemorial, and it became an early Christian ritual mentioned in the *Anglo-Saxon Chronicle*. Lammas, as it was known, was held on August the first, the start of the harvesting season. A loaf was baked from the first crop of wheat. The priest blessed the bread and used it for communion. Loaf Mass."

"Got it," Diamond said. "Lammas."

"I've baked our parish loaf each year for longer than I care to say."

He decided he'd better lavish some praise of his own on the creation in Dombey's arms. "How did you shape it so realistically, Maggie? It's a work of art." He was about as subtle as a politician doorstepping for votes but she didn't seem to notice.

"I have to confess I used a mould."

"No need to apologise. Where did you find a mould that size? Not off the internet, I'm sure."

"It was made specially for me by one of the Priest family. An artist. You won't have heard of him."

"Oh, but I have." His memory could usually be relied on. "You must mean Mervyn's brother Howard. Lived in Bathampton."

She blinked in surprise. "How on earth . . . ?"

"Agnes Douglas mentioned him the other day. Bit of a

recluse. I got the impression he was a painter rather than a designer of moulds."

"He was. He didn't usually work with metal, but he learned this new skill in a very short time. He had great talent. He could have been a sculptor if he wished." She looked at him over her glasses. "You seem well informed."

"It's a friendly village."

"It was until certain visitors took advantage and made a nuisance of themselves. I know who you are. I'm surprised you have the nerve to show your face here."

The barbed remark came from nowhere. Diamond thought it was intended for him until he saw she was eyeballing his companion. A moment ago she'd invited Bert to call her Maggie.

Dangerous.

His unctuous companion had too much of an ego to let the taunt pass. He said through clenched teeth, "That's unfair, ma'am, especially in God's house when I'm giving my time and energy to your precious harvest festival. As a matter of fact, we just decided to make your loaf the centrepiece of the whole thing, in front of the altar. We could change our minds, you know."

She gave a hoot of contempt. "The loaf belongs to the parish now. Kick it out of the door if you wish and answer to the vicar." Satisfied with that parting shot, Maggie Harrap turned her back on them and went to speak to the ladies decorating the pew ends with sprays of flowers.

Diamond noticed breadcrumbs bouncing like hail on the flagstone floor. Dombey's fingers were digging into the underside of the loaf. It was in serious danger of disintegrating. "Don't grip so hard, Bert."

The man looked murderous. His cheeks were the colour of the tomatoes ranged along the choir stalls.

"Take a deep breath and let it out slowly."

Dombey did so, eyeing Diamond as if he was a stranger.

"Another . . . and again . . . Now breathe evenly if you can."

The crisis seemed to be passing.

"Put the loaf down and we'll deal with it later. Here will do." He gestured to a convenient surface, which happened to be a prie-dieu, the vicar's litany desk. "Gently does it."

The harvest loaf survived. And so did the prie-dieu.

"Well done. Do you want to go outside for a bit and collect another barrowload?" The simple activity of moving fruit and vegetables from one place to another might have a calming effect.

Dombey nodded and started walking.

"Don't forget the wheelbarrow."

He ignored that.

Diamond used the side of his shoe to nudge some of the largest crumbs out of sight under the nearest choir stall. Then he collected the barrow and followed Dombey outside in time to see him aim a kick at a pumpkin.

"Don't take it personally, Bert. To her, you represent Claudia's noisy friends from Bath and that's all it was."

Dombey's mindset made him incapable of seeing the disturbances from the villagers' point of view. "How does she know I was at the parties? I've never spoken to her."

"She listens to everything. She was in the pub while you were chatting to the barmaid. It's not worth making an issue of it."

After some thought, he felt for one of his braids and mimicked touching his forelock. "Whatever you say, your lordship. I know my place."

"Shall we load up, then?"

"I'm through."

There was a disconnect before Diamond said, "We haven't finished. There are four more bales in there."

"Aren't you listening, chum? I've had enough."

"It's not the job. It's what else we might find out."

"I found out everything I want to know. I'm off."

13

THE COLUMBO ROUTINE had stalled. Diamond had lost his man. You can't tease out the truth if your suspect has quit the scene. Following him would be futile. It would only bring out more hostility, undoing all the goodwill cultivated in their meetings up to now.

Those parting words—"I found out everything I want to know. I'm off"—cut deep with Diamond. That was more than just an exit line. It was a taunt. Dombey had learned something useful and was refusing to share it. He must have got it from the women he'd chatted up. His whole attitude had changed.

The empty bales of straw waited inside the church, each one a call to action. Diamond couldn't risk losing the friendship of the church community, if only for Julie's sake. Feeling more annoyed with himself than with Dombey, he filled the wheelbarrow and pushed another load of garden produce up the aisle.

Before unloading, he dealt with the harvest loaf. Its position on the prie-dieu was precarious. He lifted it as respectfully as if he were one of the clergy, carried it up to the altar and leaned it upright at the centre of the top step.

"Well done Peter," Agnes Douglas said from where she was fixing ferns to one of the choir stalls.

He looked across and smiled. "Is that the right place?"

She crossed the aisle for a more private conversation. "You couldn't have chosen better. The loaf will be used on Sunday. Instead of the usual wafers, we celebrate the sacrament with real bread, blessed by the vicar, of course. Maggie bakes one each year. I'm afraid most of us take it for granted, she's done it for so many years, but she never lets us down. She has a huge Victorian cooking range and the loaf only just fits in."

"I know her secret," he said.

"What's that—the mould? When she started, she didn't use one." She glanced right and left to check whether Maggie was still there. She wasn't. Agnes still spoke in a lowered voice, not so much out of respect as from a wish not to be overheard. "Between ourselves, she wasn't much good at it when she started. Her loaves were a disaster, looking nothing like sheaves. Stalks as thick as my arm and ears of corn like sausages. She worked at it so long that the bread went flat. Mervyn said he'd seen cowpats more like the real thing. In the end he asked his brother to make the mould."

"Was Maggie offended?"

"She was tickled pink. I'm sure she fancied Howard. She was just a young thing, then, in her twenties, and he was about forty years older and didn't get out much, but still a likeable gent. She was under the illusion he thought the whole thing up himself."

"A labour of love?"

"That's putting it strongly, but she may have thought so. Howard involved her in the design and she visited him in Bathampton several times, she told me. And while she was there he made sketches of her."

"Flattering for any young woman. Did the friendship come to anything?"

"No, it fizzled." Agnes gave the smile of a woman wearing a wedding ring, sympathy mixed with self-congratulation. "Reading between the lines, there was never any thought of romance on Howard's side. The mould held more interest for him than Maggie did."

"Was he paid?"

"I expect so. Mervyn would have insisted, but Howard wouldn't have asked. The typical penniless artist, head in the clouds and no commercial sense. He didn't exhibit. Putting his work up for sale was too demeaning. He left a load of paintings when he died."

"Were they any good?"

"I've seen some and it's unkind to say so but they're rubbish. None of it was original. You've heard of painting by numbers? He worked from photographs enlarged and squared-up, but he couldn't do detail, so they look like a blur."

"He should have gone into mould-making," Diamond said. "Cornered the market in tins for harvest loaves. He might have made a fortune."

She smiled. "Wishful thinking. Most people like to shape the loaves by hand."

"Does Maggie still carry a torch for Howard?"

"Definitely not. She came to her senses quickly and realised how naive she'd been. It's a closed book now. But I don't think she ever found out the real reason why the mould was made for her. If she had, she would have torn strips off Mervyn. She has a sharp side to her character."

He grinned. "I'm aware of that. She cut Bert Dombey down to size and he went off in a huff. I'm on my own now."

She was all ears for a bit of gossip she hadn't heard. "What on earth did she say to him?"

"Something about the nerve he had to show his face here."

"That sounds like Maggie. Seeing him must have brought back the anger about the parties. You weren't here, Peter. It was a bad time."

"I've heard this from several people. What will happen when Claudia is freed?"

She turned her head once more to see if anyone was in earshot. "She already is."

Speechless, he stared at her, demanding more.

"When I spoke about this earlier, I didn't tell you everything. She was released on licence last weekend. She's treating herself to a few days at the spa in Longleat to get over the prison experience."

He struggled to take this in. Dombey had told him he'd visited Claudia at the prison only yesterday. His mystification must have been obvious. Had Dombey fed him a pack of lies? "Are you sure?"

"A hundred per cent. She called me from there. She doesn't want the rest of the village to know yet, so—please—if you tell Julie, ask her to play along."

"She will, I'm sure. Is Claudia going to show up here any time soon?"

"That's the plan. She'll make her appearance at the harvest supper, hoping to earn some goodwill, I suppose."

"Because she's hosting it?"

"Like old times. If you can come, you'll meet her."

"Try and keep me away."

His mood was transformed. When he went back to decorating the bales of straw, his brain was in overdrive. He completed the job as if he were on autopilot. Forty minutes after, when he finished, he had scarcely any memory of the wheelbarrow work.

IN JULIE'S COTTAGE that evening, he started telling the tale.

"Claudia is *out?*" Paloma piped in disbelief as soon as he shared what he'd learned from Agnes.

Bella, startled out of sleep, wriggled from under Julie's chair to check whatever emergency was occurring.

"On licence since last weekend," he said. "She's been treating herself to a week at some fancy spa."

"That's Claudia," Julie said while calming the dog with her hand.

"I'm supposed to ask you both to keep the news under your hats."

Paloma shook her head, baffled. "But Bert Dombey told you he visited her in prison yesterday. That's why he met you at Gordano services. That can't be true."

"That's what he told me."

"What a liar."

"World-class. Agnes speaks regularly on the phone to Claudia and Bert's name has never come up."

Julie was well ahead with the significance of this. "It calls everything into question. Why he agreed to meet you, why he returned to the village and what he's up to. He can't be doing it for Claudia. Was he there when you had the conversation with Agnes?"

"No, he was chatting up some of the other women."

"What's his game, guv?"

"I don't know yet. All I can say is I'm even more sure he's dangerous. But you'll want to hear the rest of what happened, our afternoon as church volunteers." Recapping the day was useful for him, too, picking the juicy bits he'd learned from everyone.

"You're a legend, guv," Julie said when he'd finished. "In one afternoon, you discover more about this village than I have since I moved here. The whole thing about Howard and the mould is new to me."

"But you knew about the harvest supper tomorrow?"

"I didn't mention it because I don't usually go and I didn't think it would be your idea of an evening out. You can't possibly miss it now with the chance to meet Claudia. We can get tickets from the shop."

"Sounds fun to me," Paloma said. "There's only one problem. I'm going to need a dress."

It was decided the two women would make a shopping trip into Taunton the next day. Diamond wouldn't be with them. He said a suit was always right for every occasion. Obviously that was where the word "suitable" came from. Julie and Paloma buttoned their lips.

"You don't look too convinced," he said. "This one is Italian cloth. The finest you can get. I collected it when I made my trip to Bath."

Almost on cue, his phone buzzed and the caller was Ingeborg. He stared at her name and asked himself if he really wanted to speak to her. He guessed some crisis had arisen in Bath Central. Without his hand on the tiller, the ship was sure to run aground. Hadn't he got enough to deal with?

He touched the green button and said, "Can't a man have a couple of days off without being hounded?"

Ingeborg said, "Guv, are you okay?"

"Hundred per cent until my phone rang."

"We had quite a debate about whether to call you. Keith thought you wouldn't welcome it and he seems to be right, but some of us disagreed. We thought you were away in Somerset with Paloma."

"I am. She's sitting opposite me."

For the cool Ingeborg, the "Oh" she uttered was out of

character, a breathy, embarrassed admission that she was at a loss as to what to say next.

He waited.

She cleared her throat. "False alarm, obviously."

"If you say so." He had an inkling what this was about.

Ingeborg still struggled for the right words. "One of us thought they caught sight of you in Cheap Street yesterday morning, but they must have been mistaken."

The inkling was confirmed as fact. "Who was that?"

He waited again.

"Out with it, Inge. Are you talking about yourself?" He was getting his own thoughts in order. He didn't particularly care which one of them had spotted him. The trip had been a risk at the time. His current mindset was all about being undercover, admitting nothing, pretending he'd been in Baskerville, but he had to snap out of it. He would never lie to his own team.

A new voice replaced Ingeborg's. They'd set this up as a conference call. "Guv, it was me that saw you."

He pictured Paul Gilbert turning redder than the fire extinguisher on the office wall. DC Gilbert, the young man with an extraordinary talent for saying the wrong thing. Years ago, the first day Paul had joined a team meeting, looking so baby-faced that Diamond had called him "son," he'd had the neck to recommend a new technique called DNA. (It was that long ago.) With everyone else holding their breath, Diamond had explained that he wasn't ignorant about forensic science. In fact, the high-ups at headquarters regularly signed him up for courses at Peel Centre. "It's called professional training. If you take the trouble to check the lists of delegates, you'll find they always put the letters DNA after my name, a rare distinction. Detective Superintendent P. Diamond, DNA. Did Not Attend."

"Paul?" Diamond said down the phone. "You thought you recognised me in Cheap Street?"

"Yes, guv." He was still known to everyone as young Gilbert, regardless of his age. He played up to it. As his career developed, he'd taken on roles requiring responsibility and courage but he still treated everyone else on the team as if they were royalty. "You must have a double. He was even in a suit just like yours."

Another Gilbert gaffe. There was clearly some sniggering on the line. Diamond knew what they all thought of his choice of clothes. "Was he with a small fellow with a big moustache he might have bought in a joke shop?"

"Yes."

"That was me, then. I'm on holiday. I'm allowed a day in Bath without being stalked by my own team."

"I didn't mean to offend you. I was worried, seeing you without Paloma. I could only think something bad had happened, like she'd been taken ill or had an accident and was in hospital."

"If you were worried about Paloma, we appreciate your concern. I was on an errand for Julie, the old colleague we're staying with, understand? Is Keith on the line?"

"I am, guv," came Halliwell's deep, support-you-evermore voice.

"How are you coping? Any problems you want to tell me about?"

"Don't you worry. It's going like clockwork here. Isn't that so, people? Shall we say it together?"

In unison, the whole team repeated that it was going like clockwork, which wasn't what Diamond had hoped to hear. He'd rather be told that they were counting the minutes for him to return to work and sort out all the problems.

After the call was ended, he wished he'd thanked them

all. It was touching that they had bothered. Touching, but troubling. They would never have shown such concern in years past. They were treating him like an elderly parent who was losing it, going on walks and forgetting where he was heading and where he ought to be.

His determination to stay on in the job had taken a hit.

IT WAS MUCH later that evening, after the table had been cleared and they were sitting in front of the fire, with Raffles asleep on Diamond's lap, shedding hairs on the fine Italian cloth, and Bella stretched out on the rug with her belly towards the heat, that Julie gave a small cough and said, "Mind if I ask something, guv?"

Diamond, too, was half asleep. It had been a long day and lifting pumpkins had given him a backache. He tried to look alert.

"You said Bert Dombey walked out on you when he was supposed to be helping you decorate the church. Was that final?"

"It sounded final to me."

"I'm wondering how you can use the Columbo technique without anyone to work on."

He smiled. "Point taken. The Columbo thing may have run its course. I don't know if you ever watched the series. There was one show where the suspect was a fitness freak. He went for a jog and poor old Peter Falk was filmed trying to keep up with him, his raincoat flapping behind him. That's persistence I can't match. I don't even know where Dombey lives. Bristol, I was told, but Bristol is huge."

"You have his phone number."

"He'll cut the call when he sees who it's from."

"Is he still your main suspect?"

"Even more so now. He'll show himself again."

Julie waited, sensing there was more to come.

"Why did he leave so suddenly?" he said. "All he'd done was amuse the women decorating the pulpit and most of that was horsing around with vegetables. But he learned something. He said so."

"Didn't he say what?"

"I've worked it out. One of them must have asked if he was coming to the harvest supper. Simple as that. He'd got what he wanted all along, a chance to get inside the farmhouse."

"Why didn't he tell you?"

"He didn't want me tagging along. He thinks he's done with me. When he turns up tomorrow he'll find he's mistaken."

Paloma asked, "What's inside the farmhouse that's so important to Dombey?"

"I don't know yet. He was there when Claudia held her parties, of course, so he knows his way around. He may be planning to steal some item of value. That's my best guess."

"Is he strapped for cash?"

"I've picked up some signs."

"When he stuck you with the bar bill in the Feathers?"

He laughed. "Hadn't thought of that, but you may be right. Other things like the grotty old van he drives. His phone is ancient, too. At least as old as mine is. He wants me to think he's as well off as his friends Fortunato and Hertzog. At one time he may have been, but he isn't any longer."

"He wants his lifestyle back?"

"We can be pretty sure he's on to something that will turn his life around. Mervyn had money and Bert has a theory where it came from. He's confident that if he can search the house, he'll find the crock of gold."

"And you're ahead of him, guv," Julie said. "You've worked that out, too. I can hear it in your voice."

"You've got too much faith in your old boss, Julie. Worked it out? I've hardly begun. I know a few things Bert seems to have missed, that's all."

THE BACK PAIN was worse the next morning. Julie produced a remedy, a support he could put around his lumbar region and fasten with Velcro straps. It had mesh pouches for two gel packs. He said he'd get it on right away but she insisted the packs must go in the freezer first. He didn't like the sound of that. "Wouldn't a warm pack work better? We can put it in the microwave and it will be ready in seconds."

"No, guv. The cold treatment comes first. I'm sure of that." Paloma agreed.

Diamond said, "I think you ladies are enjoying this."

And they were right. After the first eye-watering shock, the cold treatment took the pain down appreciably. He agreed he would not go near another pumpkin all day. He wouldn't even stoop to lift Raffles on to the sofa. Raffles was already in place, curled up and sleeping, and didn't look as if he would move.

But Diamond didn't promise to stay in the cottage. Every second counted. As soon as the ladies had left for their shopping trip, he pulled his jacket on and hobbled up the lane to the farm in search of the key witness he hadn't yet succeeded in opening up: Jim Douglas.

14

JIM WASN'T IN the milking parlour where Diamond expected to find him. The cows had been left to the tender mercy of Hamish, the "good lad, growing up fast," in Julie's words. Diamond wasn't persuaded about the "good" part, but there was no question that the charmless youth shouldered more responsibility than most kids his age. He was currently on the carousel attaching cups to the teats of a black and white cow indifferent to his attentions. It was done in seconds and he moved at speed to the next.

"On your own, then?" Diamond called up and was ignored, as he expected. A less obvious line than that was needed to engage Hamish in conversation.

He would get more attention if he could get closer. Climbing up the side of the carousel to the same level wasn't possible with a stiff back.

"I was hoping to find your dad here."

Hamish moved on to the next cow.

And the one after.

Diamond's earlier schmoozing of the boy, telling him what a grand job he did on the farm and how skilful he was on the quad bike, counted for nothing. This was one stroppy teenager.

He had to think of something more arresting. "Your dad, Hamish. It's important. Where is he?"

"Calving."

Any word was encouragement, even though the boy hadn't bothered to turn his head. So it was a pity that Diamond, the typical townie, failed to understand, picturing Jim Douglas chiselling at a sculpture. "Where does he do that? Out in the open?"

"Calving shed."

Carving must have some mysterious function on a farm, Diamond told himself, though he couldn't think what, and it didn't matter as long as he found Douglas senior. "Where's that?"

He didn't get a verbal answer. Hamish paused briefly before moving to the next cow and jerked his head leftwards, to the far end of the building.

Diamond headed in that direction, playing the word "carving" over in his head. Belatedly, he understood his mistake. Somewhere nearby, a cow was giving birth. It happened on farms. On dairy farms, it happened right through the year to keep the milk coming.

He went to the end of the shed and outside, where Julie had waited with her dog the day before. Across a strip of yard were more sheds. As if on cue, he heard a series of bellowing sounds coming from one of them. He found Jim Douglas inside, dressed in a beanie hat, waterproof overalls and arm-length plastic gloves. The shed had a communal area where a number of pregnant Friesians sat in a thick layer of straw bedding. Beyond were six individual pens. Jim was in one of them with the cow, which was fully in labour if the sound was anything to go by. Not the time to start a conversation about suspicious events in the village. Diamond turned to go.

Jim must have spotted a movement because he called out, "That you, Hamish?"

"Sorry. Hamish is milking. This is Peter Dee."

"Fuck."

Spoken more in disappointment than discourtesy.

"I can fetch him," Diamond offered.

"No time for that. I need help now."

Diamond had no idea what service he could offer. Buckets of water, perhaps. He could deal with most situations, but this?

"Get your jacket off. You'll find gloves hanging on the rail."

Diamond took off his jacket and hung it over the next pen. The gloves covered his arms to above the elbow. He was clumsy at the best of times. He had no confidence he could perform here.

The distressed cow was straining. The amniotic sac protruded from the rear end. This would be a messy business. No good using the excuse that he wasn't dressed for it. He wasn't and it didn't alter anything. Nervously, he stepped up to the pen and felt for the lever to go inside.

"Not this one," Jim Douglas said. "Her in the far corner with the others. The one with a white patch like a saddle. She started and wants help. Taking far too long."

He expected Peter Diamond to act as midwife to another cow. Another challenge altogether.

"I wouldn't know what to do."

"I'll tell you. Approach her slowly. Let her see you coming and give confidence. The hooves are out but the calf won't drop. She's been straining twenty minutes. Get a grip and when she pushes, you pull."

He saw the cow in the corner. He hadn't heard the sounds it was making because the poor beast getting Jim's attention was making such a racket. The instruction sounded simple. In his eventful life he'd never been within ten feet of a cow, let alone handled one.

But he hated seeing an animal in distress. "I'll try."

He let himself into the area where the pregnant cows were housed prior to giving birth. All were sitting in the thick straw except the one who had gone to the corner for self-protection and was standing. As soon as he started wading through the mass of bedding, the nearest ones stood and moved away.

This wasn't giving confidence to the cows or himself.

In the pen, Jim Douglas's cow seemed to be reaching crisis point. Jim was fully engrossed, making straining sounds of his own. There wouldn't be much more advice from that source.

"All right, all right," Diamond said in a tone he hoped was pacifying, as if one of his police team had cracked under stress. "We can sort this." The cow turned her head and looked at him with a large suspicious eye. At least there was communication. She appeared willing to let him try and solve her problem. He approached her back end by an indirect route as if he was making for the shed wall. She shifted position a little. Thankfully, she didn't bolt. Unfortunately her insides contracted and the calf's hooves disappeared from view.

The tail, decorated with several rings of coloured tape, was swinging protectively. Diamond grasped it gently and moved it to one side. He couldn't see anything except shreds of the broken amniotic sac. He'd have to reach inside the birth canal and locate the hooves.

No detective he had ever heard of, in fiction or the real police, had been called on to perform such a duty. Village mysteries were set mainly in people's houses, rather grand houses. Miss Marple had lived all her adult life in a village. Had she ever stepped inside a cowshed?

His legs shook.

The cow was straining again. It gave voice to a long, ear-splitting groan that spurred Diamond to action. He gritted his teeth, reached inside and located something solid.

Get a grip and when she pushes, you pull.

He slipped the other arm inside. He'd definitely found the hooves.

The cow's sides were contracting. He could feel the effort. He pulled and got no result other than a piercing twinge. He'd forgotten about his own stiff back.

"I don't think this is working," he called out to Jim Douglas.

No answer. He was on his own.

The cow seemed to be exhausted. To his alarm, it sat down in the straw, forcing him down as well. He still had the hooves in his grip and he felt some movement and pulled. The hooves came into view again. He forgot his back pain and tugged.

With one more effort, the cow raised its rear and miraculously the calf's head appeared. In the same movement, everything slid out and the entire body landed in Diamond's lap. The straw cushioned the fall to some extent.

"It's out!"

Jim Douglas didn't congratulate him but he must have heard because he shouted, "Did the cord break?"

"I can't tell. Wait."

The newborn didn't seem to be moving, although there was warmth through the wetness. Diamond eased it away from him and tried to sit up. His back gave him a sharp reminder of his muscle strain. He could see part of the umbilical cord hanging loose.

"It broke, yes."

"Should breathe on its own, then."

"It's very still."

"Clear the airways. Mouth and nostrils."

He did what he could in his inept way. A lot of fluid and mucus came out when he managed to open the jaws.

"Don't leave it lying on its side. Get it sitting upright."

He understood why. In that position, the calf would be more able to take the vital first breath.

The calf was the size of a large dog but worryingly limp. Diamond reached around the ribcage and lifted it as instructed. The legs seemed to slide underneath.

Now the cow got to her feet, turned and took an interest. She nudged the calf with her head and started licking it.

Jim called out, "You can try pushing a straw up its nose and tickling it."

This sounded like a futile remedy but it was something Diamond could do. He feared the calf was stillborn, heartbreaking after all the efforts the mother had made. Still supporting the head that the cow's huge tongue was now licking, he grabbed a piece of straw, shoved it into the nostril and moved it about.

Miraculously, the calf recoiled and then snorted.

There was life.

More mucus spilled out. The calf supported the weight of its own head. Its eyes were open. It was breathing. The legs moved.

The cow nudged the small body several times with her head, as if taking possession.

"We're okay, I think," Diamond called out.

"Male or female?"

"I can't tell."

"Is the cow interested?"

"You bet she is."

"You can back off, then. Job done, mate." That "mate" was a badge of honour.

Elated by the experience, he reached for the railing and hauled himself to his feet. His clothes were saturated, he stank and his back throbbed, but the miracle of a new life had enriched him. He couldn't remember a time when his spirits had soared so high.

By the time he had forced his legs through the thick straw he saw that Jim Douglas, too, had a living calf at his feet. He was feeding it something from a bottle and it was drinking hard.

"Should mine have some of that?" As he spoke, he realised he was getting as possessive as the calf's mother.

"Yeah. Grab a bottle from over there and get some into it."

"Right now?"

"Sooner the better, mate. It's colostrum, from the udders of other cows after they give birth. Calves aren't strong enough yet to stand and suck, not for twenty minutes."

Diamond was emotionally and physically spent. He stumbled while forcing his stiff, shaking legs through the straw bedding. Luckily the bottle didn't leave his hand.

The calf knew what to do. It practically swallowed the rubber teat on the end of the tube and sucked vigorously. The cow seemed to accept that the feed was necessary. She backed off a little way and chewed some straw.

After a short time, Jim Douglas joined him and sprayed the place where the umbilical cord had snapped. "New experience for you, I expect."

"I'm pleased it happened. It's a male, by the way."

"Pity you weren't dressed for it. We'll get you out of those clothes and into something clean. Then I'll buy you a drink."

Only now did Diamond look down at his trousers. He doubted whether the finest Italian cloth would ever clean up.

As if reading his thoughts, his new mate said, "I'm not short of suits. Miss Claudia gave me a load of clothes after her father passed on. Some of them I use, like sweaters and jeans, but suits are no use to me. He was a gentleman farmer, was Mervyn. Wore them for church. Me, I'm in overalls the year round. You're more his size than I am."

An invitation to the house where the Douglas family lived, an opportunity Diamond couldn't have engineered without seeming pushy. His efforts in the calving shed were aiding the investigation in ways he couldn't have predicted.

They needed transport, which meant visiting the tractor shed. The word "shed" didn't do justice to the size of the building. It was on the scale of an aircraft hangar and some of the combine harvesters took up as much space as private planes. Evidence of huge investment. Rows of gleaming purpose-built farm vehicles for ploughing, harrowing, drilling and tilling. Excavators, bulldozers and a variety of attachments. Each was given a generous parking area for easy access and there was a throughway along the middle as wide as two lanes of a motorway. He assumed the Douglas family car would be parked here as well, but he couldn't see anything resembling private transport. "You need to be multiskilled to know how any of these work," he complimented his new buddy.

"When they save you blood, sweat, toil and tears you master them," Jim said. "They're mostly straightforward. We'll use the Massey." He went to a board and picked a key off a hook. "We ought to be more secure, but I tell myself no thief will get far with things this size. I hope you don't object to sitting in a trailer."

"Best way to travel when your clothes are as mucky as

mine," Diamond said manfully. "I wouldn't want to mess up someone's car seat."

Which was how he found himself seated on a cushion of empty cattle feed sacks being hauled by a small utility tractor through the village. It wasn't dignified but if the trailer had been the imperial state coach he couldn't have been more proud. Better still, he was now on friendly terms with one of the key witnesses in the case he was investigating. The opportunity of learning more was a huge bonus.

The Douglas house was a modern semi on a moderate-sized estate with the wooded Blackdown Hills as a backdrop. A modest home for the hardworking and responsible family so many in the village depended on for their livelihoods. Some sense of injustice would be forgivable. If there was any, it hadn't been revealed to Diamond.

The tractor looked out of place in the street and probably upset the neighbours.

Jim released the flap and helped him down. A spasm reminded him of his back strain.

"Hurt yourself, mate?"

"It's nothing. A bit stiff from yesterday, carting vegetables into the church for the harvest festival."

"You're a man of all trades."

They removed their footwear before going into the house. Jim led the way upstairs to the bathroom and turned on the shower. Diamond started shedding clothes.

"What's the harness for?" Jim asked.

"My lumbar support? Julie insisted." As a fully fledged farm worker, he didn't want it known that he was a namby-pamby using surgical aids.

Jim offered a change of underwear, but it wasn't needed.

The finest Italian cloth had soaked up all the fluid. He left Diamond to shower.

The double bedroom was across the passage and when Diamond appeared there, Jim had opened the wardrobe to display an impressive range of suits in plastic covers. "I'll be glad to unload one of these. My son isn't interested. Take your pick. Try one for size, anyway."

Diamond picked a dark three-piece pinstripe off the rail.

"You want a white shirt with that," Jim said, sounding like a menswear salesman. "Try the trousers for size." This was a quality suit with creases sharp and straight enough to satisfy a sergeant major.

Mervyn Priest must have been a bulky man, because the trousers were loose on Diamond, but he found waist extenders on each side and tightened them. The trousers stayed up.

Jim had provided a small plastic tray for the contents of the suit pockets and a black sack for the soiled clothes. He would have made a first-class gentleman's gentleman. The shirt he offered fitted well and felt good against the skin. "Are you still going to wear your back support?"

A shake of the head. "It bulks me out too much." Vanity was winning over comfort.

Jim eyed the heap on the tray. Smartphone, keys, loose cash, a tube of Softmints, the wallet with his warrant card and another with banknotes, credit cards and miscellaneous items including the Holloway Hotel compliment slip with Bert Dombey's phone number. "That lot's going to make some lumps and bumps."

"It won't all go into one pocket."

"There's a choice of ties if you want."

"I'll do without. Don't want to look overdressed."

"Shoes?" A drawer below the wardrobe was full of them.

He'd noticed when he took off his own at the front door that they were getting an ominous wrinkled look, quite apart from the coating of mud and animal waste. There was a split developing under the edge of the left sole, so they were almost certainly a write-off.

Kitted out in Mervyn's expensive things, he could have attended a state banquet, let alone a harvest supper. There was one immediate problem: how to stay clean in the trailer he'd arrived in.

Jim had the answer. "Drive the Massey."

His insides clenched. "The tractor? I wouldn't be confident."

"Man like you can manage. You just delivered a calf." How the two skills were connected, Jim didn't explain. "I'll show you the basics."

"I've never handled anything bigger than a car."

"Baskerville is the perfect place to start. Flat roads all the way to the pub. You won't turn over."

"Don't bank on it."

"Creep along in first gear. I'll walk beside you."

The title of an old song his mother had used to sing when he was feverish as a kid and suffering nightmares. But the memory offered no comfort.

Jim Douglas was a forceful character. The decision was made. In no time at all, the ruined clothes—the back support included—were in the trailer and the tractor was switched on. Diamond hadn't noticed how deafening it was when he was being driven here.

Jim produced a rag and thoughtfully wiped the seat clean before clambering down from the cab. He yelled in Diamond's ear, "Up you get, mate. Brake's on."

To have used his back pain as an excuse would have been to sully his new reputation as the hero of the calving shed.

Getting up wasn't easy, but he managed it. The tractor's bodywork was shaking, but no more than his. He'd never been a confident driver.

The controls were in strange places. Jim climbed up behind and gave a rapid tutorial that was difficult to hear. Diamond had seen the handbrake lever go on and he had some idea of the pedal functions. One thing did get through to him: if the worst came to the worst, he could turn the key and switch off, bringing the thing to a sudden stop.

Wouldn't his team at Bath CID enjoy watching this?

Jim gave him a final pat on the back and climbed down.

Diamond released the handbrake, found first gear and inched forward.

Jim raised his thumb and started walking. At no point in the journey did he need to trot to keep up. One or two villagers along the route noticed them and waved companionably. They didn't get a wave in return unless Jim gave it. Diamond was gripping the wheel as if his hands were superglued to it.

He was relieved to reach the Feathers without killing anything. A small procession of ducks had a narrow escape.

Jim made it a memorable entrance. An announcement for all to hear. "A large beer for this gent from Bath. He just delivered a calf and drove a tractor here."

Heads turned. The main taproom was half full. Dolores the barmaid said, "He's a dark horse, then. He told me he works with a computer."

Diamond gave a shy grin and made for the nearest empty table.

Jim said something inaudible when he arrived with the beers. Diamond practically emptied his pint glass at one go. "You'll have to speak up. My ears are ringing from the engine noise."

Jim leaned close. "Tell me your name again. You said it in the shed, but I wasn't listening."

"Peter Dee."

"I was thinking we might call the new bullock after you."

"Really?" He felt his cheeks glow. "That's nice."

"Usually we give them numbers. His mother is 144. This afternoon I'll tag his ears."

"I wouldn't want him to suffer because of me."

"Government requires it."

"My name on his ear?"

"The tags. They're only for numbers, the ID and the herd. You'll have your name on the tail tape."

The back end of a bullock didn't have quite the kudos he'd first thought. But a bond had been forged with the usually silent farm manager and now was as good a time as any to take advantage. "Have you heard anything from Claudia Priest?"

"Not me. My wife does the talking, gets her on the phone sometimes. Have you met Agnes?"

Of course he'd met Agnes and Jim knew about it. Diamond remembered telling him. Was the man dense, or boxing clever? "A couple of times. When I was helping in the church yesterday she told me Miss Priest is out now. Out of prison."

Jim nodded. "Said to be coming to the supper."

"Is she back in the farmhouse already?"

"Couldn't tell you, mate. You'll have to ask someone else. I've been on the go since early."

From behind them, a voice piped up. "We're expecting her later, Jim." Dolores the landlady—a reminder that little went unheard here, especially raised voices. Also at the bar on her usual stool was Maggie Harrap, who added, "Not before three, I heard."

"There's your answer, then," Jim said to Diamond before giving him a long, searching look. "You're not press, are you?"

He shook his head.

"The place was heaving with them after the body was found. There were free drinks to be had if they thought you had anything to tell them. Isn't that true, Dolores?" This had become a three-way conversation instead of the Q&A Diamond would have preferred.

Dolores gave her professional laugh. "We did good trade, but they didn't learn much. Folk here aren't stupid."

"They cornered me a few times, the bloody jackals," Jim said. "I found the body, you see. Like that made me interesting."

"You're too modest, sunshine," Dolores said. "Abseiling down the inside of the silo wearing a breathing mask and coming face to face with a dead body is front page."

"You make it sound like I wasn't wearing anything else," Jim said. "It's my job, cleaning out the thing."

"Since when has going eye to eye with a rotting corpse been your job?"

Diamond managed to get a word in. "Did you recognise him, Jim?"

Dolores said, "If he had a quid for every time he's answered that, he could pay off the national debt."

"Not personally, no," Jim said. "I could tell from his clothes he was one of the party crowd. I never had much to do with that lot, except Miss Claudia."

"She called the police."

"Sensible. I expect they questioned you."

"Took a statement and my DNA. That's all." He looked into his drink, as if he'd said too much. "Best forgotten now, all that stuff, with the boss coming back. She won't want it talked about."

"Were you called for the inquest?"

"That was at Taunton. It was more relaxed than I expected. Coroner put me at my ease. I answered some questions about silo management and said what happened."

"Did you also appear at the trial?"

"No." He looked away as if someone might save him from the direct questioning. Jim's head-in-the-sand attitude—encapsulated in the phrase "I never had much to do with that lot"—was difficult for Diamond to accept. He was head of the second most powerful family in Baskerville, the managers of the farm, and he put long hours into making it work seamlessly, yet he seemed uninterested in anything except his duties. Agnes, who was far more involved in the dramas going on around her, must have talked to him, but he affected not to know anything, not even Diamond's name.

"Did Agnes?"

"Did she what?"

"Attend the trial."

"Bits of it. We had the farm to run."

Dolores asked Diamond, "Are you coming to the supper? Claudia's sure to want to meet you after you delivered one of her calves."

"Julie said she'd get tickets for us."

"Have you got something to wear?"

He slipped his thumb under the lapel of the tailored suit Mervyn had owned. "I was thinking this would do."

She rolled her eyes. "It's a hoedown, not a wake."

"I could leave off the jacket."

"You need a different shirt, then."

"I'll see what I find." He wasn't getting the one-to-one session with Jim he had hoped for. How was it that Hercule Poirot never had any difficulty cornering a witness and extracting the vital facts?

Dolores wasn't done. "Anyone here would lend you a better shirt. Jim would, I'm sure."

"He already gave me this. Mine got messed up."

"We've never seen Jim wearing that."

"It belonged to Mervyn."

"Ha, the penny drops. No disrespect, but you look a whole lot sharper than you did before. Even so . . ."

"What?"

"It isn't right for tonight."

Jim swallowed the rest of his beer. "I can't sit here all day discussing clothes. Got a pair of newborn calves to see to."

Diamond got up as well, far from convinced that he needed a different outfit.

Dolores said, "See you at the supper, fellas. I'm running the bar. All my regulars will be in the tithe barn tonight."

OUTSIDE, JIM ASKED if Diamond wanted to drive the tractor to Julie's cottage.

He smiled and said it was only a short walk.

Jim reminded him about his back pain and the extra burden of his sack of soiled clothes.

Airily, Diamond said the beer seemed to have cured his bad back. He plucked the sack from the trailer and set off with as much alacrity as the stiffness would allow. Already he was thinking he needed a siesta.

15

HIS SLEEP WAS interrupted by three sounds that between them would have woken anybody: barking from Bella, the door closing downstairs and animated female voices. The clock showed he'd slept more than two hours. He sat up sharply, too sharply for a sore back, groaned and hobbled across the floor, stooping to pick up clothes where he'd dropped them after dragging himself upstairs. He hadn't treated his new outfit with the respect it deserved. He'd slept in the shirt. He'd left the trousers in a heap on the carpet. The creases had survived but been joined by lots of other creases. However, they didn't look bad after a good shaking, so he stepped into them. Then he swished cold water on his face. He wanted to make an entrance in Mervyn's posh suit.

The waistcoat hid most of the wrinkles in the shirt. The jacket was in reasonable shape. He looked in the mirror, dusted himself down and liked what he saw. The shoes remained, shiny black Oxfords that must have cost a bomb. He sat on the bed, pulled one on and laced it. Ridiculous footwear on a farm, but who cared? There was a harvest supper coming up and he'd be the smartest man there, whatever Dolores thought. Defiantly he grabbed the other shoe, jammed his foot inside and stubbed his toes on something that shouldn't have been there.

A ballpoint pen. Probably dropped out of a pocket in the jacket. He tossed it out, tied the shoelaces and stood up again. The ultimate in elegance stared back at him from the mirror. The anxious stare turned into a grin.

And he was given the reception he hoped for.

"Who's this fashion plate?" Paloma said. "Julie, you're not going to believe this. He's in a new suit and it looks Savile Row."

"Not bad, eh?" Playing up to the moment, he spun on his heel and bowed.

"What a transformation," Paloma said. "Where on earth did you get it?"

"Long story." He eyed one corner of the room, now taken up with large bags unmistakably from dress shops. "Mission accomplished, then?"

"Almost," Paloma said. "We thought about getting our hair done. But the salon Julie likes was fully booked so we'll have to make do."

"It's not a problem," Julie said. "I wish I had Paloma with me more often. I'd update my wardrobe every week. How's your back, guv? Did the support do its job?"

"So well that I've left it off now."

"Will you be dancing tonight?"

"That might be a step too far."

Over tea and cake, he had the satisfaction of dumbfounding them with the story of his day.

"I can't get my head around this," Paloma said when he'd finished. "You delivered a calf?"

"I did."

"And it survived?"

He didn't dignify that with a response.

"You'll be the talk of the village," Julie said, "especially now Dolores knows about it."

"I don't want fuss."

"Julie and I did some thinking about how you should dress for the supper," Paloma said.

He'd been through this with Dolores. "Me, too. I may leave off the jacket to blend in."

"That won't be enough, Pete. After the supper they clear the tables and have a barn dance. You can't turn up in your suit."

"No argument. I've got Mervyn's."

"That's not what I'm saying. The dress code tonight will be very informal, especially the men."

"You know me, both of you. I don't do informal." He smoothed his hands down the expensive cloth. "This is good enough for me."

"Not for the dance floor."

"I won't be dancing." But he'd sensed that Paloma had other ideas.

"There's something here. We thought of you in Taunton." She reached for a blue-and-white menswear bag and pushed it his way, watching him keenly.

Julie seemed to sense the electricity in the room. Her hand moved off her lap and found Bella's collar.

Uneasy, but on his best behaviour, Diamond pulled out a plaid shirt he would have called loud even for a rave-up, followed by black denim jeans. There was worse: a red-spotted scarf, a belt with an oval cattle-head buckle and a holster. Buckskin boots with Cuban heels. Topping it off was a white leather cowboy hat, for god's sake. The full Butch Cassidy.

Button your lip, he told himself, under strain. This is for one night only. Dolores called it a hoedown. Paloma's job is in theatrical costume and she knows. He succeeded in saying, "Cool."

"I know what you're thinking, love," Paloma said. "Country dancing is hugely popular now and people dress for it. You won't be the only one."

Julie said, "After what you achieved in the calving shed, you've got to look the part."

"The real achiever was the cow."

"Well said, but when she needed help, you provided it."

He asked if he got to see their outfits and was told he'd have that pleasure later, so he raised his real plan for the evening. "Tonight is crunch time. I'm banking on Bert Dombey coming."

"Your charming psychopath?"

"The charm wore off by the end of yesterday. He got what he wanted from me and dropped me. Like I told you, the supper is his heaven-sent chance to get inside the farmhouse and come away with whatever he's after. I'm aiming to find out."

"You want Paloma to look out for him?"

"I'm not even sure he'll be at the supper. He may use the kitchen to get inside. This is where I would stake out the place if I had the team with me. How the heck do these amateur detectives manage?"

"They get help from people they can trust," Julie said. "You've got Paloma and me."

Paloma said, "Some others, surely. Jim Douglas owes you."

"He may trust me but it isn't mutual. He could be a murder suspect."

"He found the body and reported it."

"Four months late. Speaking of suspects, I'm not certain I can trust Agnes. And I haven't ruled out Hamish, the stroppy son."

"So you're forced to rely on us as backup." Out of the blue Paloma asked, "Do you want me in the kitchen?"

"With the catering party?"

"Why not? One glimpse of Dombey and I can phone you. You will take your mobile, won't you?"

Julie was smiling. "A cowboy with a phone?"

"And my warrant card. I'm never without that." Humbled by Paloma's offer, he said, "This is cruel. You just bought a party dress."

"That will keep. If I can get an apron from somewhere I can volunteer. They won't turn down an offer of help."

"I can call Maggie Harrap," Julie said. "She's in charge of the team. Mervyn gave her the job years ago on the strength of her so-called skill at baking. Mercifully there isn't much involved. It's mostly heating up pies and pasties other people have cooked. But she's a good organiser. It's a big event and she manages it well. You'll need to be there at least an hour early."

"Can you lend me an apron?" Paloma asked. "Treat me nicely and I'll make sure you two get double helpings."

PALOMA HAD ALREADY left when Diamond escorted Julie along the lane at dusk, her left hand resting lightly on his forearm. She had her white stick, folded, in her bag.

They weren't alone. This could have been a familiar scene from the old black-and-white films he liked to watch, people stepping out of their cottages and moving purposefully in the same direction, in this case towards the farmhouse and the tithe barn. He steered Julie around the puddles and other hazards. They'd agreed that Bella should have the evening off. The noise, smells and general mayhem in the hall would be sure to confuse her.

Julie was in a cowgirl outfit with a loose leather waistcoat, fringed skirt and boots. She had the authentic hat suspended by a cord from the back of her neck. Diamond self-consciously held his own in his free hand until he spotted another man emerge from his front door and jam a white Stetson on his head before marching off confidently, arms swinging, ready for a shootout with the Hole-in-the-Wall Gang.

"Putting on the hat, guv?" Julie said.

"How do you know that?"

"I can't tell you exactly. Since losing my sight, I'm more sensitive to movements, even slight changes in the air. The rest is guesswork."

"You're good at this, Julie."

"Force of circumstance. It sounds to me as if we're not the only ones on our way to the supper. This part is the old village and people here support events like this. Further out on the new estate not so many get involved."

"I expect some of the old cottages have been bought by outsiders."

"Like me? Yes, but we try to fit in. It's a good mix of village families and newcomers. I'm part of the community here in a way I never was in Bath or Bristol."

"Hey-ho," he said when the farmhouse and barn came into sight. "Some folk have driven here. There's a row of cars outside the house. Posh, by the look of them."

"One will belong to Claudia. I don't know about the others."

"They're getting looks from some of the locals."

"I hope she hasn't invited her Bath crowd," she said. "You'd think she would have learned her lesson."

"I can't believe a harvest supper would appeal to that lot."

The tithe barn was huge and probably as old as the

farmhouse. Thatched and timber-framed, with solid walls of daub and wattle, it must have been used for storing the tithes from the entire village in medieval times. Diamond and Julie joined a short line entering the double doorway at the middle of the long side. No one was checking tickets.

Julie's focused senses had plenty to absorb inside the building. The musty but pleasing smell that spoke of generations of agricultural use was joined by the whiff of wine from filled glasses and the competing odours of aftershave and perfume from the throng in the standing space along the sides. The din of excited voices was such that a five-piece band at the far end could hardly be heard.

Diamond, too, was taking stock. The floor area was largely taken up by three long rows of trestle tables set for the supper and decorated with vine leaves. Behind a bar to their left, Dolores was filling wine glasses on trays and sending nervous young men and women in aprons into the throng where they were supposed to explain to the revellers that their tickets entitled them to one free drink and after that it was cash. All the youth of Baskerville had been press-ganged into service.

Julie asked for and was brought lemonade by—of all people—Hamish.

"Can we look for more space?" she asked Diamond. "It's one of those arm-grabbing situations I told you about. They mean well but I'm uncomfortable with it."

Most people had grouped by the entrance, found others to speak to and not moved. Diamond wove a passage to the end where the band was knocking out numbers from way back. Nobody was dancing yet. A few were standing nearby keeping time with heads and shoulders. There was space to breathe here. "It's a choice," Diamond said, shouting to be heard above the drumbeat. "Stand by the entrance and get crushed or come up here and get your ears blasted."

"Nice that it's so well supported."

Some kind of commentary was called for. "They could do with someone on the door," he said. "I'm wondering if they all bought tickets. At a guess there are a couple of hundred in already and more arriving all the time. Kids running about as if it's playtime."

"Any other cowboys?" Julie said.

"At least five I can see from here. Five hats, that is. Some of the others left theirs at home."

"Cowards."

"A joker in fancy dress with a plastic police helmet looking as if he came to the wrong event. Plenty are in check shirts or blouses. Dolores was right about suits. The only ones wearing them are the really old."

"Have you spotted anyone we know?"

"Like our friendly neighbourhood psychopath? I'm watching like a hawk but he hasn't surfaced—unless he's gone straight for the jackpot and is in the farmhouse already. Paloma would have called me if he'd entered through the kitchen."

"Are you switched on, guv?"

"Always, Julie, but I can't speak for my phone." He took it from the holster. "Battery's below thirty per cent. I should have recharged the thing. If I can tell you that, it must be working, mustn't it?"

She was too familiar with his technical shortcomings to go into explanations. "Any texts?"

"No."

"Paloma may find it easier texting than phoning. Are people sitting at the tables yet?"

"Some of the seniors, that's all. A crafty few have bagged

chairs with scarves and cardigans. Some places have reserved notices, for VIPs, I expect, like Claudia."

"Is she in?"

"Can't tell. Never met her."

"I'm forgetting," Julie said. "She'll stand out. She likes to make an impression."

"Someone I do know just came in and I'm surprised he's here. Fabio Fortunato, one of Claudia's former friends from Bath. Wealth manager. Maximise Your Assets." Fab wasn't tall. He wasn't even average height, but you couldn't miss him. He maximised himself with that moustache Tom Selleck would have envied.

"Is he alone?"

"He's with a couple he seems to know. Oh, Christ, the gang's all here. Harvey Hertzog and Elaine. Claudia must have invited them, as you feared. Won't go down well with the locals, will it?"

"She does things her own way," Julie said. "I expect the reserved chairs are for them. How are they dressed?"

"Kitted out for the hoedown like us but making more of a statement. Fab is a sheriff or a marshal, mostly in black, and Hertzog has a Davy Crockett hat with a raccoon tail."

"Elaine?"

"Classy. Some sort of sequin jacket and a dark red skirt with lace trimming that looks as if she's wearing layers of petticoats underneath. She'll be a hit on the dance floor."

"Could any of them be suspects?" she asked.

"Everyone who was here on the night of the party is in the frame. The opportunity was there, but finding a motive is more difficult. We'd better decide where to sit and stake our claim."

They chose places on one of the outer rows, giving Diamond a direct route to the door if the call came from

Paloma. Julie suggested he check to see if Dombey's van was outside. When he asked if she would be okay on her own, she threatened to poke him with her white stick.

Outside, the night had closed in, and the cool air sharpened his senses. Most of the farmyard was equipped with lighting, making it easy to see what was going on. A few latecomers and some smokers were about and the line of cars had grown to about twenty. There's an old saying that the best of all hiding places is in plain sight. Not if the plain sight is a row of private cars and you have a white van to hide. Dombey would have left it somewhere more clever.

The farmhouse windows were lit and there were movements inside but no one was out here. A good moment to check the exterior. Although the front door was ajar, Diamond wasn't tempted to enter. Around the side of the large building, the kitchen was easy to spot with its steamed-up windows and smells of cooking from an extractor fan. It overlooked a paved area with two raised stone flower beds stocked with overgrown herbs fighting for survival with weeds. He brushed against a straggly rosemary bush and cursed himself for picking up the pungent scent on his cowboy jeans. No use denying where he had been.

He wasn't ready to use the kitchen door and face the helpers, so he moved on looking for another way into the house, aware that if Dombey were here he might well have done the same.

Around the next corner were glazed double doors built into a large bay window through which he could see a darkened sitting room.

The doors were locked. No sign of a break-in.

He completed the tour, satisfied that his quarry wasn't lurking here. Maybe he'd misread the signs and Dombey wasn't here at all, a troubling thought after staking so

much on catching him red-handed. No, he told himself.
The man is a psychopath. He's smart. He doesn't miss a
trick. He'll be here.

The van wasn't parked with the other vehicles in front
of the house, so where had he left it?

Any other place around the yard would be obvious. Even
at night in some area away from the lights a white vehicle
would stand out.

An idea dawned. Diamond strode away from the house
towards the farm buildings. Strong security lights came on
when he approached the milking parlour. Moving on rapidly
past the calving shed, he realised he was retracing the steps
the luckless victim, Roger Miller, had taken on the night he
met his horrible death. Some distance ahead, the two silos
were faintly silhouetted against the night sky.

Much closer, a noise as loud and sudden as a motorbike
starting up stopped him in his tracks. But it wasn't mechani-
cal. It was an animal sound. A bellow from Chummy the
bull, thankfully still in his pen.

He didn't need to walk as far as the silos. The place he
had in mind was the tall steel-reinforced building to his
left where a vehicle could be driven inside and parked out
of sight. The tractor shed.

Dazzling security lights mounted over the entrance came
on as Diamond approached. A sensor had picked up his
movement. Shielding his eyes, he stepped inside.

"Ha."

At the front, a white van stood like an unwanted guest
next to the Massey Ferguson tractor Diamond had learned
to drive.

He went over and felt the bonnet. No warmth at all. It
had been parked here for some time. He tried the doors,
front and back. Locked, of course. Any doubt that this

was Dombey's vehicle was removed when he spotted a discarded T-shirt on the passenger seat with lettering on it: almost the entire word STINKS from one of the bad-taste slogans.

Proof of ownership. His only realistic suspect had arrived early and taken the chance to get inside the farmhouse.

What now? Wait here for Dombey to return?

Too passive. The man was dangerous. Innocent, unsuspecting people were in the house, Paloma among them.

First, take the van out of the equation. His freshly learned skill had equipped him to do it. With confidence summoned by the urgency of the moment, he marched over to the board where the keys to all the vehicles were hanging and picked off the key to the Massey.

Up on the seat, he started the tractor as if he'd ploughed more fields than a Soviet-era serf, engaged the clutch and brought the big beast far enough forward to make a three-point turn. Reverse gear was a new experience with an ear-blasting beep-beep from the motion alarm. His legs flexed and slipped off the pedals and he stalled and came to a juddering halt. Not so clever, Peter Diamond. He swore, tried three times to start up again and succeeded only in filling his lungs with petrol fumes. A memory popped into his head of learning to drive in a now-obsolete Ford Anglia. Wasn't there something about flooding the engine when starting from cold?

He counted to ten before turning the key one more time. The engine stuttered into life. He held his nerve and completed the move like a professional, swinging the tractor to his left before drawing across the front of the van a couple of feet from the bumper, blocking it at the front.

That done, he collected the key to another utility tractor in the row behind and moved it forward inches from the rear of the van. Whoever said he was mechanically inept? A pity none of his team were there to admire the manoeuvre.

Still seated at the wheel, he called Paloma on his phone. "Okay to talk?"

"Briefly," she said. "We're about to serve the meal."

Shucks to the meal, he thought. "Seen anything of you-know-who?"

"Not a whisker. Sorry."

"He's here somewhere. I found his van."

"The front door of the farmhouse was open when I arrived and still is. He could have come straight in if he's got the nerve."

"He's got the nerve of Old Nick. Who else is in the house apart from you and the other helpers?"

"Claudia, I was told, in her bedroom getting ready."

"Jesus, I hope she's safe. I'm on my way." He ended the call and jumped down. Instead of returning the keys to their hooks, he pocketed them. Couldn't take the chance—unlikely as it was—that Dombey could drive a tractor equally well.

He covered the short distance across the yard in time to see a group of middle-aged women in aprons wheel a laden food trolley into the tithe barn. Shouts and applause from inside greeted them.

Paloma had been right about the front door being open. This time he marched in as if he owned the farmhouse and found himself in a hall with shoulder-high dark-stained panels that must have been there since the house was built. The way ahead was dominated by an intricately carved staircase that wouldn't have disgraced a stately home. Three flights were visible and there may have been another where it curved to the left.

He stood for a moment taking in another unusual feature.

Above the panelling to his left and right, the plastered walls were decorated as if for an exhibition, hung with antique hand tools. Some he recognised, like spades, picks, hoes and forks worn smooth from years of use. Others had purposes only a specialist would know. Collecting this lot had given joy to somebody and it sat well in a farmhouse that might otherwise have seemed too grand for its wellington boots.

His thoughts returned to the task in hand. He knew about the rooms he'd seen from outside, the kitchen and the one with the bay window. Every door he could see was closed, a reminder that the house hadn't been lived in for over a year. He tried the handle of one on the left. Locked. He had to turn a key to open it and see inside. He reached for the light switch and found a high-ceilinged room and more oak panels. At first glance, it was a formal drawing room furnished with plenty of armchairs and low tables and a well-stocked drinks cabinet, so it may well have been used on the party nights. The surfaces had a coating of dust and the air was stale. No one had opened that door in months. He was getting a sense that if Dombey was inside the building he knew exactly what he wanted and had gone straight to it.

"Looking for the little room, Mr. Dee?" a voice spoke up, polite and imperious.

He turned. Maggie Harrap, the queen of the kitchen, had appeared without making a sound—an achievement on these loose floorboards. She was wearing an apron with a floral print. By accident or design, her muslin hair covering was fixed with a band of gold ribbon that looked awfully like a coronet.

The easy answer was to agree that he needed the toilet. But that wasn't honest and it would allow this holier-than-thou lady to act as if she had more right to be here than he did. Damn it, he thought when he was over the immediate shock of being caught on the prowl, this isn't her home any more than mine. She's supposed to be in the kitchen, not acting as a security guard. He opted for the truth. "I'm looking for Bert."

She folded her arms and drew a sharp breath as if the name revolted her.

"Bert Dombey," he said.

"I know who you mean," she said. "I haven't seen that person all evening."

"If you do, let Paloma know and she'll tell me."

There was a click of the tongue. Maggie didn't take orders.

"Paloma. She's on your team." He used a lord-of-the-manor voice. "In the kitchen, where you ought to be."

"You don't need to tell me my job. I know who Paloma is. I know every one of my crew."

He took note. They weren't a team. They were a crew under the leadership of Captain Harrap.

"Is Claudia upstairs?" He was getting the measure of Maggie. She had several reputations to keep up. She wasn't just the village know-it-all. She was head cook and ship's captain. She demanded respect. Demand all you like, ducky, you won't get it from me.

"Claudia Priest," he prompted her.

She started on her stock answer again. "I know Claudia—" She stopped and shook her head, wrongfooted by this brash visitor from Bath who bandied names as if he knew them all personally.

He'd heard all he wanted. This was now an upstairs, downstairs situation. Ignoring her, he stepped past and up the staircase.

He thought he heard her say, "I don't think you should . . ." but the words were drowned by the creaking stair treads. No one could accuse him of stealth.

The stair carpet was modern, woven cord in a neutral shade that blended with the varnished wood at each side. He'd have called it beige and the supplier no doubt gave it a fancy name like biscuit-coloured. Halfway up the second flight, he noticed a darker patch about the size of a two-pound coin. He paused. The light here wasn't good. He couldn't see too well, but it wasn't a leaf. A stain, he decided. Some smaller specks were close by, as if someone had slopped coffee from a mug they were taking upstairs. Or could it be something more sinister?

It was dry to the touch. Scratching didn't shift it. Probably not mud.

He moved on.

The upper storey appeared at first to be as much of a time capsule as downstairs. Another panelled corridor with unremarkable paintings in dusty gold frames. But further along was a reassuring sign of modern life. Bathroom scents wafted from a doorway.

"Hello," he said in courtesy. "Anyone about?"

Probably not, he decided. The light was on, but the open door suggested the room wasn't occupied now.

"Are you there, Claudia?"

If she was, she wasn't answering.

Get real, Diamond, he told himself. You don't have time for this. Jack Reacher doesn't act the gentleman.

He looked in.

Empty. Towels and knickers on the floor beside the shower. A bra hanging over the washbasin.

Faintly damp footprints led him a short way up the corridor to a double bedroom that had to be Claudia's. Smelling of perfume and decorated in modern pastel shades with plenty of lights and mirrors, it was a refreshing change from the formal look everywhere else. More clothes strewn about the floor along with towels and shoes. The quilt was fully over the bed and an open suitcase had been dumped on it. Everything suggested the lady of the house had arrived only a short time ago, showered, made a quick change, put on her party face and left.

He hoped so. The alternative was nasty. He was thinking about the stain on the stairs.

Then he felt a movement against his thigh. His phone vibrating in his pocket. He was pleased to hear Paloma's voice.

"I'm at the supper," she told him. "Claudia just arrived."

"Thank god for that. She was here a short time ago."

"She's dressed to impress. Calamity Jane, they're saying. I'm not sure if that's true or a bad-taste joke. Quite a personality. Very animated, as if the prison thing never happened."

"Has Dombey appeared?"

"Not when I last looked. He'd want to sit with the others, wouldn't he?"

"Who do you mean?"

"Claudia's friends from Bath, the guy with a face like a battlefield and his partner who looked as if she's on the point of leaving him."

"Harvey Hertzog and Elaine."

"And a short guy with a ridiculous moustache."

"Fabio Fortunato. They'll be the owners of two of the posh cars outside."

"They had reserved seats and now Claudia has joined them. Sorry, but I must go. Duty calls."

"I'll come when I can."

He was torn. Everyone who mattered in this true-life whodunit was at the supper now, except the main man, the psychopath on the loose.

16

DIAMOND HAD SEEN the framed picture facing him while he was in the corridor speaking on the phone to Paloma. Seen it without looking at it. Why break his concentration to study a pesky painting when he was on the trail of a psychopath?

A tweak from his unconscious made him step closer.

Although the natural light along the corridor was poor, there was enough of the electric sort streaming from the open door of Claudia's bedroom for him to recognise the scene. He knew exactly where the painter had set up his easel: Parade Gardens, the riverside park south of Pulteney Bridge in Bath, a view popular with photographers and painters. Rendered mainly in murky greens and browns, the picture wasn't the most pleasing he had seen. The artist seemed more interested in the reflections of the trees along the bank and the tall west end of Argyle Terrace than the classic view of Robert Adam's famous bridge. The best you could say was that it was recognisable to someone who knew Bath as well as Diamond did. Impressionistic, he decided, meaning the brushwork was a dog's dinner, but he'd been caught out before making judgements on art. He was no connoisseur.

The one point of interest was the signature in the bottom left corner, deftly done with a paintbrush: H. Priest.

Mervyn's brother, Howard.

All along the wall were oil paintings in the same uninspiring style in matching frames, many of them street scenes of Bath: Belvedere, Camden Crescent, Walcot Parade. Lansdown. Even Paradise Row, Holloway, where the Hertzogs had their small hotel. This entire floor was a Howard Priest gallery.

The scenes were interspersed with a few other undistinguished daubs. Howard wasn't just a third-rate landscape artist. He was third rate at still life and portraiture as well.

Fair do. Proud parents stick their kids' scribbles on fridge doors. This was a way of honouring a grown-up member of the family who called himself an artist. Hang the collected works upstairs in a corridor all to themselves. He remembered Agnes Douglas telling him Howard had never sold anything. To be charitable, it was touching to find that the paintings had survived—which said more about the saintly Mervyn than poor talentless Howard.

But the art show wasn't Diamond's reason for being here.

In the next half-hour, he checked all three upstairs corridors for evidence of Bert Dombey. There were nine bedrooms, two bathrooms, a large linen cupboard and a dumb waiter that was probably a Victorian installation. When he leaned into the shaft, he heard faint voices from the kitchen. The mechanism hadn't seen service for years. The rope was fraying. You wouldn't use that for a hiding place unless you had a death wish.

Apart from Claudia's room and the bathroom, everything reeked of disuse. He opened wardrobe doors and looked under beds and behind curtains. Bert would be enjoying this, wherever he was.

He returned to one end and looked out of the window that gave the best view of the yard. The lights remained on and through the wide doorway of the tractor shed he could see the Massey Ferguson where he had parked it, still blocking the white van. Dombey had to be here somewhere playing a waiting game, unless he'd already found what he wanted and used some other means of escape.

The promise of a successful outcome was draining away by the minute.

On his way downstairs, Diamond was reminded of that small dark patch on the stair carpet halfway down. The clue that would solve everything or a waste of time? Every mystery had its eureka moment.

He sat on the stair below and used the flashlight on his phone for a closer inspection. One carpet stain in *Midsomer Murders* would propel Tom Barnaby to the arrest of a triple killer. Only a TV detective had such luck.

Inconclusive. So many things leave a brown mark. He scratched at the fibres in case it was only mud from somebody's shoe.

"Found something, Mr. Dee?"

That acid-laden voice again. He'd mistakenly assumed Maggie Harrap was in the tithe barn commanding her crew. She must have remained behind, directing the operation from the kitchen. She would have overheard him. At the foot of the stairs, arms folded across her apron, eyes glaring over the tops of her specs, she was suspicion in the flesh.

This called for a different response than before. Needing to marshal his thoughts, he doffed his Stetson to her, gave a cheesy grin and said, "Howdy, ma'am."

She wasn't playing the cowboy game.

He took her at her word, as if she really wanted to know what he'd found. "A mark on the stairs, that's all. I don't think it came off my boots." He straightened up and reminded her of her duties. "How's it going in the barn? Have you finished serving supper?"

She ignored his attempt to change the subject. "What are you doing up there?"

"Making a search for Bert Dombey. There are more bedrooms than I expected. This house is far too big for one resident. If you ask me, Claudia has left one sort of prison for another. Solitary confinement." He started downwards but he had to stop at the bottom because she was barring the way with her hand on the newel post.

"So you didn't find your friend?" she said.

"No, and he isn't my friend. Have you seen him?"

She looked him up and down. She wouldn't be side-tracked. "Are you working for the police?"

Right on.

Her reputation as the village Miss Marple was no exaggeration. Like a boxer riding a punch, Diamond drew breath before giving the best counter he could, and it happened to be the truth. "If I was, I'd have called for some backup and searched every shed and outbuilding by now."

"Is that a no?"

Spacing the words, he told her, "I am not working for the police." He would have said the same to his boss, Georgina. What he was engaged in here was private enterprise.

"What are you up to, then? What's your interest in Mr. Dombey?"

"Someone needs to keep an eye on him."

"What do you mean by that?"

"He's up to no good."

She would keep up the quickfire questions indefinitely if he didn't break the rhythm. As a rule he never said more than was necessary, but the present situation called for wordage. He made a snap decision to share some of his suspicions. It was not impossible she would trade information.

He launched into a discourse of his own. "Going by the way you reacted to him in the church yesterday, you and I feel much the same about Dombey. He's not the charming guy he pretends to be. At first, he thought I lived in Baskerville and could be useful to him. He fastened on to me to help restore some of his credibility here. He found out later that I'm only a visitor, but I was still useful to him. I wasn't one of the partygoers like him, so he used me for cover. He told me he wanted to find out what really happened on the night Roger Miller was killed and if possible clear Claudia's name."

"I can hear disbelief in your voice," Miss Harrap said.

"Do you want to know the real reason he's here?"

She stepped back from the stairs and allowed him to reach floor level. They were almost the same height. "And what's that?"

"He's strapped for cash. He must have had plenty in the past to keep up with the Bath crowd but it isn't there now. He can't even buy a round of drinks without it hurting."

"I noticed," she said and he remembered her perched on her favourite stool at the bar. But how could he get her to share more of what she knew and suspected?

"Rightly or wrongly, he believes Mervyn had a secret source of wealth nobody knows about, not even Claudia. He thinks it's here in the house for the taking."

"Actual money, you mean?" she said, not believing him and showing it with tightened lips.

"Or something just as valuable."

"I can't think what. Everyone knows Claudia inherited millions and bought some jewellery but I'm sure it must have been somewhere safe while she was away. She's not stupid." Finally, she was giving a little.

"And neither is Bert Dombey. He claimed to be her most recent boyfriend—and that may be true."

"They were seen together before she was arrested," she said with a nod.

"But he also said he was regularly visiting her in prison and that's a lie. I caught him out over that. He claimed he was with her at Eastwood Park this week. *This week*, when she was already released and recovering at the spa."

"Who told you she was out?"

"Agnes Douglas. Whatever the relationship amounted to, it's over. Claudia was no help to him while she was behind bars."

"Have you challenged him on this?"

"I haven't seen him all day. He gave me the brush-off yesterday after he found out about the supper. He learned that the house was being opened up, giving him his chance to get inside. And he knows what he's after."

"What's that?"

He smiled. "I said *he* knows. I didn't say I do. It's still a mystery to me."

"A mystery to us all, Mr. Dee."

"Unless it's pictures," he said. "Have you been upstairs?"

She gave an impatient sigh. "I'm far too busy down here to be wandering about the house. I only stepped out because I heard the stairs creak. I thought I had a quiet moment in the kitchen."

"Sorry," he said. "I'm not light on my feet. Paloma tells me it's like the changing of the guard when I come up to bed, and that's when I'm wearing slippers. Is she with you?"

"All my helpers are in the barn waiting for the raffle to end before they clear the tables."

"I was about to say the top-floor corridors are lined with paintings signed by Howard Priest."

"Mervyn's late brother," she said without emotion. "He died some years ago."

"It's like a shrine. Every bit of wall space. Landscapes, still lifes and portraits, all expensively framed."

For the first time, her face softened a little. "That's rather touching." A small sigh escaped her lips. "Typical of Mervyn. He was a decent man."

"So everyone tells me."

"And so was Howard in his own way, but totally wrapped up in his work. I met him a few times and visited his house in Bathampton. I believe I told you he designed and made the mould for the harvest loaf." She couldn't resist another mention of her claim to fame.

He played to her vanity. "The centrepiece of the harvest festival—and you baked it."

"It's been my job at the end of each summer for as long as I can remember." She basked in the glory without noticing Diamond had taken control of the dialogue.

"So did Howard show you his studio?"

"He did, and what a glory hole it was, everyone's idea of an artist's den, filled with canvases in various stages of completion. Tubes of paint and bottles of oil. Brushes of all shapes and sizes. Sketchbooks. Photographs. It spilled out of the studio into other rooms. You could scarcely move. I didn't envy Mervyn having to clear the house after Howard went."

"Did the stuff go into storage?"

"I expect so. Some of it had to be burned."

"Obviously not the paintings."

Her tongue clicked at the suggestion. "That would have been vandalism."

He was winding her up. "They're nothing special, are

they? Agnes told me he copied from photos, using some sort of grid."

She sprang to Howard's defence. "What does Agnes know about art? There's nothing to say an artist can't use technology. I expect Michelangelo worked with squares when he painted the Sistine Chapel."

The comparison was laughable, but he kept a straight face. "That never crossed my mind. He probably did."

She looked at her watch. "I'm needed now. Will you go to the barn? You can come through the kitchen. You're too late for the raffle, but the dancing begins as soon as the tables are cleared."

He was in two minds. He was supposed to be trying to find Dombey. The place felt empty. Maybe he'd already come and gone.

"I think I will," he said. "I left Julie at one of the tables. She'll need help."

In the big kitchen, some of the crew were washing and drying plates. He raised his ten-gallon hat to them. Paloma wasn't among them. One of the women told him she was in the barn collecting crockery.

There was just a short walk across the yard to the barn. He couldn't see much. Somewhere on his left was the bull pen and, beyond that, the tank room where the milk was stored. The cool night air in the yard was blissful after the steamy kitchen. Diamond took a deep breath.

"Will you keep looking for Mr. Dombey?" Miss Harrap asked. She'd followed him outside. She seemed to enjoy catching him off guard.

"Somebody has to. He's a loose cannon, capable of anything."

"Is it possible he had something to do with the body in the silo?"

"We can't rule it out, can we?"

"What a ghastly thought." She seemed oblivious that the thought was her own.

"He's here somewhere," Diamond said. "He can't leave without his van. I'm wondering if I was wrong expecting him to be in the house. He may be out here."

"You're not doing much for my state of nerves, Mr. Dee." She looked in the direction of the outbuildings. "It's awfully quiet. When I walked over earlier with some of the ladies, the bull made a lot of noise."

"Chummy? He picks up sounds, I was told."

"Why has he gone silent? Your boots make enough noise to waken the dead." She clapped her hand to her mouth. "A pedigree bull is worth a lot of money. Is it possible his plan was to steal Chummy?"

There were practical difficulties about stealing a two-tonne bull that even the ultra-confident Bert would find difficult to overcome. Diamond made light of it. "Rustling? With all of us cowboys in town? He'd be a brave man to try."

"I'm serious, Mr. Dee. I've seen Chummy being driven away from the farm in a trailer."

"Tonight?"

"Not tonight, but every so often. He gets loaned out to other farmers for his, em, services, and a lot of money changes hands."

"Not the amounts Mervyn was getting through." The idea amused him. "Chummy may be good at his job but he didn't pay for that milking parlour by his efforts alone."

As if to contradict him, there was a sudden snort on their left, followed by an outburst of bellowing that triggered two security lights and showed how close they were to the bull pen. Maggie Harrap's glasses flashed. She shrieked in alarm, spread both arms and wrapped herself around Diamond.

John Wayne never had to deal with anything like this.

Gripping him as if he was a surfboard, she buried her face in his shoulder and knocked the hat off his head.

Diamond did his best to sound like Wayne. "Easy, ma'am. Chummy is being chummy, that's all."

She didn't loosen her grip. Her fingers dug into his flesh. "He's still in his pen. Want me to check?"

A muffled "Nooooo!" escaped from the depths of his buckaroo scarf. "Stay with me."

Giving comfort wasn't a skill Diamond knew much about. The best he could do was appeal to her good sense. "On the other hand, if he's escaped, the middle of the yard isn't the clever place to be."

Good sense didn't work. She seemed to be having convulsions. This was all wrong. He was the townie and she the countrywoman who should have known about farm animals.

Chummy continued fortissimo. Diamond could feel the soundwaves in his boots. And he could feel the shakes from Miss Harrap from the feet upwards. She was a firmer fit than a zip fastener.

He tried levity. "Gotta get this wagon rollin', ma'am," he drawled.

"I'm petrified."

"Shucks, we can make it."

"I can't let go."

"Take a hold of my arm."

As if stranded on a rock face, she withdrew her head an inch or two from his neck to check whether such a manoeuvre was safe. Apparently it was worth risking, if indelicate. Chest to chest, belly to belly, she squirmed around him until she could get both hands on his left forearm. She gripped that like a lifeline.

"Bully for you, ma'am." Diamond would have been lost for words without his cowboy persona. "Let's hit the trail."

They took some steps towards the tithe barn. Chummy harrumphed more in regret than anger, panted a few times and finally went quiet.

After they reached the barn door unscathed, Miss Harrap said, "I should have trusted you better, Mr. Dee. I can't begin to tell you how embarrassed I am."

"It was Chummy you didn't trust," he said. "Better go in and see if your ladies need you."

The episode had brought a change of attitude. "If I can be of help with anything at all, don't hesitate to ask."

Making an ally of Miss Marple was no bad thing.

Before going inside, he straightened his hat.

And when Chummy stirred behind the tall fencing, Diamond called out, "Don't even think about it."

IN THE BARN, the tables had been cleared and stacked away to make space for the dancing. Agnes Douglas was demonstrating a talent he wouldn't have guessed at, standing in front of the band with a handheld microphone calling the steps of a square dance, village-style. She had the authentic delivery, rhythmic and hearty, untroubled that the dancing was a long way short of exhibition stuff. Taking care not to get drawn in, Diamond edged past the bystanders along the length of the room towards the spot where he'd left Julie.

She was nowhere in sight.

He looked back in case he'd missed her. Most of the chairs were still in use, ranged along the wall or closer to the dancing. People were standing three or four deep, some in groups, chatting, others jigging to the beat or keeping time with their hands. Somebody, he felt certain, would have made sure a blind woman wasn't forced to stand. He had a mental picture of Julie's outfit, the frilly blouse, black leather waistcoat and fringed skirt. She ought to be obvious.

He asked some teenagers if they had seen the blind lady before the tables were cleared. They shrugged and shook their heads.

Trying to stay calm, he took out his phone and called Paloma.

"I'm in the barn looking for Julie. Did she leave early?"

"Surely not," Paloma said. "She would have said something. When we cleared the tables, she was at the end where the band are."

"That's where I am."

"She can't have gone far."

"Who was she sitting with?"

"Agnes and some others I don't know."

"Agnes is here. She seems to be running the show." The music had stopped and the capable farm manager was in discussion with the band leader, evidently agreeing which dance would be next. From the nonchalant way she dangled the mic from her hand, she was in her element. Anyone would think she was a professional.

"Let me know when you find her," Paloma said. She didn't sound unduly worried.

An alarming thought had gripped Diamond's brain. He could be faced with a hostage situation. Dombey finds he can't escape because the van is blocked in. He's ruthless enough to seize a helpless woman and use her to bargain his way out.

Far-fetched? If a long career in the murder squad teaches you anything, it is that a killer at bay is desperate and dangerous.

Maybe he should ask for a public announcement between

dances—or was that too panicky? If Julie was here some-where, she would be mortified to be treated like a missing child.

He stared at the mass of onlookers and chatterers one more time and missed his chance. Agnes had the mic to her mouth again. Each dance lasted at least five minutes.

Nothing would be gained from standing there fretting. Best check with the people at the far end to see if she'd left the building. The doorkeeping had been almost non-existent when he'd arrived with Julie.

Speaking a series of loud "excuse me's," he threaded his way back to the entrance, while satisfying himself that she wasn't among the old folk and the non-dancers seated along that wall.

No one was on duty at the door but the smokers outside the barn were adamant that she hadn't emerged since the dancing started. Most of them knew who she was. One woman said she doubted whether Julie would have walked home alone along the dark lane. Another pointed out that for Julie the lane was always dark.

Diamond went back inside to a stately St. Bernard's waltz—stately except for the two steps that were stamped. The people of Baskerville did their stamping with gusto, and many of them were in boots. A lot of the audience, even the seated ones, joined in. All this merriment was hard to stomach.

His mind was made up. As soon as the dance ended, he would borrow the microphone and appeal for help. First he had to be there.

Once more he needed to shoulder his way through to the far end where the band was. Shoulders, elbows and hips. Find an opening and squirm through and where there wasn't an opening, create one. He wasn't so coy about body contact after doing this a couple of times already. If flesh met flesh, he didn't pause to apologise.

The St. Bernard's consisted of a few simple moves repeated many times over, but there had to be an end to it and Diamond had no way of telling how long it had been going. He didn't want to find himself stranded halfway up the hall. The last thing he needed was conversation.

So when a voice said, "Having fun, mate?" he pretended not to hear. The only person who called him mate in this place was Jim Douglas. Becoming a mate of Jim's had been a high point of his day, but this was no time for small talk. The music was getting louder, as if it was coming to an end. Acting as if he had tunnel vision, he pressed on.

But he couldn't move when his shirt was gripped by a hand used to grasping sacks of cattle feed. He was forced to turn his head and say, "Sorry, Jim. Spot of trouble." He was talking over the head of a short man, a beer glass in each hand, trying to move in the other direction.

"What's up?" Jim asked. He was still in the beanie hat he wore for work.

"My friend Julie is missing."

"Julie Hargreaves?" Jim said as if that couldn't be true.

The fabric was stretched across the whole of Diamond's back like a straitjacket. "Let go of me, Jim. I need to get to the mic and make an announcement."

"You say the blind lady is missing?"

"Of course."

"She's behind you."

Diamond was damned sure she wasn't. The group he'd just passed were sweaty middle-aged men chatting loudly to make themselves heard. Until Jim had grabbed his shirt they'd been in front of him.

"Over your shoulder, mate," Jim said and released him.

He hadn't appreciated how far Jim had turned him—right about and some more. He now had his back to the dance floor. And when he looked, there was Julie within touching distance.

She was doing the St. Bernard's waltz with a pint-sized, grinning man with an over-large moustache. Fabio Fortunato, the wealth manager. Julie, too, was smiling, enjoying the confident movement that the dance sequence made possible.

Relief surged through Diamond's veins. The cell door had opened and instead of the priest and the hangman, there was the governor brandishing the piece of paper that was not just the stay of execution, but the order of release. How was this possible? Throughout this nightmare he had made the mistake of giving little more than a glance to the dancers, thinking Julie couldn't possibly be among them. Once more, he'd underestimated her. He'd always underestimated Julie, even when she was his deputy.

She was perfectly capable of dancing when she had someone to lead her. She was coping at least as well as most other women on the floor. She had to bend low when the sequence required her to turn under Fortunato's left arm and she managed it with grace. After four more bars of rotary waltzing the dance ended. She gave a slight curtsy and smiled at her partner. He took her hand and was escorting her away when Diamond called her name.

She knew his voice at once, turned, and opened her mouth to speak, but didn't get the chance because Fortunato was quicker. "Peter Dee, as I live and breathe. I should have known I'd meet you here, my friend, but I didn't."

Diamond had to be sharp. He did a mental recap of what had been said at their meeting in Bath. He'd told Fortunato he lived in Baskerville and had money to invest and now he needed to keep up the pretence. Undercover sleuthing needed sharp wits.

"Obviously you two know each other," the small man said.

Before Julie could say Diamond was her houseguest, he cut in smoothly. "From way back. We're all Bathonians originally. I heard that Harvey Hertzog is here as well."

"So is Claudia. She heard about you. She'll want to meet you for sure. We're across the other side. Come over."

Fixed in a flash. Maximise Your Assets.

17

THE PRINCIPAL LADY and her VIP guests had prime position, ten or so chairs set close to the dance area near the bar. He'd not noticed them before when his eyes were panning along the crowd searching only for Julie. Now he could see Harvey Hertzog and Elaine at one end.

Claudia—right in the centre—looked anything but a jailbird. Not for her the pallid face and lifeless hair. The benefits of a few days in a spa were obvious. She'd been under the sunlamp and through the hairdressers and given the facial treatment. Her Calamity Jane get-up was more Hollywood than the Wild West, a classy tan-coloured suede trouser suit with fringes at the hemlines and shoulders and a scarlet neckerchief tied loosely at her throat. First impressions aren't always reliable, but to Diamond's eye she was a confident, attractive fortyish redhead with enough mischief in her smile to corrupt a saint.

"Here they come, our own Fred and Ginger," she hailed the dance partners as they crossed the floor, "and we all know how Ginger did everything he did, but backwards and in high heels. Julie, my dear, I don't know how you managed him. I've danced with Fab myself and have the broken toenails to prove it, but you made him look the complete professional. Come and sit next to me. After that you deserve a drink. And Fab, don't just stand there looking pleased with yourself. Tell me who the Lone Ranger is."

It took a moment for the penny to drop. Fabio Fortunato was seldom stumped for words.

The Lone Ranger was Diamond, or Peter Dee, as he was now introduced. "Not lone at all," Fab said, in full flow again. "Peter is no stranger. He's here, there and everywhere like a friendly puppy. You never know where he'll pop up next."

The friendly puppy image grated with Diamond. Before he could say anything to correct it, Hertzog chimed in with, "He was sniffing around at the Holloway earlier this week, weren't you, mate?"

The tall South African didn't mince his words. This was supposed to be a social occasion. Diamond had been feeling comfortable until now, pleased by this chance to meet Claudia in a group situation where he could get a sense of what she was like without it being an interrogation. What he hadn't factored in was that each of these so-called friends of hers had a different story from him. Fortunato believed he was a potential client looking to invest some dodgy money. Hertzog thought he was a friend of Julie's, wanting to rake over the ashes of Roger Miller's death. Meeting them together hadn't featured in his planning. His multiple personas were unravelling like the toilet roll in the Andrex ad. But he didn't want to think about puppies.

Hertzog's normally reticent girlfriend, Elaine, tried to assist and only made things worse. "Peter is on your side, Claudia. He was asking about you."

Thankfully for Diamond, Claudia didn't seem to have heard. She was off on another tack. "Peter Dee, did I hear right?" she asked Fortunato. "I was told a Mr. Dee came to the rescue on the farm this morning. He arrived at a crisis moment and delivered a calf. He was wearing a suit and it was ruined." She turned to Diamond. "Was that you?"

He didn't always admit to things other people said about him, but this was his best way out of the minefield. "Sounds like me."

"Tell us more," Fab said.

He downplayed it. "I happened to be passing the calving shed and overheard what was going on. Jim Douglas was trying to cope with one cow while another was in trouble nearby. He told me what to do."

"Well, the story's all over the village, Peter," Claudia said. "The least I can do is compensate you for the suit."

"No need. Jim took care of that," he said. He didn't tell her he was the new owner of a hand-me-down from her late father.

"Jim is here somewhere." Claudia looked about her as if she wanted her farm manager to join the group and sink another spear into Diamond's cover story. "You can always spot him by the beanie hat. A beanie at a hoedown!"

"We spoke a few minutes ago," Diamond said and turned a truth into another lie. "He was heading for the end where his wife is."

"Where would I be without Jim and Agnes?" she said. "They ran the business while I was banged up. You know all about that from Julie. All of Baskerville knows my sordid history. I'm the daughter everyone would like to disappear. Daddy lived here all his life and was loved by one and all."

"Hard to live up to," Diamond said.

"Impossible. Which is why I have no intention of trying." She had the confidence born of hard experience. "Prison is supposed to teach you a lesson. The only thing I learned is to watch your back and I'm still doing it." She shook with amusement and her leather fringes danced.

The rest of the group gave diplomatic smiles. Claudia was a formidable presence, happy to joke about herself, but god help anyone who joined in. This was about as relaxing as the round table at the Algonquin when Dorothy Parker was in her prime.

More talk was overtaken by a drumroll from the band and a few bars of the theme from *Rawhide*. Agnes, mic in hand, was making an announcement. "This is the moment, people. Let's have all of you cowboys and girls on the floor."

"What's this? A fancy dress parade?" Diamond asked, not liking the sound of it.

"No holding back," Agnes boomed through the speakers. "We can see who you are."

"It's all of us for sure," Claudia said, rising to the call. "On your feet, cowpunchers. Don't look the other way, Harvey. With a Davy Crockett hat, there's no escape." She took a strong grip on Diamond's wrist. "You, too, Lone Ranger. We can't let Agnes down." She'd said enough to get her entire posse on its feet, including Julie.

How Diamond wished he'd insisted on wearing the suit. He didn't need to dress up. He'd played Poirot and Columbo perfectly well without the kit. He didn't enjoy being in the spotlight at the best of times. Dressed like this he felt like a fly drowning in a bowl of cream. Yet cowboys and cowgirls were coming from all sides, some only too happy, others like Diamond dragged kicking and screaming. Well, metaphorically.

Over the public address, Agnes was enjoying herself, calling the shots for this High Noon. "Is that Wyatt Earp still propping up the bar? Leave it, Wyatt. If it isn't still there when you come back, we'll get Billy the Kid to buy you another. Buck it up, Lone Ranger. We have lassoes for malingerers. See that smile on Calamity Jane's face? This won't hurt anyone, my darlings. Face this way and form your lines. It's the Cowboy Boogie."

"A dance?" Diamond said in horror. "I can't dance to save my life."

Julie, on his left, said, "Don't worry, guv. It's line dancing. We all make the same moves. There's no contact with anyone else. When you make a mistake, nobody minds. If I can do it, I'm sure you can."

He remembered his sore back but using it as an excuse would just confirm him as a wimp.

"We'll walk it through first without the music," Agnes announced. "It's easy-peasy, a two-step anyone can do. Are you ready, cowpokes? There's one rule I must mention: safety catches on, please. No gunfighting during the dance."

With the mood as jovial as this and the lines in place, escape was not an option. He caught sight of a row of the kitchen helpers watching from the sidelines, still in their aprons. Paloma was among them, loving every second of this. She gave him a wave. She didn't get one back. He was trapped as securely as if tied to a tree stump while the painted tribe hopped round, tomahawks aloft.

This needed total concentration, like driving the tractor, except now he was listening to Agnes calling the moves while he watched what the people in the line ahead were doing. Crossing one foot behind another while wearing pointed boots risked a serious pratfall. Side, behind, side, step behind, side, hitch. A mountainous learning curve. He managed the hitch and the boogie after a fashion. The hitch was a quick lift of the foot off the ground. The boogie was a wiggle of the hips. He wasn't the only one having trouble keeping up, and the proper dance hadn't started yet. No one fell, but there were stumbles. Even the

confident cowboy he was studying in the line ahead got
it wrong and bumped the woman beside him. No contact
with anyone else, yeah? On Diamond's left was sightless
Julie, coping admirably. Elbowing her could be disastrous.
He avoided that. At the end of the practice sequence, she
was still standing and so was he.

"Top marks, cowboys and cowgirls. I've never seen better.
If I had my way, I'd pin a sheriff's star to each of your chests.
Instead I'm rewarding you with one more walkthrough
before you face the music."

The extra practice helped. Diamond completed it without mishap. He'd just about got the sequence of steps in his
head. He wouldn't have performed alone, but surrounded
by others equally out of their league, he might get through.
He might even enjoy himself.

And it was a triumph. When a clash of cymbals marked
the end, he'd achieved more than he would have believed
possible. Not a foot wrong. People around him were grinning, too. It was that moment in a dusty Western when
the entire cast turn their faces upwards in joy as the rain
finally drenches them.

He felt his right hand clasped and squeezed by Claudia.
Instinctively he reached for Julie and squeezed hers before
taking a gentle hold and guiding her back to the chairs. But
before anyone sat down, Claudia flashed her teeth again.
"Thanks, guys. The cowboy boogie is like justice—it has
to be seen to be done. We showed our faces and joined in
the fun and games."

Showed our faces. The phrase smacked of the tension
still latent in this community. And the semicircle of empty
chairs—not one occupied by a villager even after they'd
been abandoned for fifteen or twenty minutes in this over-
crowded barn—graphically marked the fault line. His first

impression of Claudia had been positive. She'd appeared to be willing to identify herself with the village as her father had. Now he wasn't sure.

He muttered in Julie's ear, "Paloma is here. Want to join her?"

She nodded. "Give me your arm."

Claudia had noticed. "I hope you're not thinking of heading into the sunset, Lone Ranger. You and I have hardly spoken. I may have a mission for you unless you're on one already." She made it sound like a sexual come-on.

"Back shortly," he said over his shoulder. "We spotted my pardner across the room."

As they crossed the floor, Julie said, "She's suspicious of you, guv. She sent Fab over to get me on the floor for that St. Bernard's waltz and he was quizzing me about what you've been up to."

That much was understandable. Claudia was whip smart and used sources like Fab to keep her informed. One thing she was unlikely to believe was the truth—that he'd only started investigating because of Julie's doubt about the trial verdict.

If Paloma had been amused by his line-dancing debut, she disguised it well. "That's another talent you've kept from me, you old rogue. Whenever we talk about dancing you say you have two left feet."

"Couldn't get out of it, could we, Julie?" he said. "How are you holding up, Paloma? Tired, I'm sure."

"We get breaks. Maggie is a born organiser and they're a friendly bunch. I can't say the same for all our customers. Some of them treat us like skivvies, not volunteers."

"And still no sighting of Bert Dombey?"

"I can't think what he's up to unless he's in the farmhouse now. Are you sure he hasn't come and gone?"

"His van was still blocked in when I last looked. I'm carrying the tractor keys." He pulled them from his pocket.

"You dropped something," Paloma said.

He'd felt it go and heard it roll across the floor. "A pen I found in Mervyn's suit pocket. It's not important."

"We can't leave it here, Pete. Someone could slip on it." She stooped and felt with her hand.

"You'll get your fingers trampled doing that," he said. "It rolled the other way." He took a step sideways, located the pen with his boot and picked it up, a dark blue ballpoint with lettering he hadn't noticed before. He pressed it open and tried the point on the palm of his hand to see if it still worked. Blue. He quite liked blue pens.

"What does it say?" Paloma asked.

"Welsh, I think. I'm not going to try and pronounce it. You can if you want." He handed it to her.

"'Caer Badon Fine Art.'"

"A freebie from a dealer, by the look of it."

"Was Mervyn into art?"

"His brother was. Maggie told me Mervyn disposed of heaps of stuff after Howard's death. I expect he used a dealer for some of it."

"Could that be how he got rich?"

"Mervyn?" He grinned. "No chance. The pictures don't sell. They're hanging upstairs in the farmhouse. I saw them this evening. Didn't care for them myself. Agnes says they're rubbish. Harsh, but I agree."

"Modern art?"

He shook his head. "Can't even use that as an excuse. Scenes, mostly, and dull as cold tea. He copied from photos, apparently."

"There's no law against that."

"It's not creative, is it?"

"We all react to art in our own way. There may be some billionaire collector who adores Howard's work."

"If there was, there wouldn't be umpteen paintings taking up wall space in the farmhouse." He glanced across at Claudia and her acolytes. "I'd better go back. She wants a chat and she may reveal something of interest."

"It may not be what you're expecting."

Over the loudspeakers, Agnes said, "Strip the Willow."

"Oh no," he said in alarm, "what's that about?"

Julie smiled. "A Scottish country dance."

He didn't like the sound of it, whatever it was.

"We need sets of four couples," Agnes served notice. Any moment she could be naming people.

"I've done my bit," Diamond said. "See you later."

He took the long way around the floor and didn't hurry. But there was no enthusiasm for stripping the willow from Claudia's set. They remained attached primly to their seats, looking more like extras in a trial scene than cowhands at a hoedown.

"This is the perfect moment to break out of the village lockup," Claudia said as soon as he approached. "I've got a bottle of wine in the farmhouse and we can hear ourselves speak there."

The invitation appeared to be for him alone. Fab Fortunato winked at him, and he pretended not to notice.

When the two of them were heading towards the exit, Claudia, with a fixed expression, said, "Remember the ending of *Shane*? He rides away from the kid and doesn't look back." When they were through the door, she said, "Phew. My parties weren't anything like that."

He didn't say a word. This wasn't the time to talk about the parties.

But she seemed keen to share her thoughts. "My father never missed a village event, but he was popular and I'm not. I shouldn't have invited the others." She shrugged. "The truth is, I couldn't face it alone."

"Understandable," he said.

"Was that your wife helping out in the kitchen—the one you were with just now?"

"Partner," he said, content to let her do the talking.

"She looks lovely, even in the apron and mob cap. You're both staying with Julie?"

"Yes."

"Another remarkable woman."

"I agree." He could have said more, but he was keeping his powder dry for the grilling he expected imminently.

The farmhouse door still stood open. "You're not security-minded?" he said.

"Why do you ask?"

"The door left open."

"What's to steal?" she said, standing in the hall with her hands spread wide. "The junk on the wall wouldn't interest a thief. It has a curiosity value, rusty old agricultural tools, but you'd have a job finding anyone wanting to pay you for them."

"Was it your father's collection?"

"Some of the stuff was there when he took over but he added plenty. He'd go to auctions and sales of farms. The old life in the country was one of his main interests. It didn't mean he was rooted in the past. He spent a small fortune modernising this place. You've seen the milking parlour, of course." She opened a door. "We'll speak in here. Care for a glass of wine?"

"I'm more of a beer drinker, thanks."

Her eyes lighted briefly on the spare tyre hanging over

his belt. "You're not getting beer from me." She gestured to an upright chair. They were in an office room. A large mahogany desk with a computer. A shelf filled with filing boxes. A cork board groaning with DEFRA regulations. He'd heard that farmers spend as much time dealing with admin as working the land.

She sat on the edge of the desk looking down on him. The small talk was at an end. "People tell me you teamed up with Bert Dombey, who isn't my number one pin-up, to put it mildly."

He'd been asking himself what her first salvo would be. He could handle this. "He seems to think he is."

"The man is deluded."

"I didn't team up with him, as you put it. He attached himself to me."

"Why was that?"

"Did you know he claimed to be visiting you in Eastwood Park?"

Her eyes rolled upwards. "Ridiculous. I wouldn't have left my cell to see him."

"I'm telling you what he said when we first met at Gordano services. He made out he was in a relationship with you, but there wasn't much passion in the telling of it."

She made a hissing sound. "You discussed my sex life when you met this stranger at a fucking motorway stop? That's so romantic."

"The talk wasn't graphic."

"Is that supposed to calm me down?"

"It's the truth."

She took a sharp breath. "Truth? Here's some truth. Regardless of whatever schoolboy fantasy was aired across the table, it was never a relationship. I slept with him once after a few drinks too many, but I was sober enough to tell myself there wouldn't be a repeat—ever. If he thinks we clicked, he's deluded, a fantasist."

"He probably is."

"What were you even doing at Gordano?"

"He told me he was on his way home from the prison."

"*You*, not him. We just established he's a lying skunk."

The focus had shifted dangerously. Understandably she was angry and this would become a shouting match if he didn't reach out to her in some way. The best he could do was speak the truth—or as much of it as he could reveal. "We fixed a meeting over the phone. I was acting for Julie. She believes you didn't get a fair trial, so I thought I'd speak to some of the people who were there."

"It was none of your business."

"I know, but Julie was troubled."

"It was none of her business either."

"Hold on, Claudia. You know each other. Julie is a neighbour and she was concerned about you. The blindness means she has hours and hours to think about an injustice, as she saw it. She couldn't do much about it other than talk to someone like me with a reputation for winkling out the truth."

"I heard." The sneering note made clear what she thought of that. "Fab tells me you call yourself a problem-solver."

"That's because I thought it was a term he would understand."

"Whose problems, his or your own? You conned him into thinking you had money to invest."

"'Conned' is unfair. He saw me coming and decided I was up for it."

"His mistake, then?"

"Yes."

"And did Harvey Hertzog persuade himself that you once played rugby?"

"That's the truth."

She shook her head. "Liar. He checked up. No Peter Dee ever played for London Welsh."

"My wishful thinking. I was trying to find something we had in common and he was seriously good at the game. But I did play before getting this beer gut."

"How can I believe a single word you say?"

"Speak to Julie or Paloma. They'll tell you I'm basically honest."

"You can tell Julie I appreciate her concern, but she should have spoken to me before setting you on my trail. She could have phoned. I was allowed to take calls in prison. I spoke regularly to Agnes about the running of the farm. Life goes on."

He was tempted to say Roger Miller's life hadn't gone on but he buttoned his lip, fascinated to hear what else she would tell him.

What she said next was worth the kicking he'd been getting. "I was guilty of manslaughter and I've taken my punishment. The last thing I need right now is someone trying to reopen my case, however well meant it may be. The man who was killed was another ex who refused to believe I'd finished with him. I should have dumped him properly but I flunked it. That's one of the hardest things in a relationship, telling the man face to face you don't want to see him again. Ever."

She was talking about a predicament he'd never had to deal with. He was trying to see it from her point of view. And then as the investigator. Could it be easier arranging for someone to die than facing the break-up scene she dreaded?

"I hosted the party," she went on in this confessional vein. "I thought up the game with the garters. I ordered and took delivery of the damned things. I knew Roger would be the first to volunteer."

"But you didn't plan to kill him," Diamond cut in. "You said at the trial that you hid the garter in the bull pen."

"And I wasn't believed." She eyed him analytically, picking her words with such care that they had an extra force. "Do you think that's true, that I'm innocent? Or did I lie about the bull pen to try and save myself from the guilty verdict? I wasn't believed by the judge or the jury. What's your verdict, Mr. Dee?"

This was a test and he'd better react the right way or he'd get nothing from her.

He had tried from the beginning to keep an open mind. She might be as innocent as Snow White or as guilty as Lady Macbeth. Until there was proof, he would resist a judgement. Even her character had to be weighed. She had a brazen manner because she'd been toughened in her youth. There was a steely indifference to the conventions most people lived by, but she hadn't had the upbringing that breeds conformity. She'd shown little gratitude for her father's financial support, but his reputation as the patron saint of Baskerville seemed to have been at the expense of real paternal love. She looked for affection elsewhere and soon discarded the men she attracted.

Her eyes continued reading every line of his face. This was their own High Noon.

He wasn't ready to commit. "I respect what you just told me. Okay, you were instrumental in Miller's death, but if I'd been on that jury, I would have demanded to know more about how the garter got into the silo."

She shot him a murderous look. "Don't piss me about.

Spit it out, man. Do you think I'm guilty or not? Your verdict, Mr. Dee. You haven't answered my question."

Nor would he. Instead, he threw in a telling observation on her trial. "It seems what really swung it was the jury being bussed out here to see the silo and watch the court official climb to the top. The judge chose a woman when he could just as easily have picked a man. The victim was male and the perpetrator may well have been male, but the image of that woman will have stayed in the jury's minds."

Her expression changed, the fierce scrutiny replaced by a frown. She hadn't expected a sympathetic take on her treatment.

His eyes held hers, watching his words sink in. "Didn't your lawyer object?"

She shook her head slowly, reflectively. "It wasn't like it happened in court. We were here on the farm in the open air, watching. People were chatting. There wasn't any formality about it."

"Your lawyer should have put a stop to it."

Claudia was clearly shaken. "Why didn't I spot this? I should have spoken to my lawyer. I can't blame her for letting it happen."

"But you can. That's exactly the kind of thing she's paid to notice. Grounds for an appeal."

"I didn't appeal."

"That puzzled me, Claudia. It made me think you were willing to take the rap whether you were guilty or not. Is that the truth of it?"

She reddened. She shifted position on the desk. The dominant forward lean gave way to a different pose, angled back defensively, hands flat to the surface. As good as a yes.

"Have you ever read Charles Dickens?"

Mystification was written across her face. She didn't answer.

"*A Tale of Two Cities*," he said. "The last line of the last chapter. Sydney Carton on the scaffold: 'It is a far, far better thing that I do, than I have ever done'?"

She remained silent.

"Evidently not," he said. "I'm making sure you weren't covering for someone else. I don't see you as a saint but I needed to ask. It was closure you wanted, wasn't it?"

Still silent, she blinked several times as if a dust cloud had blown up.

He'd never rated body language as a reliable guide but this was telling him all he needed. "You had a bigger issue—the source of the money that modernised the farm. Far too much to be accounted for by the turnover from farming. Your father had found what every farmer wants, a goose that lays golden eggs. Wisely, he told no one and certainly not you, his free-spending daughter. Was it legal? Probably not. But the evidence was all around you when you took over. In the bank as well. Am I making sense?"

She said nothing, but she denied nothing. She was fully absorbed.

"For you, a year or two in jail was a price worth paying for the jackpot in prospect. You accepted your sentence, made no appeal and had the farmhouse locked up ready to find that goose when you got out."

The colour drained from her face. "Who told you this?"

"It's not rocket science. I worked it out myself and so did someone else."

"Bert?"

"He's here tonight."

She stared with car-crash eyes. "I didn't invite him."

"That wouldn't stop Dombey. He parked his van in the tractor shed before anyone got here. I blocked it in." He dangled the ignition keys to show it was true. "He's here somewhere."

"In the house, do you mean?" Her anger had shifted away from Diamond. "He has no right. No fucking right."

18

"I WANT HIM out," she said. "He's trespassing."

It was less than an hour since Diamond had done some trespassing of his own.

Any doubts Claudia had about him were set aside. At this minute she needed help. She was angry about the invasion of her privacy. She couldn't act alone, and this able-bodied guy who could deliver a calf and drive a tractor was a better bet than her flaky friends. That was Diamond's take on it, anyway.

"We must do this right," he told her. "He can be dangerous."

Rather to his surprise, she didn't agree. "Bert? He's just a long, thin streak of piss who wears unfunny T-shirts."

"Don't underrate him. He could be gunning for you, believing you know where the money comes from."

She frowned. Her voice switched to a lower, more serious register. "Is that what he told you?"

He ducked the question. Silence did the job of words and avoided a lie.

"All right," she said in a grudging tone. "But please, if he's hiding in the house, I want him ejected. I have to sleep in this place. Shall we start upstairs?"

He shook his head. "Down here is better. If he comes down, we're sure to hear." Evading a trap of his own making, he added, "In a house as old as this, I bet the stairs creak like a ship's timbers."

If she had a suspicion he'd already used the staircase, she didn't say so.

He put his cowboy hat back on for the search. Wearing it helped him feel more the man of action. All he had in his holster was his smartphone, but he doubted whether Dombey was armed. Just a long, thin streak who wore unfunny T-shirts, wasn't he?

Claudia stayed close. She gestured to the doors along the hallway. "There are two reception rooms, a dining room, an old-fashioned boot room and a cloakroom. We can leave out the kitchen and scullery where the ladies are."

"You lead the way."

She took him to the end room with the bay window he'd already looked into from the outside. She pointed to the key turned sideways in the lock. "He won't be in here."

It was no bad thing to act the innocent. "Why not?"

"He wouldn't be able to lock himself in, would he? I secured the entire ground floor before I went to my trial."

"Smart thinking. And it simplifies our job."

To be certain, they unlocked and turned on the light. No one was there and the musty air told them the door hadn't been opened in many months.

They checked each room in the same perfunctory way. Apart from the kitchen, which they didn't enter because they could hear the ladies still inside, the cloakroom was the only one unlocked and no one was inside.

"Soon done," the Lone Ranger said, a thumb tucked nonchalantly inside his belt. "The upstairs, then."

Claudia paused at the foot of her ornate staircase. "Does Bert know something I don't about my father?"

"Hard to tell. He's interested in your money, as you know. He seems to have a theory how it was acquired."

"Which is?"

"He won't say, but when I threw out a few suggestions of my own like drugs and trafficking, none of it impressed him. Forged banknotes, stolen goods, money-laundering."

She closed her eyes briefly and shook her head as if the family honour was under attack. "None of this sounds like Daddy, anyway. He was really high-minded when I was growing up. If he wasn't so fucking sanctimonious, I might have respected him more."

"After you left home as a teenager, you never saw him again, right?"

"True."

"More than twenty years and he made sure you were never without money?"

She shrugged. "Like I said, he had this outdated sense of duty." A stillness came over her as if she might be having a second, more gracious thought about her father's staunch support. She quickly snapped out of it. "You were telling me about Bert."

"Only that he talks as if he knows something."

She gave an angry sigh. "Well, he's ahead of me if he does. It's obvious there was money on tap from somewhere. That's why I didn't sell the house when I inherited. I moved in expecting to find whatever it was, a safe full of precious stones, loot behind a secret panel, anything. I had two years living here before I was arrested. Oceans of time to search."

"And didn't you find anything?"

She eyed him with scorn. "Would I be telling you this if I did?"

There was clear frustration behind the remark. He believed what he was hearing.

"Did you mention it to any of your friends?"

"Such as?"

"Bert."

"Oh, I see what you mean." Some of the contempt vanished from her face. "We talked, I'm sure. He did a bit of a search with me one time."

"No joy, then?"

"The place is a warren, as you see. Nearly five hundred years old."

"The fifteen hundreds," he said. "Elementary maths I can manage. History was never my strong subject. Was that the Tudors?"

"Elizabeth the first."

"Was the family Roman Catholic, by any chance? I'll tell you why I'm asking."

"Save your breath, cowboy. Do you think I haven't heard of priest holes? We had one behind a panel in the kitchen. In Victorian times they extended it upstairs and turned it into a dumb waiter. I played with it as a kid, but it doesn't get used anymore."

He didn't admit he'd seen the dumb waiter already.

"The Priest family were Catholics for centuries, if that doesn't sound like a truism. They defected to the Church of England before I was born."

"Some Catholic houses had more than one priest hole. I visited one in Worcestershire that had seven."

She was unmoved. "If there were more here, someone would have found them in the last five hundred years. Stories like that are handed down through the generations."

"But would anyone have told you?"

"Daddy would have known." The confident woman suddenly sounded like the small girl of more than thirty years ago.

Diamond waited for a more thoughtful answer.

She turned a shade more pink. "I guess the history of the house wasn't high on the agenda when I was staging my teenage rebellion."

As they were climbing the stairs, he pointed out the stain before she had a chance to notice. "How long has that been there?"

She gave it a cursory glance. "No idea. I only got here this afternoon. It's not fresh, is it?"

He made a show of testing it with his fingertips. "Feels dry. Could be mud, wine, anything." He rapped on the carpet with his knuckles. Whatever was below didn't sound hollow, but neither did it seem entirely solid. This second flight of six stairs abutted a wall and the space below was boxed off by a carved wooden side panel intrinsic to the structure. "A favourite place for a priest hole was inside a staircase. Did you think of that when you were searching?"

"The first place I looked."

"And . . . ?"

"Haven't you noticed the carpet tacks?"

Another theory went down the tubes. All the way up, there were tacks in the risers as well as the treads. The heads were hammered in so deep that some weren't visible. The strip of corded carpeting hadn't been disturbed in years.

At the top, he had to pretend this was all new to him. She told him there were nine bedrooms. "My ancestors bred like rats in a grain ship," she said and then corrected herself. "That's not quite fair. The farming wasn't mechanised in those days."

"Hands-on."

"Exactly, and they needed all the hands they could get."

"Which room is yours?" he asked, already knowing the answer. "We should check that first."

She pointed to the open door. "Are you thinking he's in there waiting to pounce?"

"Is there any place he could hide?"

"A fitted wardrobe. I made some changes when I moved in."

"Let's make sure. I'll go first."

"It's in a state," she said. "I didn't have much time."

He smiled to himself. A psychopathic killer could be waiting inside and she was fretting about the clothes she'd scattered about.

He wasn't expecting to find Dombey there. His sixth sense told him the room was empty.

It was.

Claudia followed him in and started tidying the things she'd left out. "If I stay here, I want to convert the room next to this into an en suite. One fewer bedroom isn't going to bother me."

He thought of her living alone in this mansion for two years after Mervyn's death and he understood her need for company.

"When you threw your parties, the size of this house must have been useful."

Her eyes lit up. "You bet. It's not all bad memories."

"Most of your guests stayed overnight?"

"Every bedroom was in use." She gave a half-smile. "Let's leave it at that."

"Shall I check the other rooms and come back to you?"

"I'll come with you. Until we find him, I don't want to be left alone."

He was amused. "Calamity Jane shouldn't talk like that."

Quick as anything, she linked her arm through his. "And

the Lone Ranger stops being lone while I'm around, so chew on that, cowboy."

It felt like a come-on and he wasn't sure how he would deal with it, especially while checking bedrooms.

"There's something I've been meaning to ask you."

"Shoot, cowboy." She came closer, so close that their hats touched.

Not what he intended.

He straightened his hat with his free hand. "Have you ever heard of Caer Badon?"

"Should I? Is this relevant? Right now, at this time?"

Instead, he said, "I've got it in writing. Can I have my arm back?"

She flexed, laughed, and then allowed him to wriggle free. He took out the ballpoint he'd found and showed her the lettering. "It looks Welsh to me. Not the Fine Art bit, but the first two words."

She held it to the light and started trotting out obscure facts like an expert on *Antiques Roadshow*. "Caer is Welsh, and it means *fortress* or something similar, but it must have been used by the ancient Britons as well because Badon was their name for Bath. There was a battle of Badon about the year 500 between the Britons and the Anglo-Saxons. The Brits beat off the invaders and King Arthur is supposed to have led them."

His head was swimming. "I've lived in Bath most of my life and never heard of this battle."

"There you are, then. You learn something every day. Nobody knows the actual site, but Bathampton Down is one strong candidate and Bannerdown is another."

"How do you know all this?"

"It's one of Roger Miller's pens—the late, lamented Roger." There wasn't much lament in her voice.

Miller, the man in the silo. Diamond started to catch up, mortified for not making the connection. Julie had told him the guy was an art dealer when she had first talked about the incident. And Hertzog had gone into more detail when they met in the Holloway. He'd mentioned the local street scenes that were the main business. The wording on the pen should have screamed Miller. The Welsh-sounding name had put him off when in fact it placed the business squarely in Bath.

Claudia clearly had issues with Roger and his pens. "He gave me one himself after we slept together for the first time and I chucked it straight in the bin. A fucking ballpoint for services rendered!"

"I don't blame you."

"Like I was tax-deductible or something. It's one thing to promote yourself to the people you do business with and quite another to hand one to the woman who shared her bed with you."

"Was that why you split up?"

"Oh, god, so many reasons. I measure my life with the mistakes I've made over men."

"I was forgetting he was an art dealer."

"And proud to be living in Bath, which is why he gave his business this pretentious name. He told each client the story. I was never a client, but I qualified for the history lecture. How did you get yours?"

"The pen?" He grinned. "Not the same way as you. It was left in a suit Jim Douglas gave to me, one that once belonged to Mervyn. Jim said he'd never worn it. He doesn't need suits for his job."

Her mood lightened. She shook with laughter. "I can tell you a story about that. When I moved here, there was a wardrobe stuffed with Daddy's clothes. They were far too good to sling out, so I offered them to Jim and he told me they were no use to him, but when he got home and mentioned this to Agnes, she must have given him a proper earful. She's a strong personality and a frugal Scot. Can't bear to let anything go to waste. The next day poor old Jim knocked on my door looking like a spaniel that had pooped on the carpet and said please could he take them after all. You don't cross Agnes when she issues an order."

"So I discovered tonight. Nobody else would have got me on the dance floor."

"Don't be so sure of that." She popped the pen into his shirt pocket and gripped his arm again. There were no subtleties with Claudia. "Now we've solved the great pen mystery, can we check the other bedrooms?"

He looked ahead. Howard's pictures lining the corridor walls hadn't been mentioned so far. They had to be somewhere in the mix. "Do you know whether any like these were sold to Roger Miller?"

"No chance," she said at once. "He dealt in proper art. You've only got to look to know these are by an amateur. My uncle painted them. He thought he was good but he was deluded, bless him. Never sold a single one. Survived on handouts from Daddy"—she smiled self-consciously—"and so did I, come to that."

"Your father must have cared about you."

"Neither of us were good investments. When Uncle Howard died, my father had a godawful job sorting out the house in Bathampton. He was too sentimental to throw the pictures out. I suppose one solution was to frame the least ghastly ones and hang them here where hardly anyone sees them."

The check of the rooms supported Diamond's belief that they hadn't been disturbed in many months. The conversation had been more productive than the search.

"Did you see much of your uncle when you were growing up?"

"Not really. He didn't even come for Christmas and it was a good thing he didn't because all he ever talked about was art. He was OCD, poor old thing, obsessed with one painter whose name I forget, but who lived in Bathampton during the second world war. Quite famous. You'll have heard of him."

"I wouldn't bank on it." Diamond's knowledge of twentieth-century artists was on a par with his grasp of quantum physics.

After they'd completed the search and found no trace of Dombey, Claudia looked out of the window at the end. "The van is still there. What's he up to?"

No answer was possible. Diamond looked at his watch. "I must get back to the barn and see if Julie has had enough yet. What time does the dance finish?"

"Before midnight usually." She turned from the window and a different, less assertive note crept into her voice. "Peter, I've got a favour to ask. I don't want to be alone in the house tonight. He scares me."

"Dombey? You called him a long, thin—"

"That doesn't make him less dangerous," she interrupted him. "Searching for him hasn't been good for my nerves. It's given me the creeps."

"Aren't any of your friends staying over?"

"They have to be back in Bath by tomorrow. They're leaving at the end of the evening."

"I'm sure Dombey wants to make his getaway as well."

"He can't while his van is blocked in."

It was a fair point. "Maybe I should move the tractor and see if he comes out from wherever he is right now."

"You said he was dangerous and he could be gunning for me. Were you serious?"

He couldn't in all conscience deny it. "'Gunning' is a bit colourful. I've no reason to think he's armed."

"But he's still dangerous?"

What could he say to that without bringing on hysterics? "Unpredictable, anyway."

"We found that out this evening. He's one jump ahead of us."

"He may be two jumps behind," he said. "There's no way of telling. Listen, I must see that Julie is okay. Paloma will have finished in the kitchen and I hope they found each other but I want to be sure. Are you going back to the barn to see Fab and Harvey?"

"I suppose I should."

"We'll go together."

"Will you stay the night?"

"I want to get Dombey on the move if I can. Freeing the van should do it."

THE BARN DANCE had reached the point when all the lights were dimmed except a glitterball and "Home on the Range" was being played at a funereal tempo that allowed couples to shuffle about the floor in close holds, a far cry from the cowboy boogie. Diamond found Paloma and Julie seated just inside the door. They were ready to leave. "I'm leg-weary," Paloma said, "and Julie wants to get back to the cottage and let Bella out for a few minutes before we all get our heads down."

He said he needed to stay on for a while. If he got back late, he'd keep Raffles company on the sofa downstairs. He didn't mention Claudia's appeal for a night watchman.

"You wouldn't be treating yourself to a late drink before the bar closes?" Paloma said.

"Now you mention it, I haven't had one all evening."

But he wasn't going to get it. He had a couple of tractors to shift and he wanted to be in the shed when Dombey showed. So he escorted his ladies outside.

"Got your phone?" Paloma said.

He patted his holster. "Faster on the draw than the Sundance Kid."

"Be sure to call for backup if you need it."

"Is that an offer?"

She smiled. "Anyone but us. Julie and I will be out to the world."

He kissed each of them lightly.

Julie said, "Take care, guv." And it wasn't the empty phrase it often is.

AFTER THE STEADY drumbeat from the barn, the tractor shed was as silent as a sleeping cat until Diamond started up the Massey Ferguson and returned it to its correct place in the line-up. He doubted whether anyone was about. Even Chummy was quiet. He returned the key to its hook and moved the other tractor. The van was good to go, as they say.

But Diamond wasn't. He needed to get out of sight immediately and keep watch. Helpfully, he was spoilt for choice. He climbed into the cab of a combine harvester, high up in shadow under the lights, with a clear view of the van.

Minutes passed. He was glad of a pause in his hectic evening after escorting Julie to the supper, rearranging the tractors, twice touring the farmhouse, being caught, quizzed and squeezed by Maggie Harrap, joining the VIPs at the hoedown and getting corralled for a line dance by Agnes. But the big development had been meeting Claudia.

His mind wasn't made up about her. Anyone released

from prison has to choose what to say to people. Her way was to be as hard on herself as her meanest critic. She was the daughter past praying for, with a sordid history, guilty of manslaughter, for which she accepted her punishment. She had no alibi, wanted no pity and was angry about the attempt to clear her name.

She'd appeared to be ironclad. But there were signs of frailty, especially in her dealings with men. Her father had failed to help her through adolescence and allowed her to leave home at the first opportunity, yet she still called him Daddy. She saved her contempt for blokes of her own generation. Even with them, she was torn. She craved their company, invited sex and treated them as disposable. With some, this worked. She couldn't handle pathetic creeps like Roger Miller and Bert Dombey, who wanted a relationship and became a nuisance. She'd confessed to being inept at dumping them. The way she'd spoken about Miller showed no regret and no conscience over his horrible death.

Cold-blooded? She must have seemed so to the judge and jury. Yet she was also unsparing about herself.

Speaking to Diamond about the trial, she had ducked the overriding issue of whether she'd lied about placing the garter in the bull pen rather than the silo. When pressed, she'd deftly turned the question around and challenged him to say what he believed.

It was a reversal that rocked his confidence by planting a larger doubt in his mind. If she had lied to the court, all bets were off. She was a killer and he the mug who had wasted his time opening old wounds. He'd be forced to admit he hadn't cut it as a lone sleuth. He could only function as a team player with his squad in support along with all the resources of forensic science. Paloma's words—"Be sure to call for backup if you need it"—were more telling than she had realised.

He shivered. The night had closed in. His breath was condensing, misting the glass he was trying to look through. A low moment. He'd started this quest reluctantly as a favour to Julie. Rapidly it had become a cause, his chance to prove his worth without assistance from the police. And it came home to him now how committed he was.

He needed keenly, urgently, desperately to make a success of this. No one else knew the crises of confidence he'd suffered through his long career. He'd learned to manage them, often buoyed up by colleagues like Julie. This time he was going it alone. Failure was unthinkable.

He heard the heavy drumbeat from the barn reach a peak and then stop. It didn't start up again. The sounds that followed were car doors slamming. People were leaving.

Was this the trigger Bert Dombey needed?

He could hope.

More minutes passed.

He took out his undercharged phone. He didn't want it to run out of juice completely, so he wouldn't use it just to keep boredom at bay. He never had. But it was still a rarely used aid. He wanted to make a search. Claudia had tried to tell him about Howard Priest's obsession with one particular artist who lived in Bathampton during the war. She couldn't recall the name. A search engine might help.

He googled *Bathampton artist* and got a page of references to an art group that was currently functioning there. When he scrolled down, a more intriguing result came up. A print was being offered for sale and the title was *Bathampton c1940–1* by Walter Richard Sickert. He'd heard of Sickert. Anyone interested in the history of crime has heard of Sickert. Was that the name Claudia had tried to remember?

He started a new search and was inundated with websites with speculation on Sickert's supposed secret life as Jack the Ripper. He knew all about that, had read the books and didn't believe a word of it. He wasn't interested in what happened in Whitechapel in 1888. Right now, he needed more about the Bathampton connection. Persistence paid off. A summary of Sickert's life stated that he had died there in 1942.

He'd had a long, rich life as an artist. Studio assistant to Whistler, he was despatched to Paris on an errand to meet Edgar Degas, who became a major influence. His scope as an artist was exceptional: drawing, painting, etching, engraving, lithography, sculpture and photography. His subject matter ranged over portraiture, nudes, still lifes, landscapes, seascapes and interiors. He'd painted Queen Victoria, George V and Edward VIII, given lessons to Winston Churchill, been painted by him and done his own portrait of the great man. Others who had sat for him included Lady Eden, Lord Beaverbrook, Peggy Ashcroft, Hugh Walpole and Israel Zangwill. It was a lot to take in.

Then the shed lights went out. Infuriating. Either they were on a timer or someone had deliberately cut the power. He rubbed a clear patch in the windscreen and couldn't see anything except a section of yard through the large open doors, the mud overlaid with silver by moonlight. The attraction was lost on him. Being plunged into darkness had altered everything.

He might spot his man coming in. He would lose sight of him inside.

He paused the phone and returned it to the holster.

The advantage of being up here had gone. He'd be better

off at ground level. He opened the cab door and climbed down, needing to feel his way with each step of the ladder. The Cuban heels added to the difficulty.

Back on floor level, he could make out the shapes of the farm vehicles. He was less safe here than in the cab but he could pick his position. He chose to stand near the doors.

He moved a short way and froze.

Someone was approaching. He could hear them in the yard. Light, stealthy steps.

A torch beam picked a path through the ruts and cow-pats.

He darted behind the nearest piece of farm machinery, which was a digger with rubber tracking. Helpful cover. Crouching, he waited to see if he'd guessed right and this was Dombey.

A figure was silhouetted in the doorway. The torch dazzle stopped him from telling who it was.

19

THE BEAM OF light panned across the shed picking out vehicles, but Diamond was under no illusion that farm machinery was the focus. What mattered was the flesh and blood it might conceal. Tense and motionless, crouching out of sight behind the excavator's undercarriage, the flesh and blood drew shallow, quick breaths. Whoever was holding that torch wanted to be damned sure no one was about. They wouldn't move from the doorway until the last piece of machinery had been checked.

He knew when it was his turn. The shadow of the digger spread over the wall behind him, tyrannosaurus-like. He kept as still as the track rollers he pressed against.

Time stood still. Even so, he knew deep down that the inspection took too long. Then, to his horror, he heard the scrape of rubber on the concrete floor, slow, deliberate steps of someone wearing trainers. The torchbearer was coming for a closer look.

Making a run for it was not a serious option. He would only be trapped at the far end of the building. He remained where he was, hoping fervently that the steps would halt.

They continued their inexorable tread. And suddenly he wasn't in shadow anymore. He was caught in the glare.

"Out you come, cowboy. I don't know what's more obvious, the hiding place or the hat." He knew the voice. She'd come right round the digger and was a few yards off.

He turned his head. "Jesus, Claudia, I thought you were Bert."

"Flattery will get you nowhere."

He stood up and braced his legs to stop them cramping.

Claudia said, "I hope you're not planning to spend the night here after you promised to keep me company." She'd changed clothes. She was in a pink sweatsuit that may have been her nightwear.

He felt his cheeks redden enough to compete with her hair. "I don't remember promising anything."

"Point one: you said he's dangerous."

"True, but—"

"Point two: I told you I don't want to be alone."

He didn't make an issue out of who said what. His version wouldn't be accepted. Claudia owned this place. Right now, she owned him. What she wanted, she got.

"If Bert really was here, you would have found him, wouldn't you?" she said. "Which means I'm not safe in the house on my own."

"We searched," he said. "He wasn't there."

"Two hours ago."

"Would you mind not pointing the torch?"

She lowered the beam, took a step closer and said with more warmth and even a hint of seduction, "Come back to the house. I'll make coffee and we'll talk about it."

He didn't jump at the offer. There was a game being played here. He doubted whether she was truly afraid of Dombey. This invitation was about more than him. "I moved the tractor. Bert's van is free to go now. He could be waiting for us to leave so he can drive away."

Her tone changed. "What the fuck does it matter if he does?"

A telling point, brutal and possibly true. Maybe Dombey the psychopath hadn't harmed anyone. Maybe he was a bunny rabbit waiting to scuttle off to his burrow.

With his confidence draining like water through sand, Diamond made an effort to reason with her that he decided was pathetic even as he spoke the words. "We don't know what he might have found. He was here early. He had plenty of time to search the house."

"There's shit all to find," she said. "You saw for yourself."

A few trenchant words demolished the case he'd been diligently building all week. He was supposed to be helping her find the truth.

Anticlimax seeped through every vein in his body. Everything she'd said or failed to say screamed that she was guilty of Roger Miller's death. He struggled for words. "Okay. I hear you."

THE KITCHEN HAD been left immaculate by Maggie and her helpers. Every item of crockery cleaned, dried and stacked on the big farmhouse table for return to the suppliers.

Claudia poured the coffee. Diamond, perched unhappily on a high stool, was in urgent need of energy and asked for sugar.

"I didn't think anyone took it these days." She went to a cupboard, took out a fresh packet and tore it open. Then she gave an impatient sigh. "Next you'll ask for a fucking spoon."

"An ordinary one will do."

She might have smiled. He hadn't meant to be amusing.

He stirred in his usual two sugars, followed by two more. "I don't know what you expect from me."

She gathered her hair and swished it behind her shoulder. "That's not what a damsel wants to hear from her knight in shining armour."

What? This was bizarre. He should tell her to cut the bullshit but he didn't. The detective in him needed to keep her onside and get to the truth. So he sidestepped her comment instead of squashing it. "Haven't you noticed what I'm wearing?"

She laughed. "More Lee Marvin than Sir Lancelot. All right, Lone Ranger. You can get your kit off. I won't stop you."

"Can we be serious, Claudia?"

"I'm serious. I brought you here because I need cover. Take that any way you want."

He didn't even try. "Be straight with me. Are you afraid of Bert?"

"More to the point," she ducked the question with her usual disregard, "are you afraid of me? I haven't had a man in eighteen months."

Now Diamond laughed, but it was a forced laugh. He'd not been propositioned in twenty years and the reason she gave was no compliment. "In case you didn't notice, I'm in a long-term relationship."

"That's a problem?"

"It's not a problem for me. I sleep with Paloma."

From the look she gave him, she was deciding whether to throw her coffee at him.

He tugged the conversation back to reality. "I can check that all your doors are locked before I go and that's my best offer." Then the sugar rush got his brain working again. "Wait, there's a better way."

"Which is?"

"Not what you're thinking." He could be high-handed, too. After all the hassle he'd endured, this idea was neat.

She watched him finish his coffee. No more was said before he took his mug to the sink. "This will work better in the hall—if it works at all."

He crossed the kitchen, stepped into the hall and ran his eyes over the layout like an estate agent making a valuation. Claudia stood leaning against the door frame holding her unfinished coffee, prepared to be unimpressed.

Surrounded by Mervyn's collection of ancient agricultural tools, Diamond took out a more modern device, his smartphone. How smart, he couldn't guarantee. It had been low on juice at the start of the evening.

He felt in his pocket for his wallet. When he'd first called Bert Dombey, he hadn't saved the number. What a good thing he still had the compliment slip he'd been handed by Elaine. He keyed the digits in, pressed green, jammed the phone to his ear and heard the beeps connect. For a man who wasn't well known for his competence with mobiles, this was bordering on genius.

"Who are you calling?" Claudia asked.

"Listen up. If he's in the house and it rings, we've got him."

"And if it isn't, am I supposed to feel safe?"

He held the phone away from his ear. No one had answered, but he thought—or fancied—he could hear a ringtone from inside the house, so faint it could be wishful thinking.

Claudia started to say something else and he told her to shut up and listen. Basic courtesy was suspended.

"Upstairs."

He climbed to the third flight, dialled again and waved to her to stay silent.

Definitely the notes of a ringtone. He'd expected to trace it to an upstairs room. Instead, it was coming from below.

"Hear that?"

Claudia was now at the bottom of the stairs looking up. "You're closer than I am."

"But you heard it too?"

"'Bohemian Rhapsody,'" she said. "Only a few bars."

"Is that Dombey's ringtone?"

"Could be. It's the bit when Freddie sits at the piano and sings to his mamma about killing a man. Typical Bert, wanting that on his phone. Have you seen his T-shirts?"

She didn't get an answer. In any other situation, Diamond would have taken an interest in this new instance of the man's dark, psychopathic humour. Right now, it was a side issue. His focus was on the staircase. He came down to the second flight, crouched, flattened himself awkwardly to the stairs, pressed his ear to the carpet and touched redial.

"I don't get it," he said after hearing the notes more sharply, yet still low in volume. "I checked before for a priest hole. The carpet is tacked all the way up. Do you know when it was laid? It's in good condition, which is why the staining is so obvious."

She had remained downstairs, as if unwilling to encourage him. And yet she hadn't called off the hunt. "I expect my father had it done. It was in place when I came to live here."

"There must be a space under here. Is there a broom cupboard behind all that carving where you're standing?"

"If there is, it's new to me," Claudia said. "This is crazy. Are you saying he's hiding under the stairs?"

"His phone is." He returned to the ground floor. The staircase appeared solid, supported by beams thick enough to be ship's timbers and infilled with intricate wood carvings of what looked to him like sylvan scenes of shepherds and their flocks with a few nymphs looking on. Any means of entry would have been obvious. He tapped with his knuckles and got a sound testifying to the thickness of the wood. Frustrated, he thumped the panel with the flat of his hand.

"Careful," Claudia said. "This house is five hundred years old."

He turned to look at Mervyn's display of farm tools. "I can use that sledgehammer."

"You're joking, I hope."

"On the stair treads, not the carving. Do you want this mystery solved?" He was impatient. He believed she knew more than she was saying. "It stands to reason there's some space inside."

"I'm not having my stairs sledgehammered."

"They can be repaired."

"I want you out of here now." The force of the words left no doubt that she was serious. He could have mistaken some of what she'd said before as role-play but she wasn't speaking lines now. Eyes blazing, she was up for a fight.

He risked a flippant comment. "That's a sudden turn-around. A few minutes ago you were too damn scared to spend the night on your own."

"And you offered to check that everything is locked."

"The offer stands."

Her fists stayed clenched. "Will you listen to me? If you're right and there's a priest hole inside, it was built by a master craftsman to save lives. An expert made it and it will take an expert to find it."

"No sledgehammer, then." But he hadn't caved in completely. "Bert Dombey is no expert and he got inside. God knows what he found." He marched back up, two stairs at a time. "I want another look at that stain."

Forensic science has an entire subsection on the nature of stains, their composition, their patterns and what can be learned about the incidents that caused them. Blood spatter can speak volumes if you have the knowledge and means to analyse it.

Diamond had neither. The stain could be coffee, oil, ink or any other fluid and he wouldn't know. He was unable to tell how and when it had got there. The only certainty was its placement here, above the main supporting beams of the staircase, the very heart of the structure. What if it literally marked the spot? He visualised a section of the staircase opening to reveal an inner room. Then reality weighed in to remind him that the carpet was tacked to each stair from top to bottom.

The problem with the stain was that it had taken all his attention. He hadn't looked minutely, Sherlock-style, at the entire tread. This time, kneeling two steps down with his nose almost touching the fabric because, unlike the great detective, he hadn't brought a magnifying glass, he studied three much smaller spots he supposed were spatter marks. And when he'd learned nothing useful from them, he turned his attention to the tacks. Four either side and four more on the riser, all hammered home cleanly. Not one was bent. And there were no telltale holes in the fabric from earlier tacking.

Then a new theory dawned.

He was looking at the angle between tread and riser. He couldn't tell for sure whether there might be a break. The fibres knitted together where the wood behind them joined and gave the effect of a continuous run down the six stairs of the flight. That could be an illusion.

"Get me a knife." An order, spoken firmly, as if to one of his team. Force the blade under the carpet and he could lever out the tacks.

She flung back defiance. "Who the fuck do you think I am?"

"Behind you on the wall." He'd seen them earlier, strong, sharp-pointed blades once used to bring relief to bloated sheep.

She made no move, so he ran downstairs and grabbed one himself. He picked off a pair of pincers as well.

Claudia had already ordered him out of the house. She reached for his sleeve to stop him but he was away like a snatch-and-grab man.

Back on his knees upstairs, he shoved the blade behind the carpet and pulled. The tacks resisted the first try and the second before he loosened one. He pincered it out, forced the knife farther in and levered out the others. He grabbed the entire piece of carpet and yanked it free. Success!

The carpet hung loose. It was divided right across. Deliberately. The edges of the two strips had been wedged so tightly into the angle that no one could have told they were not joined.

He'd found the way in. The method may have lacked the finesse of Sherlock Holmes, but it was effective. Next came the real test, devised five centuries ago.

Would the stair move?

It was solid oak and tightly constructed. He tried pressing his fingertips under the nosing of the upper tread. Wouldn't lift. Flattened his palms to the riser panel and pushed. Damned thing didn't shift a millimetre. There had to be a way. Claudia was right about one thing. A master carpenter had made this. The mechanics would not be obvious.

He searched for anything else that might do the trick. A button disguised as a knot in the wood. Any sort of imperfection. There was none. No hidden fastening. No screws. No wedges.

He stood up, jammed his foot in the angle of the stair

and put more pressure on. It didn't even creak. He kicked the thing and dented the toe of his cowboy boot.

Claudia shouted, "I'll sue you for the damage you're doing."

The banisters, then. Maybe the trick lay with one of them. Use it as a lever, or twist it.

No joy. Each one was attached top and bottom.

The Elizabethan carpenter had outwitted the twenty-first-century sleuth. The sledgehammer was the only option left.

Halfway down the lowest flight, he stopped.

Claudia stood at the foot of the stairs holding another item from the wall display. A sickle with a vicious curved blade. She wasn't about to hand it to him.

Some calm was wanted here. "What do you hope to achieve with that thing?"

"Sanity," she said. "You're destroying my home."

"But I found the priest hole."

"Bollocks."

"I mean it. There's a cut in the carpet where the stair can be raised."

"I don't believe you."

"Come and see."

A frown showed she was interested even though she didn't move.

He set out the facts in a way meant to intrigue her. "Your father had a secret. Agreed? We spoke of this, didn't we? I think he always knew about the priest hole. He laid the carpet to cover it up."

She tried to appear indifferent without realising she had lowered the sickle a small way.

"He thought up some way of locking the loose stair. I haven't been able to shift it yet."

She continued to stare at him, eyes widening.

His words were making an impact, so he talked on. "Dombey appears to have found the way in. Seems he was using his phone as a flashlight and dropped it in there."

She found her voice and used it to belittle him. "If Bert got in so easily, what does that say about you?"

He was tempted to point out that in the two years she'd lived here, she hadn't even found the stair, but you don't taunt someone holding a weapon that can slice you up.

"Believe me, Claudia, I'm trying to help." All the time he watched that blade. Here on the stairs, he couldn't dodge out of range. "Who knows what may be inside? Anything we find is yours if it hasn't been taken already."

The hostility remained. "You're obviously hopeless at this. I'll find someone who knows how these things were made."

"That could be a mistake," he said, wishing he didn't sound so much like a prissy lawyer. "It's your father's secret and he guarded it from everyone. There must have been good reason."

"If you think I'm going to let you sledgehammer your way in, you're mistaken. Face it, Mr. Dee, you're out of ideas."

Nobody spoke to Diamond like that with the exception of his boss, Georgina. Pride was at stake now. He dug deep for inspiration. "If you'll allow me to pass, there's one last thing I'd like to try."

"Without more damage?"

"If this doesn't work I'll leave you in peace."

For all her resistance, she was as eager as he to solve this mystery. She stood back with the sickle so loose in her hand he could have snatched it away. He walked across to the panel below the second flight. If he was right, the priest hole was behind it.

He'd already concluded that the surface was impenetrable,

constructed from a slice of oak sawn from a tree trunk so large it must already have been centuries old when it was felled.

The carving formed the centrepiece of a design that elevated the entire staircase to a work of art. Grassy slopes, hedges, grazing sheep, a distant church spire, birds in flight across a clouded sky, all chiselled by a master in the dark stained wood. Oak is hard to work, but wonderfully durable.

His attention was above eye level, on the stringer, the sloping strip like a skirting board that hid the side view of the stairs. Nothing was visible of the carpenter's work. The underpart was hidden behind the carver's art, a strip running the length of the flight of stairs and carved with a pattern of hundreds of birds flying in formation, starlings, probably, performing their evening show, swooping and soaring in their mass celebration of twilight.

He ran the tips of his fingers over the part he could reach.

"What are you doing?"

"Nothing destructive."

The wood was as black as ebony and carved so finely that touch was more use than his other senses. He might as well have been blind. Pity he didn't have Julie with him.

"Do you want a chair to stand on?" The offer surprised him. He didn't think Claudia's hostility had drained away.

"A torch would be more helpful. I can reach, but I can hardly see."

"Use your fucking phone."

Stupid. He'd talked about Dombey using the flashlight and forgotten he could do the same himself.

The beam picked out more detail. The carver's artistry was revealed, the way thousands of starlings had been suggested when in fact only a few were fully formed by the cuts. Imagination filled in the rest from dense areas of unworked wood depicting the swirling mass. So clever. All done by autosuggestion. It takes an artist of genius to guide the perception of the person viewing the image.

But he hadn't found what he was looking for. It was never going to be obvious. He continued to examine the surface.

Claudia said, "Getting anywhere?"

Without turning his head, he said, "I might if you put down the scythe you're holding. It worries me."

"It's a sickle." There was no sound of her doing as he asked.

Then the tip of his second finger found a slight difference in texture in one of the unworked areas representing the dense mass of starlings. A patch about the shape and size of a ten-pence coin. He had run his hand over it several times already without feeling it there. The difference wasn't apparent to the naked eye, even under the flashlight. He scraped with his fingernail to locate an edge.

Perfectly round.

His first thought was that someone had repaired the wood by filling a knot-hole. Whatever the addition was, it was sited with undoubted skill flush with the surface.

He turned to Claudia. "I need a knife again."

"Oh, yes?" she said on a rising note laced with sarcasm. The curved blade of the sickle was high in front of her again, a giant question mark casting doubt on her innocence, his ability to handle the challenge and the worth or uselessness of this new discovery.

"I'm not asking you to fetch the damned knife. I'm telling you I'm making a move to fetch one off the wall."

She didn't budge.

"Look, have I threatened you at any stage? We're on the same team. I need something sharper and harder than my fingernail."

She still barred the way to the wall with its array of potential weapons, so he took a step towards her, palms upwards. "You want to get into the priest hole, right?"

No answer.

"This is your chance."

Finally she saw sense, swayed a little, lowered the weapon and took the two steps backwards that allowed him to pass her.

He unclipped a small bone-handled knife that might have been for pruning. Careful to point the blade downwards and show no threat, he crossed in front of her again and reached up. As far as he could tell, the imperfection he'd found was level with the stair he'd uncovered.

He worked at the edge, testing for movement until a flake of something dropped on the back of his hand. Varnish. Over the centuries, many coats must have been applied. No harm done to the carving, he told himself. Then the point of the blade nudged something harder than wood. He twisted the knife and prised out the round metal head. He gripped it between thumb and forefinger and pulled. It came out with surprising ease.

A steel skewer about nine inches long that he held up for Claudia to see.

"A hole is drilled right through the carving and into the stair. Neatly done. Locks it completely."

She took the skewer from him for a closer look. "It doesn't look old."

"I don't suppose it is. Your father will have installed it for extra security. He didn't want his secret discovered by some berk like me simply lifting the loose stair. Shall we go up and see what's in there?"

20

B EFORE ANYTHING ELSE, Diamond collected the pincers and clipped them back in position on the wall along with the knives he'd used. This wasn't just about housekeeping. Claudia was left in no doubt that handing over her weapon was a precondition to lifting the lid on her father's hiding place. She handed him the sickle and he fastened it in place.

At the foot of the stairs he gestured to her to go first, more for self-protection than acting the gentleman.

"It's the one with the strip of carpet hanging loose," he told her.

"Stop fussing."

She was calmer than he expected. He'd got her down as a volatile personality, yet here was a family secret about to be revealed after years of searching and she was in no hurry. Perhaps she didn't want her excitement showing. Or she was nervous of what she would find.

Or she already knew.

Slowly, with a sense of ceremony, she folded back the carpet and uncovered the stair. Tucked her fingertips under the tread and lifted. There wasn't even a rasp of wood on wood as two stairs came up together and revealed a cavity big enough to climb into and about five feet in depth, as safe a hideout as any persecuted priest could have hoped to find.

Diamond used the flashlight again.

It should have been a moment of triumph. It was not.

The light showed them what was deep inside: the blood-covered corpse of Bert Dombey.

"Oh my god!"

Claudia straightened her fingers. The stairs slammed shut. She reached for the stair rail and steadied herself.

Diamond froze. Like any other detective on a case, he routinely thought ahead, inventing scenarios, trying to predict outcomes. You don't ever want to be unprepared. This one had caught him so far off guard that he deserved to be shot at dawn. It changed everything.

"You okay?" he asked Claudia. The macho man-in-control was hiding his own turmoil. "Want to sit down?"

"I'll be all right."

"We have to report this."

"Now?"

"It's a crime scene."

He knew what was going through her head. This couldn't be worse for a convict fresh out of jail on licence.

He was about to say he could give her an alibi but he stopped himself in time. He'd only met her after the supper was over, and Dombey's van had been parked in the tractor shed all the time. There was no certainty how many hours the body had been here. "I'm going to take another look. You may want to turn away."

She nodded. "I saw enough. I need a strong drink."

"Easy on the intake, then. It's going to be a long night."

His own part in this would take some explaining to the police, poking his nose into a case that was supposedly done and dusted and telling no one he was a serving officer. They would soon discover he had teamed up with the man who was now the corpse.

He waited for Claudia to vanish downstairs for her drink before lifting the lid on Dombey's body. Another breach of protocol. He should have dialled 999 already. The case wasn't his baby now. It was a major incident. But he'd never been a slave to the rules. He wanted to be forearmed with some idea how this might have happened.

First impression, unscientific, melodramatic and horribly real. The eyes, bulging in death, glared at him and gave it to him straight: *Fuck you, Dee. I was no psychopath. I was an innocent man you pursued and harassed when you should have been on the trail of the real killer. This look I'm giving you will haunt you for the rest of your wretched life.*

Second, more professional impression: the body lay face up in a cavity built into the well of the staircase, arched over a stack of filled plastic sacks. There were no visible wounds but there was bleeding. He'd been cut for sure. Whether stabbed, slashed or beaten was not obvious. Nor was it possible to tell if the killing had taken place inside the priest hole or whether the body had been dumped there after death. It was wearing another of the notorious T-shirts, black with white lettering, the letters streaked with blood. A final rebuke from a troubled soul: PISS OFF I DON'T WANT TO KNOW.

Third: the space was bigger than he expected and clearly used for storage. Some of the bags had been ripped open, the contents exposed. Photos, mostly large, some spattered with blood. Sheets of thick paper probably used for art. Canvases. Almost certainly Howard Priest's effects.

I guessed right about that, he thought, needing to console himself. Wrong about everything else but right on one thing.

There was enough here to keep a scene-of-crime team busy for the next week and more. He was careful to avoid touching anything, knowing he was implicated more than enough already with his prints all over the staircase.

He left the priest hole open and joined Claudia downstairs. She was in the kitchen with a bottle and glass on the table in front of her. Brandy, going by the bottle shape.

"Go easy on that. You want to keep a clear head."

"My house. My drink. I'll do as I want, thanks." The shock hadn't mellowed her.

He picked up the phone and got through.

"They'll send a patrol car first," he told Claudia after he'd made the call. "The people who ask the tough questions come later."

"You're not telling me anything I don't know." She poured herself more brandy.

He drew a long breath, deciding how to word his next statement. "Here's something you don't know. I'm a serving police officer myself."

Her lower lip jutted out so far he could have played hoopla with it.

He wasn't put off. Now was a better time to explain his presence than when the place would be swarming with police. "I'm off duty, right? You'll have to believe me on that. I'm visiting Julie, like I said, and she wanted my opinion on your case, which I knew nothing about. I'm a guest here, a private person."

"A fucking undercover cop." She spat out the charge.

"I wouldn't call it that."

"I would."

"People get uncomfortable when a policeman is around, so I didn't announce myself, that's all. If I was a prison guard, I wouldn't go out of my way to tell you."

"You wouldn't fucking need to. I'd know."

She might not have meant to be amusing, but he grinned. "A tax inspector, then. I'm not here because of my job. There's no agenda."

"That's horseshit. You put yourself about like a wasp at a picnic." She was definitely taking pleasure in smacking him down.

"Better to be sociable than sneaky, isn't it?"

"Do the filth know who you are?"

He hated that expression but he let it go by. "I just gave my name on the phone." Cue another admission. She had to be told. "It isn't Dee, by the way. I'm Peter Diamond."

She rolled her eyes in disbelief. "That's not sneaky, then? Going under a false name?"

"It was possible some of your friends from Bath would have heard of me. Like I just said, I prefer to be anonymous."

"You'll have to front up when the law gets here."

"That's why I'm telling you now, so it doesn't come as a shock."

"It will take some believing when they see your cowboy suit." Some of the disgust went out of her eyes as she relished the prospect.

"God, yes. I keep forgetting what I look like."

"They know me anyway," she said. "They wanted me banged up for ten years. This time they'll make sure."

"Want my advice? Be honest with them," he said. "Tell it straight."

"Coming from you, that's rich." She reached for the bottle again.

He couldn't go on warning her to stay sober. She'd lost all respect for him anyway. These minutes of waiting for the wail of the patrol car had to be used profitably. "Who do you think did it?"

"Some evil bugger with a massive grudge." She was starting to slur her words but there was sense behind them.

"Someone who knew him well?"

"I'm not naming anyone." She shut her mouth and glared.

Collapse of conversation. Diamond had to give it CPR. "Bert wasn't all that well known in the village."

No response. More work was needed.

"The only reason for any of the locals to hate him is that he was one of your crowd who treated the place as a nightclub. Scarcely enough to justify killing him."

She rose to that. Couldn't resist. "There haven't been any parties since I was banged up."

"Okay. If it isn't one of the locals, who is it?"

She was just about sober enough to duck that one. "How would I know? I've been out of it for two years."

"Must be someone who was here tonight," Diamond continued to press her, keen to extract something new before she was taken into custody again. "Someone confident of coming in here. Your friends from Bath know the inside of this house better than any of the villagers."

"You think so?" She yawned the long vocal yawn of a few drinks too many.

"I'm certain. It's not looking good for Fab and Harvey. What time did they arrive tonight?"

"How would I know?"

"They could have told you."

"We had better things to talk about."

"You were late getting here, you told me. You had to get dressed in a hurry. They could have been here and carried out the murder before you arrived. Let's not forget Hertzog's partner Elaine as well."

"She's a nobody."

"Not from what I saw," Diamond said. "She runs that hotel. Hertzog is a good talker, but she's the boss."

"It sounds to me like you know them."

"Visited, that's all. I had a day in Bath and looked them up."

She squinted at him through her alcoholic haze. "What the fuck for?"

"He was one of the three who played your garter game. I wanted his account of it."

He'd given her something else to hammer him with. "So you drove all the fucking way to Bath to meet him? And you expect me to believe you're not here because of your job? I wasn't born yesterday."

"I didn't say I wasn't interested in what happened the night Roger Miller was killed. I'm extremely interested. Three played the game and two are dead now. Has that crossed your mind?"

"Not until you said it."

"Hertzog had better watch out."

"Are you going to warn him?"

"I won't get the chance. They'll be well on their way to Bath by now, and they'll be questioned tomorrow. Nasty surprise when they ask what it's about . . . or maybe no surprise at all."

She yawned again. She was losing interest. "I'm tired. How long will the heavy mob be?"

"Depends where they were when they got the shout. They won't hang about."

"Can't keep my eyes open."

"A strong coffee would be better than the stuff you're drinking. Want me to put the kettle on?"

"Shoot yourself," was what Diamond heard. With the slurring, it could have been "Suit yourself." For all the insults she had slung at him, she seemed to understand that they were in the same sinking boat. At least they were still talking. Each of them viewed the other with a mixture of resignation and suspicion.

He got up and filled the kettle. "There's something I wanted to ask you. You were trying to think of the artist your uncle idolised. Was it Sickert?"

"All right, clever clogs, how do you know that?"

"He's about the only artist I've heard of, and I only know about him because some people think he was Jack the Ripper."

"Load of codswallop."

"That disposes of that, then."

"There's no need for sarcasm. People have milked that rumour since before I was born. For fifty years, nobody bothered to check where Sickert was when the murders happened. He was in France, for fuck's sake, on a family holiday in Normandy. There are letters to prove it."

"I'll take your word for that."

"You don't have to. You can read it in black and white. His life story is in the front room with a load of other Sickert stuff. My uncle knew more about Sickert than anyone alive. He had books piled shoulder-high and Daddy brought them here to sit on a shelf with his own fascinating collection on tractor maintenance and how to improve your wheat crop. No one can say we're not cultured."

IT WAS AFTER midnight and they were on a second coffee when the police hammered on the front door. Two constables, male and female, unbelievably young, in heavy-duty, flame-retardant, high-visibility tactical body armour bristling with pouches containing radios, batons, torches, first-aid kits, power banks, evidence bags, CS sprays, handcuffs and probably a banana each to give them the energy to stand up. One also had a submachine gun.

What followed would have been risible in any circumstances. Diamond, under strong protest, being made to stand at gunpoint with his palms flat to the wall while his holster was searched. Claudia laughing so much that she fell off her chair and had to be helped up. The constables suspecting they had been brought here on a nuisance call from two well-tanked jokers at a party.

After Diamond was allowed to produce his warrant card and order was restored, he took the officers upstairs for a sight of the body and suggested they radioed headquarters. Some tiresome to and fro of information followed before he got to speak to Jack Crandley, Taunton's senior detective, who had joined the voices. He outranked Crandley and they knew each other's names but they had never worked together.

"I'm confused," Crandley said. "Tell me this is real."

"It's happening now. We're at the Baskerville farmhouse with the body of a man called Bert Dombey."

"How come you're already there?"

"Long story. You'd better get here sharpish."

"But if you're in charge—"

"I'm not. I happen to be staying in the village. You'll need a statement from me because I found the body and made the call."

"Have you sealed the scene?"

"Are you listening, Jack? I'm not in charge. You are."

BY THE TIME Crandley arrived, Claudia was asleep on a sofa in one of the sitting rooms and Diamond was relying on caffeine to help him ignore what time it was. The young constables had made the right calls. There was police tape across the stairs, a doctor was on his way and so was a crime scene team.

Memory can be unreliable, but Diamond believed this was his first meeting with Crandley. When he saw the man, he knew he was right. In police canteen parlance, he was knee-high to a grasshopper. Back in the last century, when Diamond had joined the Met, everyone was his own height or taller. Male recruits had to be at least five-ten and females five-four. The rule had been steadily eroded in the 1990s to keep up numbers.

"Sorry if I sounded confused when we spoke," Crandley said. "I was in bed."

"Getting an early night?"

"Trying to."

"Isn't that always the way?" Diamond said wearily, thinking something less sympathetic.

"But my head is screwed on now." As if to demonstrate, the inspector turned it through as much of its axis as his neck muscles could manage. "Where is she?" This was a man in a hurry.

"You mean Miss Priest? Taking a nap, as far as I know."

"Gone to bed?" he piped in surprise.

"Bed is unlikely. No one can use the stairs. When I last saw her, she was heading for a sofa."

"You let her out of your sight?" Crandley had difficulty containing himself.

"It's her house."

"That's beside the point. She could be on the run by now."

The carping annoyed Diamond. He wasn't used to taking stick from someone of Crandley's rank. "She's in no state to run anywhere. She took brandy for the shock, far too much of it. Do you want to view the body?"

"I'd rather view Claudia Priest."

"There are three large sitting rooms off the hall."

Crandley flapped his hands at the two constables and they went off to check. "I know this place. I was here a couple of years ago when she was done for manslaughter. Hadn't heard the bitch is out on licence until I checked on the way here. Another parole board cock-up. At liberty less than a week and now this. Who discovered the body?"

"I told you on the phone. I did," Diamond said and added, for balance, "with help from Claudia." There had been more resistance than help, but he didn't like the rush to judgement she was getting.

Crandley snorted in disbelief. "Help or hindrance?"

"She didn't interfere."

"How did you know about the priest hole? I bet she didn't tell you."

"Old house, old enough to have one. Bert Dombey—the victim—hadn't been seen for a long time, so I called his phone and we heard it ringing under the stairs."

"Cool. Who heard it first?"

"We both did."

The woman constable returned. "A red-haired lady is asleep in the front room, sir."

Crandley's look was a mixture of relief that Claudia was still in the house and pique that he was wrong. "Get back in there and use your cuffs if she resists."

"Don't you want to see the body?" Diamond said.

Crandley must have sensed by now that his certainty of Claudia's guilt wasn't shared. As they crossed the hall, he said, "Only one person could have known the existence of this priest hole and she's the owner of the house."

"She claims she didn't," Diamond said.

"She grew up here. She owns the place. Of course she bloody knew."

All this certainty was getting under Diamond's skin. "I spent time with her in a search and she seemed as keen as I was to find it. I don't believe she was play-acting."

"Trust me, she's devious. I've seen a heck of a lot more of her than you have."

"But you're wrong to say nobody else knew about the priest hole."

"How come?"

"There's Dombey, for one."

Crandley took that in slowly.

Diamond said. "How else did he get in there?"

The inspector was unimpressed. "She killed him and dumped the body inside. I wouldn't put anything past her."

"When you see the corpse you may have a different opinion."

The tension between the two was high—which was more than could be said for Crandley. He needed to go one stair higher than Diamond to see inside.

He peered in. "What a dog's breakfast."

"Fair comment."

"Have you been in?"

Now it was Diamond's turn to unload his scorn. "I may look an idiot dressed like this, but I know better than to disturb a crime scene."

"Someone needs to verify death."

"A doctor, not you or me. That's organised. Anyway, it's obvious he's dead. Bloody obvious, in fact."

Crandley eyed the state of the victim. "Can't argue with that."

"That's my point. The violence appears to have happened in there and not outside. He's cut in several places. If someone dragged him upstairs or down, there would be blood evidence."

Crandley pointed to the stains on the nearest stair.

"I saw that," Diamond said. "If you look closely there's a spatter pattern and the direction is outwards from the priest hole. Looks to me as if it was made in the course of the attack or just after. It's dry, by the way."

"Is there blood on her clothes?"

"She changed," Diamond said. "She was in fancy dress earlier, like me." He regretted the words as soon as they were out of his mouth.

Crandley gave a superior smile. "And disposed of her bloodstained garments already, no doubt."

"I expect they're in her room upstairs."

"Which we can't reach." Crandley appeared to give the matter some thought, which had to be an improvement. "You may be right about the murder being done right here below us. If Dombey got wind of something valuable hidden here and was smart enough to find the secret entrance, he would have been inside, head and shoulders visible, an easy target for anyone armed with a knife or a cutting implement. She would be spoilt for choice between what's in the kitchen and all over the walls in the hall."

"She—or anyone else."

"Huh," Crandley said with a sneer. "She's worked on you, has she? The same thing happened two years ago. It really got to me. People who should have spoken out were silent. She had four months after the killing to soften up the witnesses." He continued between gritted teeth, "There's no way she can wriggle out of this one. This is murder."

"It's your case, not mine," Diamond said, "but I advise you to hold fire until you've questioned everyone."

"I'll do it my way, thanks." He drew back from the priest hole and turned to go downstairs. "You and I both know how long the CSI nitpickers take, however straightforward the evidence is. This one will keep them interested for weeks. I'm not giving her the chance to consult with her clever friends and concoct an alibi."

"Are you taking her into custody?"

"You bet I am. She's on licence and a danger to the public. She can spend the rest of tonight in a police cell and I'll question her tomorrow when she's sober and I've caught up on my sleep."

Not much more could be said. "A danger to the public" was the crucial wording. Diamond knew it was written into the law. Whether Claudia was really a danger was a matter of opinion, but Crandley was the SIO with the right to conduct the case as he chose. His call. He would confer later—after getting his beauty sleep—with the probation officer and the parole board. Diamond couldn't pull rank. Any influence he had was over now this was an official enquiry.

The next few minutes would haunt him for days to come. Just as the scene-of-crime team arrived at the farmhouse, Claudia was taken out, handcuffed, struggling and needing both officers to restrain her. And it wasn't Crandley who bore the brunt of her anger. She turned her face to Diamond and yelled, "Arsewipe, giving me that crap about being on my side when all the time you were a fucking undercover cop. Like an idiot I believed you, all the lies about coming here as Julie's guest. You're a fucking two-timing, scum-sucking snitch. Everything you say is crap. You're lower than the dogshit on my shoe. I hope you burn in hell."

21

AT BREAKFAST, HE told the story of the previous evening, glossing over Claudia's language at the end by saying she'd given him a "right mouthful."

"And that hurt," Paloma said.

"A bit."

"A lot. I see it in your eyes."

"I can take a putdown. The reason I feel gutted is that I'm out of it now. It's an official investigation."

"You'll have to make a statement, won't you?"

"Done. I sat at the kitchen table with some gormless DC after Crandley had left with Claudia. It was a late night." He looked at Julie, who was biting her lip, holding back her emotions. She'd always believed Claudia was more of a victim than a perpetrator.

With an effort to be professional, she said, "You couldn't have tried harder, guv."

"But with no result. She's back at square one, in custody with the same blinkered detective in charge, except the rap will be murder this time."

"Will it stick?"

"It doesn't look good. Dombey had sniffed money and

needed some badly. If Claudia caught him red-handed in the priest hole, she may well have attacked him."

"When would this have happened?" Paloma asked.

"When she arrived at the farmhouse yesterday. She could easily have lied about getting there late."

"Before you were there?"

"Before any of us were there."

"Is that likely?"

He hesitated.

"Will the charge stick? That's what Julie asked," Paloma pressed him.

On edge, feeling the pressure, he said testily, "I'm trying to answer." More seconds ticked by. "The motive is there. The opportunity. And the means—all those farm tools. I can't argue with any of that. She's hot-tempered and she has a police record. She's right in the frame. I can't fault Crandley." He tapped his fingers against his chin. "And yet I'm not fully persuaded."

"Why not?"

"It's hard to judge anybody the day you first meet them, but I got the impression she's living with a massive secret, so big that she was willing to spend time in prison to preserve it. She asked me straight out if I believed she was guilty of manslaughter. Pressed me hard."

"How did you answer?"

"Wriggled out with difficulty. I honestly hadn't made up my mind. I disappointed her. She seemed to hope I'd discovered someone else was responsible for Roger Miller's death. She seems as keen as we are to find out what happened that night."

"If that's right, she's innocent."

"Yes—if I haven't misjudged her."

"And is the big secret out in the open now? Was it the priest hole? How did she react when you started the search?"

"Cool, surprisingly cool. She kept a tight hold on her emotions. But we'd both heard Dombey's phone ringing. Even when I found the cut in the carpet she stayed downstairs. When I couldn't get the damned stair open and wanted to use a sledgehammer, she was horrified. She told me to leave. She said she'd get an expert in next day."

"It's a listed house. That sounds reasonable enough."

"It wasn't all reasonable. At one point she threatened me with a sickle. But by then I wasn't giving up for anybody. I looked for another way to unfasten the dodgy stair. Finally, I found the skewer in the carving at the side of the staircase and pulled it out."

"What did she say to that?"

"Not much. I was dry-mouthed and I feel sure she was as well. I insisted she lifted the stair herself to see inside."

"And then?"

"Shock, horror. We saw the body and she let go and the stairs slammed shut."

"Do you think she already knew what was in there?"

"I was too shocked to notice. It's not surprising she didn't want a second look. She made no objection when I called the police."

Paloma said, "I can understand her feelings. Look at it from her point of view, Pete. You're a stranger who appears out of the blue wanting to root out her family secret, which could well be something illegal. She's in a bind because she needs your help. She's searched for years and found nothing. But can she trust you? I wouldn't."

"Aw, thanks!"

"If she is a killer, you're lucky to have got out alive. Dombey didn't."

"I must take some blame for egging Dombey on. If I hadn't got him involved in decorating the church, he might not have heard about the supper."

"He would have found out, regardless of you," Paloma said. "Don't beat yourself up, Pete. Nothing you said or did made anything worse."

"Come on," he said. "If we're honest, things are a lot worse now."

"Not because of you. Chill, it's out of your hands."

"I get that. Don't rub it in."

"Look on the bright side. Some positives came out of yesterday. You earned respect with the locals by delivering a calf and driving a tractor. You danced a St. Bernard's waltz."

"Got a new suit," Julie added.

"He's wearing it," Paloma told her. "Dapper, but I quite liked him as a cowboy." Then she surprised Diamond. "And you won the star prize in the raffle."

He blinked. "The first I've heard of that."

"Didn't we tell you we bought you a ticket? The numbers were drawn while you were out of the room. A magnificent pumpkin too big for Julie or me to bring back."

He raised a smile. "You're having me on."

"We're not."

He knew the serious tone in Paloma's voice. This was no joke. The Somerset giants were having sport with him. His lower back contracted. There was a danger of going into spasm. "I'm not lifting one of those monsters again—ever."

"We thought you'd say that, so we arranged for Hamish to bring it over in a wheelbarrow. He'll do the lifting."

"Tell him not to bother."

"We can't offend the whole village."

"Watch me when he brings it." The mention of Hamish

triggered something in his tired brain. He'd almost forgotten Hamish existed. "Where was he last night?"

"Helping Dolores at the bar," Julie said. "He brought me a lemonade."

"I didn't see him after, did you?" He flushed as soon as he spoke the words. Another blindness gaffe. "Sorry. Wasn't thinking. I was going to ask what use a pumpkin is."

"Don't start me off, guv. Pumpkin soup, pumpkin puree, pumpkin pie, roast pumpkin—"

"All right, all right."

"The seeds are full of nutrients and you can make a planter out of the husk."

Paloma was laughing. "That's next weekend looked after."

"Every weekend for months to come."

Paloma sensed that he'd suffered enough. "So we can all have a quiet day and make the most of being in the country. Did you get any sleep at all on the sofa?"

"I would have slept on the floor if necessary. I was done for. Raffles may have lost some sleep. There wasn't room for the two of us. Where is he?"

"Curled up in Bella's basket."

"See? I cause trouble wherever I go. Where's Bella?"

"On the sofa," Julie said. "I don't know where she spent the night."

He said a morning walk would revive him. He felt hungover despite not finishing a drink all evening. The ladies were sympathetic.

THE ENTIRE VILLAGE seemed to have a hangover. Large black birds he couldn't name were strutting the street, pecking at dried cow dung, reluctant to take flight even when he got near. His steps took him past the shop and the pub. The scene-of-crime van was parked in the farmhouse yard and a figure in a hooded forensic suit was putting something in the back.

"Keep out, Diamond," he thought. "It's case closed for you. You're lucky to have played private eye for almost a week. If you have any sense at all and value your real job, you'll count your blessings and think of other things like Bath Central and the team you hold dear."

Most good intentions are short-lived. This one was measured in seconds. "How's it going in there?"

"Long job," the SOCO said.

"Has a pathologist been by?"

"Last night."

"Any conclusions?"

He was given a hard stare. "Who are you, exactly?"

What could he say to a question like that? The village busybody?

This called for candour. He dug his warrant card from his pocket and showed it. There was no reason why this guy shouldn't know the truth. He admitted he wasn't the SIO. DI Crandley was busy at Taunton nick interviewing a suspect. He didn't say he was on the team, but it was implied and believed. Perhaps the new suit swung it.

SOCOs aren't usually talkative. This one was a rare exception. "They don't like giving much away before the autopsy, as you know, but there are deep cuts to the upper body as if he was stabbed. At least one of them must have got the heart. The right hand has a defensive wound, so it's clear he was attacked."

"While he was inside the priest hole?"

"For sure. The angle of the cuts tells the story. He would have been trapped in there four feet lower than his killer, with uneven footing, really vulnerable."

"Approximate time of death?"

"I'm glad you say approximate. The medic said sometime between late morning and early evening."

"Has the body been removed yet?"

"First thing this morning. Gives us a chance to get at what was underneath. It's surprising how big the space is. There's a hidden part you can't see from the opening. It's been used to store art materials, enough to open a shop. Canvases, sketchbooks, rolls and stacks of paper, frames, brushes, tubes of paint. A nightmare, frankly, because everything has to be listed and recorded and a lot of it was trampled on during the attack."

"Have you found the weapon?"

"Not yet. It's a right mess in there."

"A knife, I suppose."

"We don't know yet. Some of the cuts appeared to be in pairs and in alignment, as if it was a double-bladed weapon."

"Strange. Like scissors?"

"We're trained not to guess. The post-mortem should reveal more. They'll measure everything."

"Has anyone checked the farm tools hanging in the hallway?" Diamond asked.

"We're concentrating on the priest hole."

"What's going on right now?"

"We're removing the top layer, everything that might have traces of blood or anything else, and that's a painstaking process. Each item is listed, photographed, videoed and marked on a diagram before we lift it, and the lifting is a performance in itself, keeping every goddam sheet of paper horizontal before we bag it up and label it."

"May I see what you've brought out so far?"

"Look in the van if you want, but for Christ's sake don't touch anything." The SOCO swung the door wider and showed stacks of canvases in plastic covers, initialled and dated. "All of these are squared off with red lines. I wouldn't call them paintings."

"Squared off for copying?"

"I wouldn't know. I'm an evidence gatherer, not an artist."

A different bagged-up item caught Diamond's eye, a large black book with the word *Ledger* in faded gold lettering. "What's that for?"

"There were several like that in there. A record of his sales, by the look of it."

"Don't bank on it. If he's the artist I think he is, he never sold anything. Have you opened it?"

"God, no. We're just the dogsbodies. We don't do anything as technical as that. Someone in the lab might." He paused for thought. "If you know who the artist is, you'd better speak to my boss."

"I can if he's interested. You guys deal in certainties. I happen to know there was an artist in the family called Howard Priest, that's all. Shall I go in?"

"Why?"

"To tell your boss."

"Using your phone, I meant. We don't let anyone inside. Our number's on the side of the van."

The feeling of being an outsider hit him like an Arctic gale. "If I can't see him, I won't bother. What's the point, when I've spoken to you?"

The SOCO seemed to sense he'd caused offence. "I'm sure he'd like to hear it from you, sir."

Diamond looked into the van again. "That's all right, then. I see some spare bunny suits here. I'll grab one and step into it." He had ripped the plastic cover open before the guy uttered another word. He kept talking while tugging the forensic suit over his clothes. "This is meat and drink to me. I'm a crime scene regular. I know all about do-not-cross tape and I'll sign the security log if you're keeping one. I won't go anywhere near the stairs. There are a couple of helpful things I must say to your boss. I'll remind him about that farm tool collection. In fact, I can check it for him. I know what should be there." The over-shoes went on and he marched away from the bemused SOCO and straight into the farmhouse.

"WHERE DID YOU get these?" Paloma asked him.

He had dumped three hefty books on Julie's kitchen table. All were studies of Walter Sickert's life and work.

"The farmhouse. Claudia said I could borrow them."

"You were supposed to be going for a walk."

"I know. The door was open, so I popped in. Didn't interfere with the men in white overalls."

She shook her head slowly. "You've got to let go, Pete. It's out of your hands now." Her face had creased into what he could only think of as a *Goodbye, Mr. Chips* look. He could almost hear the violin.

"I need something to read, that's all."

She switched to the gentle mockery he knew and enjoyed. "Come off it, Lord Peter. You're just as involved as you ever were. Taunton Police won't appreciate you interfering. Isn't that true, Julie?"

Julie was pouring coffee. "Will somebody tell me what we're talking about?"

"Three books on Sickert, the artist," Diamond said. "There's a bookcase full of them in the farmhouse. They belonged to Howard, I was told—"

"—who was fixated on Sickert," Julie said, seamlessly taking over. "I can join the dots now. Mervyn hid How-ard's paintings in the priest hole and you think they were the secret source of all the money he spent modernising the farm, but it's a mystery because Howard never sold anything. Am I getting warm?"

"Extremely," Diamond said.

Paloma said, "I'm not with you on this. Mervyn was selling off Howard's pathetic paintings and claiming they were Sickerts? And people were taken in, people willing to part with big bucks? I can't believe that. Collectors aren't so easily fooled, you know. They look for provenance, a record of ownership going right back to the artist. It doesn't wash, Pete."

"I hear you," he said. "How the money was made is a mystery in itself."

"With no connection to Howard."

"Except for one thing." He felt in his pocket and took out the ballpoint that had come with the suit. "Remember this?"

"Of course I do. It dropped out of your pocket when you took out some keys. What was the name on the side?" She read it aloud again. "Caer Badon Fine Art. We thought it was Welsh."

"Actually an ancient name for Bath."

She frowned. "All right. Not many people know that, but how does it help?"

"I showed it to Claudia and she knew straight away where it came from. It's company merchandise. Roger Miller's company."

"The man in the silo?"

"Buying and selling pictures was his job. He lived in Bath, isn't that right, Julie? You told us this the day we arrived here."

Julie nodded. "Bennett Street."

"*Comprenez?*" Diamond said to them both. "This pen is proof of the link to Mervyn. He and Roger Miller were doing business while Mervyn was alive, long before Claudia came to live here."

"Neat," Paloma said with a touch of admiration. "You're on the ball, Peter Diamond. I would never have made the connection myself. But . . ."

He waited for the follow-up.

When it came, she was deferential. ". . . is there any way of proving Mervyn was selling Howard's paintings to Miller?"

"For big money," Julie added.

"Passing them off as original Sickerts," Paloma said.

"If that was really the scam," Diamond said, "it's unlikely there are bank records of large sums changing hands. They would have covered their tracks. Miller may have paid for the farm machinery himself instead of making direct payments."

Julie carried the tray of coffee to the table. "I find it hard to believe Mervyn was into something like this. Everyone here looked up to him as the soul of honesty."

"When did he start spending money on a big scale?" Diamond asked. "Was it after Howard died in 1993?"

Julie laughed. "Over thirty years ago. It was long before I got here. I was a rookie DC working with you, guv. You'll have to ask someone who was here at the time, like the Douglases."

"Good idea."

Paloma placed her hand on the books. "So how do these come into it? You'll never have time to read them."

"I flicked through the illustrations. I know damn all about Sickert apart from the daft Jack the Ripper theory, but his pictures tell you a lot. He was into everything from famous people like kings and prime ministers to down-and-outs and working girls. He painted fashionable places like Venice and Paris. Music halls, theatres, churches. News stories of the time like Amelia Earhart's aeroplane flight and a notorious murder."

"I thought you just dismissed the Jack the Ripper stuff."

"I did. This was another case, twenty years after, paintings of a nude on a bed with a clothed man beside her said to be inspired by a murder in Camden Town. I've heard of it myself, so it must have been big at the time."

"Does it matter?"

"I'd like to know whether Howard's stuff is remotely similar."

"I thought he painted street scenes."

"From all I've heard, he was willing to try anything Sickert did."

"Are you going to tell Inspector Crandley?"

"I'm not muscling in on the murder enquiry. They have more on their minds than Mervyn Priest."

"But what if you can prove that Miller was killed because of his dealings with Mervyn?"

He spread his hands. "Miller's death is another case. Crandley has moved on."

22

THEY WERE HAVING a sandwich lunch when there was a knock at the door. Julie insisted on going herself.

Her two guests heard a familiar adolescent croak. "Give us yer car key."

Diamond was at Julie's side immediately.

Hamish had arrived. A huge wheelbarrow stood in the road behind their car. It had to be huge because it was loaded with a pumpkin big enough to house Cinderella, Prince Charming and the ugly sisters.

"Christopher Columbus! That thing can't fit in my car."

"It's for you," Hamish said.

"Would your mother like it?"

"She don't want it. She grew the fucker."

"Do you know anyone else who would?" A damn fool question. Who in Baskerville would want a thing that size? Who in the world?

Then his desperation bred an inspiration. "Tell you what. Why don't we divide it up? Julie, have you got a handsaw?"

She looked puzzled. "I think so. In my broom cupboard. I've never used it."

"Should be sharp, then. Hamish will make short work of

this. He's the strong man of the village. We'll slice it up and offer it around the houses. Or, better still, leave it outside the shop for people to help themselves. And Hamish . . ."

There was a grunt.

"You get to pick the first slice. In fact, we can let you have as many slices as you want."

An ideal solution. The curse of the pumpkin would be shared and Hamish was the next recipient. The drooping jaw drooped lower and the eyes glazed over. The grouchy teenager thought he had completed his errand. He hadn't expected a new one.

"Come in and help, Hamish. We can't have a sightless lady feeling in her cupboard for a sharp saw."

Julie pointed to the broom cupboard door and Hamish, programmed to respond to orders, rummaged inside while Paloma collected a carving knife and a roll of tinfoil from the kitchen and took them outside. Resigned to this extra task, Hamish brought out the saw, tipped the pumpkin from the wheelbarrow with a thump like an earthquake and started systematically destroying it. The first cut would divide it in half and the second and third in quarters.

Diamond could see this would be hard work. Some vocal encouragement was wanted. "This young man is a credit to modern youth. Last night he was handing out drinks. Today, it will be pumpkin slices. His parents must be proud as punch. I wish you could see the muscles on him, Julie. You'd go all of a quiver. He won't stop until the job is done. The saw will go blunt before he runs out of energy."

The monster was bisected. The two halves tumbled apart.

Julie said, "Gorgeous smell."

The honeyed words were helping. Hamish paused, but only to tug off his shirt and display more of those muscles. He had heard the commentary.

Paloma had her phone out. "It says here that the scent of pumpkin is a sexual turn-on. Seriously. Some scientists in Chicago researched it. Don't ask me how, but it seems pumpkin has a direct pathway to the pleasure centres of the brain."

Diamond took over the baton. "We could bottle this and sell it for a fortune. After Hamish has finished, he'll reek of the stuff. It won't be safe for him to walk home without an escort."

Hamish had cut through one of the halves. He was sweating so much that his own aroma blocked out any erotic stimulation.

Diamond kept up the flattery. He was buttering up the sullen youth for some vital questions. "Look at all those beautiful seeds. They can have a piece of foil to themselves. We'll make a present of them to Hamish. They're full of nutrition, good for the skin, the hair, everything. Not that he needs much improvement. I'd call that hair lustrous, wouldn't you, ladies? Do you take anything for it, Hamish?"

There was a shake of the head. Hamish paused in the sawing and used his free hand to sweep the lustrous hair from his acne-studded brow.

"We should have thought of this last night," Diamond went on. "We could have left a large plate of slices near the bar. Ah well, they all got their drinks thanks to Hamish and his team." He moved smoothly into police interview mode. "Where did you get to after supper, Hamish? I don't remember seeing much of you then."

"Cleared the tables," Hamish said.

"For the dancing? Of course. And after that? I don't suppose you joined in. Too old-fashioned for a streetwise young guy like you. Where did you go? Not home for an early night, I'm sure."

"Hung about outside." Basking in all the good opinion, Hamish was talkative by his standards.

"Bit of a smoke and a chat, eh? I won't ask what else was being passed around. Tell me, did you go inside the farmhouse at any point in the evening?"

"What for?"

"That was going to be my next question."

Hamish ran his sweaty finger along the smooth edge of the saw. He didn't often make eye contact. "Stayed outside, didn't I?"

"Did you? I don't know. The reason I asked is you could have seen something and not realised how important it was. We all know why the police were called."

"Didn't see shit."

"Okay. How about earlier, before the supper started?"

"In the barn, wasn't I?" The way he turned statements into questions was a habit of speech, nothing notably suspicious.

"Getting your instructions, I expect. Who was in charge—your mother?"

"Dolores."

"The lady from the Feathers? I'm getting the picture now. I saw her myself pouring the drinks, a free glass of wine for everyone who bought a ticket. You waiters must have been there good and early. The party couldn't start without you. And you'd already done a day's work. Did you come straight from the milking?"

"Nah. Changed my clothes, didn't I?"

"What a hectic schedule. How did you manage to get the cows milked as well?"

"Dad dunnit."

"Jim did the milking? You weren't there?"

"I done the herding."

"Bringing them in from the field on your quad bike. Got you. What time was that?"

"Five."

"And then you went home and spruced up for the evening while your dad managed the milking. I saw him later when the dancing started."

Hamish seemed to decide that the questioning was over. He steadied the quarter of pumpkin with his left hand and started sawing again. Paloma was cutting each huge slice into smaller ones and stacking them on foil.

Diamond waited for a chance to start the questions again. The bouts of sawing weren't lasting so long now.

"Some time in the afternoon a white van arrived at the farm and was parked in the tractor shed. Did you see it, by any chance?"

Hamish was breathing heavily. He shook his head.

"Don't you park your quad bike with the tractors?"

"Nah."

"It's kept somewhere else?"

"Cowshed."

"I'm sure you would have noticed the van driver. He was wearing a white T-shirt."

Hamish said, "Piss off."

For a moment Diamond saw red. Then he understood and almost hugged the lad. "You saw the words on the shirt?"

The truth of this was so obvious to Hamish that he didn't dignify it with an answer.

"Splendid. This is the guy who was killed. Where did you see him?"

"Outside."

The goodwill was running out. "Where exactly?"

"Yard."

"Which part of the yard? This really matters, Hamish. Was it anywhere near the house?"

A leading question. It wouldn't have been allowed in court.

He got a nod.

"The front?"

"Nah."

"Round the side, then? I need your help here." But Diamond simultaneously asked himself whether it *did* matter precisely where Bert Dombey had been spotted. The point at issue was that Hamish had seen him. He must have been telling the truth because he had quoted the first two words from the T-shirt, which he wouldn't otherwise have known.

"Any idea what time this was?"

"Dunno."

"Yes, you do. Before milking?"

He was rewarded with a shrug. Not a totally indifferent shrug, but an admission that Diamond was right. The sighting must have been before the cows were milked.

"Which is when?"

"Five."

"But you had to collect the cows from the field, so it must have been quite a bit earlier. About four-thirty?"

Hamish pondered the matter. "Quarter past."

Hard work, but worth the effort.

Diamond allowed the sawing to resume. They were running out of foil and he had run out of questions.

"We're in danger of over-catering here," Paloma said.

She had half filled the wheelbarrow with wrapped slices, more than enough for everyone likely to call at the shop. Three-quarters of the pumpkin had not been used. The unused pieces stood on the verge like milestones.

"Let's go, then."

Hamish set off like a greyhound, bent on emptying his wheelbarrow and escaping.

Some way behind, Diamond, Paloma, Julie and Bella followed.

"What was all that about?" Paloma asked Diamond in a tone that signalled she already knew the answer.

"Dividing up the pumpkin?"

"Putting Hamish through the wringer."

He knew exactly what she was on about. He put the best spin he could on his answer, sounding as positive as if he'd discovered a new law of physics. "We now know Dombey arrived during the afternoon and didn't go into the farmhouse until four fifteen at the earliest."

Paloma wasn't having any of it. "Before Hamish appeared, you told us—I remember your exact words—'I'm not muscling in on the murder enquiry.'"

"I'm not. That's DI Crandley's baby. No way will I interfere."

"Oh yes? Questioning a witness? Checking on the murder victim's movements?"

"Taunton Police will get to the truth without help from me, or they should do. It may take longer, but I have every confidence."

"Admit it, Pete, you can't resist poking your nose in."

"When an opportunity like that presents itself, I can't," he said, and threw in a red herring. "I don't want to alarm you, but it's about self-defence."

"Self-defence?" Paloma stopped walking. "What on earth are you saying—that you're in danger?"

"Could be. You'd be surprised how often the person who reports the crime turns out to be the perpetrator. Crandley knows this as well as I do. Right now, Claudia is in the frame, but my fingerprints, footprints and DNA are all over the scene. She regards me as a snake in the grass. I let her believe I was rooting for her when all the time I was a cop. If she can shop me, she will."

"That's nuts."

"To you and me, maybe, but to Crandley, who needs desperately to get a result, I'm next in line after Claudia. He won't rule me out. Corrupt cops make all the headlines these days."

She was starting to look concerned and so was Julie. "Oh, Pete! You don't even have a motive."

"The motive they're working with is personal gain. You could pin that on an archbishop and it would stick. Shall we move on? Hamish will be out of sight."

They caught up with him outside the shop. It was sod's law that Miss Harrap was taking another turn as shop manager and came out to see what the fuss was about. Diamond expected fireworks. But when she spotted Paloma, one of her catering team, she couldn't have been more helpful. She sent Hamish to fetch two folding tables from inside.

"In the early days of the shop, we offered light refreshments out here during the summer months," she said. "That's why we still have the tables. If only there were more helpers, we'd do it now."

Diamond offered to unwrap a few slices so that people could see what was on offer, but Miss Harrap didn't agree. She said there were wasps about. Coming from the most waspish woman in Somerset, that was rich, Diamond thought.

She turned back to Paloma. "This is so generous of you."

Paloma pointed out that she hadn't won the pumpkin herself, but that didn't get through. All the goodwill was flowing her way, so she gave some back. "You're doing us a good turn, Maggie."

Diamond drew a sharp breath, unsure whether Paloma was on first-name terms. He'd won the right himself two days ago by going into raptures about the harvest loaf. He'd forgotten Paloma had become one of the inner circle.

"My dear, you put in such a good stint last night considering you're a visitor. And now this kindness. While you're arranging the slices, I'll find a large piece of card and a marker pen and make a notice."

When Miss Harrap was out of earshot, Diamond said, "I wasn't expecting this when she first came out. It's all down to you."

"Or the scent of the pumpkin," Paloma said. "She could be making a play for you."

"Hamish, more likely," he said.

But the flattery had worn thin. Hamish snapped the tables open, stood them in place and without much grace started heaping them with handfuls of the slices.

"Hold on," Diamond told him. "You heard the lady. These need arranging."

Hamish didn't even give him a look. As soon as he'd emptied the wheelbarrow, they wouldn't see him for dust.

"Anyhow, we don't need all of these. You can deliver some to Dolores for the pub."

"Fuck that," Hamish said. "Bull needs mucking out."

"Is that your job?"

"I'm late."

It was almost certainly true. Chummy needed attention and Chummy was the most valuable living creature in the village.

"Okay," Diamond said. "Leave the wheelbarrow with me and I'll return it when we're through."

Hamish was off.

Diamond called after him, "Thanks for the help. You're a star." It was doubtful whether he heard.

"Magnificent," he said to Maggie Harrap when she returned with the notice. The lettering was neat, even if the line along the bottom was not: *Donated by Paloma and friends.*

Visibly pleased, she propped the card on the nearest table.

This was a good moment to get serious. She could be a useful ally. "Did you know I was with Claudia last night when the body was found?"

She blinked, ambushed by the question. She knew, of course. Most of the village would know by now and nothing escaped the Miss Marple of Baskerville. Keen interest lit up her usually guarded face and she wanted to have this conversation, only on her own terms. After a pause for thought, she said, "Tell me more."

Clever. Three short words put him on the receiving end. Her hesitation was all he had got from surprising her and he wasn't sure how much to read into it. She had to be a suspect for Dombey's murder, a plausible suspect. She'd been in the farmhouse kitchen most of the afternoon and evening when the killing had taken place. The opportunity had been there. But would she reveal a motive? He'd heard nothing more damning from her than the annoyance everyone shared about the man.

Suspect or ally, she had never shown any sign of being as approachable as she was right now.

"We found him in a priest hole under the stairs," he said, trading information. "I knew he was here on the farm somewhere because I'd seen his van. He didn't own a posh car like the other weekenders. He was strapped for cash and he thought the answer to his problems was hidden in the farmhouse."

"You spoke about that once before and I didn't understand what you meant," she said and straightened her glasses as if seeing him more clearly would help.

"The source of Mervyn's wealth."

"What do you know about that?"

"Only what I hear from various people."

"You didn't hear it from me. Who gave you this idea?"

He wasn't going to name his sources. "It's self-evident, isn't it? State-of-the-art facilities in the dairy. A pedigree herd. All the posh farm machinery. The funding of your shop, come to that."

"The shop belongs to the community, not me, Mr. Dee."

"Mervyn was the controlling shareholder, isn't that right, Julie?" he called out.

Julie was helping Paloma arrange the pumpkin slices on one of the tables. "So I believe."

"And did Mr. Dombey find the pot of gold he was looking for?" Miss Harrap was living up to her reputation, asking the questions in the penetrating tone of St. Mary Mead's resident detective.

"If he did, it must have been stolen by his killer. All I saw in the priest hole were art materials. Mervyn used it as a store for his brother's old junk."

"Do you mean canvases?"

"Paint tubes and brushes. Sketchbooks. Photos of local scenes. A lot of it trampled on by Dombey."

She clicked her tongue as if the murdered man should have had the decency to die without damaging the artefacts.

He said, "You used the phrase 'a glory hole' the other day when you told me about Howard's house and that sprang to mind when I looked in." She didn't open up, so he added, "A godawful job for the crime scene people."

"No doubt."

"I was talking to one of them, trying to make order out of chaos. He let me look inside his van and it was such a contrast, everything neat and tidy. Actually, it wasn't just art stuff. They found some ledger books."

"Found what, did you say?" Her eyes widened.

"Ledger books, as in accountancy."

"Strange."

"I thought so," he said. "You told me he never sold any of his work, so they can't have been used to keep records."

"Did you look at them?"

"They won't let you touch anything. The one I saw in the van was wrapped and labelled. They may have found a bloodstain on it."

"And there were others in the priest hole?"

"So he said. It'll take days to get everything out."

She cleared her throat. "Is the, em, body . . . ?"

"Still there? No. That was the first thing they took. They'll do a postmortem and we may hear more."

"It's all very upsetting." She shook her head. Like Miss Marple, she contained her emotions mostly and they were revealed more in her face than her speech. "Did you speak to the inspector?"

"He spoke to me. He seems to have his mind made up."

"About Claudia?"

He nodded.

"Tell me, Mr. Dee, how did she react when you opened the stairs and found the body?"

"I think she was as shocked as I was, but I wasn't watching her. I was too startled to notice anything else."

"I can understand."

This was going well—up to a point. It had been all one way. She was assembling the facts as expertly as any detective in his team. "I do remember inviting her to lift the loose stairs for a first look and we both got one glimpse and she let go and it slammed shut."

"What happened next?"

"She said she needed a drink. I was left there alone. I opened it for a second look."

"She was downstairs by then?"

"In the kitchen drinking brandy."

"And didn't return?"

"I joined her presently and phoned the police."

"Did she act as if she knew all along what you were going to find?"

He continued to answer, but less freely. "I don't think so. She was horrified, like me." He said nothing about Claudia's tantrum in the kitchen when he'd admitted being a policeman. That was a secret known only to Claudia and the Taunton CID team. "The police arrived pretty soon and took over."

"How was Claudia when they took her away?"

"Angry would be an understatement. I don't like to think what they'll hear from her."

"She can't turn the blame on you."

"Oh, but she can. I was the one who found a way to open the priest hole and I invited her to lift the loose stairs and look. Without my encouragement, her fingerprints wouldn't be there."

"Unless they were there already," Miss Harrap said with a meaningful look. "What will you do next?"

"I'd better find out more in case I do become a suspect. I'm wondering whether you can point me in the right direction. I know you were busy with your team in the kitchen. I'd like to discover who else was around, if only to save my own skin. You may be able to help me. I'm told you miss nothing that goes on."

She frowned and primly drew her collar to her throat. "I don't know where you heard that."

He wished he hadn't said it. He'd worked hard to cultivate her as an ally. It was high time he got something in return. "If you can remember anyone at all behaving suspiciously, it could be important."

"The only person who springs to mind was you, Mr. Dee."

"Oh?"

"If you recall, I saw you on the stairs and asked if you were looking for the little room."

"So you did." The blood surged to his cheeks, blameless as he was. "I was looking for Bert Dombey at the time." Which only made it worse. "Didn't I tell you why?"

You could have cut the atmosphere and wrapped it in slices like the pumpkin.

Julie was fully fifteen yards away, but she must have been listening. Just like the old days, she came to his rescue. "We've set out the slices and there are still plenty left. Did you want to take them to the pub?"

"Right you are, Julie," he said, struggling to recover his poise. "Not that I'm gasping for a pint, I'll have you know." He turned back to Miss Harrap. "Shall we see you in there?" And he barely stopped himself from adding, "As usual."

23

THE PUB WAS empty except for the same two old men in cloth caps playing cribbage. They seemed to be a fixture. They didn't look up from the cards when Diamond trundled the wheelbarrow past them.

The barmaid and landlady Dolores was a joy to meet again after the tense session with Miss Harrap. She was more than happy to take the rest of the pumpkin slices for her customers. She pushed a table against the end of the bar and told Diamond to unload them there. She chalked the words HELP YOURSELF on a blackboard and propped it in place. "They won't need any more invitation than that."

"A pint or a strong black coffee?" she said. "You look shell-shocked, my dear, finding the stiff under the stairs. Last night is one to forget, eh?" Like everyone else, she knew all about it.

"The beer, if you please," he said. "Your village will be in the news again. I'm surprised the media aren't here already."

"They won't be long," she said. "Someone will have tipped them off by now. Extra business for me is the way I look at it. I defrosted all the burgers I was keeping for the weekend." She pulled the pint and slid it in front of him. "They'll be after you. If you don't want to be pinned to the wall, you'd better drink up fast."

There were things he needed to find out first.

"Good for business last night?"

"About the usual. I don't turn much of a profit after paying my helpers. It's unofficial, but I like to give them a fiver each."

"Your waiters? I saw young Hamish among them."

She smiled. "His mum makes sure he joins in. It does them good to speak to adults even if it's only 'Red or white?'"

"Did they help you before the party started?"

"They were Trojans. As well as unpacking the wine glasses there were things to collect from the kitchen. Nibbles. Guacamole. One of the ladies had made an enormous dip and there were bowls of it to offer round."

He had the answer to one of his questions. He needed to be certain. "You're speaking about the farmhouse kitchen? Hamish and the other waiters went in there?"

Dolores folded her arms defiantly. "There you go again. Questions all the way. Do you double up as a quiz-show host, by any chance? Of course they were there, coming and going most of the evening."

"I saw Hamish a few minutes ago and he wasn't saying much, as usual. I hope he had nothing to do with the killing."

"God help us, what a morbid thought." But Dolores didn't rise to Hamish's defence. She asked a question of her own. "Do we have any idea what time it happened?"

"Late afternoon, probably. He admits he saw Bert Dombey alive and near the farmhouse at about four fifteen."

"Hamish volunteered this?" she said in some surprise.

"Not exactly." He smiled at the memory. "I had to wring it out. Unless you know better, it was the only sighting of

Dombey before he was killed. I don't suppose he came in for a drink."

"Definitely not. Did they speak?"

"Hamish doesn't speak much to anyone, does he? He would have been on his quad bike, on the way to collect the cows for milking."

Dolores shook her head. "He's just a kid. I can't think of anyone except Claudia who might have wanted Bert dead."

"You knew him a bit."

She wagged a finger at him. "You'd better not be serious. I speak to all my customers, good and bad. Barmaid, it's in my job description, look it up. Some of them are tossers. Doesn't mean I would stick a knife in them. I was far too busy anyway. If you want my opinion, this has nothing to do with the villagers. It's about the weekenders, Claudia's mob. Bert was one of them and there were others here yesterday."

"Hertzog and Fortunato?"

"Not forgetting the silent woman."

"Elaine?"

"They all vanished into the night before the body was discovered."

"So did everyone else. The hoedown was well over." He tried a different approach. "You told me you've had this job for nine years."

"Did I? And you remember? What are you, my love—the secret police?"

Much too close to the truth. He grinned uncomfortably, and he was sure it showed.

"Or an ex-cop recently retired and still going through the motions?"

His nightmare. She'd really hit home this time.

Then she broke into a broad smile. "Only joshing with

you, sunshine. You've come over all pink. What did you want to ask me?"

It was a relief to get back on script. "I was thinking you must have been here when Mervyn was alive. I keep thinking he's the key to all this."

"Him? He was getting on in years then and well respected. A father to everyone. A father figure, at any rate." She giggled. "I don't mean he sired little Mervyns. We all looked up to him."

"You must have chatted to him many times in here."

"Funnily enough, hardly ever. He did his drinking at home. Came in sometimes and bought a bottle of scotch to take out. Didn't linger. Towards the end, that was a habit. If he wasn't an alky, he wasn't far off."

"Any idea why?"

"Couldn't swear to it, but things changed after the Douglases took over the day-to-day management of the farm. Gave him more time to think, I reckon. I always thought of him as a family man who lost his family. For a time, he made do with all of us instead, but the ones he really wanted were his wife and daughter, one dead and the other free as a bird and wanting to stay that way. Sad. I'd see him most mornings in the summer sitting outside the shop in dark glasses with a black coffee in front of him, staring into space."

"Hungover?"

"What do you think?"

"It must have come as a shock when he overdosed."

"Huge. Totally unexpected. None of us knew he was taking sleepers. The drink and the drugs were a deadly cocktail."

"Did he leave a note?"

"Nothing. The coroner told the jury to bring in an open verdict."

Diamond was interested. Open verdicts beg questions. "So his suicide was unproven?"

"In the eyes of the law, I suppose. But we all knew better. The church was packed for the funeral."

"Did Claudia come?"

"No. She only surfaced after she was told about the will. I don't think she expected to be left anything. Hey-ho. Looks like new customers."

Two strangers had just entered, one carrying what was obviously a camera bag.

The media had caught up.

"Better drink up and return the wheelbarrow, hadn't you?" she said to Diamond with a wink.

He didn't need telling. On his way out, he heard one of the pressmen ask if the pumpkin slices were any good.

Dolores said they were freshly cut, like some of her customers.

Outside, a Land Rover was coming his way, the word PRESS displayed on the windscreen. The driver stopped and lowered the window. "Excuse me, sir."

Diamond didn't expect a "sir" from anyone. He had to think what it was about. From the pressman's point of view, a fellow in a smart pinstripe couldn't be mistaken for a rustic even when pushing a wheelbarrow.

He avoided eye contact.

"Have I missed the farmhouse?" the driver asked.

Without a word, Diamond pointed in the wrong direction, grasped the handles again and moved on, making it clear he was either the village idiot or too grand to answer damn fool questions.

They were closing in. The last thing he wanted was media attention. He had important things to do before it became impossible to move about with freedom. He and

Paloma would be leaving in the morning, so if he got his movements right, he might outfox the newshounds. He didn't underestimate them, but he had some experience of lying low.

His motive for returning the wheelbarrow wasn't good manners. He could have left it anywhere. No, it was a prop in a rather important drama, an excuse to go looking around the farm buildings and finding at least one of the more talkative members of the Douglas family. Agnes was the more likely. Jim roamed widely and could be out in the fields.

She wasn't in the tractor barn. Dombey's van was gone, no doubt transported to the garage where forensics examined vehicles. Diamond wheeled the barrow towards the milking complex. The cows had long since been milked and returned to their grazing, but it was possible someone was still in the tank room. A pair of wellington boots stood outside. A smaller size than a man would wear.

He parked the barrow by the door and let himself in. Two huge metal tanks dominated and the walls bristled with electronic controls. He could hear the movement of liquid. At this stage of the day, it might be the automatic washing system cleansing the insides of the tanks. He had to shout to be heard.

"Anyone about?"

Agnes appeared from behind the second tank, wearing a white coat and mob cap. "What the heck . . . ?"

She may have said something stronger. He didn't catch the words over the sound from the pumps.

He made the kind of pacifying palms-spread salute you would give to a Sioux warrior brandishing a hatchet. "I was looking for you."

She pointed to the door and it could have been an

invitation to speak outside. More likely she was telling him to get the hell out.

He went.

And waited.

Presently, she appeared at the door, no longer wearing the coat and cap, and told him he should know better than to march in there in his day clothes. "It's strictly regulated by the Food Standards Agency." She sat in the doorway and reached for the boots.

He made a grovelling apology and pointed to the wheelbarrow. "I promised to return this." Without drawing breath, he added, "And I'd love to talk to you about yesterday. Did you hear I was with Claudia when the body was found?" Daft question. By now everyone in the village knew. But it got straight to the point.

"I'm not a lawyer, you know," she said as she pulled on the second boot. "If you're in trouble, speak to an expert."

"It's Claudia who needs help. The police kept her overnight and don't have any other suspect. She was shocked and horrified. I think she's innocent."

"Tell the police, then. Don't tell me." She stood up, shut the door behind her and started walking away as if no more needed to be said. Her manner towards him had changed and tank-room protocol was not the reason.

He followed, speaking to her back. "She's her own worst enemy. She talked herself into a manslaughter sentence two years ago and now she could be on trial for murder."

She kept walking. "She's the one in need of a lawyer, then."

He wasn't giving up. "You know what she's like, Agnes. She's spent most of her life up against authority. She'll ignore their advice, lose her cool, and get deeper and deeper into the mire. That's what happened last time."

"What am I supposed to do?" Agnes said over her shoulder.

"When we spoke of this before, you sounded more sympathetic."

She did at least turn and speak to him. "Listen. Claudia is my employer. Three of us in my family depend on her. I don't know what to think about her now and I'd be a fool to mouth off about it."

It was a telling point. In her position, he'd feel vulnerable. "If, as I believe, someone else killed Dombey, then it would help your family to have them unmasked." He was starting to sound desperate.

"I don't know anything about this. I was too busy all day yesterday to know what happened in the house."

"I saw that myself and all credit to you," he said. "You organised and fronted the entire event. But you must have some idea what was in Claudia's mind."

"Don't involve me," she said and it sounded like a warning.

He was starting to think there was more to this than job insecurity. She was afraid of being implicated in the murder. "This is just between ourselves. You know her better than anybody here. She phoned you regularly from prison."

"Only on farm business."

"But you knew in advance that she was out and planning to be here for the harvest supper along with three of her friends from Bath. You told me you visited her solicitor to collect the keys of the farmhouse and open it up for the caterers."

"So?" She looked away towards the fields as if whatever he said next wouldn't interest her.

"Did you see her when she arrived? Do you know what time it was?"

"We spoke briefly. She was in a hurry. It was getting late and she had to get dressed."

"Were her friends already here?"

She let out an impatient breath. "I don't know why you're asking me these questions. My advice to you, Mr. Dee, is to keep your distance. When are you leaving us?"

"Tomorrow morning."

"I won't see you again, then. Goodbye."

He had one more card to play. "I can save you a journey. I can return the keys to Claudia's solicitors in Bath. You still have them, do you?"

She folded her arms. "I may live out here in the sticks but I'm not thick. I know what you're planning. The only people with right of access now are the police and the forensics team. They have *all* the keys."

"Including the set you had?"

"Keep up, Mr. Dee."

He didn't believe her.

BACK IN THE cottage, he apologised to Julie.

"Whatever for?" she said.

"I let you down. You were hoping I'd unravel the truth about Claudia. She's in a worse situation now than when we arrived."

Julie knew his moods of old. On a bad day in the office, Diamond could crash a computer by looking at it. "That's not your fault, guv."

"If I hadn't started on this, she'd be enjoying her freedom."

She shook her head. "How do you work that out?"

"I stupidly convinced myself Bert Dombey caused Roger Miller's death. I had him down as a psychopath and I spent far too much time with him trying to tease out the truth."

"Wearing your Columbo raincoat."

Julie's attempt to lighten his mood fell flat. He continued laying out the case against himself. "He probably was a psycho. He was excessively focused, but not a killer. He was hellbent on finding the source of Mervyn's wealth and I egged him on."

Across the room, Paloma had been listening. Well organised as always, she was starting to collect things for the journey home. "That's not the whole story, is it, Pete? You tried to keep him in the dark about the harvest supper. It wasn't your fault he found out."

He wouldn't let himself off the hook. "I encouraged him to help decorate the church. He got chatting with the other helpers and that's how he heard about the supper."

"Stop beating yourself up, love. You didn't know he would break into the farmhouse and get murdered."

"And you don't know all the facts. He didn't break in. The place was wide open for the first time in two years. Agnes Douglas had driven to Bath early that morning and collected the keys from Claudia's solicitor."

"Agnes?" Julie said. "Was she involved in this?"

"She was. Exactly how much is an open question. She was acting under instructions from Claudia. They'd been in regular telephone contact throughout Claudia's time in prison. She was told to open the farmhouse so that the kitchen could be used to prepare the supper."

"Agnes had a busy day. She was the MC for the dancing."

"Don't I know it." He rolled his eyes. Self-mockery can be an antidote to misery.

Julie said, "She's an amazing person. She runs that farm. Jim is a big support, but Agnes makes all the decisions."

Diamond hadn't mellowed enough to say a word in favour of Agnes. "Getting back to Bert Dombey, the front door of the farmhouse was open, so he walked through like I did and I guess his killer did. He knew his way around from all the parties he'd attended. He'd cultivated Claudia—that's the way he will have thought of it—and he shared her belief that her father had hidden something there. He was smart enough to work out that the space under the stairs was the most likely place."

"He still had to find the priest hole and how to unlock it," Julie said. "Nobody else had."

"The focus of a psychopath is extraordinary. Once a goal is in his sights he'll go for it like no ordinary mortal. So-called professionals like me are not in the same class. Yes, he worked out where it was and how to get in. He was inside and searching when he was murdered. That's my belief. Forensics may come up with a different theory, but it looks to me as if he was standing in the priest hole with his head and shoulders visible when he was killed, an easy target for someone wielding a sharp weapon."

"Meaning a woman?" Paloma said and saved him from sounding sexist.

"Or anyone. A youth. An old person, even. They had the advantage if they avoided being grabbed by the arms and pulled inside—and that doesn't seem to have happened. Knowing Dombey, as I do, he would have been concentrating wholly on the search he was making, totally unaware of someone coming up the stairs. The first he'd know of it would be the thrust from the murder weapon."

"Horrible. Were there other stab marks?"

"Several more. It looked to me as if they were twin wounds and my thought is that the killer used something with a double blade, like sheep shears. Do you know what I'm talking about?"

"One of the antique farm tools?"

"Yes, in times past, the sheep were sheared with sharp

blades like scissors, but bigger and joined at the handle so that they sprang open after each cut. Some were on the wall downstairs, easy to grab and use."

"Wasn't it found at the scene?"

"Not when I checked. I asked the SOCO and he said the space was so cluttered that getting everything out was a slow process."

"They worked through the night," Julie said. "Someone told me in the shop. Maggie, our resident lookout."

"The stuff that interests them most will have been taken to the lab," he said. "Anything bloodstained or likely to hold some DNA. There were layers of canvases and paper, but the materials underneath are going to be less useful than this first crop. I doubt if they'll have a second night in there. They'll seal the place and come back tomorrow and each day until the job is done."

"Hoping their tests will lead them to the killer," Julie said.

"Crandley hopes so, for sure. Claudia's DNA will be picked up. And mine. And Mervyn's. If anyone else's is found, they'll have questions to answer."

"But not for some time," Julie said. "The wheels grind slowly."

"How are you going to return these?" Paloma said. She was looking at the books on Sickert.

"I haven't finished them yet."

"Bit late in the day for a long read, isn't it? We've got to pack our stuff in the car if we're making an early start tomorrow."

Julie said the last thing on Claudia's mind at this time would be a few borrowed books. She offered to return them after life in the village returned to normal.

If ever, each of them was thinking.

24

PACKING HER MULTI-POCKETED leather weekender bags had taken most of the afternoon for Paloma. Throwing things into his ancient suitcase was a five-minute job for Diamond.

Time before supper for a fast and final browse through those books. On the front of *Sickert: A Painter's Life* were two black-and-white photos, a smiling dark-haired man with film-star looks and a grizzled veteran continuing to face the world with amusement. Diamond went straight to the back and the chapter entitled "Bathampton."

The painter had lived there in a grand Georgian town house on the north-eastern slopes of Bath in the last years of his life, 1938 to 1942. Although in his late seventies, he was still at work. A colour plate showed his oil painting of the white stuccoed front of the house. Pictured on the drive were eight figures in mid-Victorian costume he must have added from his imagination unless he used models in hired clothes. Even to Diamond's untutored eye, the artistry was markedly better than anything on the walls of the farmhouse. Mervyn's brother, Howard, might have tried to paint in the same style, but he hadn't produced anything in this class.

Sickert must have caused a stir in buttoned-down Bathampton. He was everyone's idea of the eccentric artist, with an unruly white beard stained by the cheroots he smoked. He dressed in a sailor's peaked cap, gaudy ginger tweeds with a tailcoat and carpet slippers or gumboots, depending on the weather. Although very famous, he was frequently in debt (his friend and former pupil, Prime Minister Winston Churchill, took time out from running the war to arrange a handout from the Royal Bounty Fund). But he was generous with his time, always happy to talk to the local children. He gave a weekly unpaid lecture at the Bath Art School and then pottered about the city getting lost and eventually hailing a taxi and overpaying with five-pound notes. The saving graces in his life were his third wife, Thérèse Lessore, and, of course, his art. He painted to the end of his life.

Diamond turned to a second book, *Sickert in Bath*, intrigued that there was enough material for a large-format volume running to several hundred pages. Much of it was taken up with the picture section. There was scarcely a view of the city the prolific artist had not painted, and some several times over. As if this wasn't enough, he was turning out portraits, still lifes and interiors.

Not all the work in the book was from his last years. Sickert had spent two summers in Bath during the first world war, in 1917 and 1918. He'd rented the Lodge on Entry Hill and worked from a studio in the centre, at 10 Bladud Buildings. "Bath is it," he wrote to a friend. "There never was such a place for rest & comfort & leisurely work. Such country & such town."

Leisurely work. The book told another story.

A street scene painted in 1917 and owned by Tate Britain was analysed to show the tortuous stages each painting

went through. *Belvedere* was a view looking down Lansdown
Road towards the city centre. On the facing page was a
preparatory sketch. Sickert had drafted the scene in pen
and ink and watercolour on squared paper.

A caption explained how he would first draw the main
features in pencil or charcoal in a squared sketchbook. Later,
in his studio, he would enlarge the sketch on thin drawing
paper, working with the squares to keep the proportions
right. Then he blackened one side of a sheet of newspaper,
pinned it to the canvas with the new drawing over it and
went over the outline with a stylus to make the marks. As
an extra check for accuracy, he referred to photos he had
taken at the scene, projecting the image on to the screen
using an epidiascope.

Only then would he start the oil painting.

The process sounded more like science than art to
Diamond. The text explained that these were techniques
Sickert had first used for portraits and later applied to
landscapes. His mentors, Whistler and Degas—he liked
to drop the names into a conversation—each used photography as an aid.

Overleaf was a surprise, a far less painstaking render-
ing of the same scene, the main colours blocked in, purple
shadows spread across the cream road surface, dark-toned
brown and black buildings at either side with green foli-
age rising above the roofs and the pale blue and mauve of
Beechen Cliff in the background. If this hadn't borne his
signature, you wouldn't have known it was Sickert's work
without reference to the more polished version two pages
back. Diamond had never professed to know much about
art but the word "slapdash" came to mind. Whether the
painting had been a mock-up to get the tones right or a
potboiler done for a quick profit was not explained.

It had sold in 2015 for almost £30,000.

Sickert was a bankable artist. The more carefully wrought version of *Belvedere* had been a bequest to Tate Britain. Its true value would run to six figures.

Diamond studied each of them like a connoisseur, a connoisseur of the criminal mind. He returned to the slapdash effort. The style and execution was not dissimilar to Howard's.

A light-bulb moment.

The answer to the mystery that had bugged him all week was here in front of him. Wicked old Mervyn, stuck with his legacy of several hundred of his brother's mediocre paintings, had found a way of turning some of them into a handsome profit. They could pass for preparatory studies.

What a pity there wouldn't be time for the rest of *Sickert in Bath*. There was an awful lot of it. He'd be up all night if he tried to read the entire book.

As if he needed convincing how much there was, he thumbed through the text, watching the pages race past. Then there was another game-changing moment. He glimpsed a mark in the margin somewhere in the early part of the book. It was gone so quickly that he had to thumb the pages a second time, only more slowly. And there it was: a blue line against a paragraph someone had decided was worth noting:

> *In 1917 Sickert painted the same scene in reverse, looking up Lansdown Road from the Assembly Rooms towards the row of buildings called Belvedere. The picture was left in his studio at Bladud Buildings after he returned to London in 1918. Its survival is something of a miracle. In 1925, seven years after the Sickerts had left, the landlady found the canvas and was about to consign it to the dustbin when somebody*

*mentioned that it was probably a Sickert. Much to
her credit, she handed it over to the Victoria Gallery.
Who knows how many more scenes of Bath the artist
scattered in his wake? He was not overly careful about
his work, once completed.*

No question who had marked the paragraph. Mervyn
had seen the potential in the idea of some lost Sickerts. It
was a good bet that the blue line was made with the pen
Diamond had in his pocket, the freebie from Roger Miller.

Over supper, when he told the ladies about his discovery, Julie said, "There you are, guv. Just what you said this
morning. You could be right about Mervyn selling some of
his brother's paintings and passing them off as Sickerts."

"Inferior Sickerts," he said, enjoying his new reputation
as an art expert. "Until I saw the picture section in the first
book, I doubted whether anything Howard produced could
be passed off as genuine. Now I can believe it, having seen
some of the stuff Sickert turned out. From what I can tell,
he liked to rough out a painting to get the colours right.
Then he'd put it aside, not realising some Sickert fanatic
would want to own it."

Paloma as always was being cautious. "Who would want
to buy a second-rate trial piece?"

"You have to understand the mentality of collectors, my
dear. They'll buy anything." And don't I sound a pomp-
ous twit, he told himself. The only surprise was how mild
Paloma's rebuke was.

"Get off your high horse, Pete."

"Okay, okay. The way I see it, Mervyn looked for a dealer
in Bath townscapes—"

"—and found Roger Miller," she completed the sentence
for him.

"Er, yes. Miller had cornered the market in selling Bath scenes. This was years before he joined Claudia and her party set."

"And ended up in a silo, poor bloke."

He was more nettled than she was. "Do you want to tell it, or shall I? He will have dealt in Sickert's work and I'm sure he will have been approached by serious collectors ready to stump up good money for an unknown Sickert."

"But they're not fools," Paloma said. "They won't buy any old rubbish, even if it has the signature. Like I said before, they want to know the provenance."

"I have an idea about that," he said.

"What's that?"

"I need to check something first."

"Be like that."

Silence slapped down like a wet dishcloth.

Only one person in the room could lift it.

"Could Howard have known Sickert personally?" Julie asked.

"That's a thought," Paloma said, her interest rekindled. "We checked on him, didn't we? He was born in 1925, so he would have been thirteen when the Sickerts came to live in Bathampton."

"Forty miles away," Diamond pointed out. "He lived here."

"Forty miles is nothing to a teenager," Paloma said. "We all know about teenage crushes. He could have cycled to Bathampton. Or hitched a lift. People did in those days."

He thought about it, starting to be persuaded. "You're right. They could have met. The old painter was happy to talk to anyone about art, young people in particular."

"You *have* done your homework," Paloma said.

"The bits that interest me."

Julie was linking things up. "The reason Howard chose later to live in Bathampton must have been the Sickert connection."

"We can all agree on that. He was obsessed."

"What happened to all the art stuff after Sickert died?" That was easily answered. The book had covered it. "His widow, Thérèse, moved to London and died just a few years later. Everything passed to Thérèse's sister, who founded the Sickert Trust to deal with both their estates."

"How about the things that weren't of much value, like the unused canvases and the tubes of paint?"

"Good point," Diamond said, sensing where Julie was going with this. Her insights were as valuable as they had always been. "I expect a lot of it was dumped."

"Put into jumble sales, more like," Paloma said. "Not much was wasted after the war. Anything that could have been put to use will have been snaffled by the locals. I daresay some of Sickert's things are still in people's lofts in Bathampton. What made you ask, Julie?"

"I was thinking of what was found in the priest hole. Up to now we've assumed it was Howard's stuff. Could any of it have belonged originally to Sickert?"

Paloma snapped her fingers. "Smart thinking."

Diamond weighed the suggestion, unsure whether he dared to run with it. "I like it, Julie. Howard will have been alert to any art materials he heard about."

After they'd eaten, he carried some plates to the dishwasher and then returned to his reading. The book he hadn't yet opened was a thick paperback, a collection of articles about Sickert by a variety of writers taken from various academic publications. Many had obscure, unfathomable titles. There was no index. He sighed and was about to put it down when he remembered his trick with *Sickert in Bath*.

He thumbed through it from front to back in search of another mark in the margin. Then he bent the book the other way and checked all the pages with even numbers.

It had been too much to hope. And of course he hadn't checked the margins on the left side. They were too close to the spine. He'd have to search page by page and he didn't have the energy for that.

He was left glaring at the contents page. And then the gods smiled on him again. He noticed a small, neat tick in blue ink against one of the titles: "Between the Lines: Some Observations on W. R. Sickert's Idiosyncratic Choices of drawing paper." The writer was Risto Raitio, professor of paper science at Helsinki University.

Paper science? Was that really going to be helpful?

Encouraged but far from confident, Diamond found the article and started reading. It was based on research at the Walker Art Gallery in Liverpool, which had the world's largest collection of Sickert's drawings. In 1948, the Sickert Trust had offered the Walker three hundred items found in his studio and they had since acquired more. Professor Raitio was more interested in the choices of paper than the art. Sickert had often used the first drawing surface that came to hand for a quick sketch—the backs of envelopes, laundry books, postcards and newspapers. But the kind he went out of his way to use was accountancy paper—ironic for a man who was hopeless with money.

Many of these sheets were roughened along one edge and discoloured by oxidisation and traces of glue, suggesting they had originally been bound. Sickert was unusual in using ledger books for drawing rather than the sketchbooks most artists used. Far from being put off by all the coloured lines, he used them as an aid to recording

*the image accurately. Moreover, they were helpful when
he transferred the sketches to larger, squared paper, or
his canvases.*

Another puzzle was solved. The ledger books in the
cellar weren't for Howard's accounts. They were for sketching. Sickert drew in ledger books. Howard, his disciple,
would have used the same method. He would have got in
a supply of his own.

Or were they his own? The cover of the one Diamond
had seen in the crime scene van had looked decidedly
antique, the gold lettering on the cover faded and barely
legible. Bold thought: Was it possible Howard had obtained
a set that had once belonged to Sickert and been acquired
by someone in Bathampton after his death?

A pulse throbbed in his temple.

In Julie's overgrown back garden she and Paloma were
watching the sun set when he joined them.

"Is Bella with you?"

"In the long grass somewhere," Paloma said.

"She'd enjoy a walk," he said.

"She would—or you would? What are you up to now?"

"I thought I'd take a last stroll up the village street. If I
collect her lead, do you think she'll come?"

"Try and stop her," Julie said. "It's on the coat hook
inside the door, guv."

"I may be some time, as brave Captain Oates said when
he stepped out into the blizzard."

"He's up to something," Paloma said to Julie. "Don't go
knocking on people's doors. It's far too late for that. They'll
think you're the police."

"I am." And long may it continue, he was tempted to
add. If this week away had taught him anything, it was

how much he valued his job and the people he worked with. He'd been right all along about the spectre of retirement. He'd cling to his job until he was booted out.

As if she read his thoughts—and she probably did—Paloma said, "You won't want to hear this, but I've been giving thought to your future. *Our* future, in fact."

He gave a guarded "Really?"

"I know you've been agonising all week over what Georgina said, the sudden interest in your age."

"Agonising? I wouldn't put it as strongly as that."

"Brooding, then. And we know your reaction. I think it colours your attitude to life in the country. You won't even think about our future while you've got the job in Bath."

"It's not just the job," he said, sensing what was coming. "It's the people. The team. I'm away from them for a few days and I'm thinking how much I value them as friends, as well as colleagues. Over a long period, I've got to know their insecurities as well as their strengths and they know mine." He turned to Julie. "You remember Keith Halliwell?"

"Of course," she said. "Lovely man."

"He won't mind you knowing this. A couple of years ago the subject of modern art came up and Keith got so emotional he had to leave the room. None of us could understand why. He told me later that his dad had been an artist, a good one, good enough to submit work for the Royal Academy. The problem was that he painted in the traditional style and it had dated. The fashion was for the modern stuff. He couldn't change. Each year he'd lug several beautifully painted canvases to London and each year he'd have to bring them home again. One day Keith called at the house and found his dad had hanged himself. No suicide note, just a freshly opened letter from the RA saying regretfully . . ."

"That his work had been rejected again?" Julie said.

Diamond nodded.

"That's awful."

"He's been my deputy all these years and I didn't know, but I do now. How can I walk away when we're as close as we are? He helped me get over my own personal tragedy, as you did. You'd quit the team because of my boorish behaviour, but you helped me pull myself together after Steph was murdered. The worst thing I've ever had to go through. I wouldn't have managed without you."

"You would," Julie said without hesitation, "but it would have taken longer."

"And I remember your words when I wanted to handle the inquiry myself. 'Your heart won't accept what your head tells you.'"

"Is that what I said?" She smiled faintly.

"Your exact words. I've heard them in my head a thousand times since."

"Then perhaps you should listen to Paloma."

The silence that followed was like a river about to burst its banks.

He controlled himself enough to say, "I hope you two aren't ganging up on me."

"Is this about the retirement thing?"

Paloma nodded. "Let's leave it for later. Look at Bella. She's ready for her walk. And take care. Here in the country every other person owns a shotgun."

25

BELLA WAS OFF duty, on the end of a five-metre retractable lead, making good use of her freedom to wander, behaving like any other pooch, zigzagging to every interesting scent along the route, yet somehow going the way Diamond wanted.

She seemed to know instinctively that they would be heading up the street and past the cottages, the farm, the community shop and the Feathers, towards the field with the twin silos.

The village was eerily quiet and there was a chill in the air. Warm summer evenings were just a memory now. No vehicles were outside the farmhouse and there was no bobby on duty. The SOCOs had spent all of last night bringing out the top layer of physical evidence from the priest hole. What was left—and there must have been plenty—could be removed with less urgency. After so much attention in the past twenty-four hours, the grand old building stood empty of people again with the added indignity of do-not-enter tape defacing the front door.

The pub may have had some life inside but you wouldn't have known. The curtains were drawn. A few crates of empties were stacked by the door. Dead men.

It was difficult to escape the feeling that Baskerville was suffering the hangover from hell.

Bella reached the gate of the silo field and turned to look for the slowcoach on the end of her lead.

He caught up, released the shoot bolt, swung the gate open and let her off the leash to wander freely, knowing she would come when called. He was here to walk the route Roger Miller had taken on the night of his death, as nearly as possible reconstructing it after dark. All the focus on the second killing didn't mean he'd lost sight of the first.

It seemed inescapable that the killings of Miller and Dombey were connected. Both were Claudia's friends. Both had slept with her and been discarded like yesterday's papers. Both had met unnatural deaths on her farm. Claudia was the common factor. She would find it difficult to shake that off under interrogation from Jack Crandley. She needed someone in support of her, even if it was the two-timing arsewipe she blamed for her arrest.

At the field's edge he had to decide whether to go by the vehicle route, a track of sorts that followed the perimeter hedge, or the quick way across the middle. Miller would have gone the quick way, blast him.

The silos stood silhouetted against the night sky, but the ground was impossible to see. Stumbling blindly over humps and dips in soggy turf was not Diamond's idea of fun. Miller had probably used the flashlight from his phone. Diamond had his mobile with him and typically hadn't recharged it in days. The small amount of power remaining had to be saved for an emergency.

Surely any sane person would assume a pitch-black rutted field would be off limits for a party game? This wasn't musical chairs or hunt the thimble. It was a commando course.

However, the experience confirmed one thing: Miller had been desperate to win. He must have been hard as steel or thick as a plank—or acting on information. Diamond was more certain than ever that someone—presumably the killer—had tipped him off.

A hidden hollow caught him off guard. Arms flailing, he lost his balance and tripped. On his knees, he grunted in annoyance, relieved to be unhurt. Bella was beside him in seconds, wetting his cheek with her warm tongue. Her care was heartening. Gratefully he fussed her up, fitted the lead again and let her act more like the guide dog she was and steer him safely towards the silos.

He could almost hear a voice say, "Good thinking, guv."

How he wished he'd lived up to Julie's expectation and cracked the case by now. She deserved better.

They reached the first silo, black as sin at this time of night. This was the brute he had scaled on the first morning of their visit. He wouldn't be climbing the ladder a second time. He didn't need reminding that there were a hell of a lot of rungs and the hatch at the top was easy to open. He'd done enough reconstructing for one night.

Also he remembered that as he had made the climb another inner voice—more like Georgina's than Julie's—had warned him how stupid he was even to think of unpicking someone else's investigation. In his usual bull-headed way, he'd ignored the wise words and decided this was his one and only chance to go it alone, have fun playing his favourite TV sleuths and winkle out the truth. Stupid, self-serving and wrong.

But was he wrong? He'd learned things. He'd formed a theory of sorts. He didn't yet have proof. Without access to forensics, he wouldn't get it unless the killer confessed to him.

Justice—and Claudia—would have to wait for DI

Crandley to come to his senses and pursue the real perpetrator.

For the killer, the trek across the field and the climb would have been less demanding, coming here earlier by daylight, without any time pressure. A reasonably fit person, male or female, could have managed it and slung the garter out to the middle, an action that had appeared so inoffensive nobody had classed it as murder, even with the knowledge a man had died a cruel death.

So sneaky and so clever.

How did that same creep feel now, he wondered. Fulfilled? Triumphant? At ease with their conscience? Or quaking in their shoes? The second murder hadn't been clever at all. There was desperation about it, blood evidence and plenty of it. Probably DNA and prints as well. Was Dombey's death planned like Miller's or had he been killed in panic because he had found out too much?

For Diamond, this return to the scene had been a rounding-off, a chance to weigh up what he had learned and get things straight in his head. He believed he knew the truth now. He looked at his watch. Past bedtime for Baskerville.

He had one card left to play. Earlier in the day he had dangled bait in front of his suspect. The next hour or two would tell whether it brought a result.

"Let's go, Bella."

An evening mist had settled over the field. He couldn't see anything of the village.

It may have been Bella's training that made her decide to avoid the cross-country route. Diamond was wholly in agreement. The perimeter track was safer and just as quick. He stepped out briskly.

After a few minutes, the outline of the village emerged

as a blur that could have been one of Walter Sickert's more slapdash landscapes.

By stages, he could make out individual buildings, the nearest row of cottages with the church tower behind. The taller barns and sheds of the farm. And then, as he got closer, the farmhouse itself.

It could have been a trick of the eyes that made him think a light flickered briefly at one of the large leaded windows upstairs. He kept looking and it didn't happen again.

The village street was in darkness when they reached it. Ten was the witching hour and it was way past that. The blinds were down at all the pub windows. Dolores would have closed and gone home.

Their movement into the farmyard triggered the motion sensors. The dazzle was a shock, but it didn't put Diamond off. He had business here. An appointment with a killer.

"This way, Bella."

They marched up to the house. Under the floodlights the reflective tape across the main door screamed at them to keep their distance. Not Diamond.

He got as close as he could without putting the door in shadow. It was closed, the taping apparently undisturbed.

Bella sniffed at the step and took an interest.

"What's that, doggie? Someone been this way?"

Bella gave two sharp yaps, a response that sounded positive. And then she growled.

The larger-than-life shadow of a head and shoulders spread across and beyond the door.

A man's voice from behind said, "Looking for a way in, Peter?"

Diamond snapped his hand to his side like a guardsman. He knew who it was before he turned. The way the last syllable of his name had rolled off the tongue was pure

Somerset. This had to be Jim Douglas. Salt-of-the-earth, reliable Jim, his ally from the calving shed, the last person he'd suspect of being involved in murder.

"Not at all," he answered in as calm a tone as he could manage. "Making sure it's secure, that's all."

"Not your job, is it?" The mildness of the rebuke was a reminder that the two were supposed to be on the best of terms, but there seemed to be sarcasm in play as well.

"A few strips of police tape aren't going to put someone off if they really want to get inside," Diamond said, equally civil. "What are you up to, Jim? I thought farmers went to bed early."

"Saw a light at an upstairs window, didn't I?"

"Really?" He swung around to face Jim, his heart pounding. He couldn't go on with the deadpan talk. "I saw something too while I was walking the dog. A flash, like a torch."

"Which window?"

"Top floor, round the side." He'd already decided it was the large one overlooking the staircase. He didn't say so.

"Same as me," Jim said. "Someone's inside."

"Do you have the keys?"

Jim hesitated before answering, "No. Why should I?"

"Don't tell me you came out and left them at home."

"Never had 'em" On the defensive, Jim sounded awfully like his surly son.

"Your wife had them. She told me herself she drove all the way to Bath and collected the set held by Claudia's solicitor."

"What Aggy gets up to is no business of mine."

Diamond wasn't having that. Keys don't only open locks. They bestow power. The Douglas family had got used to running the farm. It would suit them nicely to have the freedom of the house. "Don't fuck me about, Jim. I need to get in. This is a bloody emergency."

"Keys are in Aggy's handbag."

"Someone is lying, then. She told me she handed them to the police."

Jim shook his head but the creases around his haunted eyes showed he'd been caught out.

"Stop bullshitting. I can see the bulge in your pocket."

Guiltily, Jim covered the bump with his right hand.

"Come on," Diamond said. "Out with them." Force of personality had won this small battle.

Red-faced, Jim took out a large bunch, held them in his palm, picked the one that looked the biggest and most likely and held it ready. "If it's bolted on the inside we're fucked."

"This isn't the door they used," Diamond told him. "The police tape hasn't been touched since it was stuck in place. We'd better go round the side."

Jim seemed pleased to get out of the glare of the lights.

Diamond followed with Bella, his brain in overdrive. Jim's every move needed watching.

The others with the means to have entered the house were Agnes and Hamish. Diamond was inclined to discount Hamish as a gormless youth struggling with his hormones and doing the minimum unless he was given instructions.

His mother was mentally the strongest of the three. Agnes was a go-getter, confident enough to plan and oversee the harvest supper, used to dealing with Claudia and running the farm. She would feel she had an absolute right to enter the farmhouse.

Whether any of the Douglases would resort to murder was the overriding question. Why would they?

They passed the kitchen garden with the overgrown

rosemary Diamond had sidestepped before. "We'll look at the kitchen entrance."

"Taped up, just like the front," Jim said, gesturing with his open hand. He seemed to know already.

Diamond stepped right up for a close look.

On inspection he saw that the strips across the kitchen door had been cut through between the frame and the door itself all the way along the opening, down the side and top and bottom. The tape still adhered to the wood.

Neat and almost invisible.

"See that?"

Jim nodded.

"Whoever is inside cut the tape and used a key to get in."

"Who do you think is in there?"

"There's an old saying, Jim: a murderer always returns to the scene of the crime." He paused for that to sink in, interested to see the reaction.

Jim was as blank-faced as a baseball player watching cricket.

"'Always' is an exaggeration," Diamond added, "but there's a grain of truth in it. In their minds, they relive the incident over and over, wanting to be certain they made no mistake. A nervous killer might want to cover his tracks in some way. Or search for something he left at the scene."

Jim seemed to decide this was too personal. He kicked the suspicion back where it came from. "Found the body, didn't you?"

"Me and Claudia together."

"She killed him, I heard." Said as prosaically as if it was all in a day's work.

"Not while I was there."

"She's at Taunton being questioned."

Diamond nodded. "She was out on licence, so they can hold her indefinitely as far as I know."

"Their prime suspect."

"Always was."

"It's a wonder they didn't take you off to Taunton as well."

"I gave them a statement. They can come back and question me any time."

"But you won't be staying much longer."

The Star Chamber, Baskerville style.

Diamond gave a disarming grin. "Didn't expect any of this to happen."

"So what do you think? Did she do it?" An honest question. Jim's desire to know appeared genuine. Maybe the worst he was guilty of was lying about the keys.

"Claudia? I've never thought so. When I was with her, she didn't act as if she knew the body was there already." In the next few minutes he was going to need Jim's unwavering support. He had to trust him. "I have a strong suspicion who it is, but I can't prove it, so I keep my mouth shut."

"Best way," Jim said. "Best way. Are you going in?"

"Can you find a key that fits?"

"Help yourself." He handed the bunch across. About a dozen of different sizes. Old houses have many locks.

Diamond found a smaller version of the front door key. He tried it in the lock and it turned. The kitchen door swung inwards, leaving the short ends of the tape stuck to the frame.

"I can look after the dog," Jim offered.

"She doesn't need looking after." He fastened Bella's lead to a cast-iron boot scraper at the left of the entrance. "Stay." Then he turned to Jim. "Not you. I want you at my side."

26

ENOUGH LIGHT TO see by was streaming through the window. With the security lamps in the yard activated, Diamond knew he could count on twenty minutes without touching a switch in the house. Before stepping fully in, he checked either side. The big kitchen could have been made for an ambush, tall cupboards, hidden corners, a laundry room and high, broad shelves above eye level.

Jim, close behind, understood the need to do this properly. The bond between the two was back to its calving-shed best.

Satisfied it was safe, they crossed the kitchen floor, eased open the door to the entrance hall, stopped and listened.

The only sound was from outside, the church clock striking eleven, until a grandfather clock only ten feet away echoed the chimes and surprised them both. Diamond wouldn't want to admit his blood ran cold with the shock.

They went through to the heart of the house.

First impression: it looked as if the decorators had moved in. Plastic sheets were laid between the front door and the stairs. The walls either side of the door were stripped of all the historic farm tools. The entire collection must have been bagged up and delivered to the forensics lab. Most wouldn't have been any possible use as a murder weapon, but SOCOs are trained to resist making assumptions. Personally, Diamond still reckoned the unusual cuts in the corpse had been made by sheep shears.

He nudged Jim and pointed upwards. Most of the antique staircase was draped in plastic sheeting. Only the priest hole itself was not covered.

They couldn't do anything about the creaking of the stairs as they went up. The timbers of a galleon rounding Cape Horn wouldn't have made more noise. Whoever else was trespassing here would know for sure that others were in on the act.

Nobody showed.

They stopped below the stair with the stains. The sheeting had been rolled back and yellow evidence markers were in place.

The priest hole was a deep, dark void. The lighting from outside didn't reach here. Diamond took out his phone, tried the flashlight and was much relieved when it still had enough power to show them the cluttered interior. Some things had changed since he was here last. Everything of the bloodstained top layer had been removed, yet there was still enough on view to furnish an art studio, although so trampled it looked like bomb damage: drawing boards and canvases jutting out at strange angles; palettes, empty frames, some broken; a large, heavy easel on its side; sketchbooks and ledgers; scores of paint tubes and bottles of oil. Some of the oil must have been spilt because fumes of turps or white spirit wafted up and made Diamond's eyes water.

What next? Jim's mind was made up. He extended his open hand to the hole like a car salesman inviting a buyer to step in for a test drive.

Diamond shook his head. He'd already behaved improperly by entering the house. He could justify that in his own mind. He knew better than to corrupt the nucleus of the crime scene.

Jim's puzzled face said it all. They were in here to find who the hell had flashed a torch at the window. Why bother if they didn't check this purpose-built hiding place?

And he had a point. The talkative SOCO had said the interior was larger than you could see from the stairs. Diamond was no expert on priest holes but he knew they were sometimes built with a second inner chamber where the priest had a chance of fooling his pursuers even after they had found the first.

He reached as far in as possible without touching anything and inched the flashlight closer to check for a cavity below the angle of the stairs. It was impossible to tell from above.

Then a single paintbrush rolled off a canvas and dropped out of sight behind a palette.

"Did I do that?"

Jim shook his head.

"It can't have moved by itself," Diamond said. The self-imposed silence wasn't needed now. "She's got to be down there."

Jim stared at him, wide-eyed. "*She?*"

Days of keeping his suspicions to himself had been a strain. Usually everything was shared with his team. Unburdening was a huge relief. Diamond leaned right over the priest hole and called out, "You'd better come out, Miss Harrap. We know you're there."

No response. Nothing else moved.

"Do you want us to call the police?"

At that, the canvas jerked, a movement that couldn't possibly have been automatic. It nudged a sketchbook beside it and that dislodged another paintbrush. The process was slow to start but quick to develop, like the ice shelf breaking up. Small objects moved. A bottle of oil tipped over, lost its stopper and leaked on to a sheaf of photographs.

Jim said, "Goddammit!"

A thin, pale hand had snaked out of the debris. More canvases were thrust aside and the head and shoulders of Maggie Harrap burst through like a diver coming up for air. Wisps of her silver hair had come adrift and her glasses were askew. She blinked in the flashlight.

"Wise move, Maggie," Diamond said. "It's all over."

"It isn't," she said.

She had something in her right hand and he couldn't work out what it was. Not a gun, for sure. And not a knife. It looked like an aerosol with a two-inch silver tube projecting from the top.

Jim said, "That's a blowtorch."

"How right you are, Mr. Douglas," Maggie said in a voice devoid of emotion. "No modern cook should be without one." She squeezed the trigger and a half-inch blue flame sprang from the end.

In this mass of highly flammable materials, she had a lethal weapon.

"You'll kill yourself," Diamond said.

"Yes and I'll take you with me."

Jim leaned in and made a grab but she swung the butane-filled canister out of reach. The flame touched a roll of drawing paper and scorched it. Tiny tongues of fire spread along the edges.

Jim didn't hesitate. He vaulted into the priest hole, stooped and grabbed Maggie's wrist, forcing her to drop the blowtorch. The instant the finger pressure stopped, the flame was out. With his free hand he snatched up the roll of burning paper and hurled it behind him and away from the tinderbox he was standing in.

But the oily photographs were already alight and the flames were spreading. Everything down there was fuel for fire.

Jim was heroic. Years of farming had made him strong. He got his hands under Maggie's armpits and pulled her clean out of the rubble. Almost in the same movement he grasped her by the waist and raised her above his head like a dancer performing a pas de deux—except that his partner wasn't performing like a ballerina. She was struggling and screaming.

Diamond bent over, caught one of her flailing arms and dragged her upwards. His sore back objected with a stab of pain, making him yell, too. He didn't have a fraction of Jim's strength, but he managed to raise her enough to perch her on the stair.

She didn't need telling to raise her legs clear of the flames. He helped her up. The fight had gone out of her. She leaned on the banister rail and vomited.

"Get out while you can," he shouted. All their lives were at risk and Jim's wouldn't last many seconds more unless he was rescued.

Smoke billowed upwards. The gap in the stairs had become a chimney. Diamond's eyes felt as if acid had been hurled at him, but he forced himself to look in again and there was a brief window of clarity.

The entire floor covering of wood, paper and canvas seemed to be on fire. Jim had propped the big studio easel against one of the vertical timbers that supported the staircase. He was using the main crosspiece as a foothold to get above the flames. It was sturdy enough to take his weight, but it would soon be ablaze. The heaped canvases below him were already glowing red. If he remained there he would be roasted like meat on a spit.

More smoke billowed up and blocked Diamond's vision. He reached in and his hand came in contact with a piece of loose fabric hanging free, the hood of Jim's fleece jacket. He took a hold with both hands.

You've got to drag him out, he told himself. You're going to feel his weight. Your back will hurt like hell but you won't let go.

Jim's fingers had found the exposed edge of the stair. He hoisted himself higher while Diamond tugged, hoping to God that the fabric wouldn't rip. Getting leverage from his thighs, he tried to straighten up. Jim was a lot heavier than Miss Harrap but inch by inch he was raised higher until he was able to grab the nosing on the other side of the stair, getting enough purchase to hoist his torso high enough to flop on to the tread and let the staircase take most of his weight.

Still grasping the hood, Diamond descended two stairs backwards to get a better position to tug his man free of the rising flames. Even when he'd succeeded and Jim was fully supported by that top stair, the danger wasn't over. His trousers below the knee were on fire. Diamond ripped off his own jacket and smothered the flames.

His brave companion was totally spent.

The fire, on the other hand, was gathering strength.

Diamond knew what he had to do. He couldn't get Jim upright and he was incapable of carrying him. His only option was to lower the large, limp body downwards stair by stair, sliding and bumping over the plastic covering.

At floor level, he used one of the ground sheets to tug

him across the floor and through the kitchen. He flung open the door, bundled him outside and gasped the clean night air.

There was a movement at his side. He felt Bella's tongue licking the soot from his face.

Sometime after—he was too exhausted to tell how long—Agnes Douglas came running round the side of the house. He told her to call the fire service. She said they were already on their way and so was an ambulance. The sound of her voice brought Jim out of his stupor. "We won't need the ambulance, love." He sounded hoarse and the effort of speaking made him cough.

"Don't count on it," she told him. "They'll be the judge of that."

"I thought you were at home."

"I was. Maggie Harrap called me and I called some others. We've got her in the tithe barn recovering. She was distressed but she did the right thing. We'll get you guys over there. It's a make-do sick bay."

THE NEXT HOUR was a blur. Between bouts of coughing and shallow sleep, Diamond registered that he was lying on a trolley with an oxygen mask attached to his face. Paramedics had taken over. Jim was beside him for a while and then wheeled away. People came and went. Paloma used some wipes on his face. He told her Maggie Harrap ought to be under arrest and he tried to get up and go looking for her. Paloma put her hand on his chest and pushed him back against the pillow. She said Maggie had been sedated and wasn't going anywhere. He was able to answer some questions from a senior fireman. In turn, he asked a question of his own. He was told that the farmhouse was gutted beyond reconstruction. The seat of the fire, the wooden staircase, had been in the worst possible place. They had been extremely fortunate to get out. The police had been informed and a sergeant from Jack Crandley's team was on his way. He managed to raise a grin. "One of the team, eh? Jack won't lose any sleep, then."

27

THE AIR REMAINED heavy with the smell of burning when Diamond stepped out of Julie's cottage soon after dawn and marched up the street. Paloma had wanted him to get a proper rest, so he'd told her he'd slept like a baby and it was essential this baby saw Maggie Harrap and got a few things straight before Jack Crandley arrived and whisked her off to Taunton.

The farmhouse was a tragic sight, a smouldering, blackened shell holed in the roof and surrounded by broken tiles and pools of water. A fire tender remained outside and a few weary firemen were on watch, and so were some early risers from the village, a couple of dog walkers and a jogger.

Diamond didn't linger. He moved on to where a community support officer was on duty, yawning, at the door of the tithe barn. Mercifully, the wind had blown in the opposite direction overnight. The thatch could so easily have caught a spark.

He waved his ID and went in. The nurse he met inside took more convincing than the PCSO that he had a right to enter. She folded her arms and barred the way. Obstructive officials were never a problem for Peter Diamond. He congratulated her on shielding her patient so well and then put on the face he used for funerals and said it was possible other people had been trapped in the farmhouse and Miss Harrap was uniquely placed to tell him where to find the bodies. Pure invention and it worked.

She was alone in the nearest corner of the barn in a wheelchair and wrapped in a red blanket, misleadingly insignificant and unthreatening in the big space. She was washed and had loosened her silver hair and wasn't wearing her glasses. The usual severe look had softened. "I wasn't expecting you, Mr. Dee," she said. "I thought the police would get here before anyone else."

If he wanted the truth from her, he had to come clean. In as disarming a way as he could manage, he told her his real name and owned up to being a senior detective, making clear he wasn't officially on the case.

She took the information calmly. "I had my suspicions when I caught you on the stairs in the farmhouse on the night of the supper," she said, treating him as if he was the guilty party. "I asked you directly if you were working for the police and you denied it."

"I gave you an honest answer," he said. "I was working for Julie, who felt—rightly as it turns out—that an injustice had been done."

"To Claudia?" She shut her eyes tightly as she spoke the name but they soon opened again. "That's true. I feel more distressed about her than about the men I killed."

Simple as that, the admission of guilt—as if she knew he had worked everything out. The blowtorch had burned through the wall of deceit between them. After her reckless conduct, any pretence of innocence was impossible.

"I don't suppose I'll get a chance to tell her."

"You can have your say in court."

"She'll think I'm a callous bitch and I am, but I do have

a conscience, believe it or not. Each day she was locked up distressed me, too. I hadn't expected her to take the rap. Is that the expression?"

He wasn't here to debate the morality of her conduct. "Shall we go back to the start of all this, the reason you resorted to murder?"

She turned her head, as if the far end of the barn held more interest. "You wouldn't understand."

"Try me. I'm sure I do, but I want to hear it from you. Does it have to do with Howard?"

She faced him again. The answer was in her eyes. He'd touched a raw nerve, a secret bigger than the fact that she was a serial killer. She had owned up to the murders, yet still wanted to conceal her motive.

He was confident he knew. Now he had to commit. "We've spoken before about the harvest loaf you make each year. You must have been in your twenties when you started."

The resistance remained but she mellowed a little. The loaf gave her status. He'd found before that speaking about it was a way of getting through her reserve.

"At the beginning, you shaped them by hand and then, at Mervyn's suggestion, Howard offered to make a mould for you. You went to see him at Bathampton, which must have been quite an adventure, meeting an artist. He was in his sixties, with a white beard, and you felt safe with him. You visited more than once and he persuaded you to model for him."

She gripped the sides of the wheelchair. "Who told you this?"

"Agnes."

"She talked about me? She knows nothing."

"Howard sketched you in one of those ledger books he

used. I'm sure he told you at the time about his obsession with Walter Sickert."

She clicked her tongue and said, "Richard."

"Excuse me?" Diamond said, distracted.

"Howard always spoke of him as Richard Sickert. That's the name he preferred. Only ignorant people call him Walter."

"Well, that's new to me." He was only too pleased to be one of the ignorant if it loosened her tongue.

And it did. "Howard was still in his teens when they met at Bath Art School. Richard lectured the students every Friday morning and offered him lifts back to Bathampton by taxi. You used the word 'obsession,' but it was more about being influenced by a great painter. He applied the methods to his own work."

"Like working with photographs?"

Mistake. Her lips tightened as if she'd pulled a drawstring through them. "How do you know that?"

"About Sickert? Agnes told me first and then I learned more from some books I borrowed from the farmhouse."

"That woman is a blabbermouth."

He knew about the rivalry between the two. At one time, they must have been close friends. "Anyway," he said, "Howard slavishly copied Sickert, his way of working, his colours, his subjects, even the strange habit of sketching in ledger books."

"There's nothing criminal in that," she said. "I've seen students in galleries making copies."

"You're right. The crime comes when someone sells off a copy as an original. I don't think Howard was ever on the make, but his brother was. After Howard's death, Mervyn inherited everything. Among the pictures and materials were those dusty old ledger books we saw in the priest hole. They had once belonged to Sickert."

"You're not telling me anything I don't know."

"Tell me how Howard acquired them. I don't think they were a gift. My theory is that they were thrown out when Sickert's house was sold. Nobody thought they had any value."

"They were given to a local accountant," she said. "Eventually they got into a junk shop in Bathampton and Howard saw that some had been used for drawing. He knew exactly what they were and bought the whole lot for five pounds."

"Exciting."

"He showed them to me as if they were the holy grail. Most of them hadn't been used but some were filled with unfinished sketches and some were thinner than the rest, with pages removed."

"Rejects?"

"Not necessarily. When Mr. Sickert used a sketch as the basis of a painting, he would tear it from the binding and mount it on card. The Walker Gallery in Liverpool has the biggest collection of his drawings in the world and Howard went there and studied them, many on the ledger paper. By looking closely at the torn edges any expert could prove they were taken from the books he now owned."

"Did he tell the gallery?"

"He told me." There was immense pride in the claim. The old artist had taken the young woman into his confidence.

"Did Howard sketch in the ledger books himself?"

"Only the spare ones."

"And he made the drawings of you."

She gave him a guarded look that told him what he needed to know.

"Did he give them to you?"

"No, they were preliminary studies for a painting."

"On the lined paper, just like Sickert. And of course he

took photos of you, as his master would have done. Sickert used the camera as an aid for almost fifty years."

She had turned as pale as a two-day corpse, seemingly shocked that Diamond knew so much.

He came to the crux of the case. "You posed nude for Howard. That's what all the killing was about. Your reputation. I'm a town person myself. I live fairly anonymously but in this small village everyone knows everyone else's business. They will have known you posed but they assume it was only a head and shoulders sketch. You're so respectable that nobody can imagine you undressing for a man you scarcely knew. As for photographs . . ." He let his voice trail off.

"Please, I've never mentioned this to anyone," she said in a whisper, as if she could hang on to her secret.

He didn't spare her. "He asked you to pose in positions Sickert's models had taken up. I've seen illustrations in the books and they were graphic. One is called *L'Affaire de Camden Town*. A naked woman on an iron bedstead, legs apart, nothing left to the imagination, obviously a sex worker, with a clothed man standing over her and a chamber pot under the bed in case the squalor isn't obvious enough."

"Don't," she said in a strangled voice.

"How did he persuade you? Did he seduce you first?"

She shivered and drew the blanket tightly against herself. "Absolutely not. There was nothing like that." She paused, remembering. "It was the day he'd finished the mould for the loaf and presented it to me. It was a thing of beauty and I couldn't thank him enough."

"Right. I get it."

"He told me about being a student and disciple of this great artist, Richard Sickert, and how he had learned so much from him. He showed me examples in books and one of them was that picture you just mentioned."

"To reassure you they were art with a capital *A*?"

"He took me into a room where everything was ready and set up, exactly as in that picture. The bed, the bedclothes, even the chamber pot."

"The man?"

"Was Howard himself. The camera was an old-fashioned Kodak of the sort Mr. Sickert had owned, the kind that took black and white pictures. It was on a tripod and it had some sort of timer that allowed him a few seconds to get in position before the picture was taken."

"Professional."

"I thought so, and I still believe it."

"So you agreed to pose?"

She looked away, her expression calm. This memory wasn't causing her pain, or even regret. "He made me feel appreciated. I wasn't particularly good-looking. I was used to men ignoring me. Howard was courteous and considerate, treatment that was new to me."

"You were young."

"And trying not to appear so," she said.

"How many did he take?"

A tear rolled down her cheek. "I wasn't counting."

"Did you ask what he would do with them?"

"I trusted him. And he didn't betray my trust. He behaved impeccably throughout. He'd already told me they were for his private use as an artist and no one else would ever see them."

Diamond had toyed briefly with the idea that she had killed Howard as well as the others. Clearly not. She clung to her respect for him.

"Did he show you the finished painting?"

"No, and I didn't ask to see it. I don't suppose it looked anything like me."

"Are you sure it existed?"

"I know it did because eventually Mervyn told me. After Howard died, everything was left to him. Most of the paintings were scenes of local places and he had them framed and hung them upstairs in the farmhouse."

"I saw some of them. I'm no expert, but to my eye they weren't very well done."

"They were broad-brush studies in the style Mr. Sickert taught him, working from the sketches and photos."

"From sketches on lined paper in the ledger books?"

"At some point Howard must have told Mervyn those ledgers had belonged to Mr. Sickert and were priceless, so he kept them, along with the other stuff."

"Stored them in the priest hole?"

"And he didn't tell a soul. Until that dreadful day he broke the news to me, I assumed he'd disposed of everything after Howard's death except the paintings on the wall."

"Everything including the photos?"

She sighed heavily. "I had a secret fear that they still existed somewhere. Howard fully intended to keep his promise but he scarcely ever threw anything out. I worried that Mervyn had come across them during the clear-out. I couldn't sleep. I was on zolpidem for months, but nothing was said and I began to hope they were destroyed. A few years passed and then Mervyn started spending money on the farm, upgrading the machinery, rebuilding barns and so on. He told no one where the money came from."

Diamond was impatient to move the story on. "You suspected he was selling Howard's paintings, passing them off as Sickerts?"

"It had to be something like that. I watched him over many months and he made occasional trips to Bath, to see a dealer, as it turned out."

"Roger Miller, correct?"

She hesitated. Perhaps he was pushing too hard. "That's right. Roger was one of Claudia's Bath friends and I never suspected what was going on at the time. He had a big success selling a couple of local scenes Sickert painted and he found a rich client in the Far East, a collector eager to buy anything by the same artist."

"How do you know this?"

"Mervyn told me later."

"But there had to be some trickery going on to pass off Howard's inferior work as Sickert's."

She said in an icy tone, "Inferior to your eyes, perhaps."

"I can see where this is going. A dealer would want provenance, a record of continuous ownership going right back to the artist."

"Mervyn was able to supply it, as good as," she said. "Howard had been a devoted student when Mr. Sickert gave his weekly lecture at the Bath Art School. His name is on the roll."

"You really researched this."

"Some of the old ledger books contained original sketches Sickert made, with notes on colour and other details in the artist's handwriting. Any expert would authenticate them."

"Gold dust to Mervyn."

"Of course. A lot of the sketches never became paintings. Sickert never did any more with them. But Howard did. They were a gift from God for him. He applied Sickert's methods and worked them up into paintings."

"Which Mervyn sold as undiscovered Sickerts?"

"Exactly."

Diamond shook his head. He needed more convincing. "Howard wasn't in Sickert's class as a painter. Any expert would spot the difference."

"He wasn't selling them as the finished works. Sickert liked to rough out a painting first to try out the colours and the composition. He called these paintings 'pochades.' You can see examples in the books showing how he progressed from a sketch to a masterpiece. They're preparatory studies and some of them look a mess to the likes of you and me, but they all have a value to collectors."

"How much does a finished Sickert fetch? A six-figure sum?"

"Easily. His major works are worth millions. They're in galleries throughout the world. The Tate put on a retrospective exhibition in 2022. Of course the ones Howard did aren't in that class, but they used Mr. Sickert's colour range and had the hallmarks of his style and they were backed up by the authentic pencil sketches in those ledger books."

She paused and looked into the distance, remembering.

"He was a perfectionist. He went to great pains to do everything in the Sickert style. I told you he used an antique camera. He followed the technique to the letter, transferring the image to the canvas. He wasn't doing this to fake the work, you understand. He was learning from Sickert."

"Pochades, you called them?"

"Yes. They fetched enough to allow Mervyn to modernise the farm."

"From this fanatical collector? Did you speak to him about it?"

"I had to know for certain. I was worried sick when I first became suspicious of what was going on. It meant he'd kept the ledger books and . . . probably other things from Howard's effects." The words "other things" brought colour to her cheeks.

"The photos?"

She squeezed her eyes shut, as if in pain. "I could think about little else. Mervyn had the reputation of being a good man but I knew he wouldn't like being asked. This was after he retired. One morning I plucked up courage and asked if he'd sold off some of Howard's work. He was sitting outside the shop and I'd served him his strong black coffee, his 'morning-after medicine,' as he called it."

"Dolores told me about the whisky habit," Diamond said.

"Only he wasn't drunk at the time. He knew what he was saying and he knew exactly what was troubling me." She drew a long breath before going on. "He laughed and made a lewd remark I won't repeat and told me I would never get the photos back because they were his nest egg. He'd had an offer for the picture and the photos and sketches were part of the package."

"The provenance?"

"Yes."

"Big shock for you."

"Huge. My world collapsed. He was vile to me. This was the man everyone loved. Next morning I put him to sleep."

Diamond tensed so suddenly that the back pain returned. "Literally?"

By this time, she had nothing to gain by concealment. "I'd kept a supply of sleeping tablets after Howard's death. I crushed a large number and added them to his coffee. They taste bitter and in strong, black coffee they weren't obvious. It takes half an hour before they work. The doctor who examined the body said Mervyn must have got home, drunk more whisky and gone to bed. The combination of alcohol and the drug killed him and nobody suspected it was anything but suicide."

"You got away with murder."

She didn't rise to that.

"If you'd stopped there," he said, "no one would have found out."

"That was my hope. I hadn't got the photos back but the immediate crisis was over. The farmhouse was locked up until Claudia decided to come and live there."

"You hadn't bargained for that."

"What made it worse was when the parties started and one of her friends was Roger Miller. I recognised him at once, unluckily for him. He'd been to the village a few times visiting Mervyn in the days when they were doing business."

"That wasn't luck," Diamond said. "He made sure he was one of her group."

"You mean he knew she was Mervyn's daughter and the new owner of the farm?" Her eyes narrowed and then opened wide. "I hadn't thought of that. He let everyone think he was besotted with her. How cynical."

He didn't comment. He wasn't there to make moral judgements. He waited for her to recall what she did next. Sharing a long-held secret can be a kind of liberation.

She said, "I don't suppose you or anyone else will understand my state of mind when it became clear that those intimate photographs of me existed. Howard had promised me faithfully that no one else would see them, but he didn't destroy them and after his death they were waiting to be discovered. He didn't intend it but that was the reality."

"More than you could endure?"

"My privacy was violated. They were in—what's the phrase?"

"The public domain?"

"Yes—and anybody might see them. These days it's so simple to make copies of any photo. There are scanners, photocopiers. You can even use a phone. It only wanted one person with a sick mind to get hold of one of those

photos and pass it around the village and . . ." She shook
her head. The shame was beyond words. "They were never
meant to be pornographic but that's what people would
think. I couldn't bear that. Everyone knows who I am. I
do more than my share of volunteering in the shop, the
church and the parish council. I'm not massively popular, I
know that, but I've earned respect here. That's my identity.
It was hard-earned and it's my reason for living."

Her motive in a nutshell. Fear of character assassination.

She said, "I was terrified that on one of the party nights
this art dealer would search the house for Howard's prop-
erty."

"The danger was back."

"Yes, I was beside myself with worry. I overheard him
in the pub chatting to Dolores, asking questions about
Howard. And then Claudia played into my hands by thinking up that silly garter game. The first I knew of it was
when the Parcelforce man came with the packet of garters
addressed to Claudia. The shop was their drop-off point
for the village and I was on duty that morning. When
Claudia collected them, she was very open. She told me
the garters must be inside and ripped open the packet and
dangled one of them in front of me, shaking with laughter.
I could never be like that. She said they weren't for herself
but a game she was planning for the next party. She even
offered to let me wear one and join in if I wanted. I think
she was joking."

He could picture Claudia running rings around the staid
Miss Harrap without knowing she was playing with fire.

"On the day of the party I kept a close watch on her.
Early in the afternoon she walked over to the bull pen. Ten
minutes after she came out, I went in and found the garter."

"That was brave, considering you're terrified of Chummy."

A joyless smile twitched across her face. "You mean my performance with you on the night of the supper? That was an act, Mr. Diamond, in case you had your suspicions about me."

"You fooled me."

"I got something right, then. Do I have to tell you the rest?"

"You moved the garter to the silo. Quite an effort, climbing up the side. I tried it myself."

"I'm not decrepit and neither am I overweight."

Ouch! He let that pass.

"When Mr. Miller came into the shop to collect the dozen red roses he always ordered in advance for her, I told him about the garters. I said he was such a good customer that I would give him a helpful tip for the game."

"To check the silo?"

"There are two, you see. I had to be sure he knew which one."

No remorse that she'd sent him to be buried alive. Her self-interest crowded out everything.

"In some ways," he commented, "this was similar to the killing of Mervyn Priest, hands-off and remote-controlled. You weren't present at the scene. You made the preparations and let events take their course."

She nodded.

"Time went by and the immediate crisis was over. Claudia was blamed for Miller's death, which suited you perfectly."

"She brought that on herself."

Earlier she'd expressed some regret about Claudia but in this last bitter account she was unforgiving. He didn't challenge the change of tone. Her narrative mattered more.

"But you weren't in control last night, when Bert Dombey came to the farmhouse to try and find Mervyn's secret."

"He caught me off guard. He was clever, I give him that. We hadn't seen him in months until he turned up yesterday with you. He must have worked out where to look and how to unlock the priest hole. Cleverer than me, you see. I got to the farmhouse early myself to start my kitchen duties, heard some sounds and went to investigate and there he was inside the staircase, with only his head and shoulders showing, rummaging through Howard's effects for anything of value. Well, Mr. Diamond, you know how I reacted."

"Grabbed the sheep shears off the wall and attacked him."

"I acted on impulse, angry and alarmed at the same time. He was an easy target and those shears were sharp. Only after he fell dead did I stop to think what I'd done. Most of the blood was in the hole. In the pressure of the moment I didn't notice the spots on the stair carpet. I was wearing an apron that I took home later and destroyed. I closed the stairs and took the shears down to the kitchen and washed every drop of blood from them. Then I hung them back on the wall where they came from. I checked everything a second time and found the rod sticking out of the panel in the side of the staircase, so I pushed it home and locked the stairs, telling myself no one else alive knew how to get inside."

"You didn't expect to get away with it?"

"I'm not that stupid, superintendent. I'd bought myself some time, that's all. But I miscalculated, didn't I? You and Claudia found the way in the same night and called the police. My luck had well and truly run out."

"Not completely," he said. "They made the mistake of arresting Claudia, which *did* buy you some time—time to go back in and make a search for those indecent photos.

They troubled you more than the killing of three men. As I said before, your reputation in the village was the driving force behind these murders. So you added arson to your CV and destroyed a grand old building and would have added two more of us to your tally if Jim hadn't jumped in and grabbed you."

"Three more," she said. "I would have gone up in flames as well. Good thing, too." She turned away from him and rearranged the pillow.

Interview over.

"NO APOLOGY?" PALOMA said when he returned to the cottage.

"None. Jim saved her life and got burned in the process and she didn't once ask how he was getting on."

"Do we know?" Julie asked.

"I called the hospital. He's recovering well. He'll be sent home this afternoon."

"Has Claudia been released?"

"By now she will be. I called Jack Crandley and told him Maggie Harrap will confess to everything. He claims he'd worked it out and was about to release Claudia anyway."

"What a liar."

"I didn't challenge him on that. This job isn't simple. We all make mistakes."

Julie said, "Your charitable side again."

He said, "But you know there's another side."

Paloma asked Julie whether she thought Claudia would sell the farm now that her house was destroyed.

"I can't speak for her, of course," Julie said, "but I know it was insured and she never felt comfortable in it, so I reckon she'll have a house built here to her own design."

"And stay on?"

"That's my hope. People are going to find out she was unjustly kept in prison. The noisy parties made her unpopular but they appreciate the fact that she kept the farm going through that time and gave them job security. I'm sure Jim and Agnes feel that way. She's the sort of person who wants to be liked. I hope that will persuade her."

Paloma said, "There's sure to be sympathy. Even some partying may be forgiven."

THEY LEFT AFTER lunch. Now that the harvest was in, much was changing in Baskerville. An Octoberish chill had set in. "Busy week," Paloma said as the car headed along the lane.

"A week—is that all it was?" he said. "I'll be glad to get back to the office for a rest."

"Now you know what life as a private detective is like."

"It's different, I can tell you that."

"Julie and I were confident you'd get to the truth," she said. "We knew you'd make a good job of it."

"A job," he said. "Not a good job. Another life lost. A fine old building burnt down. People's lives changed forever."

"When it gets written up, it will be a good job," Paloma said.

"You're forgetting," he said. "This case was off the record. There's no pesky paperwork at all."

A perfect opening for Paloma. She allowed him to make the turn into another narrow lane before saying, "Oh, I wasn't speaking about you writing up the case."

He frowned. "I don't follow you."

"Your biographer."

"My *what*?"

The car bounced against the verge. Raffles shrilled in protest from the pet-carrier on the back seat.

"Careful," Paloma said. She wasn't shaken. She'd already braced herself. "You must have thought about it. How many murder cases have you solved over the years? At least twenty. Someone is going to write a book and you may be sure they'll include this one. You won't be able to keep it off the record."

He was lost for words. The blood pressure had soared.

"You only have to look at those books of famous detectives on the shelf at home. *Fabian of the Yard*, *Famous Feats of Detection*. Your career is crying out for the treatment."

"Over my dead body," he said.

Paloma smiled. "If they have to wait for that, they will, and if you don't ease up on the work, it won't be long."

"I'm not allowing some hack writer to make money out of me. I'd rather do it myself."

"What an excellent idea," she said as if it hadn't crossed her mind.

"Except I'm far too busy. I don't have the time."

"You will when you stop work." She didn't pause. "You've got some wonderful stories in you and you'd enjoy reminding yourself about them. What's more, it's the perfect excuse to stay in touch with the team and talk about old times."

"Maybe," he said.

"If it's not too late."

"What do you mean?"

"That hack writer could be working on it now, reading up your cases in the press, interviewing people you once worked with like, em, like John Wigfull."

A name guaranteed to inflame him, the sneaky DCI who had regularly undermined him when he was new to Bath.

"Didn't he become the official press officer after he retired?"

"Incredibly, he did. He always had an eye for the main

chance. But I haven't seen him in a while. He wasn't much good." A worse thought struck him. "You don't think ... Oh, no. There must be a law. He'd have to get my permission."

"I don't think so. They simply market it as the unauthorised biography."

She'd said enough. As every countryman knows, after sowing the seed you need to be patient.

"Oh, Christ," he said. "Not again." He'd spotted signs of life approaching them along the narrow lane, a canopy of hot breath swirling above the hedge in the cool morning air. He braked, pulled over and remembered to draw in the wing mirrors. "There's room, I think. They shouldn't do any damage."

But they weren't cattle. They were people dressed in straw hats adorned with flowers and ribbons. Waistcoats striped red and white with tiny bells attached to them. Skinny trousers, buckled shoes with more bells. One carried an accordion, another a drum and another a hobby horse. As they approached the car, the drummer started up and some of them made a small show of jigging.

"The Morris men," Paloma said, and clapped.

Someone sang, "Come and join us. Come and join us. Come and join our happy throng."

Diamond muttered, "Not in a million years."

"You could do it," Paloma said. "You know you could. In my wildest dreams I never pictured you as a dancer. Now I know better."

"Definitely a one-off."

"Come on. You're not the stick-in-the-mud I took you for."

When he was sure the Morris men had all gone by and Paloma's fantasy had passed as well, he started up again and tried moving forward. The wheels didn't respond.

He turned to look at the heavily packed rear of the car. "Do we have any cardboard left?"

Raffles stirred again and made a strange sound deep in his throat that definitely wasn't purring. It was as good as a "Not again!"

They both got out and looked at the rut the embedded tyre had made.

Diamond said, "I think this is where we came in."

A NOTE ON SOURCES

THE STORY IS, of course, fiction, but the reader may care to know that the artist Sickert did live on Entry Hill in Bath for two summers in 1917–18 and used a studio at 10 Bladud Buildings. For the last years of his life, from 1938 to 1942, he rented St. George's Hill House (since renamed) in Bathampton. He did much to encourage local art and artists and gave a weekly lecture at Bath Art School. All of this is detailed in Philippa Bishop's *Walter Richard Sickert (1860–1942) Painter of the Bath Scene* (2007), which can be found online in the publications of the History of Bath Research Group.

Sickert's elaborate process from sketch to finished work is examined in Alistair Smith's 2021 article at the Tate.org.uk website, "Walter Sickert's Drawing Practice and the Camden Town Ethos." The artist's use of ledger books for sketching is described by Keith Oliver in an essay, "Drawing played a varied, vital role in his practice'— Sickert's Paper," in the exhibition catalogue for *Sickert: A Life in Art*, held at the Walker Art Gallery, Liverpool, 2021–22.

I am also indebted to the entertaining biography by Matthew Sturgis, *Walter Sickert: A Life*, HarperCollins, 2005.

Incidentally, in a final section entitled "Postscript," Sturgis forensically examines and dismantles the theories linking Sickert to Jack the Ripper. He begins with a tongue-in-cheek quote from the artist himself: "Oh it is splendid to be accused of things. I have been accused of everything and have always pleaded guilty."

Acknowledgments

M Y SON PHIL looked at the script and brought much of the dialogue into the twenty-first century. His skill with words makes me proud. A number of professionals made creative suggestions that improved the book as it went through the editing process, notably Juliet Grames of Soho Press, USA; Rosanna Forte of Sphere, UK; and my long-term copy-editor, Mari Roberts, who likes the series enough to have delayed retirement to work on this one. Not least, I wish to thank my literary agents, Vanessa Holt in the UK and Jane Gelfman and Cathy Gleason in the USA. They have managed my career almost from the beginning and made it possible for me to realise my dream of being a full-time author. To say I'm enormously grateful to everyone mentioned here is an understatement.

Peter Lovesey